BUREAU FOR PARANORMAL • RESEARCH AND DEFENSE •

B.P.R.D. HELL ON EARTH: COMETH THE HOUR

created by MIKE MIGNOLA

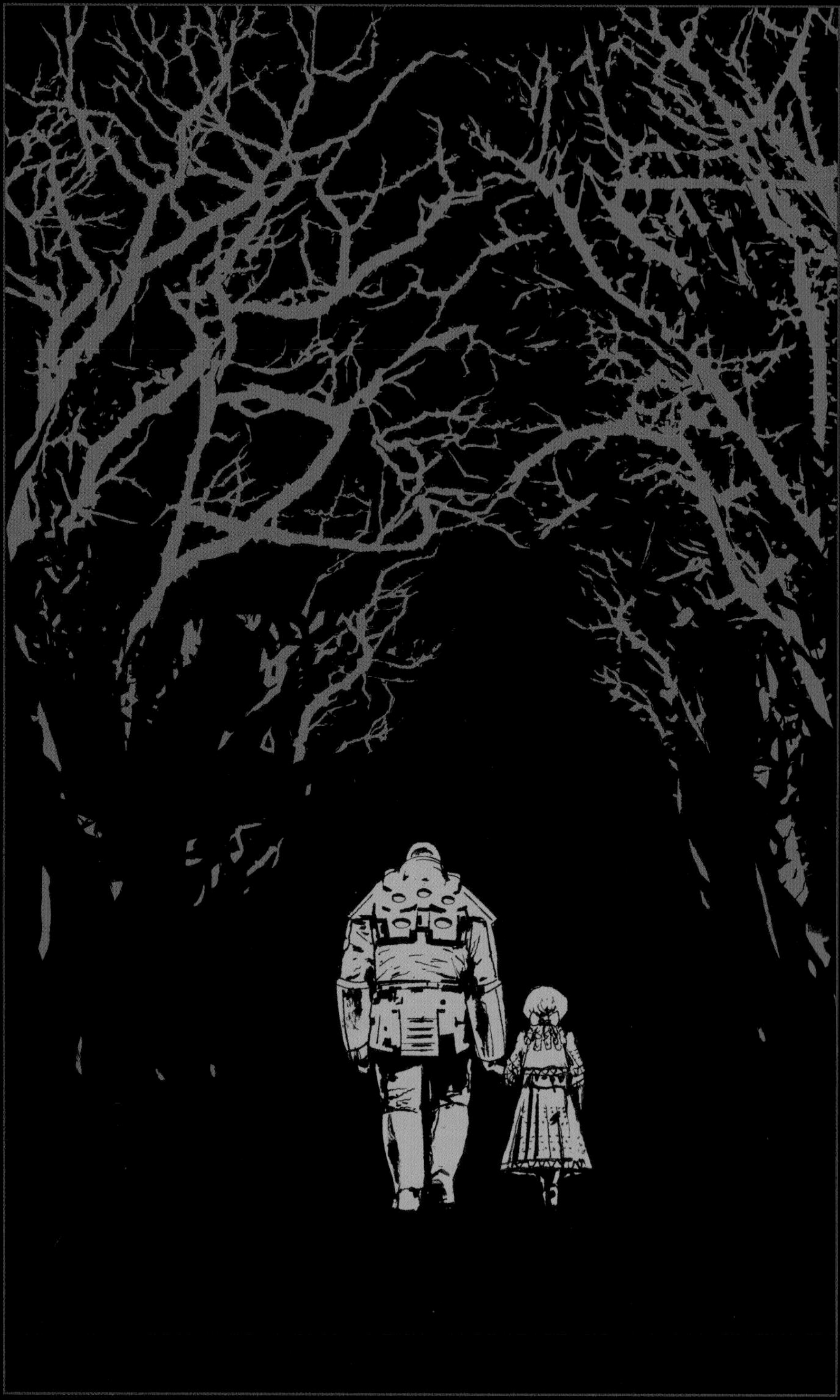

With the Black Flame dead, Kate Corrigan, Liz Sherman, and the BPRD face a problem no one imagined—an earthbound Ogdru Jahad, spilling new nightmares across the landscape as it barrels toward Colorado and Bureau headquarters. But is the real threat this living vessel of the original darkness, or a little Russian girl in a pretty white dress . . .

MIKE MIGNOLA'S

B.P.R.D.™
HELL ON EARTH
COMETH
THE HOUR

story by **MIKE MIGNOLA** and **JOHN ARCUDI**

art by **LAURENCE CAMPBELL**

colors by **DAVE STEWART**

letters by **CLEM ROBINS**

cover by **LAURENCE CAMPBELL**
with **DAVE STEWART**

chapter break art by **DUNCAN FEGREDO**
with **DAVE STEWART**

publisher **MIKE RICHARDSON**

editor **SCOTT ALLIE**

associate editor **SHANTEL LaROCQUE**

assistant editor **KATII O'BRIEN**

collection designer **PATRICK SATTERFIELD**

digital art technician **CHRISTINA McKENZIE**

DARK HORSE BOOKS ®

DarkHorse.com   Facebook.com/DarkHorseComics   Twitter.com/DarkHorseComics

B.P.R.D. Hell on Earth Volume 15: Cometh the Hour

This book collects B.P.R.D. Hell on Earth #143–#147.

Published by Dark Horse Books
A division of Dark Horse Comics, Inc.
10956 SE Main Street
Milwaukie, OR 97222

International Licensing: (503) 905-2377
Comic Shop Locator Service: (888) 266-4226

First edition: March 2017
ISBN 978-1-50670-131-8

10 9 8 7 6 5 4 3 2 1
Printed in China

Library of Congress Cataloging-in-Publication Data

Names: Mignola, Michael, author. | Arcudi, John, author. | Campbell,
    Laurence, 1969- artist. | Stewart, Dave, colourist, artist. | Robins,
    Clem, 1955- letterer.
Title: B.P.R.D. Hell on earth. Volume 15, Cometh the hour / story by Mike
    Mignola and John Arcudi ; art by Laurence Campbell ; colors by Dave
    Stewart ; letters by Clem Robins ; cover and chapter break art by Laurence
    Campbell with Dave Stewart.
Other titles: Cometh the hour
Description: First edition. | Milwaukie, OR : Dark Horse Books, 2017. | "This
    book collects B.P.R.D. Hell on Earth #143-#147"
Identifiers: LCCN 2016043703 | ISBN 9781506701318 (paperback)
Subjects: LCSH: Comic books, strips, etc. | BISAC: COMICS & GRAPHIC NOVELS /
    Horror. | COMICS & GRAPHIC NOVELS / Fantasy. | FICTION / Action &
    Adventure.
Classification: LCC PN6727.M53 B259 2017 | DDC 741.5/973--dc23
LC record available at https://lccn.loc.gov/2016043703

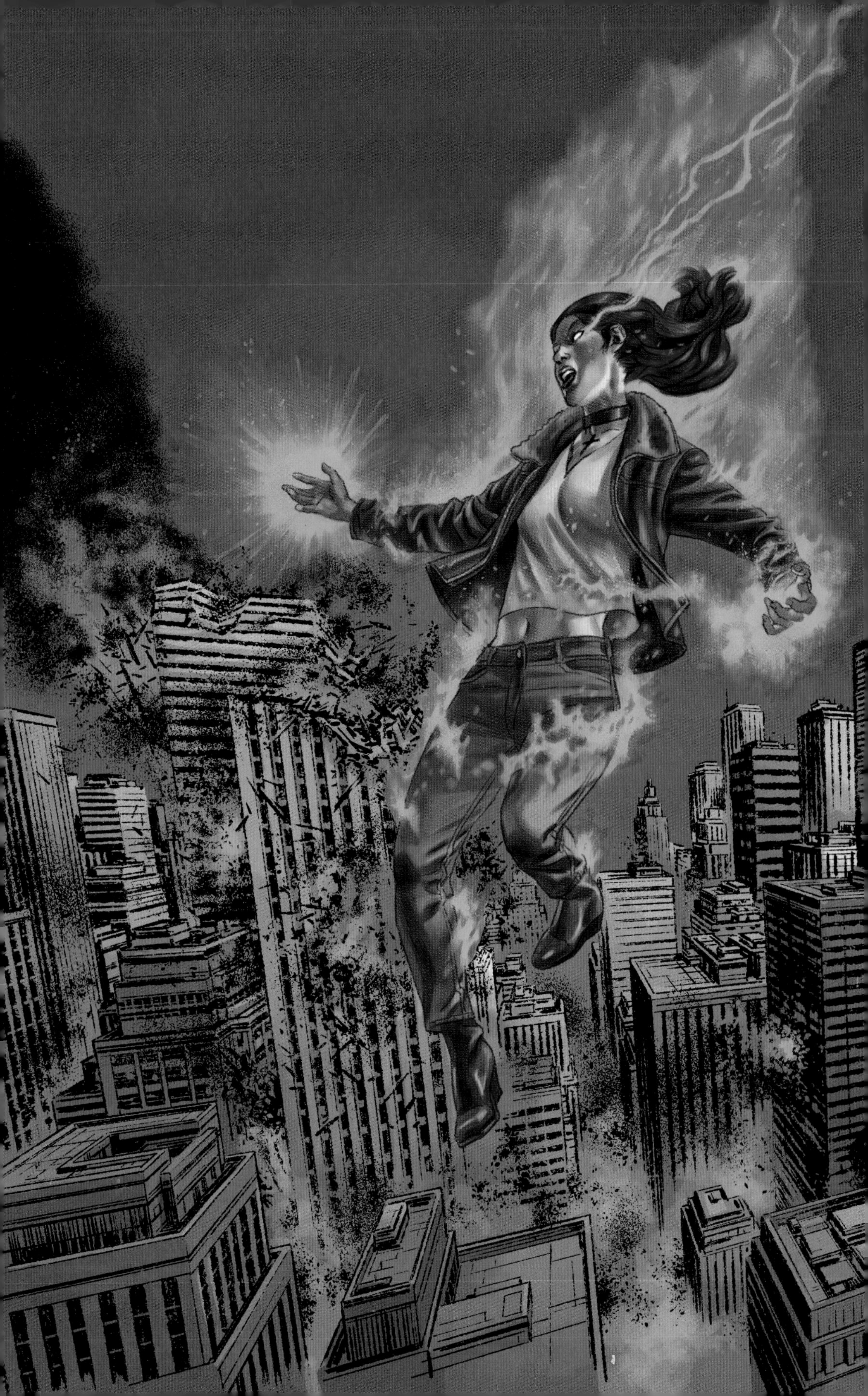

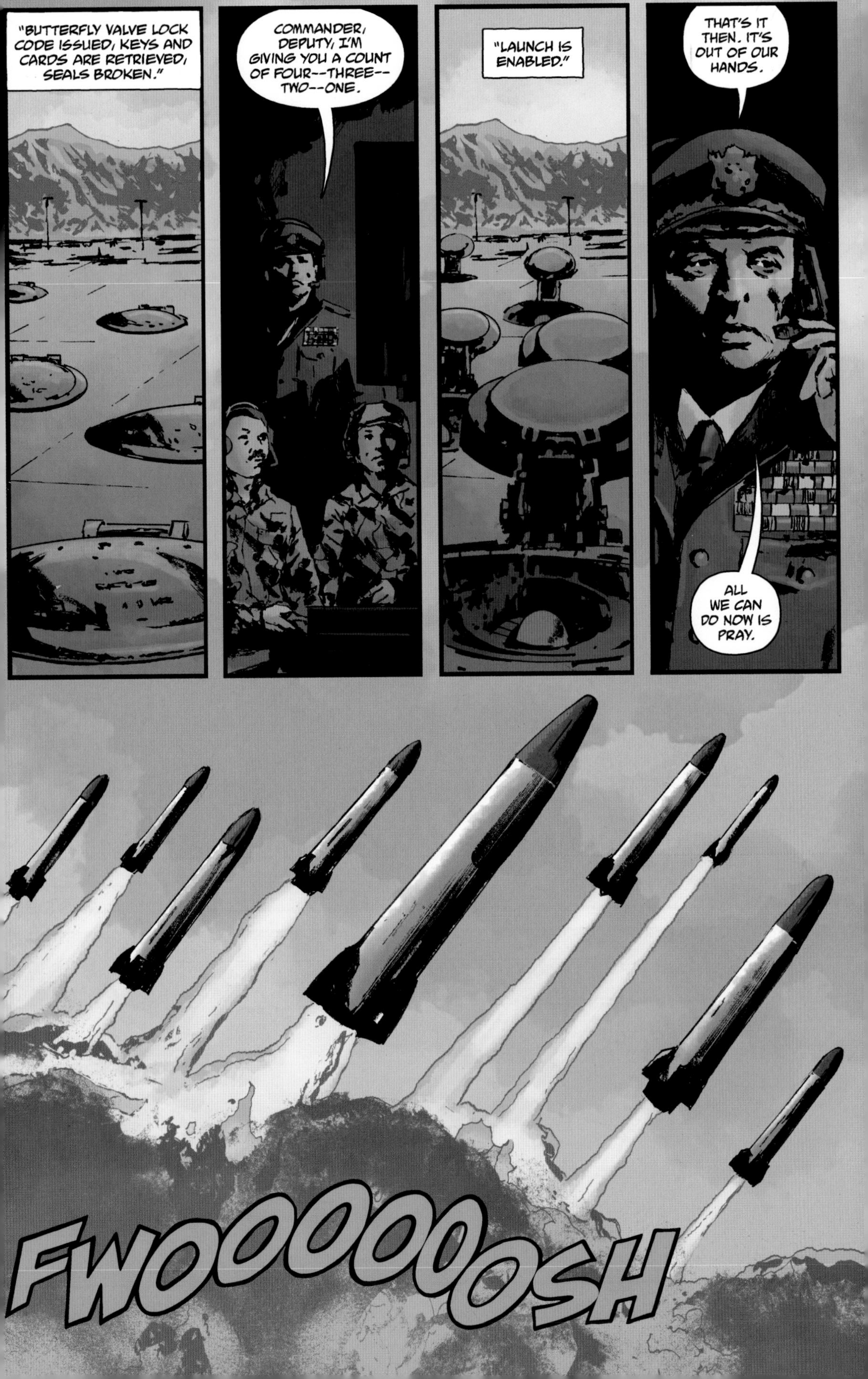
"BUTTERFLY VALVE LOCK CODE ISSUED, KEYS AND CARDS ARE RETRIEVED, SEALS BROKEN."
COMMANDER, DEPUTY, I'M GIVING YOU A COUNT OF FOUR--THREE--TWO--ONE.
"LAUNCH IS ENABLED."
THAT'S IT THEN. IT'S OUT OF OUR HANDS.
ALL WE CAN DO NOW IS PRAY.
FWOOOOOOOSH

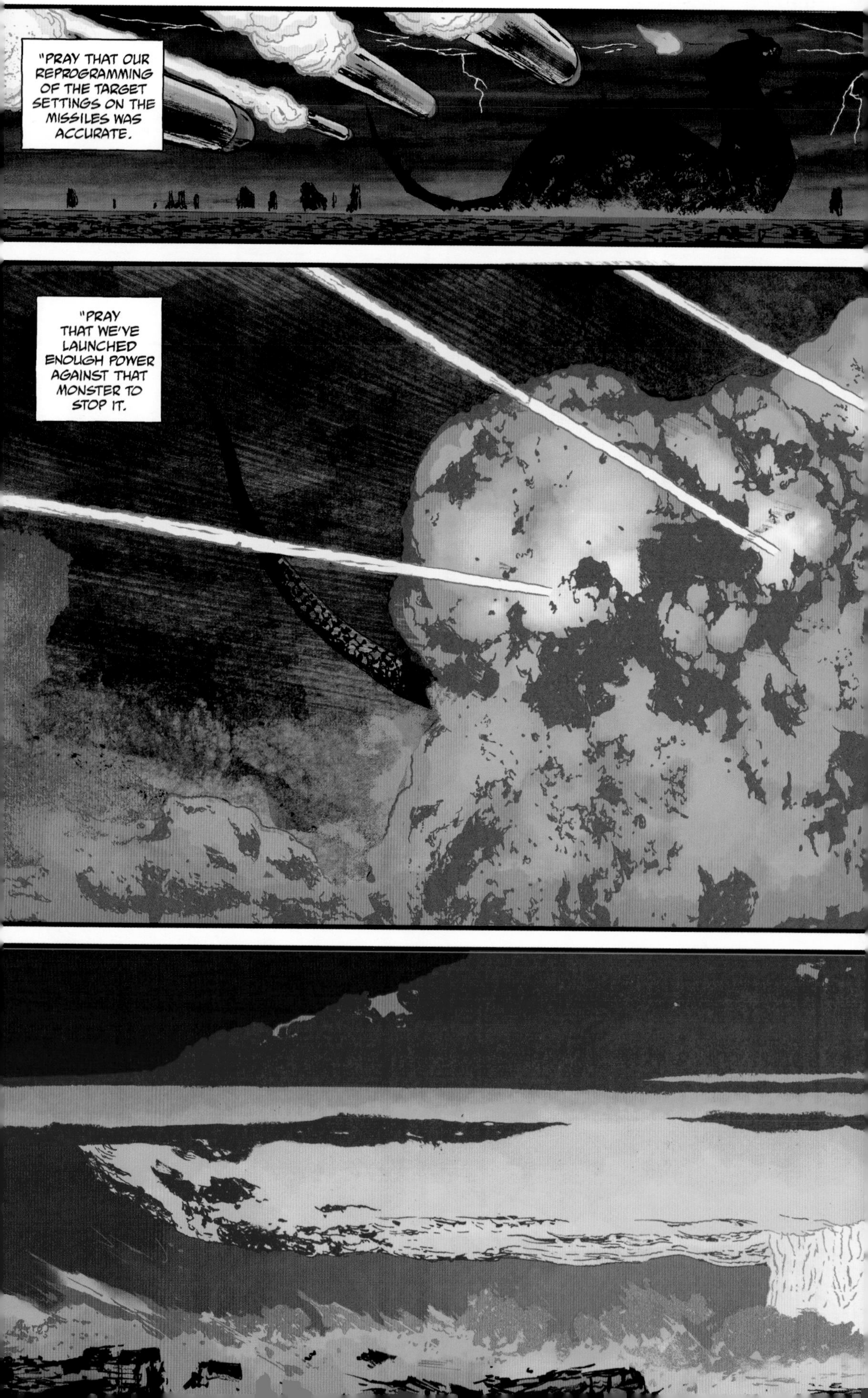
"PRAY THAT OUR REPROGRAMMING OF THE TARGET SETTINGS ON THE MISSILES WAS ACCURATE.
"PRAY THAT WE'VE LAUNCHED ENOUGH POWER AGAINST THAT MONSTER TO STOP IT.

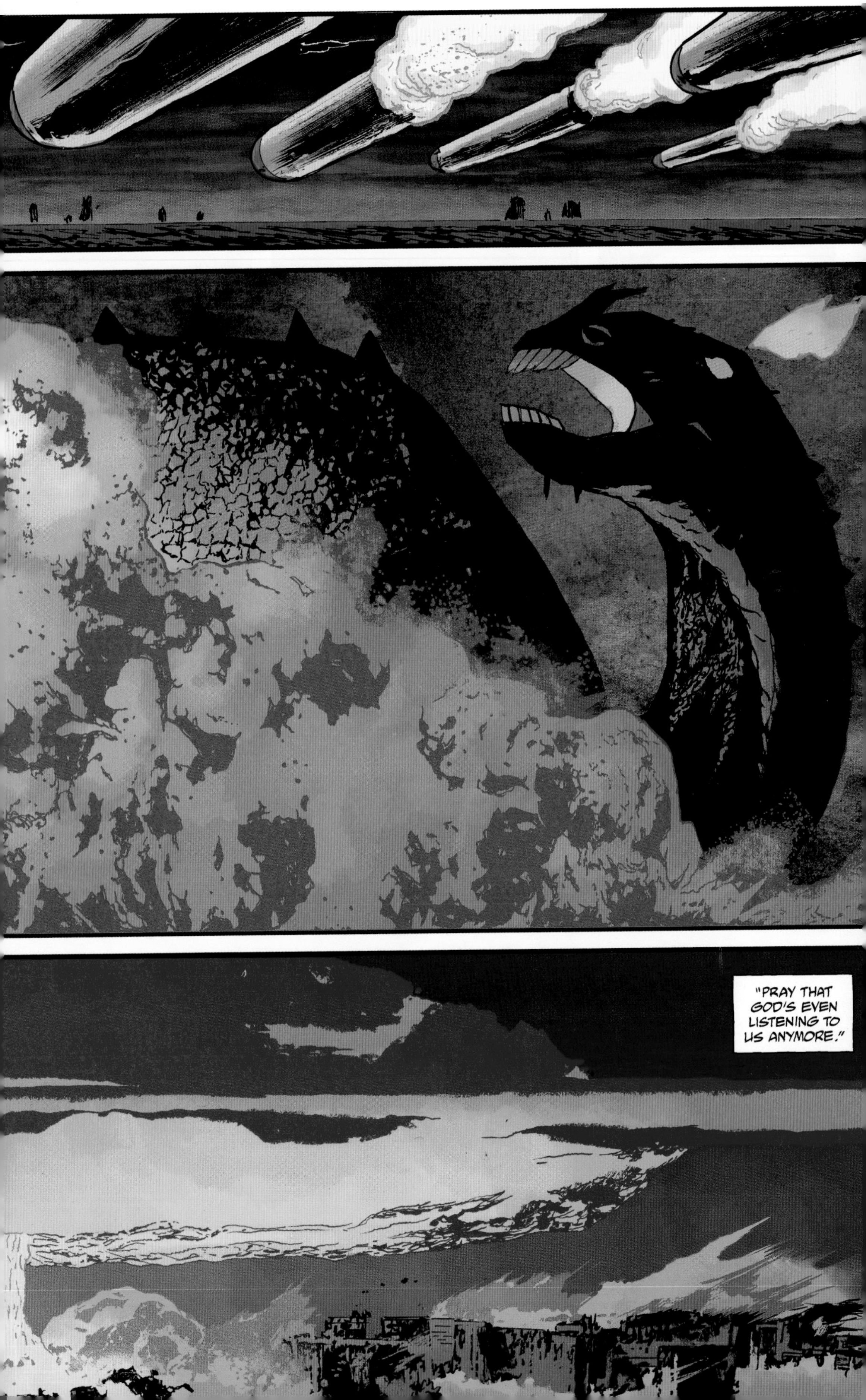
"PRAY THAT GOD'S EVEN LISTENING TO US ANYMORE."

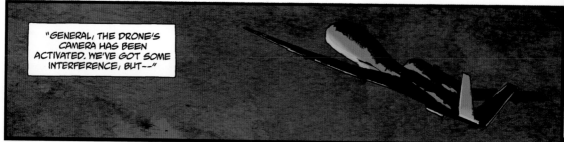

"GENERAL, THE DRONE'S CAMERA HAS BEEN ACTIVATED. WE'VE GOT SOME INTERFERENCE, BUT--"

WELL, CAN YOU FIX IT? WHY THE HELL DO WE HAVE A *DRONE* THERE IF WE CAN'T GET A *VISUAL?*

I THINK WE... *THERE,* GENERAL! *GOT IT!*

WHY, LORD?

ROOARR

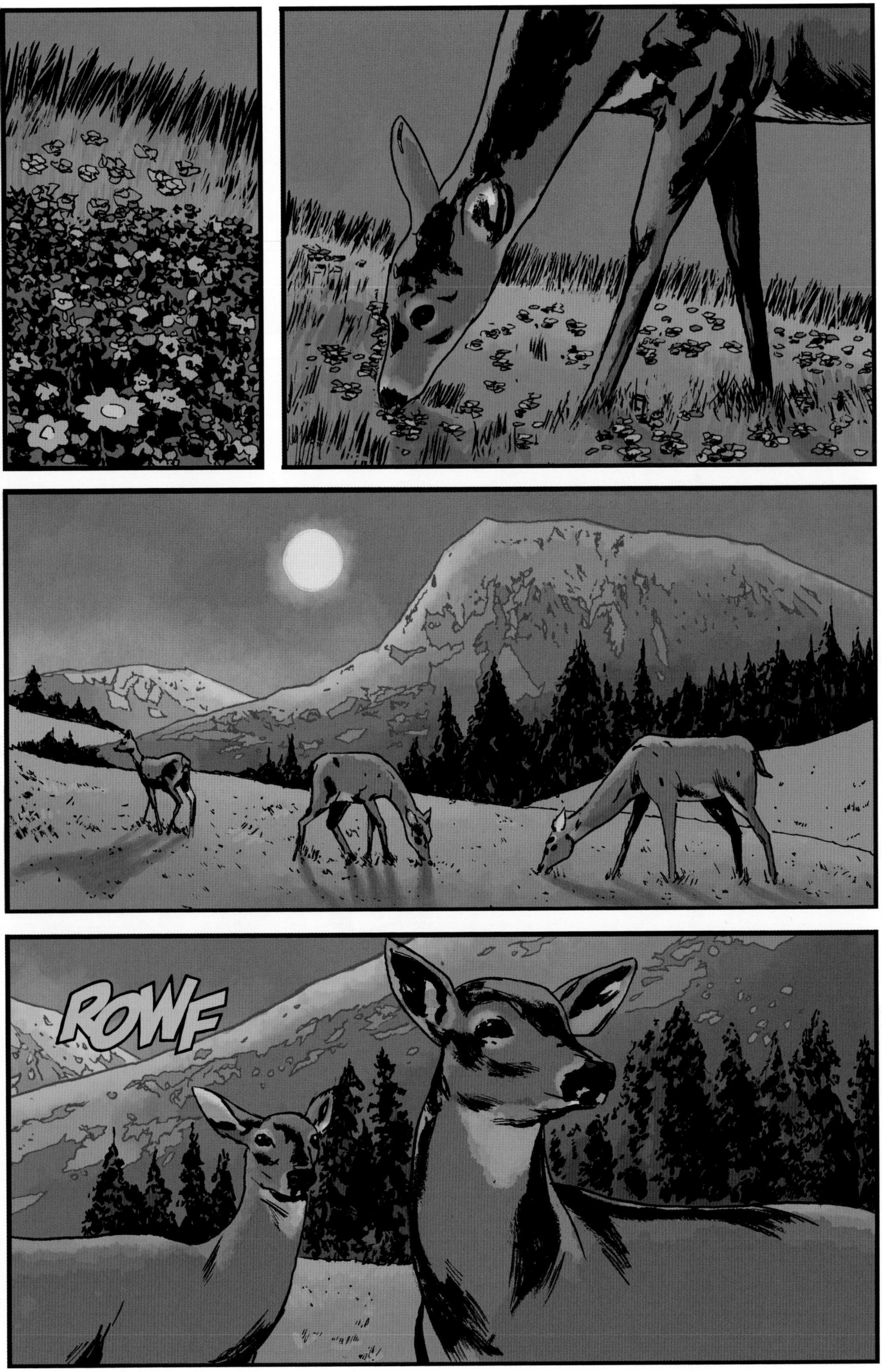
ROWF

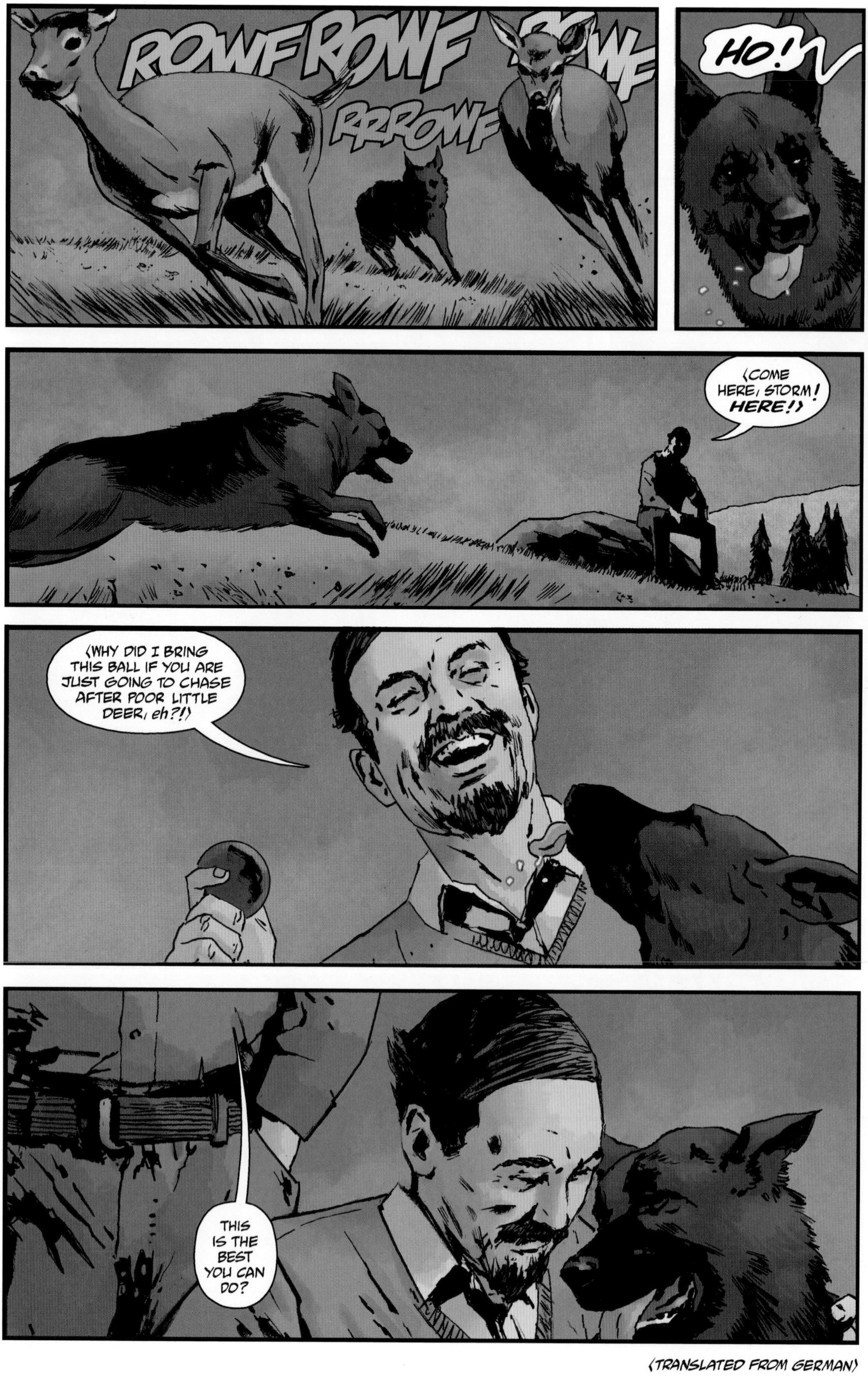
ROWF ROWF
ROWF
RRROWF
HO!
⟨COME HERE, STORM! HERE!⟩
⟨WHY DID I BRING THIS BALL IF YOU ARE JUST GOING TO CHASE AFTER POOR LITTLE DEER, eh?!⟩
THIS IS THE BEST YOU CAN DO?

⟨TRANSLATED FROM GERMAN⟩

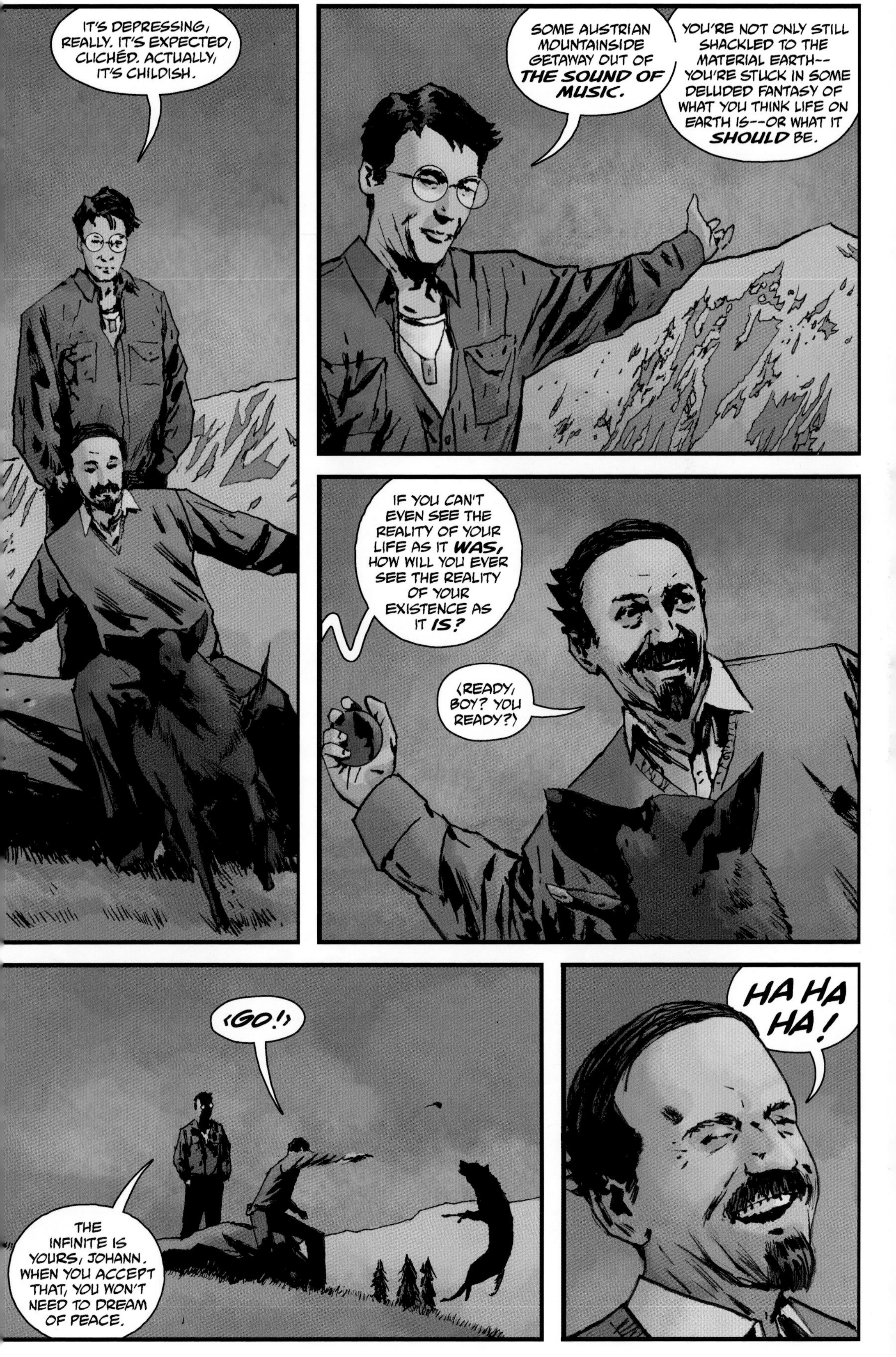
IT'S DEPRESSING, REALLY. IT'S EXPECTED, CLICHÉD. ACTUALLY, IT'S CHILDISH.
SOME AUSTRIAN MOUNTAINSIDE GETAWAY OUT OF THE SOUND OF MUSIC.
YOU'RE NOT ONLY STILL SHACKLED TO THE MATERIAL EARTH-- YOU'RE STUCK IN SOME DELUDED FANTASY OF WHAT YOU THINK LIFE ON EARTH IS--OR WHAT IT SHOULD BE.
IF YOU CAN'T EVEN SEE THE REALITY OF YOUR LIFE AS IT WAS, HOW WILL YOU EVER SEE THE REALITY OF YOUR EXISTENCE AS IT IS?
‹READY, BOY? YOU READY?›
‹GO!›
THE INFINITE IS YOURS, JOHANN. WHEN YOU ACCEPT THAT, YOU WON'T NEED TO DREAM OF PEACE.
HA HA HA!

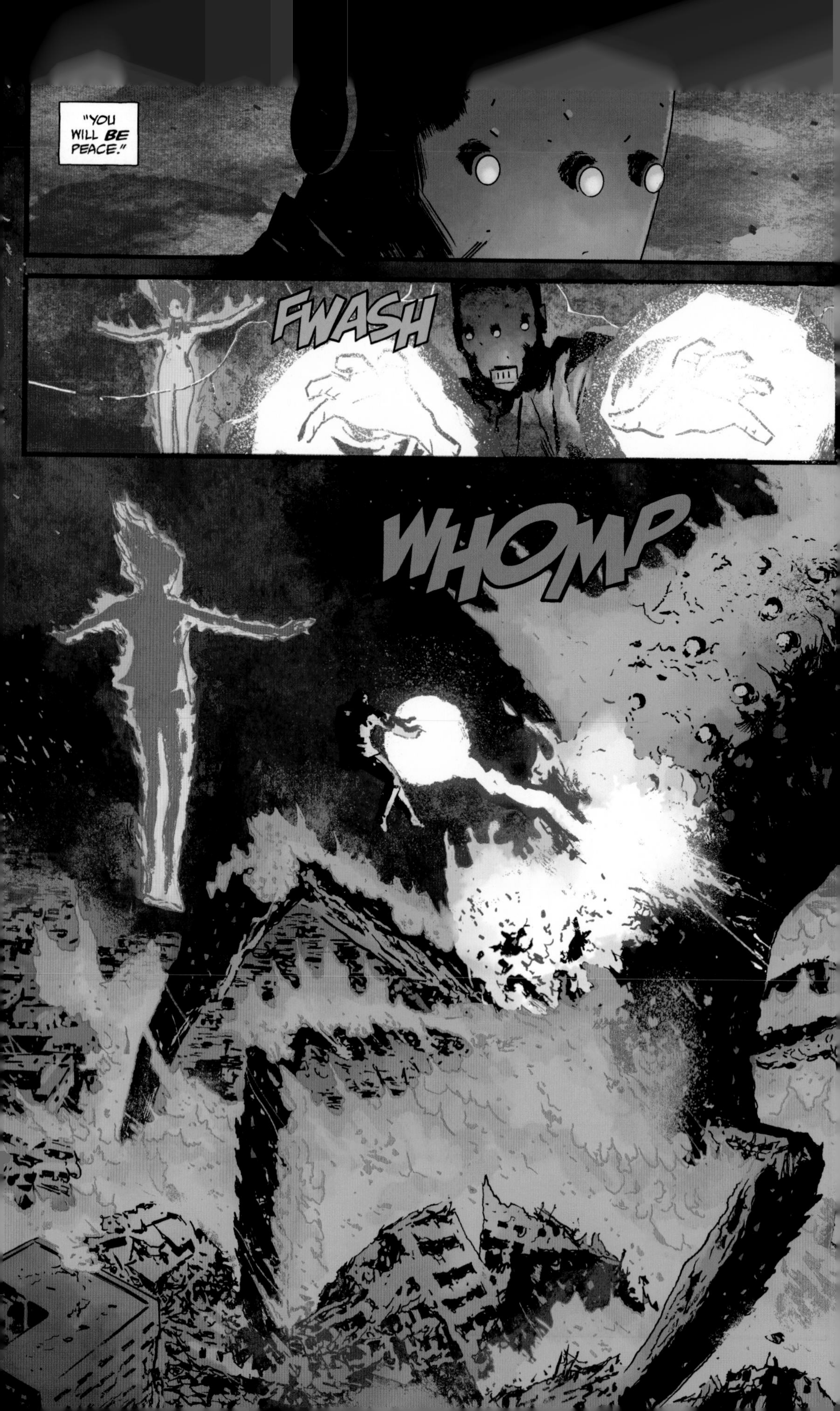
"YOU WILL BE PEACE."
FWASH
WHOMP

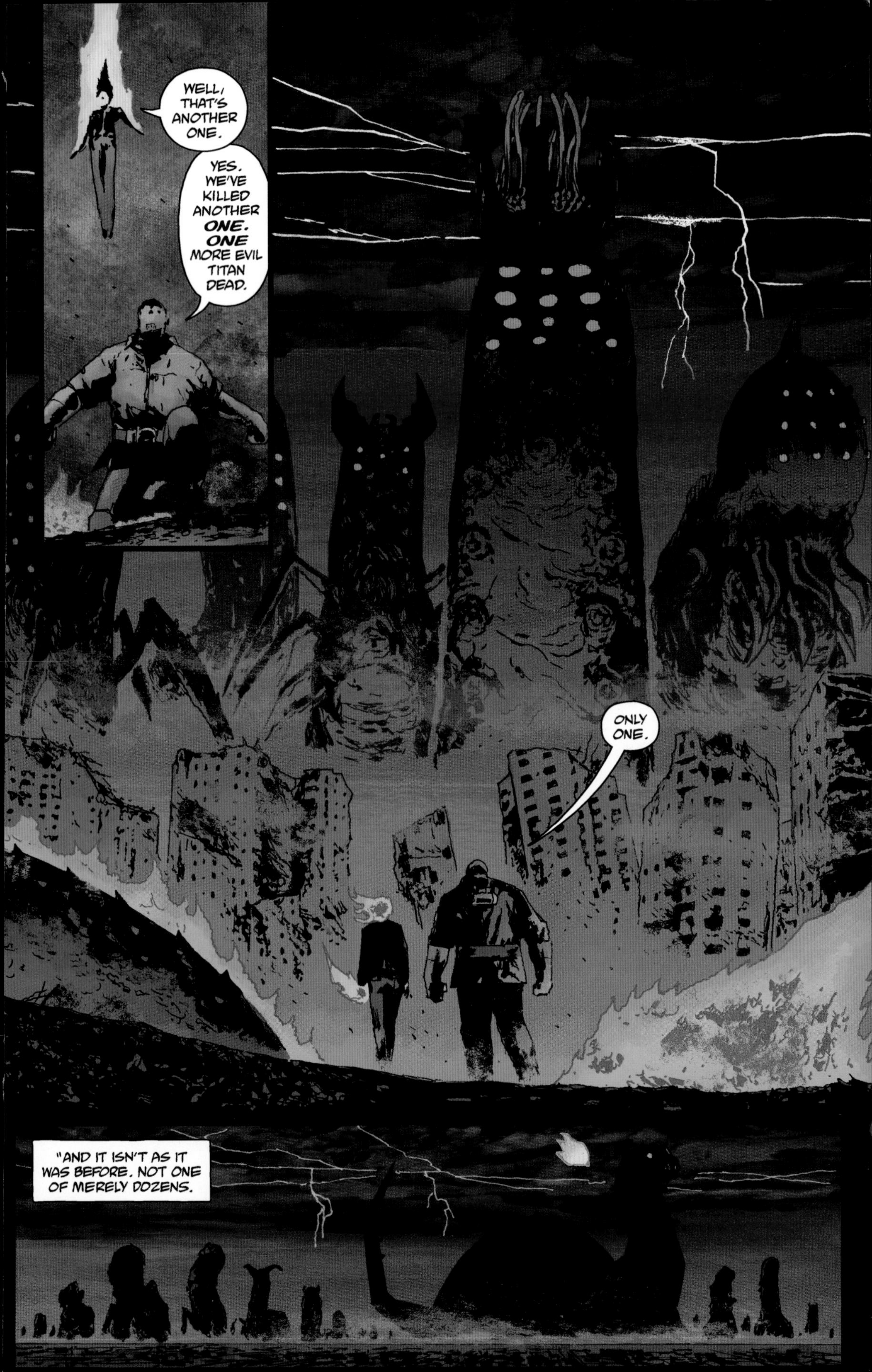
WELL, THAT'S ANOTHER ONE.
YES. WE'VE KILLED ANOTHER ONE. ONE MORE EVIL TITAN DEAD.
ONLY ONE.
"AND IT ISN'T AS IT WAS BEFORE. NOT ONE OF MERELY DOZENS.

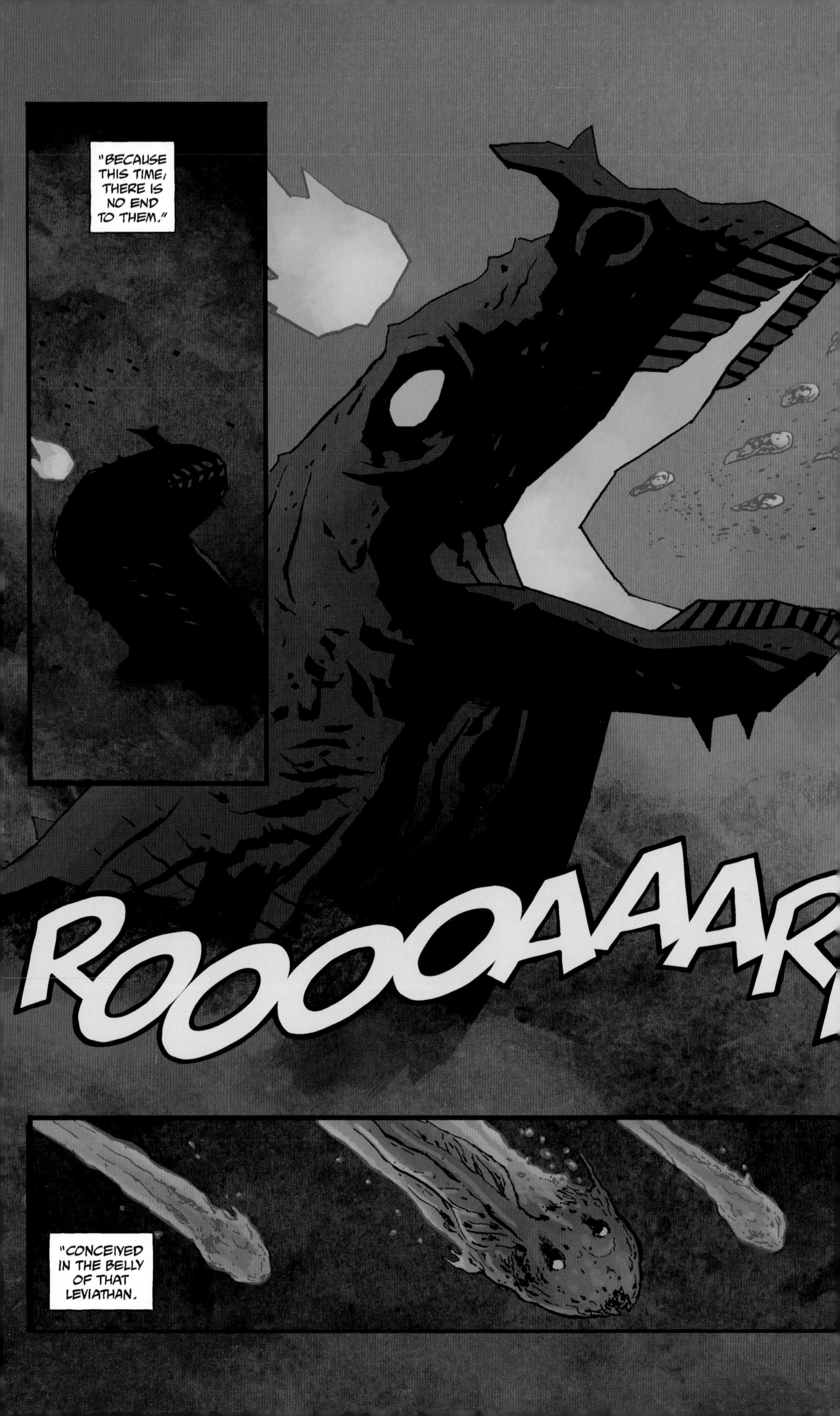
"BECAUSE THIS TIME, THERE IS NO END TO THEM."
ROOOOAAAR
"CONCEIVED IN THE BELLY OF THAT LEVIATHAN.

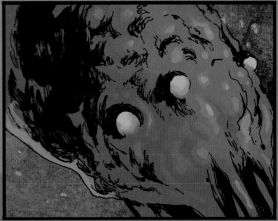

"SPEWED OUT HOUR AFTER HOUR."

BWHOOOOM

"A LEGION OF MONSTERS BORN EVERY DAY."

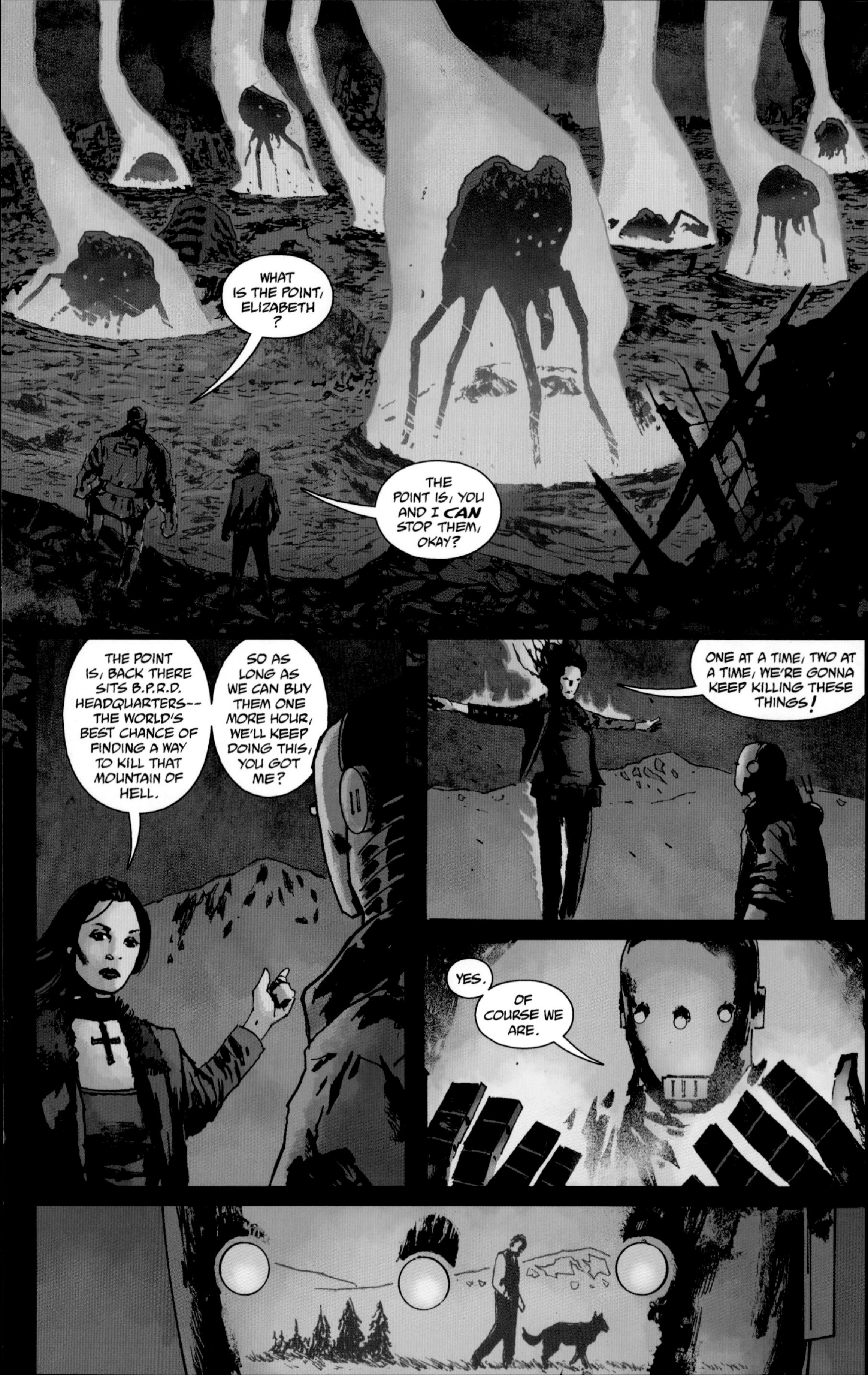
WHAT IS THE POINT, ELIZABETH ?
THE POINT IS, YOU AND I CAN STOP THEM, OKAY?
THE POINT IS, BACK THERE SITS B.P.R.D. HEADQUARTERS-- THE WORLD'S BEST CHANCE OF FINDING A WAY TO KILL THAT MOUNTAIN OF HELL.
SO AS LONG AS WE CAN BUY THEM ONE MORE HOUR, WE'LL KEEP DOING THIS, YOU GOT ME?
ONE AT A TIME, TWO AT A TIME, WE'RE GONNA KEEP KILLING THESE THINGS!
YES.
OF COURSE WE ARE.

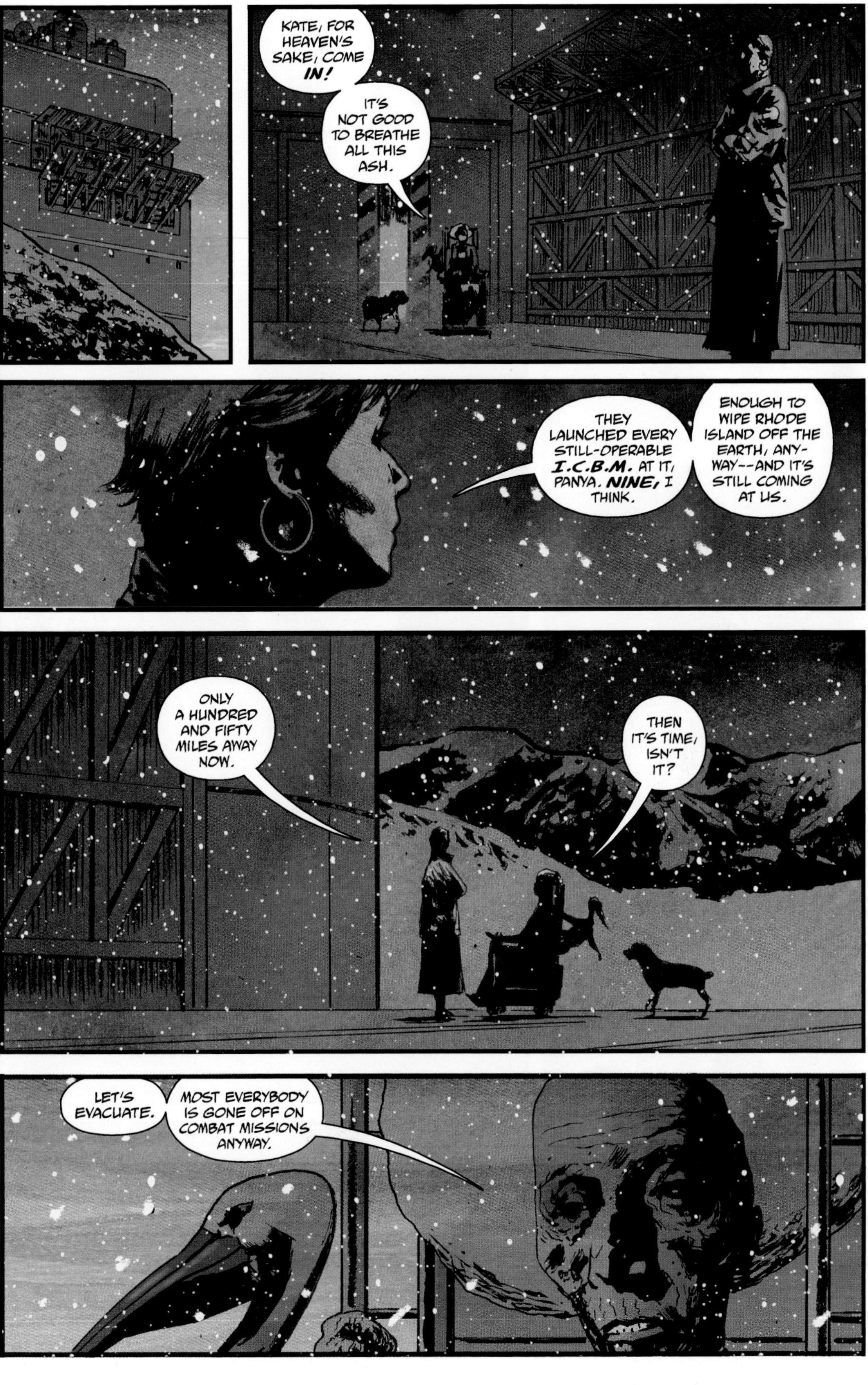
KATE, FOR HEAVEN'S SAKE, COME ***IN!***
IT'S NOT GOOD TO BREATHE ALL THIS ASH.
THEY LAUNCHED EVERY STILL-OPERABLE ***I.C.B.M.*** AT IT, PANYA. ***NINE,*** I THINK.
ENOUGH TO WIPE RHODE ISLAND OFF THE EARTH, ANY-WAY--AND IT'S STILL COMING AT US.
ONLY A HUNDRED AND FIFTY MILES AWAY NOW.
THEN IT'S TIME, ISN'T IT?
LET'S EVACUATE.
MOST EVERYBODY IS GONE OFF ON COMBAT MISSIONS ANYWAY.

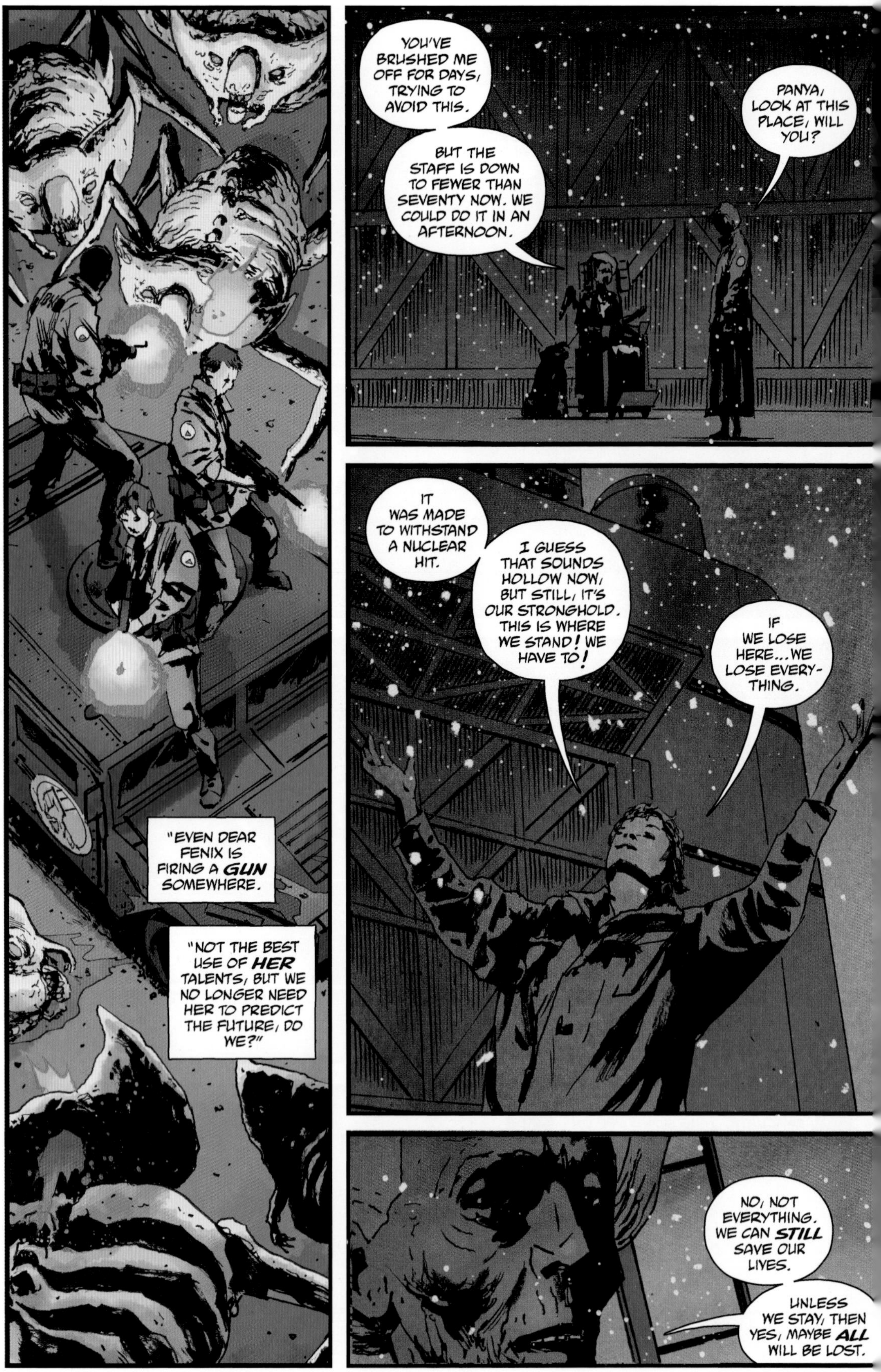
"EVEN DEAR FENIX IS FIRING A GUN SOMEWHERE.
"NOT THE BEST USE OF HER TALENTS, BUT WE NO LONGER NEED HER TO PREDICT THE FUTURE, DO WE?"
YOU'VE BRUSHED ME OFF FOR DAYS, TRYING TO AVOID THIS.
BUT THE STAFF IS DOWN TO FEWER THAN SEVENTY NOW. WE COULD DO IT IN AN AFTERNOON.
PANYA, LOOK AT THIS PLACE, WILL YOU?
IT WAS MADE TO WITHSTAND A NUCLEAR HIT.
I GUESS THAT SOUNDS HOLLOW NOW, BUT STILL, IT'S OUR STRONGHOLD. THIS IS WHERE WE STAND! WE HAVE TO!
IF WE LOSE HERE... WE LOSE EVERYTHING.
NO, NOT EVERYTHING. WE CAN STILL SAVE OUR LIVES.
UNLESS WE STAY, THEN YES, MAYBE ALL WILL BE LOST.

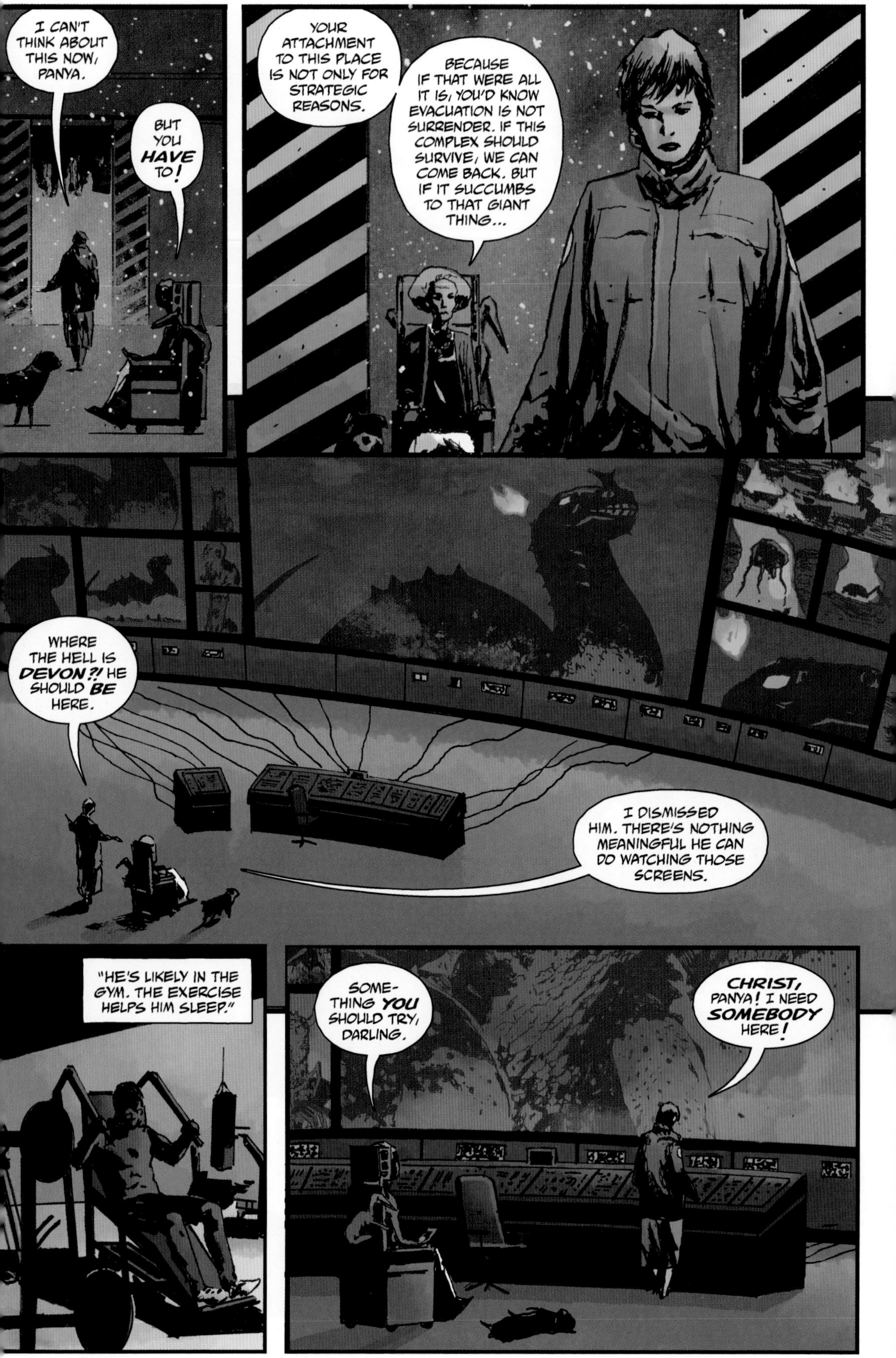

I CAN'T THINK ABOUT THIS NOW, PANYA.
BUT YOU *HAVE* TO!
YOUR ATTACHMENT TO THIS PLACE IS NOT ONLY FOR STRATEGIC REASONS.
BECAUSE IF THAT WERE ALL IT IS, YOU'D KNOW EVACUATION IS NOT SURRENDER. IF THIS COMPLEX SHOULD SURVIVE, WE CAN COME BACK. BUT IF IT SUCCUMBS TO THAT GIANT THING...
WHERE THE HELL IS *DEVON?!* HE SHOULD *BE* HERE.
I DISMISSED HIM. THERE'S NOTHING MEANINGFUL HE CAN DO WATCHING THOSE SCREENS.
"HE'S LIKELY IN THE GYM. THE EXERCISE HELPS HIM SLEEP."
SOME-THING *YOU* SHOULD TRY, DARLING.
CHRIST, PANYA! I NEED *SOMEBODY* HERE!

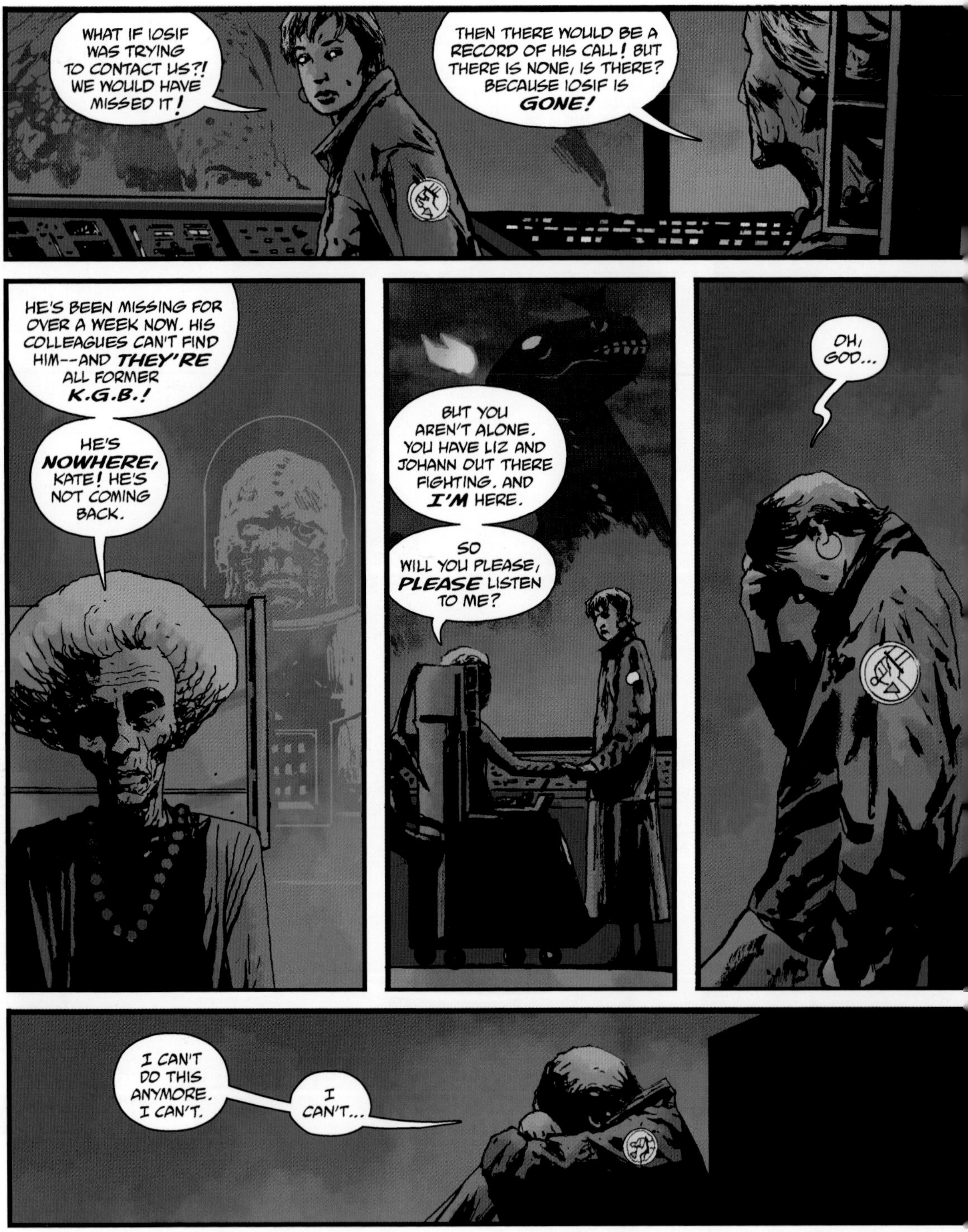
WHAT IF IOSIF WAS TRYING TO CONTACT US?! WE WOULD HAVE MISSED IT!
THEN THERE WOULD BE A RECORD OF HIS CALL! BUT THERE IS NONE, IS THERE? BECAUSE IOSIF IS GONE!
HE'S BEEN MISSING FOR OVER A WEEK NOW. HIS COLLEAGUES CAN'T FIND HIM--AND THEY'RE ALL FORMER K.G.B.!
HE'S NOWHERE, KATE! HE'S NOT COMING BACK.
BUT YOU AREN'T ALONE. YOU HAVE LIZ AND JOHANN OUT THERE FIGHTING. AND I'M HERE.
SO WILL YOU PLEASE, PLEASE LISTEN TO ME?
OH, GOD...
I CAN'T DO THIS ANYMORE. I CAN'T.
I CAN'T...

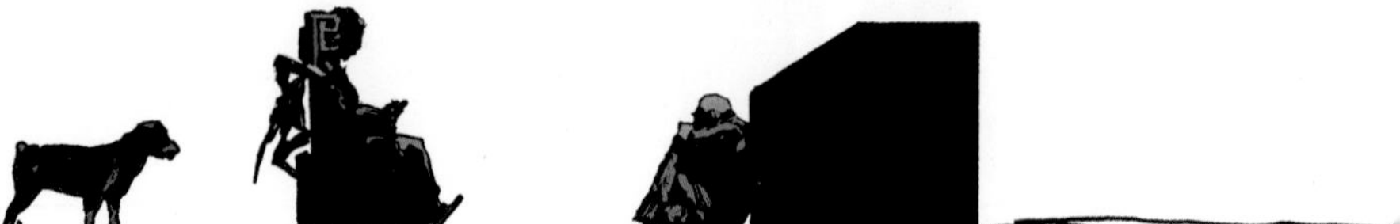

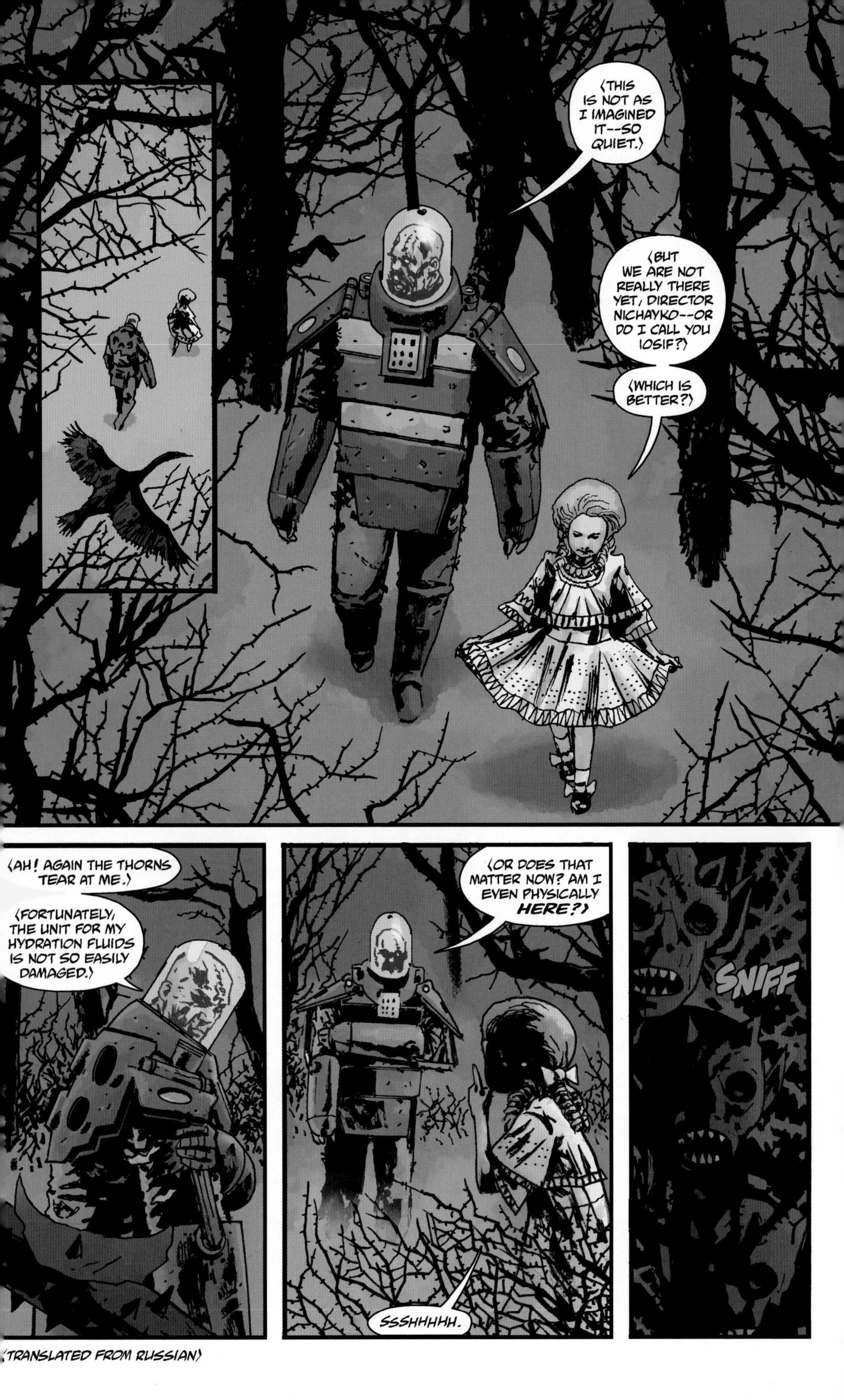

‹THIS IS NOT AS I IMAGINED IT--SO QUIET.›
‹BUT WE ARE NOT REALLY THERE YET, DIRECTOR NICHAYKO--OR DO I CALL YOU IOSIF?›
‹WHICH IS BETTER?›
‹AH! AGAIN THE THORNS TEAR AT ME.›
‹FORTUNATELY, THE UNIT FOR MY HYDRATION FLUIDS IS NOT SO EASILY DAMAGED.›
‹OR DOES THAT MATTER NOW? AM I EVEN PHYSICALLY *HERE?*›
SSSHHHHH.
SNIFF

‹TRANSLATED FROM RUSSIAN›

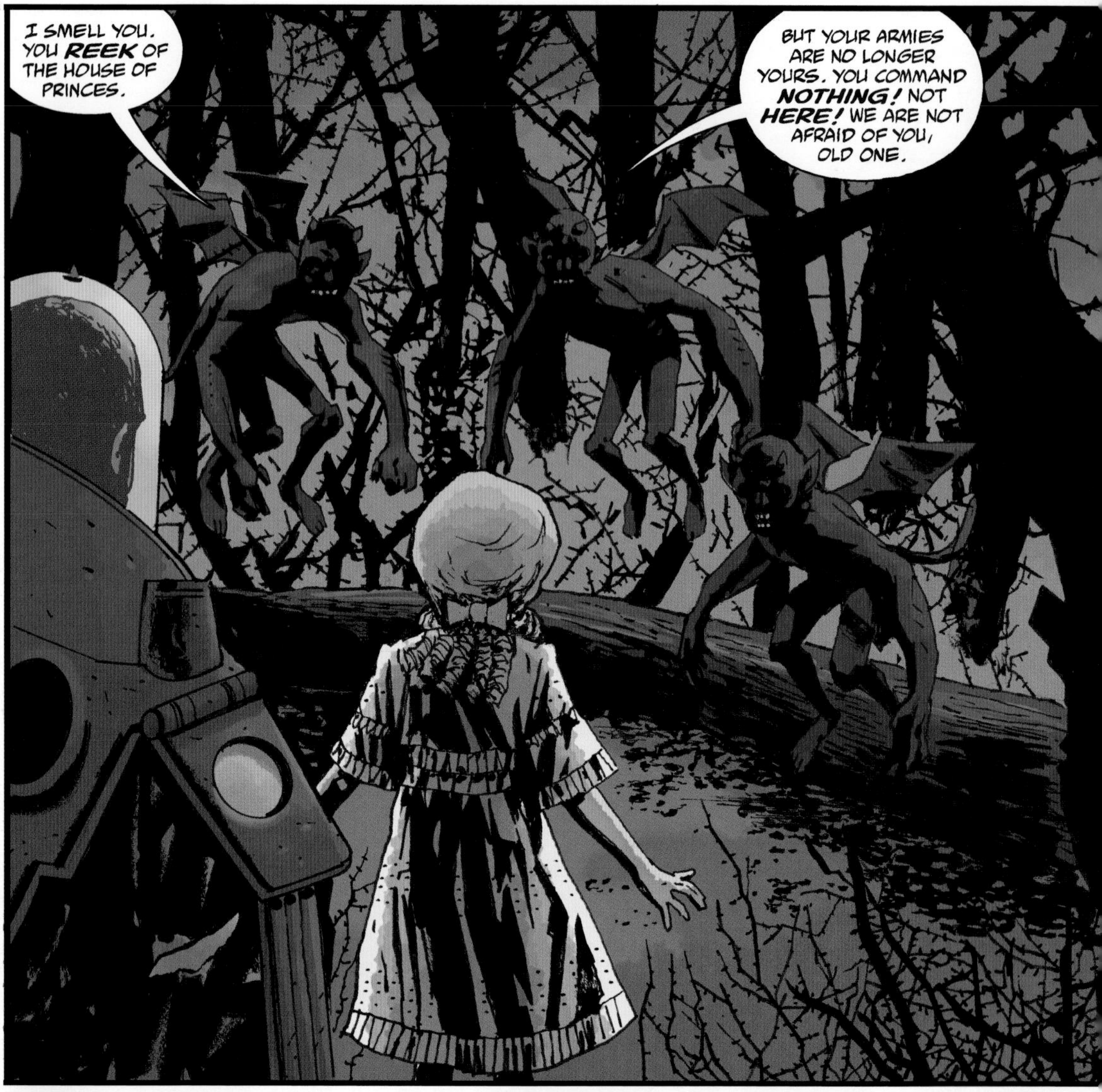
I SMELL YOU. YOU REEK OF THE HOUSE OF PRINCES.
BUT YOUR ARMIES ARE NO LONGER YOURS. YOU COMMAND NOTHING! NOT HERE! WE ARE NOT AFRAID OF YOU, OLD ONE.

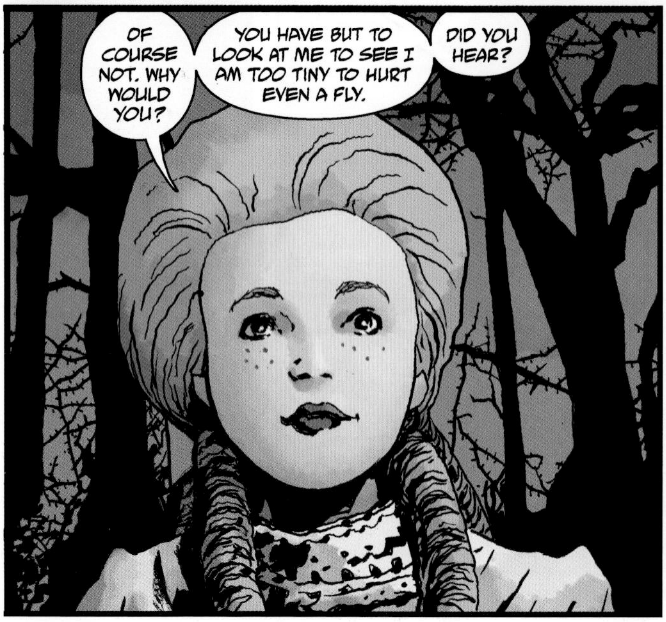
OF COURSE NOT. WHY WOULD YOU?
YOU HAVE BUT TO LOOK AT ME TO SEE I AM TOO TINY TO HURT EVEN A FLY.
DID YOU HEAR?

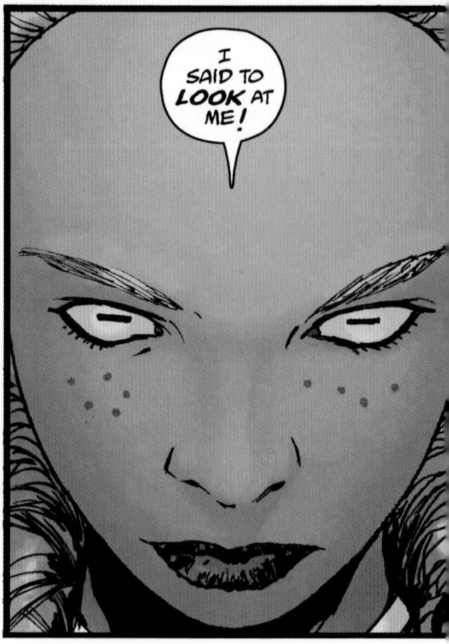
I SAID TO LOOK AT ME!

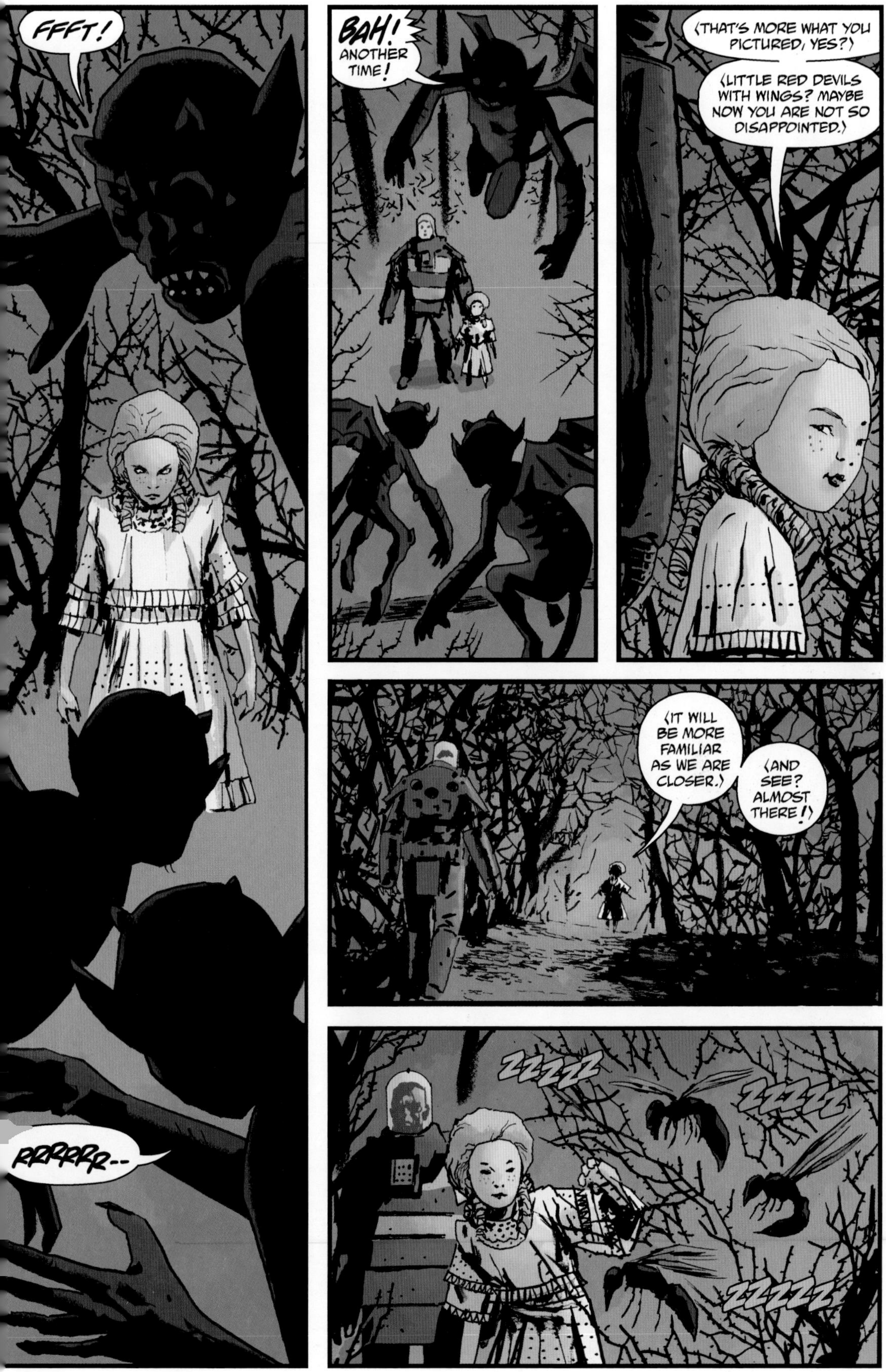
FFFT!
RRRRRR--
BAH! ANOTHER TIME!
⟨THAT'S MORE WHAT YOU PICTURED, YES?⟩
⟨LITTLE RED DEVILS WITH WINGS? MAYBE NOW YOU ARE NOT SO DISAPPOINTED.⟩
⟨IT WILL BE MORE FAMILIAR AS WE ARE CLOSER.⟩
⟨AND SEE? ALMOST THERE!⟩
ZZZZZ
ZZZZZ
ZZZZZ

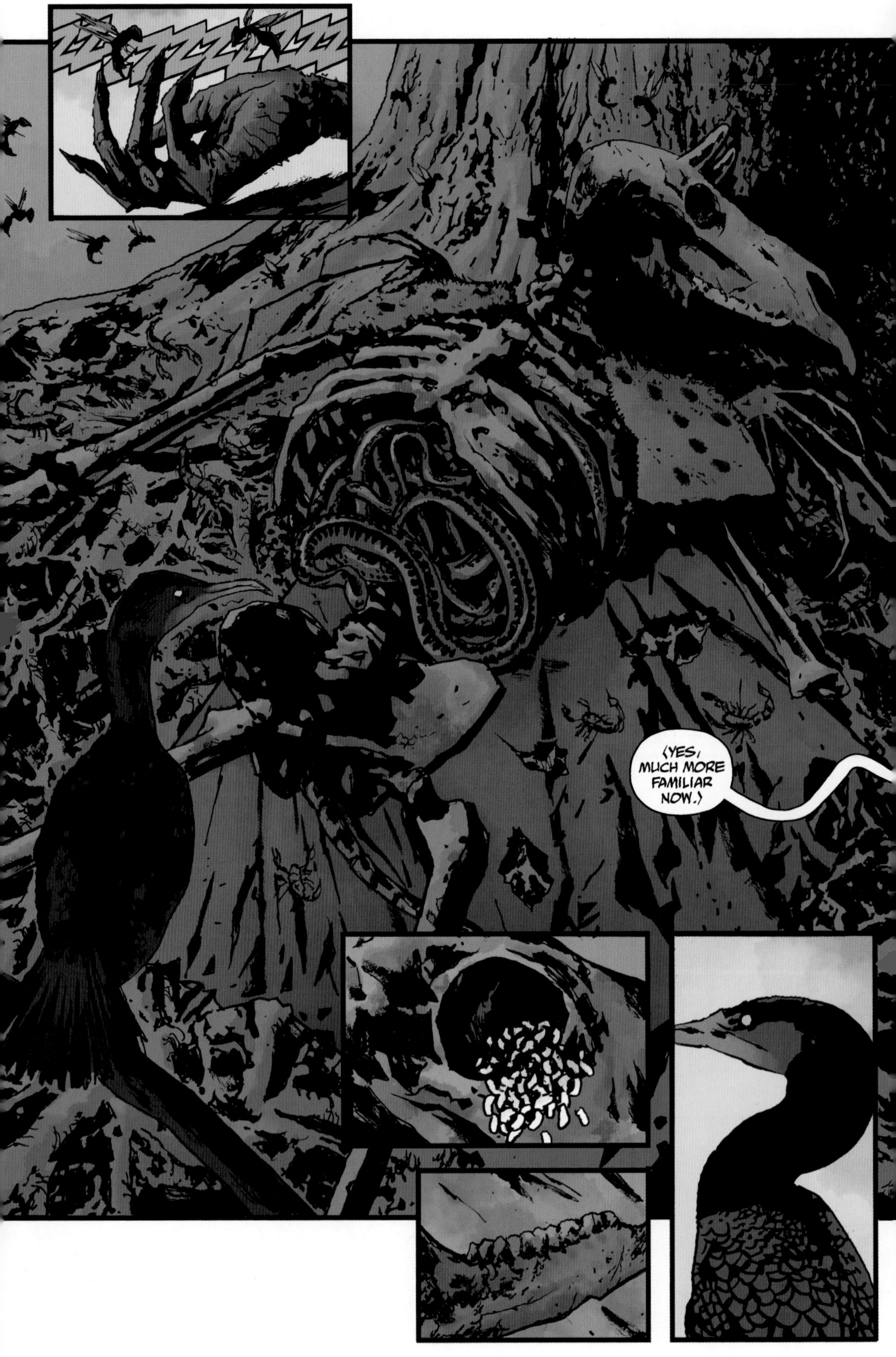
‹YES, MUCH MORE FAMILIAR NOW.›

⟨AH, BUT I KNOW HIM! IT IS THE TINY *KING*, AMDUSIAS!⟩

⟨SO LITTLE LEFT OF HIM, BUT HIS ARROGANCE SURVIVES.⟩

⟨THEN IT'S TRUE. WE *ARE* IN HELL.⟩

⟨*AM* I HERE IN FLESH, OR HAVE YOU KILLED ME AFTER ALL?⟩

⟨*SO* DRAMATIC, IOSIF.⟩

⟨AND *YOU*, LITTLE WORM. *HUSH!* I AM HERE ONLY TO VISIT.⟩

SSSSS

⟨ALL THE WHILE I WAS IMPRISONED, HOW SO I ENVIED YOU, AMDUSIAS.⟩

⟨BUT LOOK HOW THINGS HAVE TURNED OUT.⟩

⟨AH, YOU SEE THIS?⟩

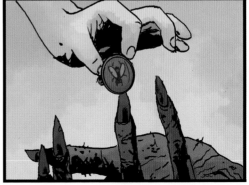

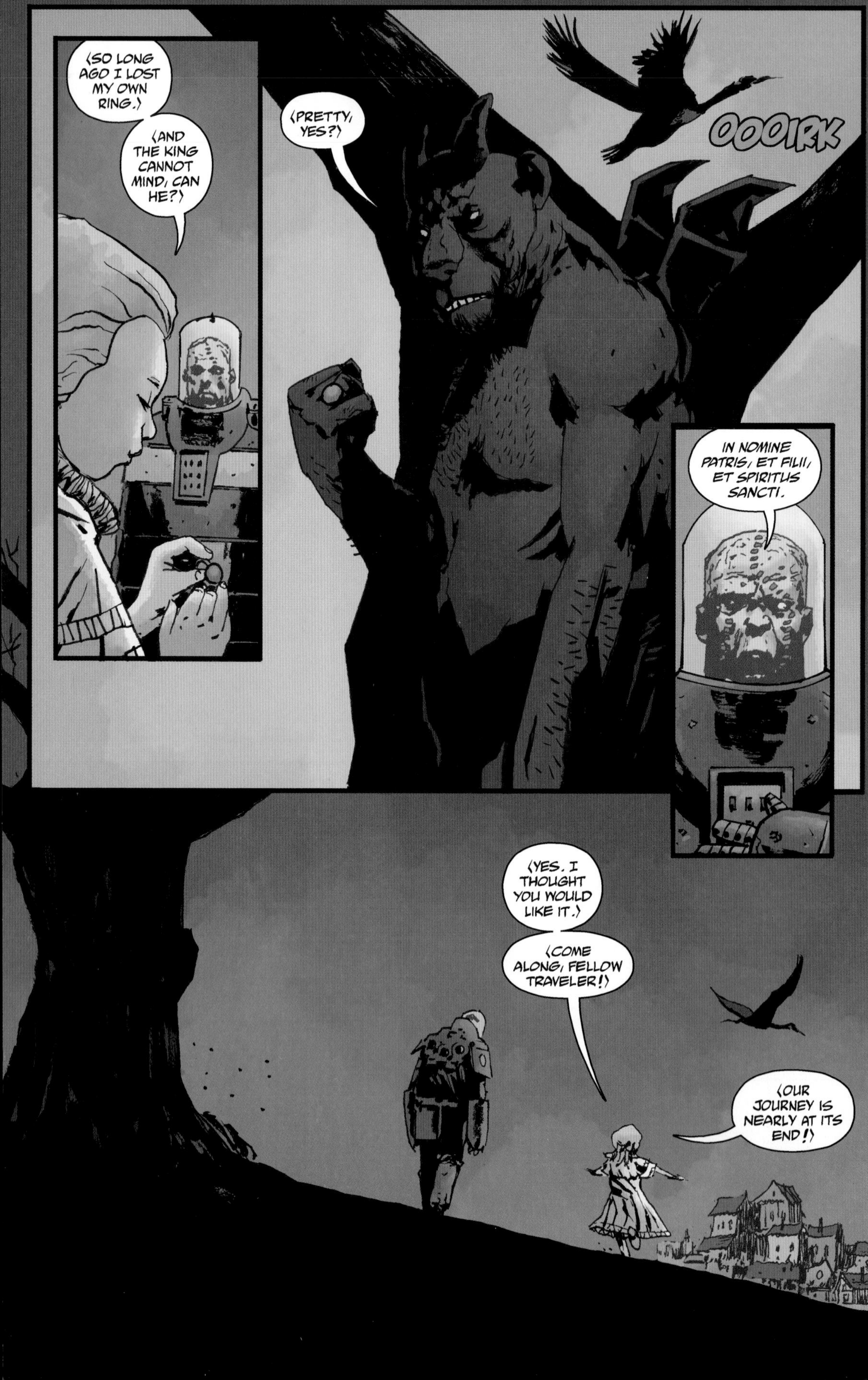

⟨SO LONG AGO I LOST MY OWN RING.⟩
⟨AND THE KING CANNOT MIND, CAN HE?⟩
⟨PRETTY, YES?⟩
OOOIRK
IN NOMINE PATRIS, ET FILII, ET SPIRITUS SANCTI.
⟨YES. I THOUGHT YOU WOULD LIKE IT.⟩
⟨COME ALONG, FELLOW TRAVELER!⟩
⟨OUR JOURNEY IS NEARLY AT ITS END!⟩

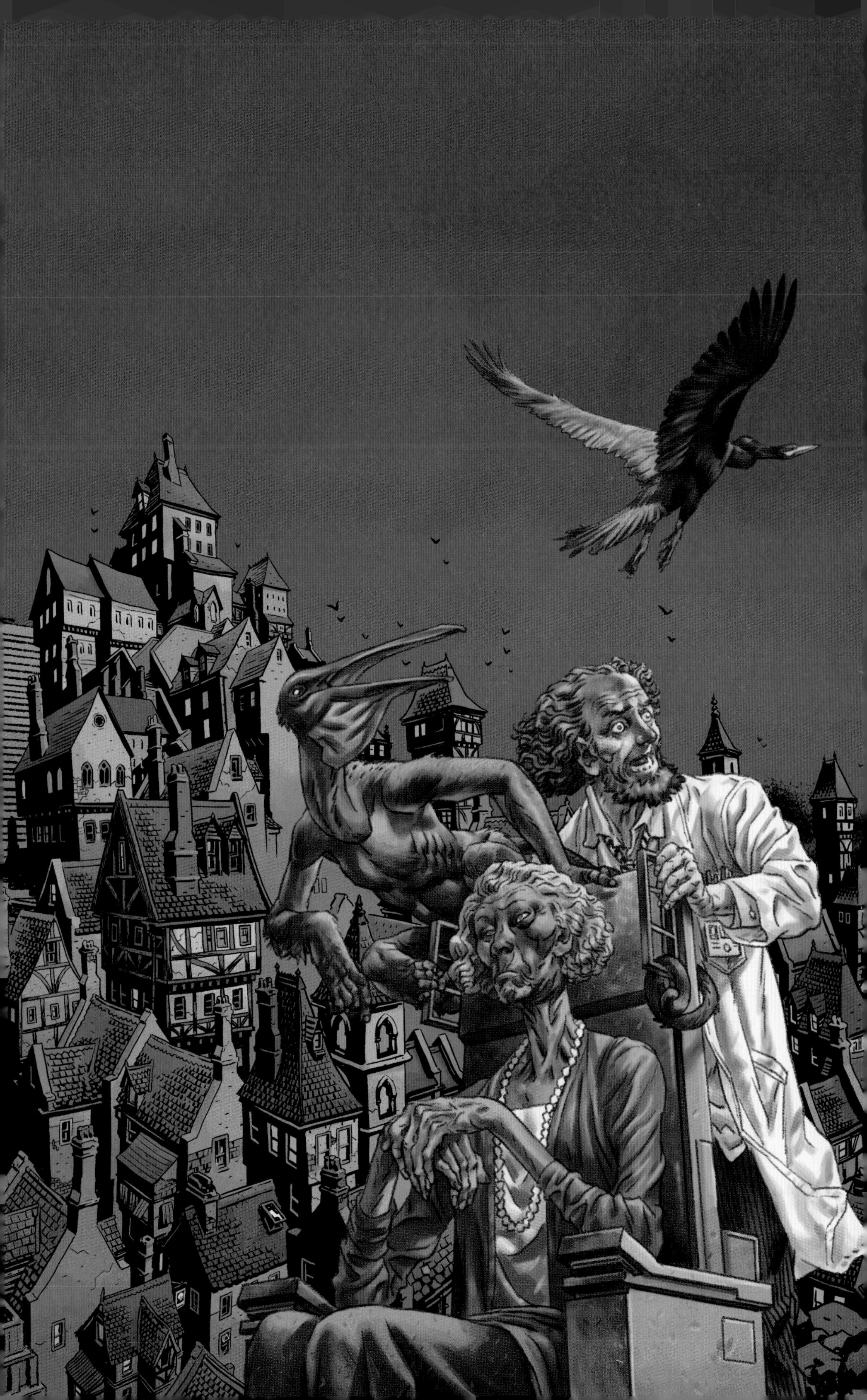

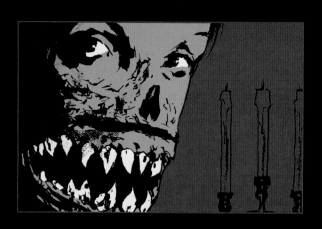

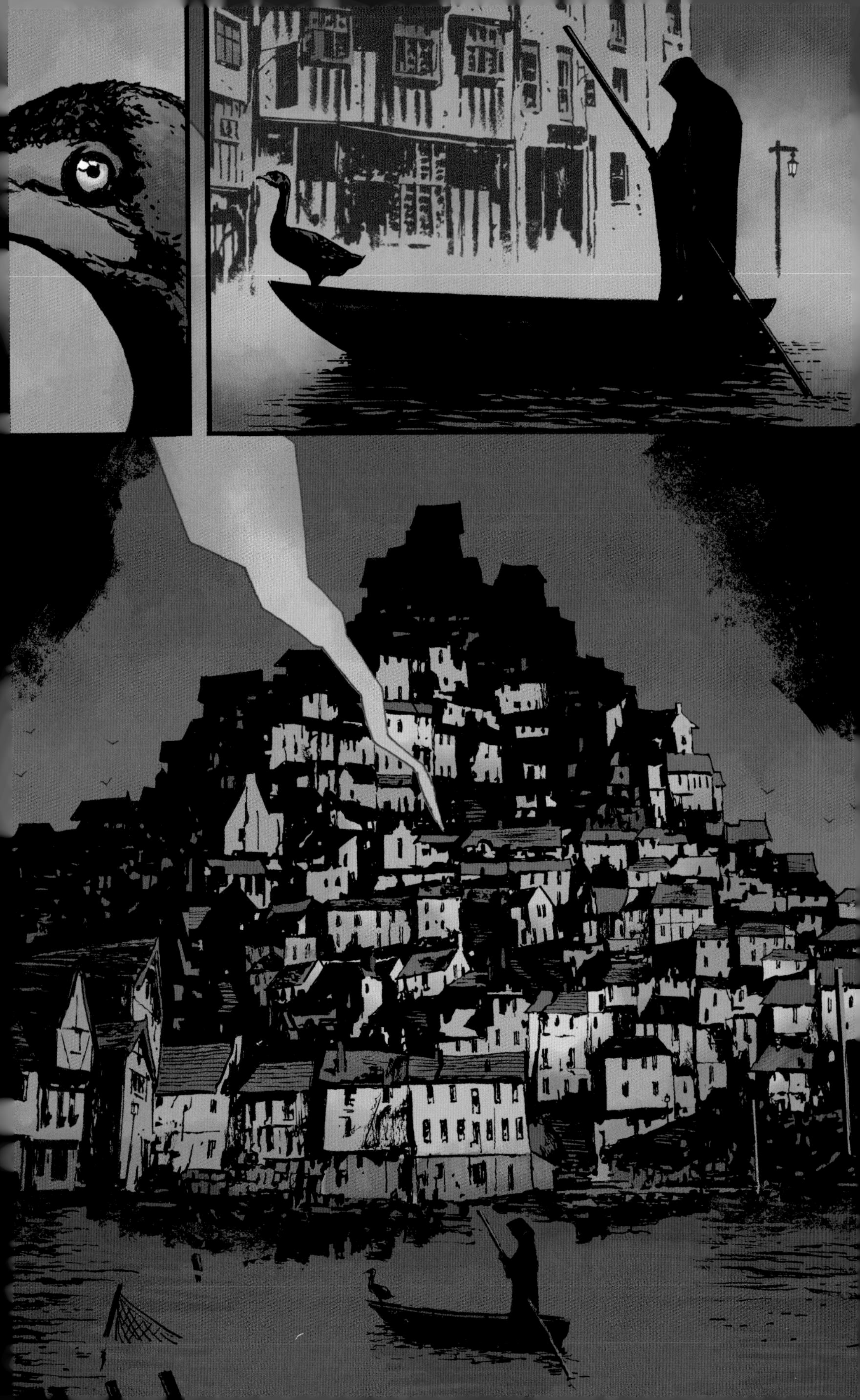

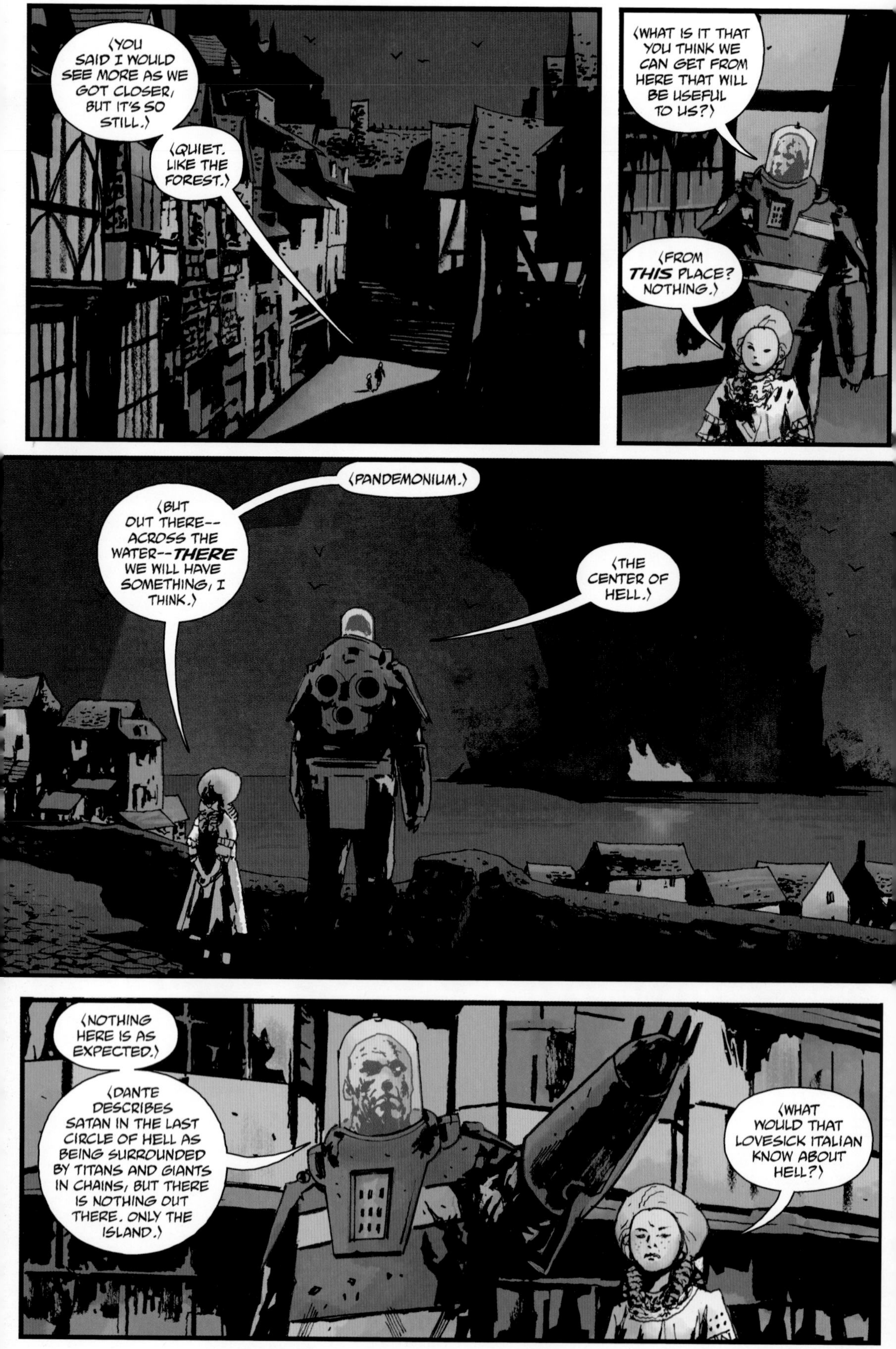
⟨YOU SAID I WOULD SEE MORE AS WE GOT CLOSER, BUT IT'S SO STILL.⟩
⟨QUIET. LIKE THE FOREST.⟩
⟨WHAT IS IT THAT YOU THINK WE CAN GET FROM HERE THAT WILL BE USEFUL TO US?⟩
⟨FROM *THIS* PLACE? NOTHING.⟩
⟨BUT OUT THERE-- ACROSS THE WATER--*THERE* WE WILL HAVE SOMETHING, I THINK.⟩
⟨PANDEMONIUM.⟩
⟨THE CENTER OF HELL.⟩
⟨NOTHING HERE IS AS EXPECTED.⟩
⟨DANTE DESCRIBES SATAN IN THE LAST CIRCLE OF HELL AS BEING SURROUNDED BY TITANS AND GIANTS IN CHAINS, BUT THERE IS NOTHING OUT THERE. ONLY THE ISLAND.⟩
⟨WHAT WOULD THAT LOVESICK ITALIAN KNOW ABOUT HELL?⟩
⟨TRANSLATED FROM RUSSIAN⟩

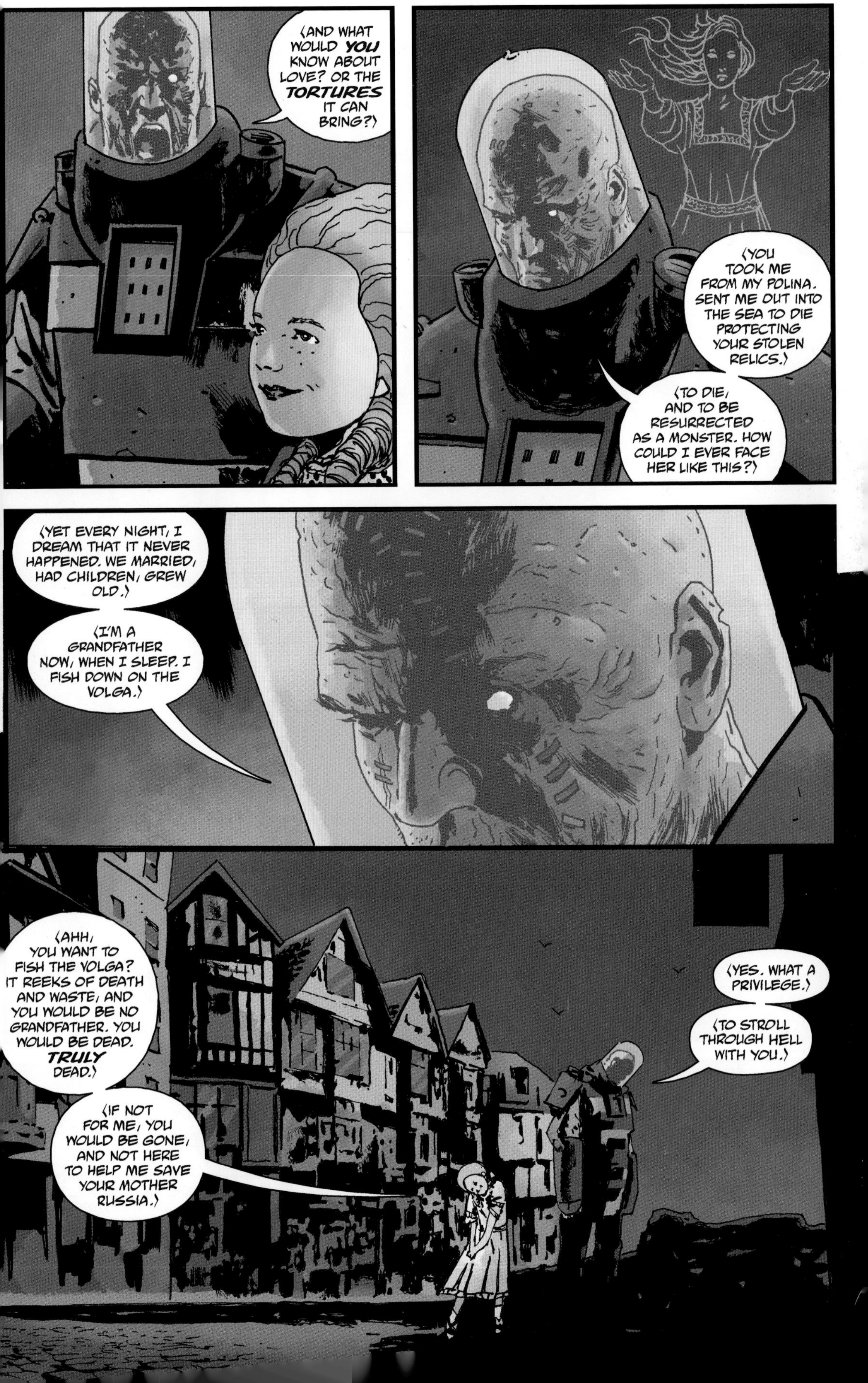
⟨AND WHAT WOULD YOU KNOW ABOUT LOVE? OR THE TORTURES IT CAN BRING?⟩
⟨YOU TOOK ME FROM MY POLINA. SENT ME OUT INTO THE SEA TO DIE PROTECTING YOUR STOLEN RELICS.⟩
⟨TO DIE, AND TO BE RESURRECTED AS A MONSTER. HOW COULD I EVER FACE HER LIKE THIS?⟩
⟨YET EVERY NIGHT, I DREAM THAT IT NEVER HAPPENED. WE MARRIED, HAD CHILDREN, GREW OLD.⟩
⟨I'M A GRANDFATHER NOW, WHEN I SLEEP. I FISH DOWN ON THE VOLGA.⟩
⟨AHH, YOU WANT TO FISH THE VOLGA? IT REEKS OF DEATH AND WASTE, AND YOU WOULD BE NO GRANDFATHER. YOU WOULD BE DEAD. TRULY DEAD.⟩
⟨IF NOT FOR ME, YOU WOULD BE GONE, AND NOT HERE TO HELP ME SAVE YOUR MOTHER RUSSIA.⟩
⟨YES. WHAT A PRIVILEGE.⟩
⟨TO STROLL THROUGH HELL WITH YOU.⟩

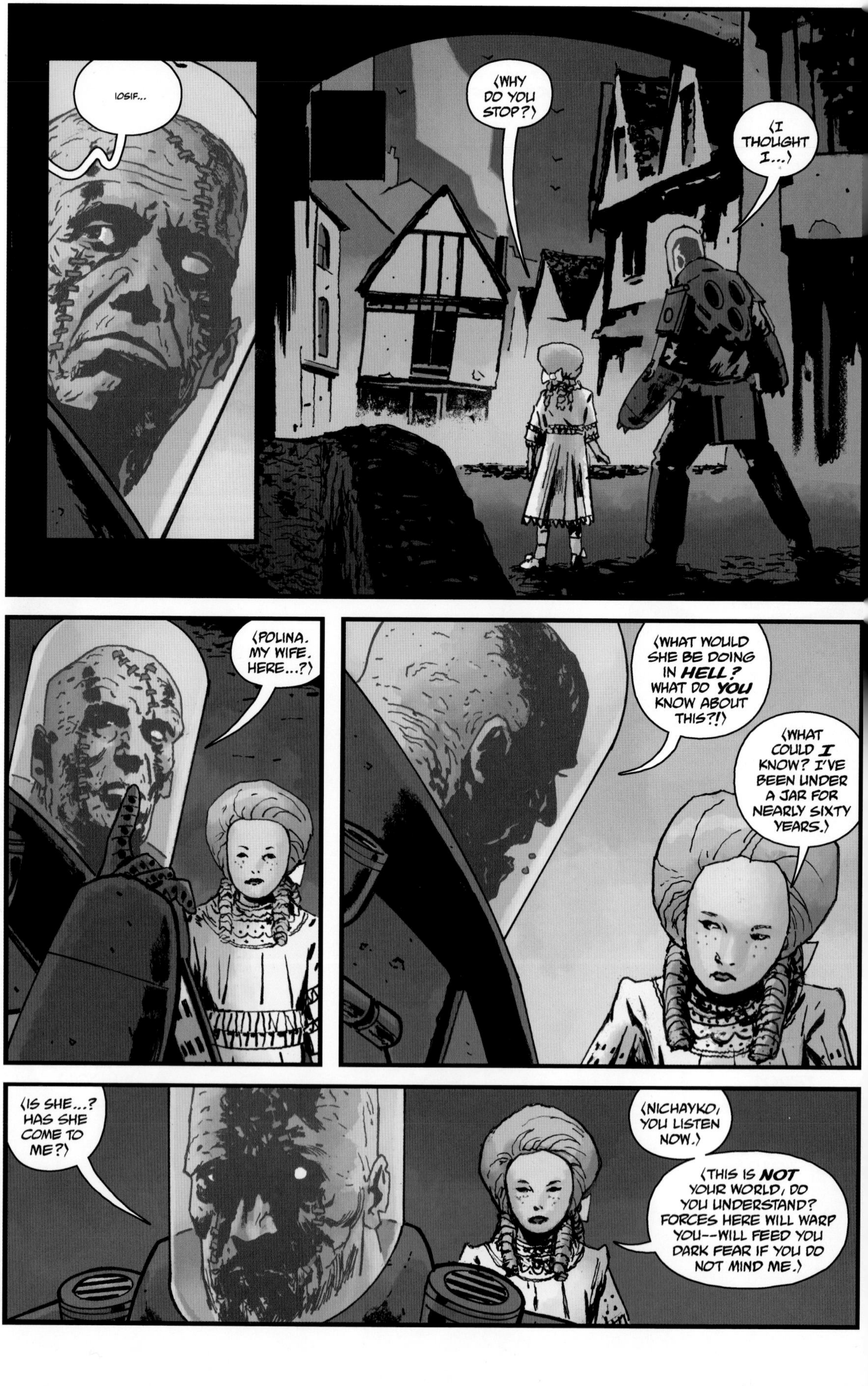
IOSIF...
⟨WHY DO YOU STOP?⟩
⟨I THOUGHT I...⟩
⟨POLINA. MY WIFE. HERE...?⟩
⟨WHAT WOULD SHE BE DOING IN HELL? WHAT DO YOU KNOW ABOUT THIS?!⟩
⟨WHAT COULD I KNOW? I'VE BEEN UNDER A JAR FOR NEARLY SIXTY YEARS.⟩
⟨IS SHE...? HAS SHE COME TO ME?⟩
⟨NICHAYKO, YOU LISTEN NOW.⟩
⟨THIS IS NOT YOUR WORLD, DO YOU UNDERSTAND? FORCES HERE WILL WARP YOU--WILL FEED YOU DARK FEAR IF YOU DO NOT MIND ME.⟩

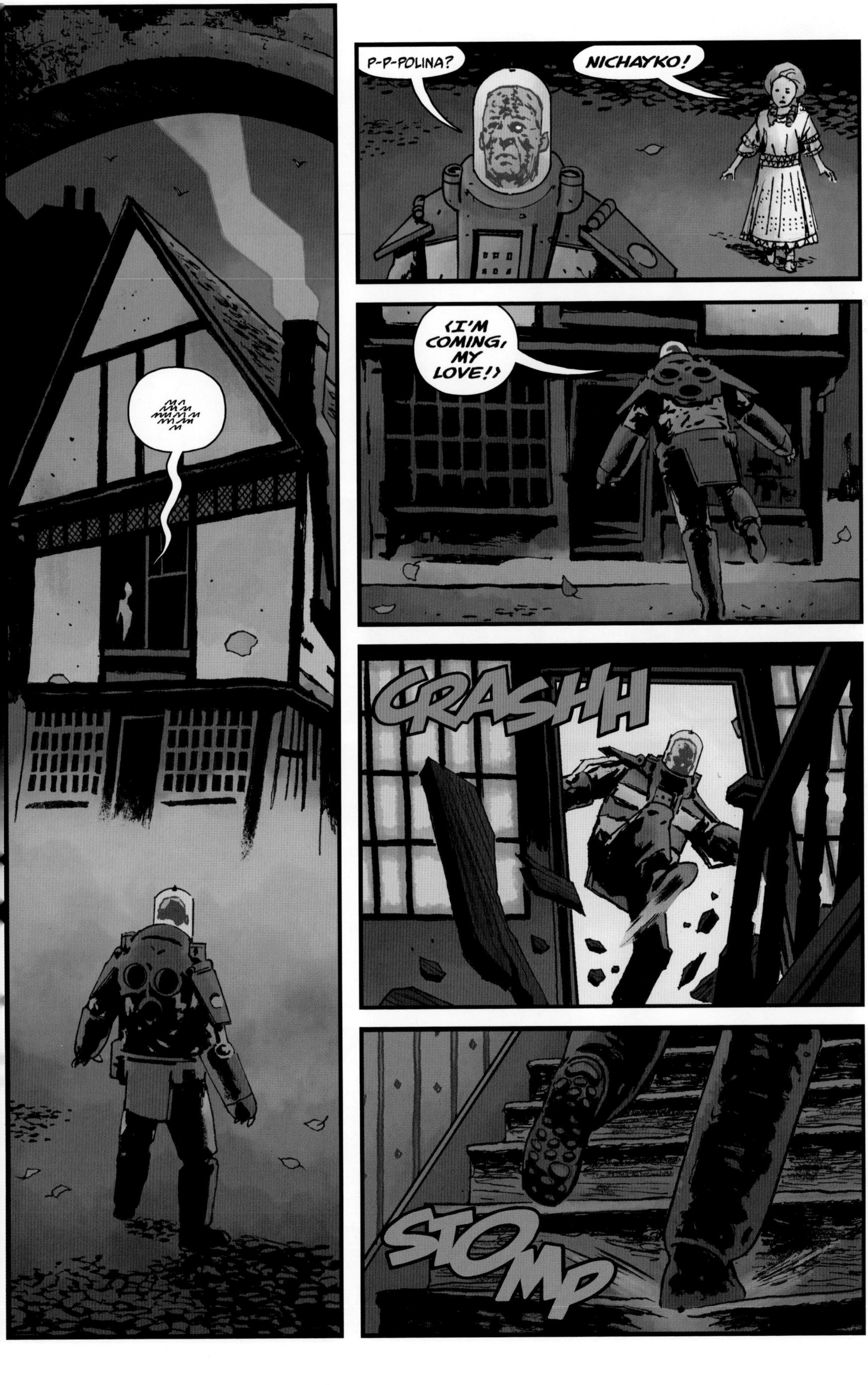
P-P-POLINA?
NICHAYKO!
‹I'M COMING, MY LOVE!›
CRASHH
STOMP

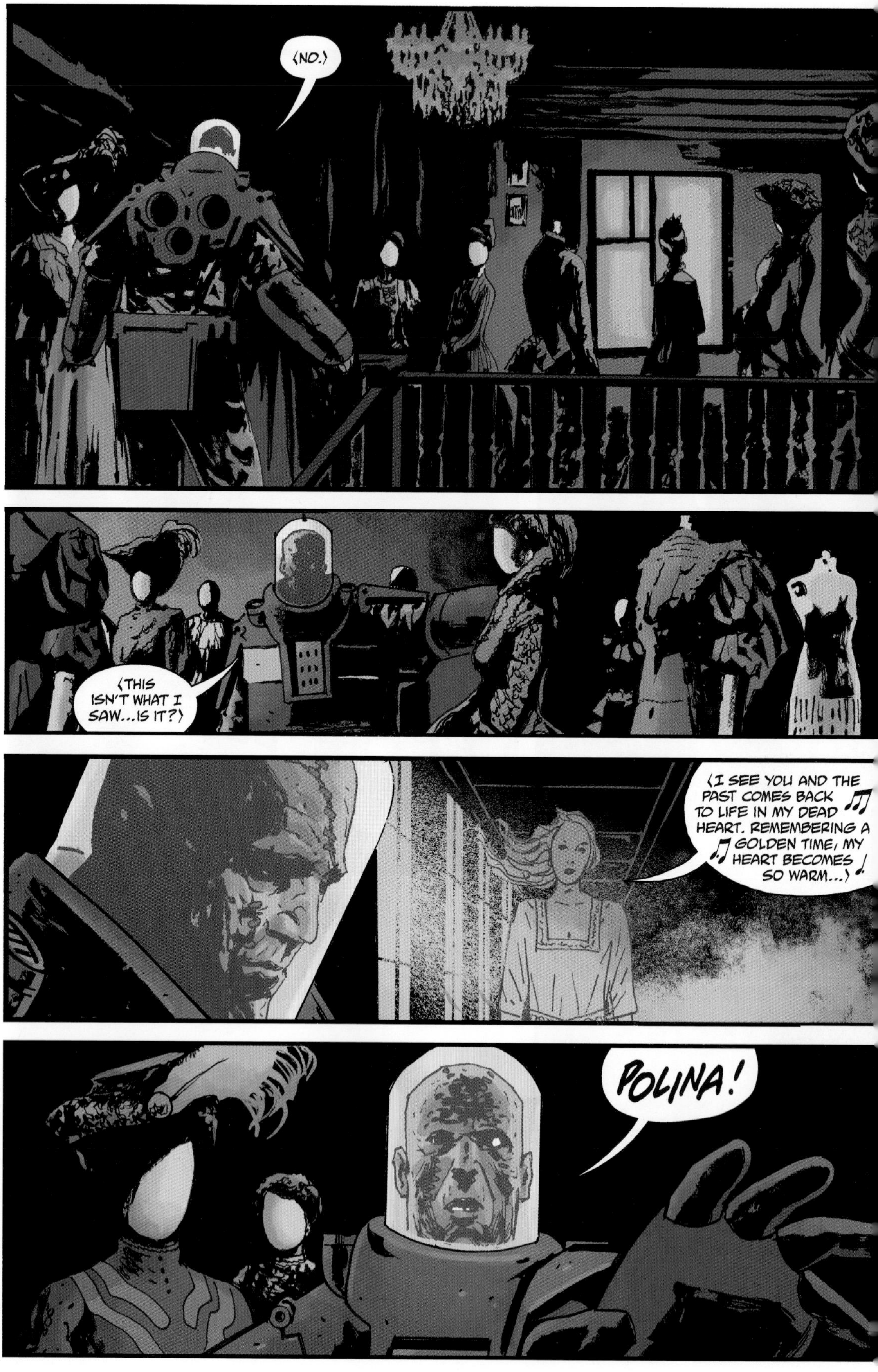
⟨NO.⟩
⟨THIS ISN'T WHAT I SAW...IS IT?⟩
⟨I SEE YOU AND THE PAST COMES BACK TO LIFE IN MY DEAD HEART. REMEMBERING A GOLDEN TIME, MY HEART BECOMES SO WARM...⟩
POLINA!

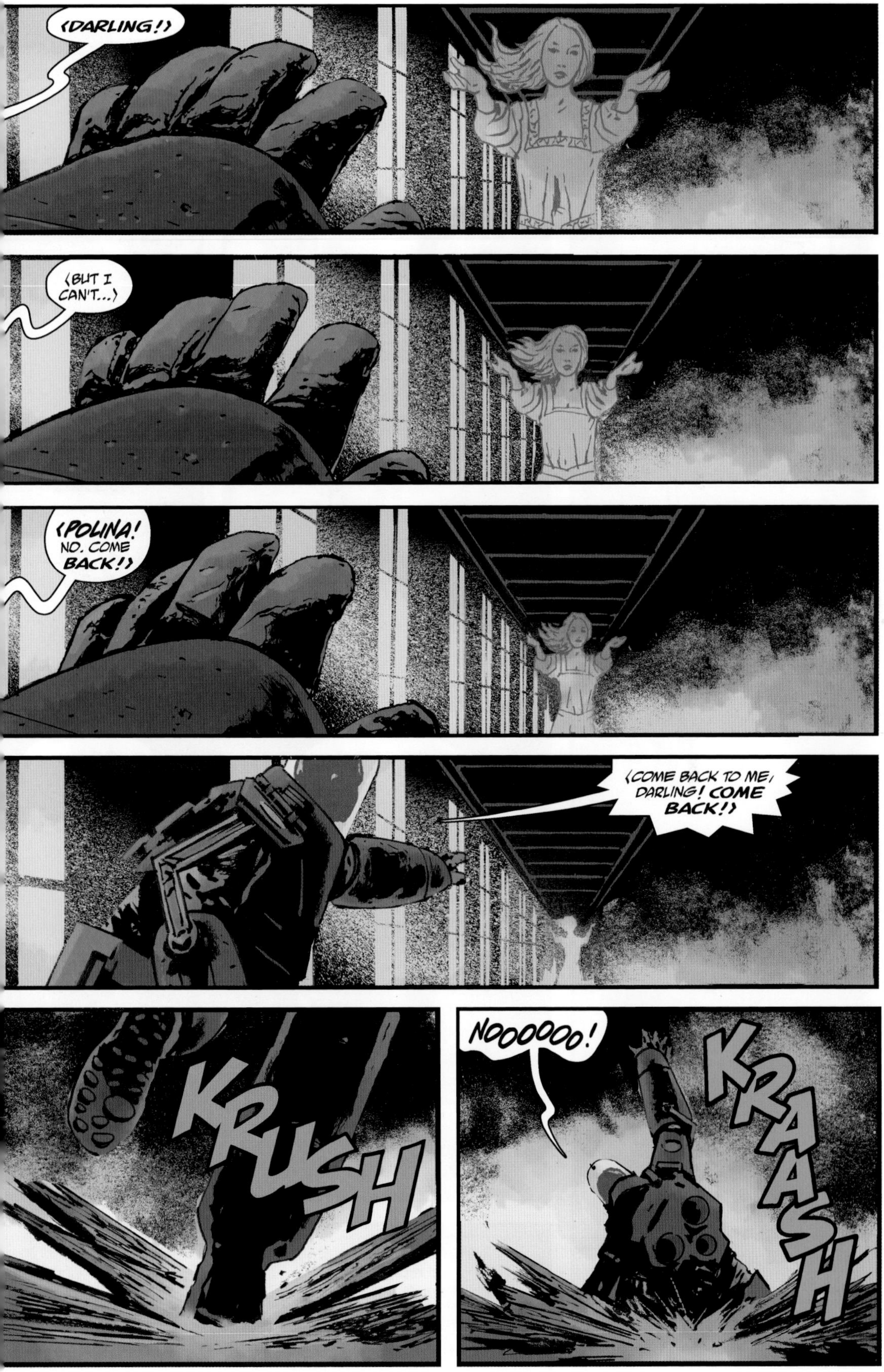
‹DARLING!›
‹BUT I CAN'T...›
‹POLINA! NO. COME BACK!›
‹COME BACK TO ME, DARLING! COME BACK!›
KRUSH
NOOOOOO!
KRASH

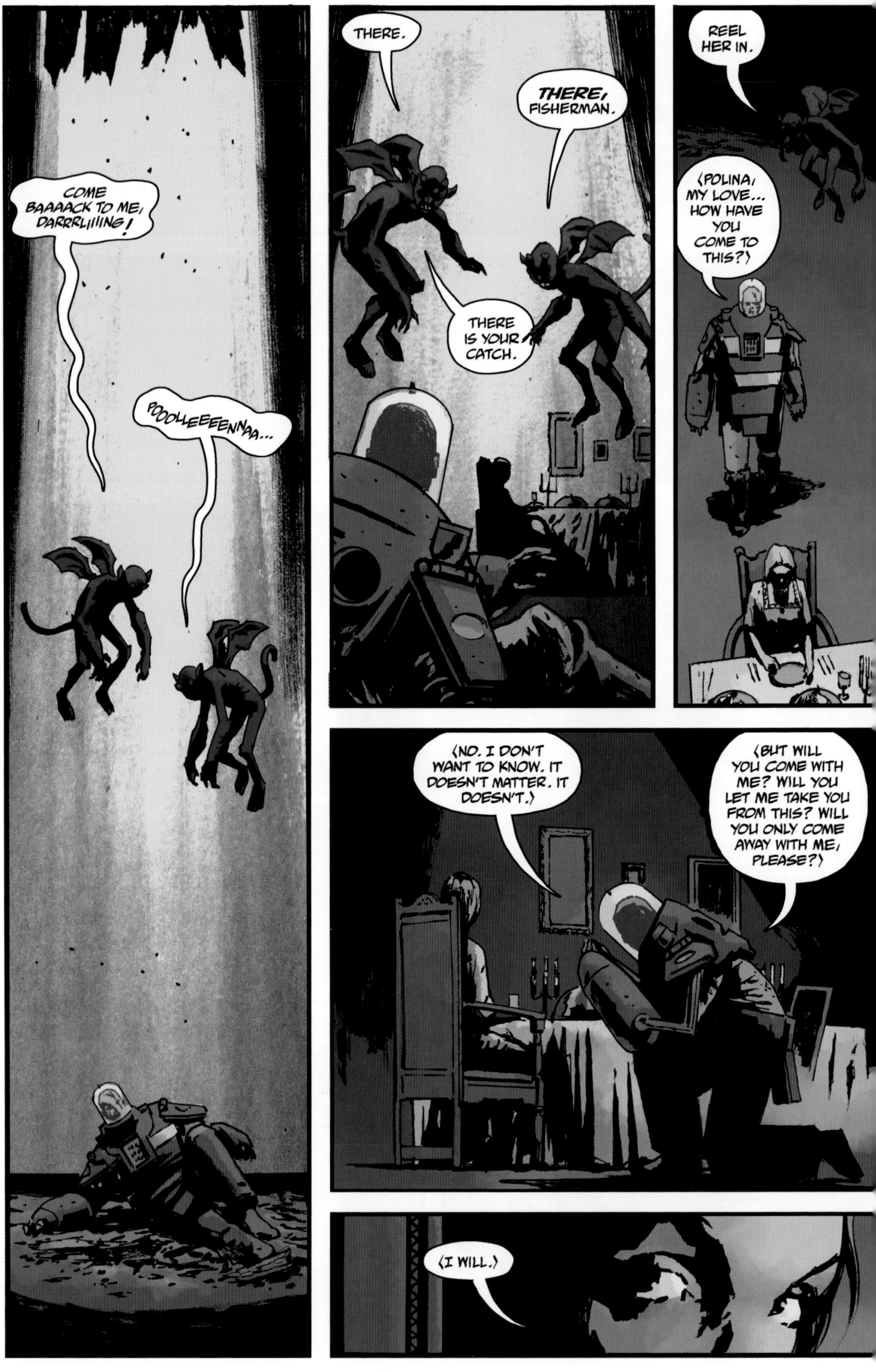

COME BAAAACK TO ME, DARRRLIIIING!
POOOLLEEEENNAA...
THERE.
THERE, FISHERMAN.
THERE IS YOUR CATCH.
REEL HER IN.
⟨POLINA, MY LOVE... HOW HAVE YOU COME TO THIS?⟩
⟨NO. I DON'T WANT TO KNOW. IT DOESN'T MATTER. IT DOESN'T.⟩
⟨BUT WILL YOU COME WITH ME? WILL YOU LET ME TAKE YOU FROM THIS? WILL YOU ONLY COME AWAY WITH ME, PLEASE?⟩
⟨I WILL.⟩

〈WHEN MY BELLY IS FULL!〉

NO! NO!

LIE-LIE-LIE-LIE!

〈THIS IS LIES! ALL MONSTROUS LIES!〉

EEEEEEEE!!

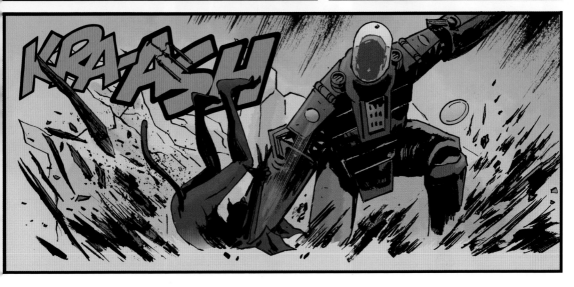

KRAASH

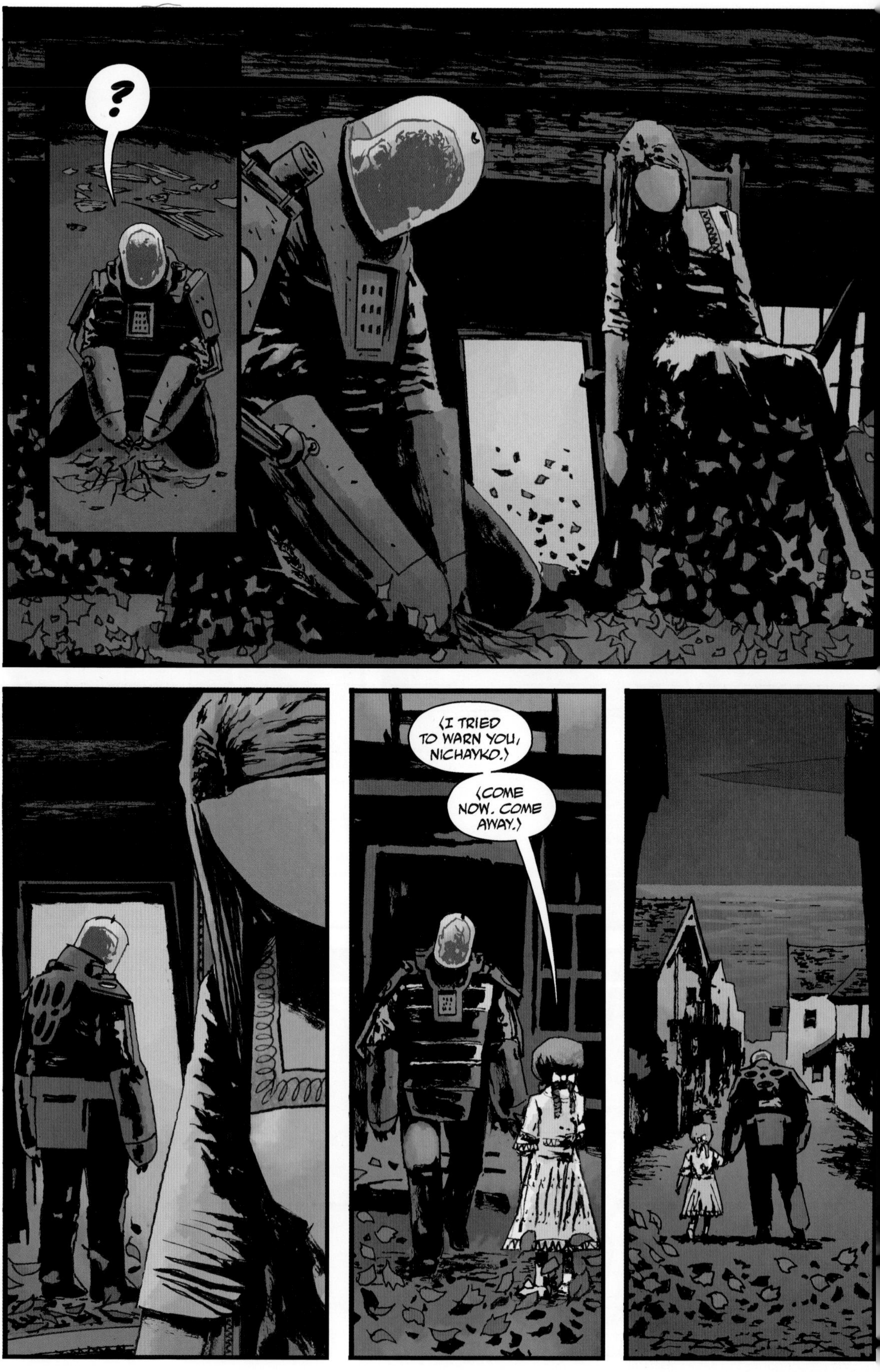
?
‹I TRIED TO WARN YOU, NICHAYKO.›
‹COME NOW. COME AWAY.›

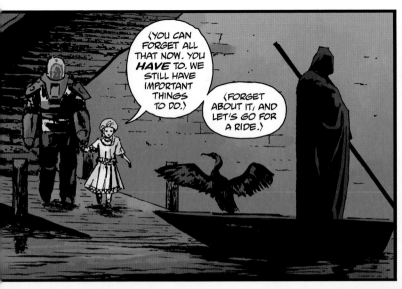

⟨YOU CAN FORGET ALL THAT NOW. YOU **HAVE** TO. WE STILL HAVE IMPORTANT THINGS TO DO.⟩

⟨FORGET ABOUT IT, AND LET'S GO FOR A RIDE.⟩

SQWERK

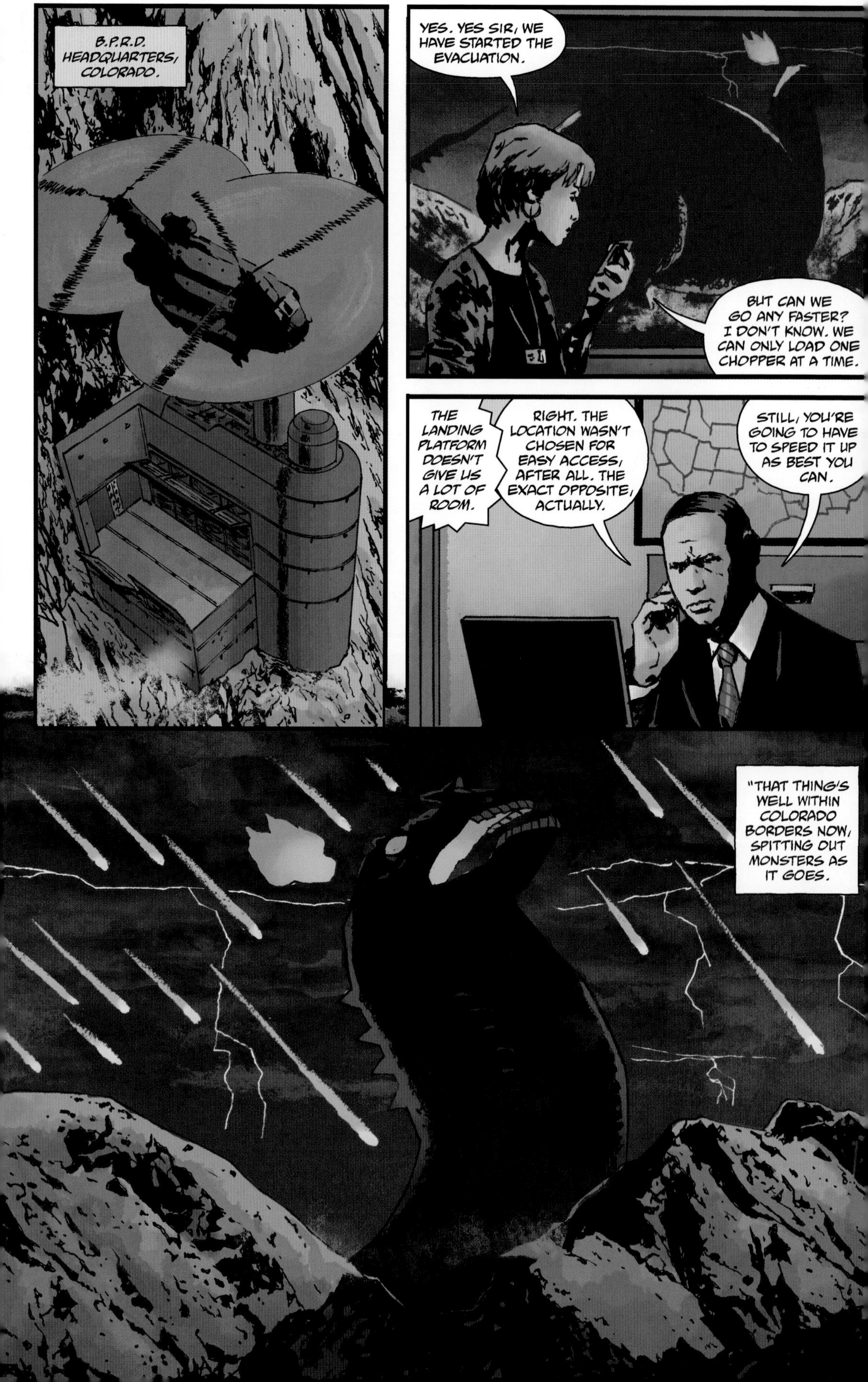
B.P.R.D. HEADQUARTERS, COLORADO.
YES. YES SIR, WE HAVE STARTED THE EVACUATION.
BUT CAN WE GO ANY FASTER? I DON'T KNOW. WE CAN ONLY LOAD ONE CHOPPER AT A TIME.
THE LANDING PLATFORM DOESN'T GIVE US A LOT OF ROOM.
RIGHT. THE LOCATION WASN'T CHOSEN FOR EASY ACCESS, AFTER ALL. THE EXACT OPPOSITE, ACTUALLY.
STILL, YOU'RE GOING TO HAVE TO SPEED IT UP AS BEST YOU CAN.
"THAT THING'S WELL WITHIN COLORADO BORDERS NOW, SPITTING OUT MONSTERS AS IT GOES.

"AND THERE'S NO WAY LIZ AND JOHANN CAN STAY AHEAD OF THEM."

ALL RIGHT, TOM, BUT IF YOU WANT US TO PICK UP THE PACE ON THE EVACUATIONS, HOW ABOUT GETTING US ANOTHER CHINOOK SO WE CAN **PLATOON** THEM?

I'LL SEE WHAT I CAN DO.

THANKS, TOM.

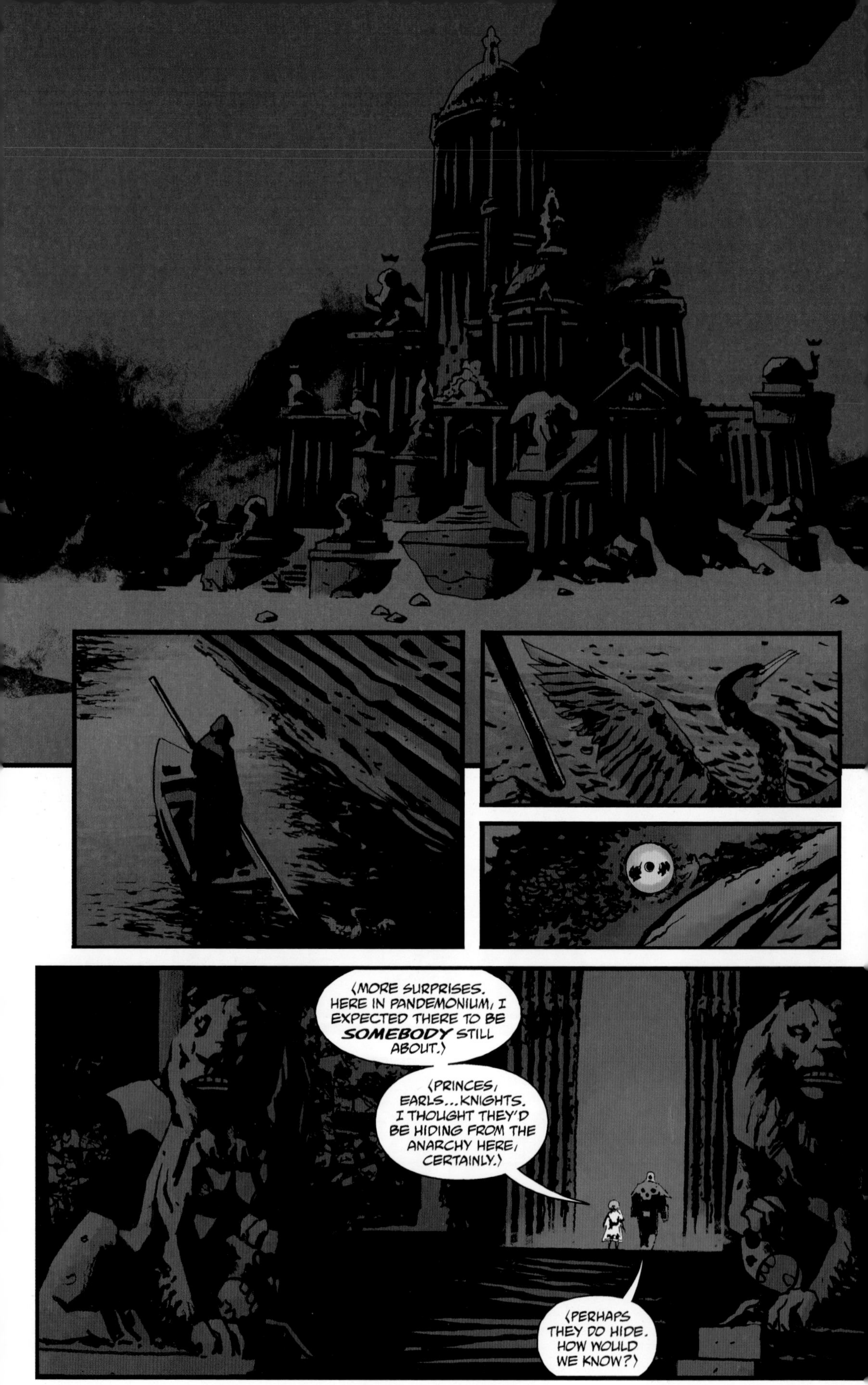

⟨MORE SURPRISES. HERE IN PANDEMONIUM, I EXPECTED THERE TO BE *SOMEBODY* STILL ABOUT.⟩
⟨PRINCES, EARLS... KNIGHTS. I THOUGHT THEY'D BE HIDING FROM THE ANARCHY HERE, CERTAINLY.⟩
⟨PERHAPS THEY DO HIDE. HOW WOULD WE KNOW?⟩

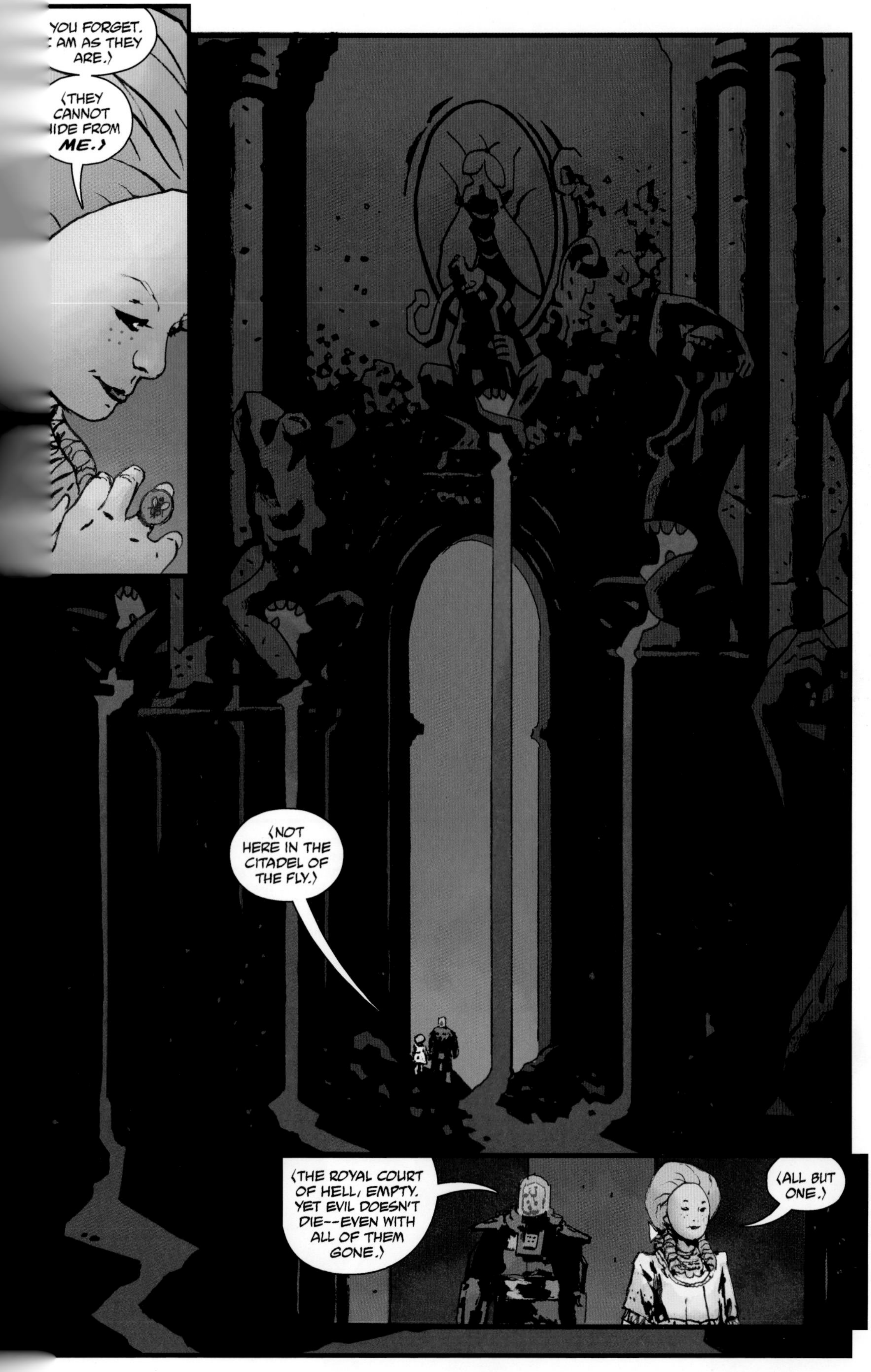
(YOU FORGET. I AM AS THEY ARE.)
(THEY CANNOT HIDE FROM ME.)
(NOT HERE IN THE CITADEL OF THE FLY.)
(THE ROYAL COURT OF HELL, EMPTY. YET EVIL DOESN'T DIE--EVEN WITH ALL OF THEM GONE.)
(ALL BUT ONE.)

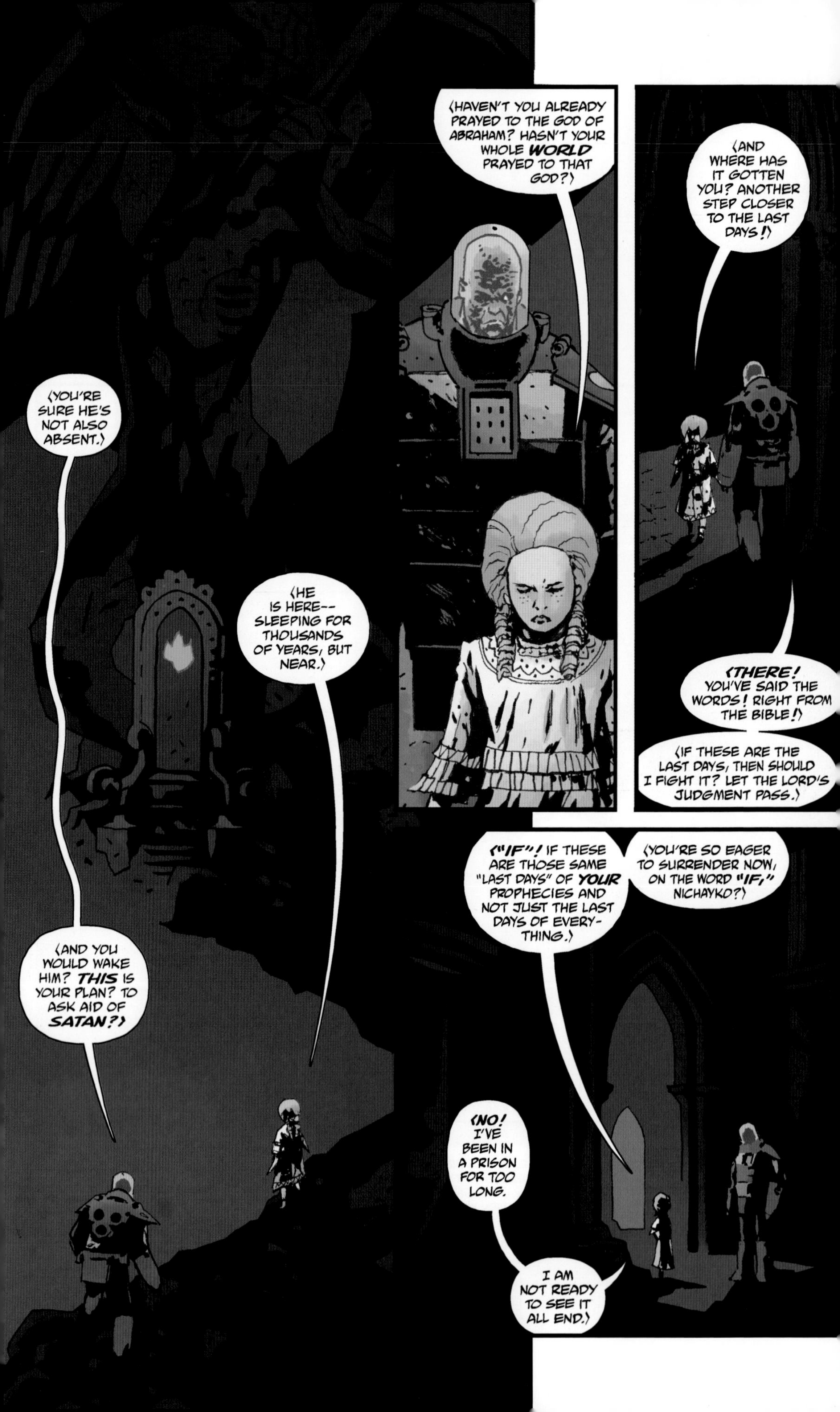

‹YOU'RE SURE HE'S NOT ALSO ABSENT.›
‹HE IS HERE-- SLEEPING FOR THOUSANDS OF YEARS, BUT NEAR.›
‹AND YOU WOULD WAKE HIM? THIS IS YOUR PLAN? TO ASK AID OF SATAN?›
‹HAVEN'T YOU ALREADY PRAYED TO THE GOD OF ABRAHAM? HASN'T YOUR WHOLE WORLD PRAYED TO THAT GOD?›
‹AND WHERE HAS IT GOTTEN YOU? ANOTHER STEP CLOSER TO THE LAST DAYS!›
‹THERE! YOU'VE SAID THE WORDS! RIGHT FROM THE BIBLE!›
‹IF THESE ARE THE LAST DAYS, THEN SHOULD I FIGHT IT? LET THE LORD'S JUDGMENT PASS.›
‹"IF"! IF THESE ARE THOSE SAME "LAST DAYS" OF YOUR PROPHECIES AND NOT JUST THE LAST DAYS OF EVERY-THING.›
‹YOU'RE SO EAGER TO SURRENDER NOW, ON THE WORD "IF," NICHAYKO?›
‹NO! I'VE BEEN IN A PRISON FOR TOO LONG.
I AM NOT READY TO SEE IT ALL END.›

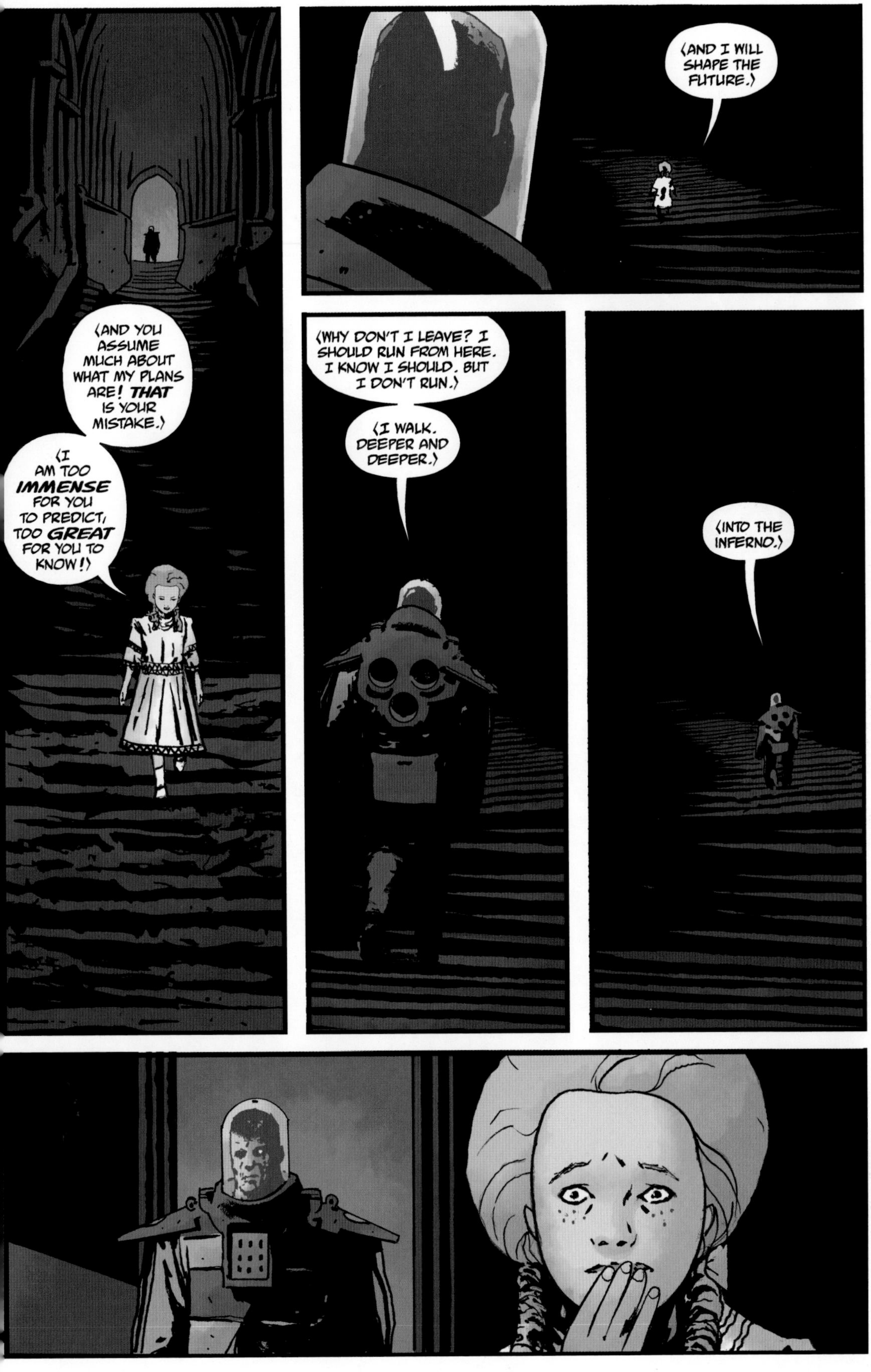

⟨AND YOU ASSUME MUCH ABOUT WHAT MY PLANS ARE! **THAT** IS YOUR MISTAKE.⟩
⟨I AM TOO **IMMENSE** FOR YOU TO PREDICT, TOO **GREAT** FOR YOU TO KNOW!⟩
⟨AND I WILL SHAPE THE FUTURE.⟩
⟨WHY DON'T I LEAVE? I SHOULD RUN FROM HERE. I KNOW I SHOULD. BUT I DON'T RUN.⟩
⟨I WALK. DEEPER AND DEEPER.⟩
⟨INTO THE INFERNO.⟩

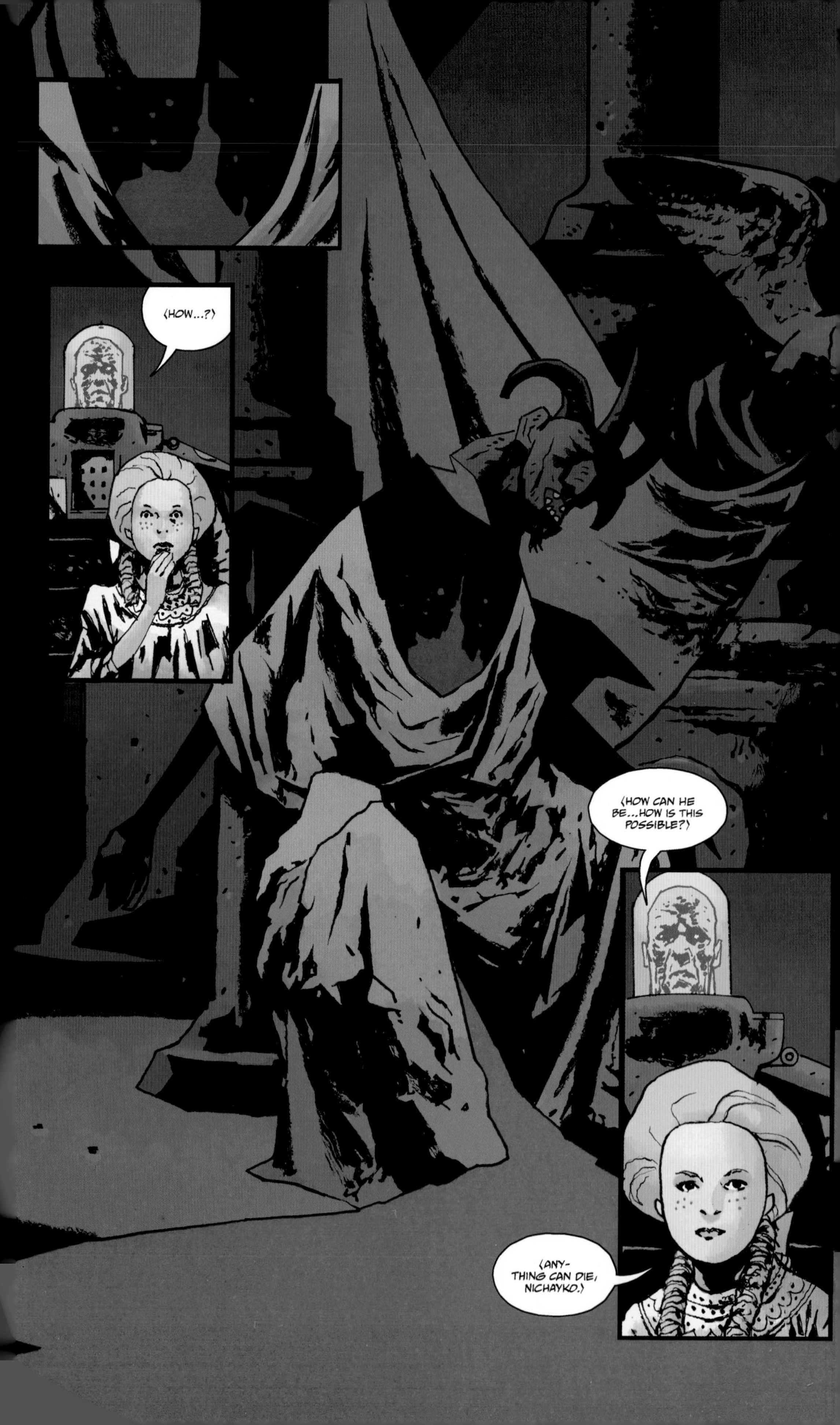

‹HOW...?›
‹HOW CAN HE BE...HOW IS THIS POSSIBLE?›
‹ANY-THING CAN DIE, NICHAYKO.›

⟨EVEN THE KING OF THE WORLD.⟩

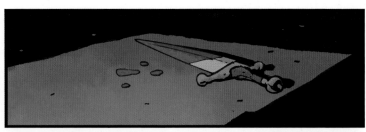

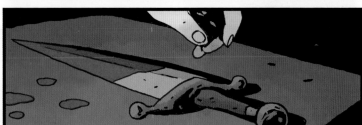

⟨IS THAT...?⟩

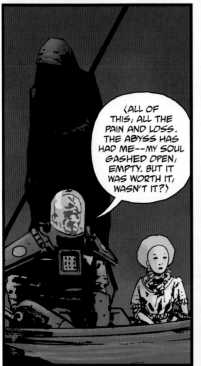

⟨ALL OF THIS, ALL THE PAIN AND LOSS. THE ABYSS HAS HAD ME--MY SOUL GASHED OPEN, EMPTY. BUT IT WAS WORTH IT, WASN'T IT?⟩

⟨THAT DAGGER... SOMETHING SO POTENT AS THAT *MUST* HAVE THE POWER TO HELP US!⟩

PUÒ ESSERE. E POI ANCORA...

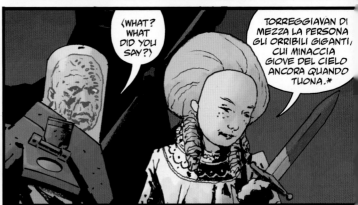

⟨WHAT? WHAT DID YOU SAY?⟩

TORREGGIAVAN DI MEZZA LA PERSONA GLI ORRIBILI GIGANTI, CUI MINACCIA GIOVE DEL CIELO ANCORA QUANDO TUONA.*

*FROM CANTO XXXI OF "HELL" BY DANTE

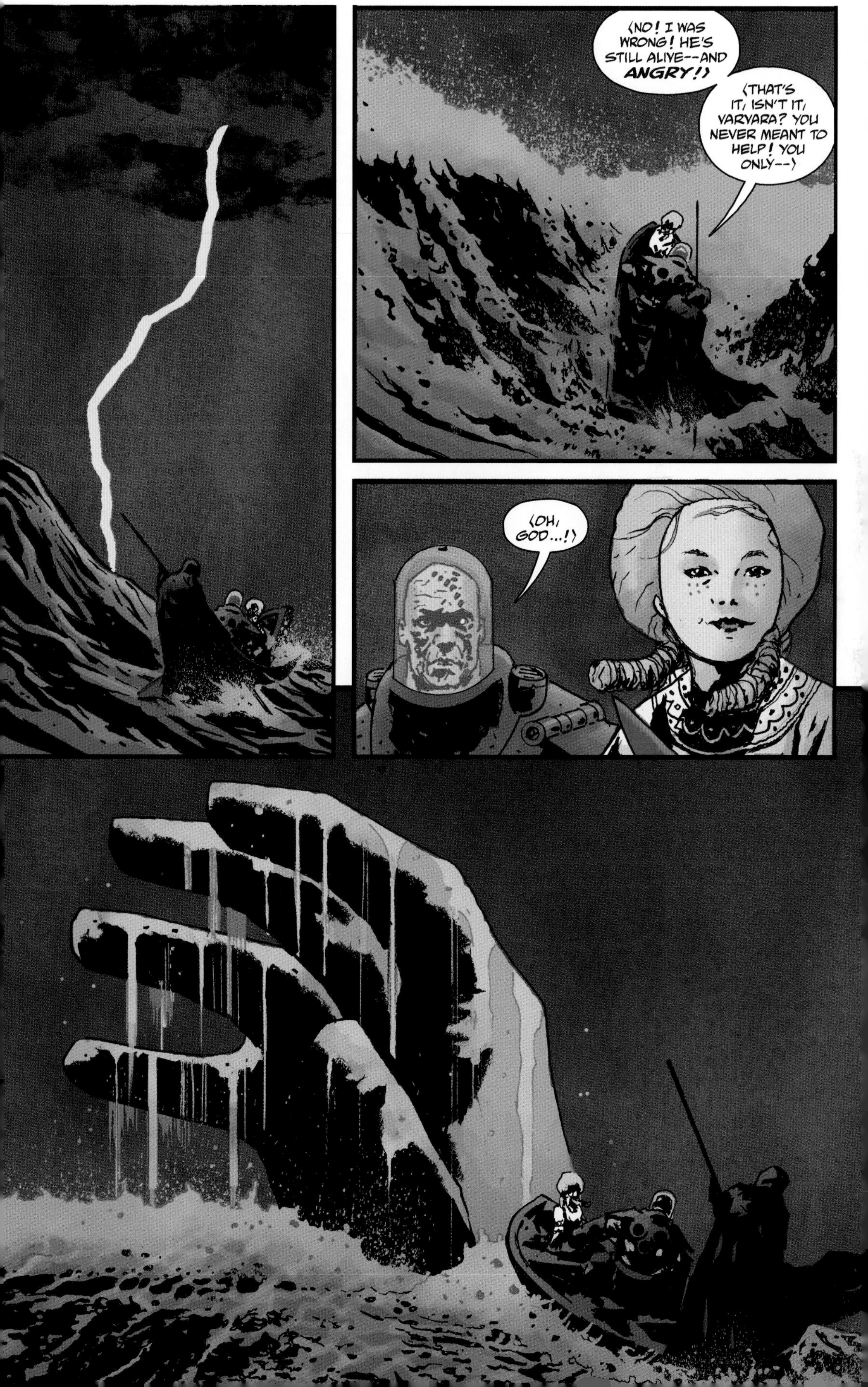

⟨NO! I WAS WRONG! HE'S STILL ALIVE--AND ANGRY!⟩
⟨THAT'S IT, ISN'T IT, VARVARA? YOU NEVER MEANT TO HELP! YOU ONLY--⟩
⟨OH, GOD...!⟩

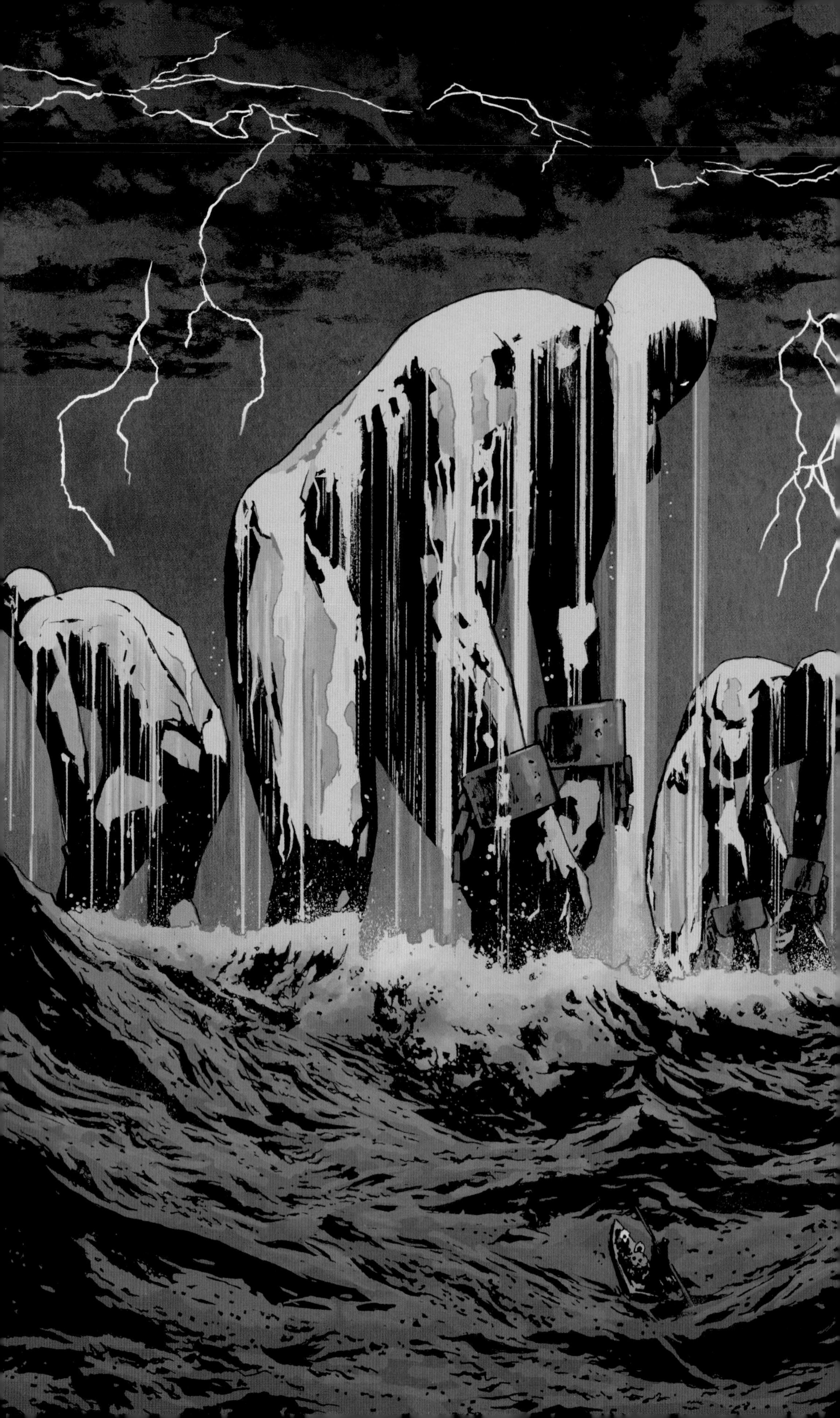

CHAPTER THREE

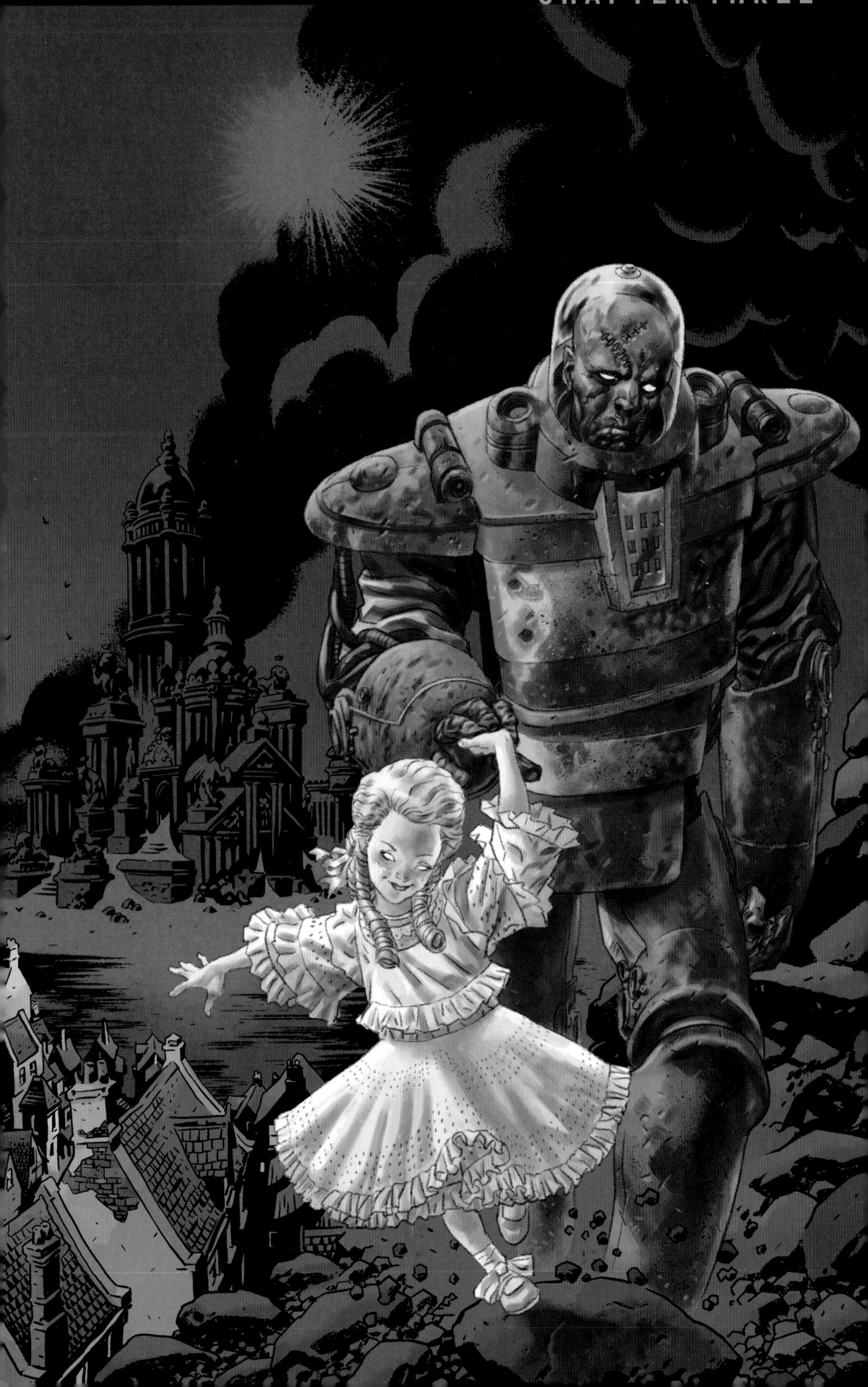

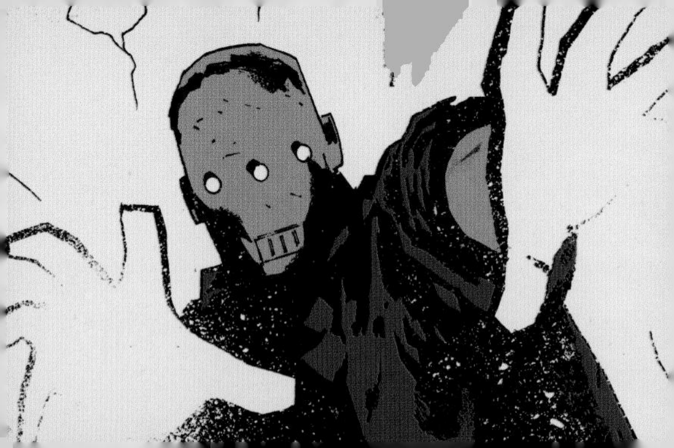

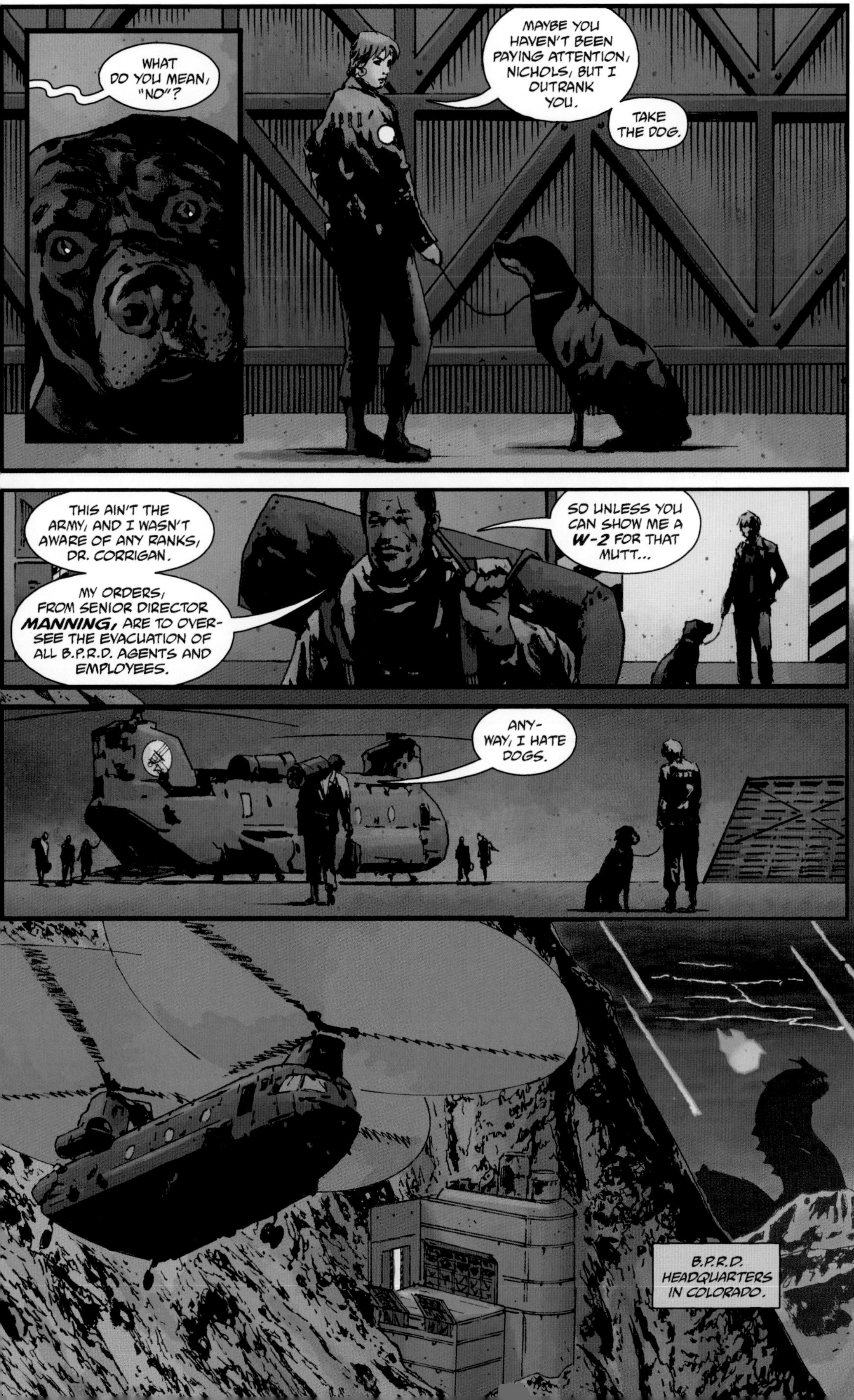
WHAT DO YOU MEAN, "NO"?
MAYBE YOU HAVEN'T BEEN PAYING ATTENTION, NICHOLS, BUT I OUTRANK YOU.
TAKE THE DOG.
THIS AIN'T THE ARMY, AND I WASN'T AWARE OF ANY RANKS, DR. CORRIGAN.
MY ORDERS, FROM SENIOR DIRECTOR MANNING, ARE TO OVERSEE THE EVACUATION OF ALL B.P.R.D. AGENTS AND EMPLOYEES.
SO UNLESS YOU CAN SHOW ME A W-2 FOR THAT MUTT...
ANYWAY, I HATE DOGS.
B.P.R.D. HEADQUARTERS IN COLORADO.

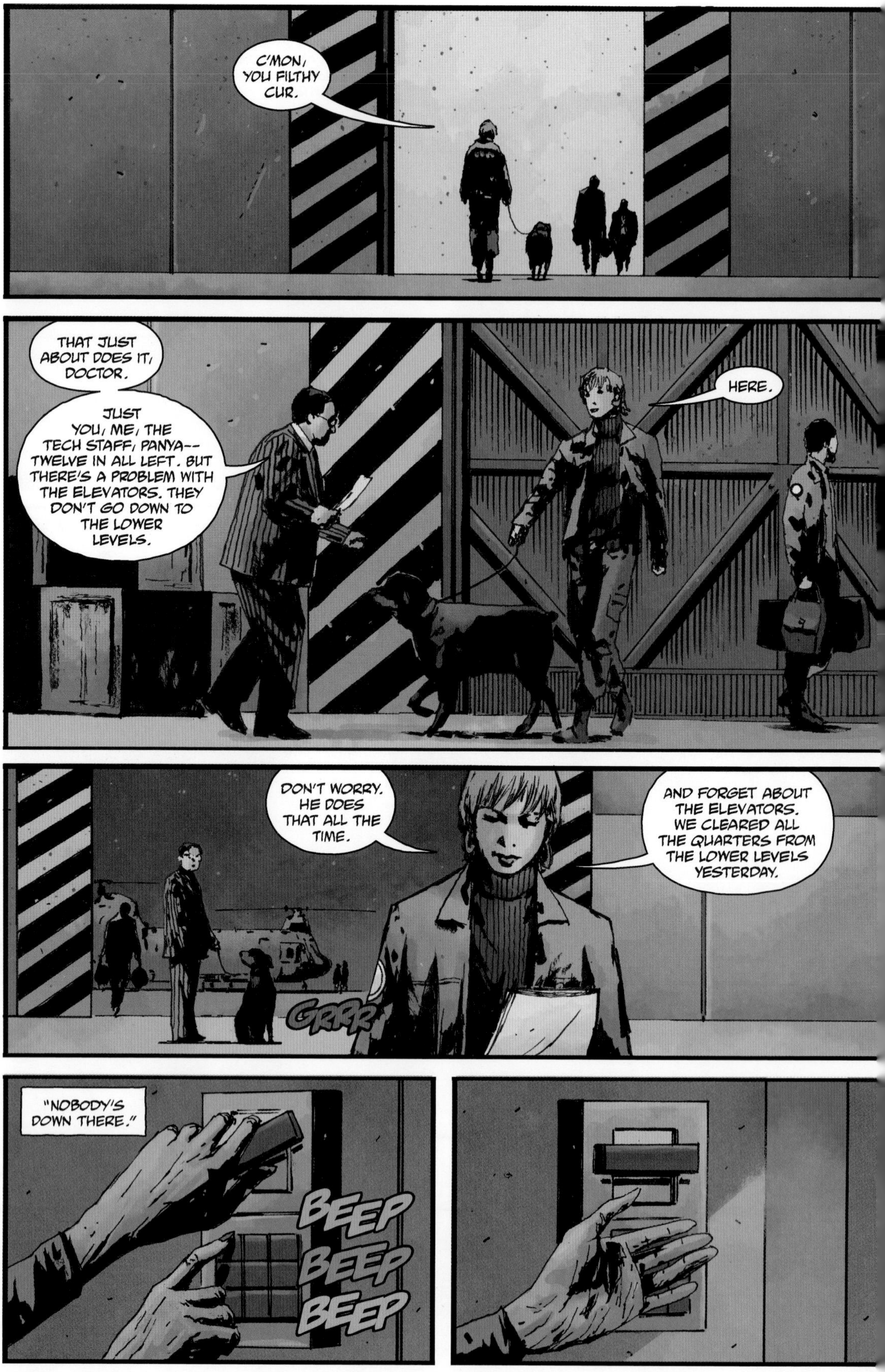

C'MON, YOU FILTHY CUR.
THAT JUST ABOUT DOES IT, DOCTOR.
JUST YOU, ME, THE TECH STAFF, PANYA-- TWELVE IN ALL LEFT. BUT THERE'S A PROBLEM WITH THE ELEVATORS. THEY DON'T GO DOWN TO THE LOWER LEVELS.
HERE.
DON'T WORRY. HE DOES THAT ALL THE TIME.
GRRR
AND FORGET ABOUT THE ELEVATORS. WE CLEARED ALL THE QUARTERS FROM THE LOWER LEVELS YESTERDAY.
"NOBODY'S DOWN THERE."
BEEP
BEEP
BEEP

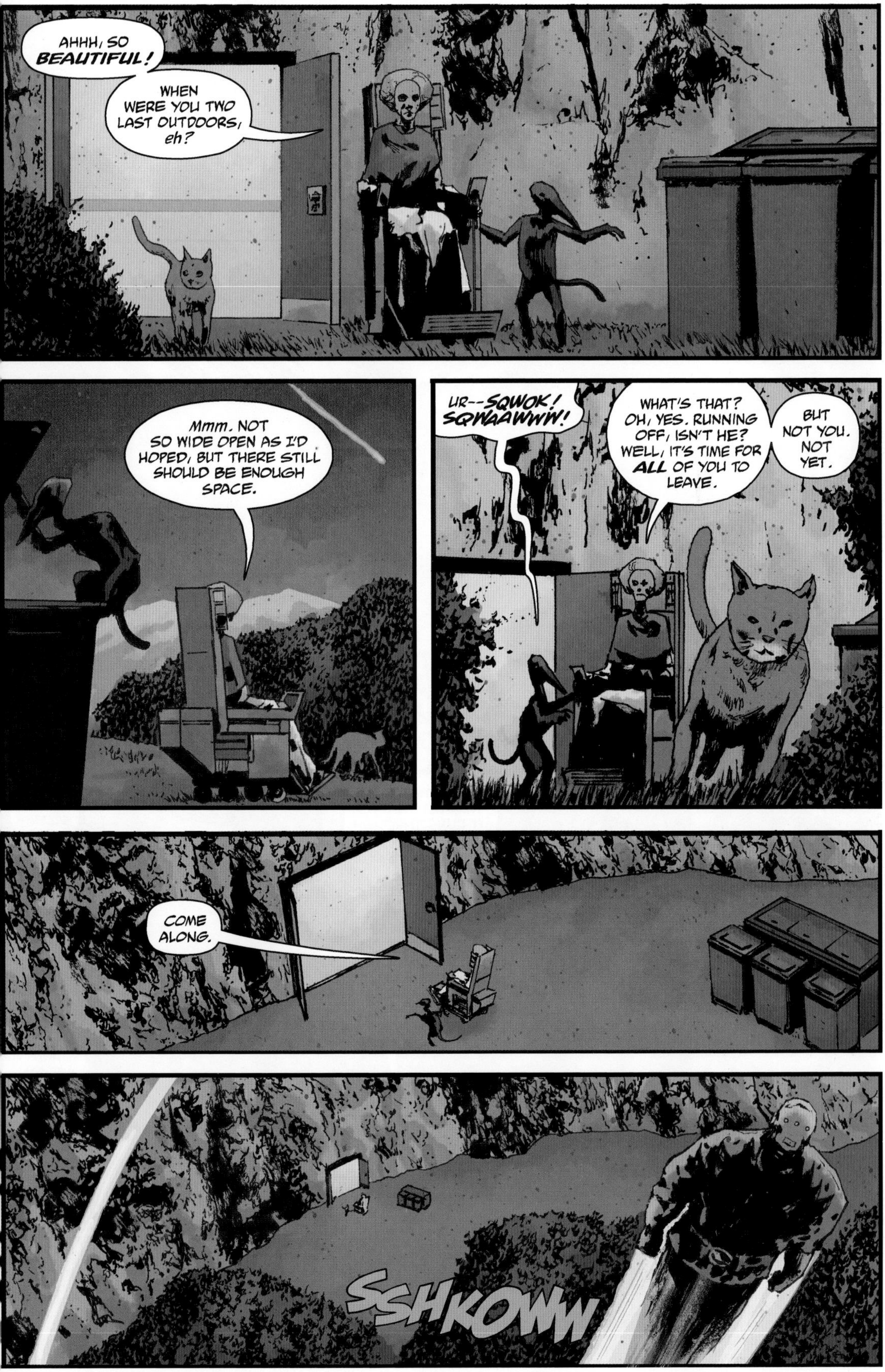
AHHH, SO **BEAUTIFUL!**
WHEN WERE YOU TWO LAST OUTDOORS, *eh?*
Mmm. NOT SO WIDE OPEN AS I'D HOPED, BUT THERE STILL SHOULD BE ENOUGH SPACE.
UR--**SQWOK! SQWAAWWW!**
WHAT'S THAT? OH, YES. RUNNING OFF, ISN'T HE? WELL, IT'S TIME FOR **ALL** OF YOU TO LEAVE.
BUT NOT YOU. NOT YET.
COME ALONG.
SSHKOWW

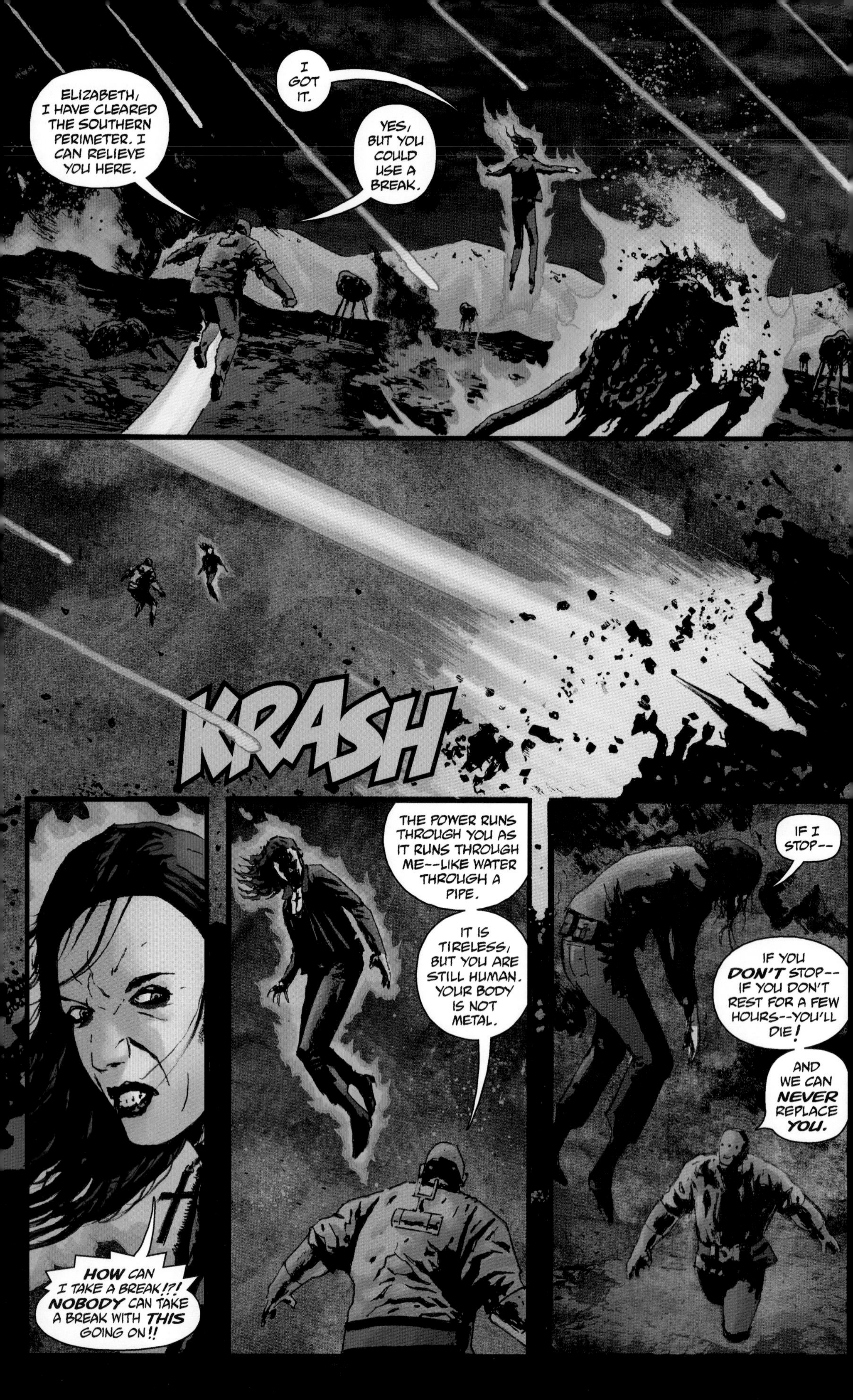
ELIZABETH, I HAVE CLEARED THE SOUTHERN PERIMETER. I CAN RELIEVE YOU HERE.
I GOT IT.
YES, BUT YOU COULD USE A BREAK.
KRASH
HOW CAN I TAKE A BREAK!?! NOBODY CAN TAKE A BREAK WITH THIS GOING ON!!
THE POWER RUNS THROUGH YOU AS IT RUNS THROUGH ME--LIKE WATER THROUGH A PIPE.
IT IS TIRELESS, BUT YOU ARE STILL HUMAN. YOUR BODY IS NOT METAL.
IF I STOP--
IF YOU DON'T STOP-- IF YOU DON'T REST FOR A FEW HOURS--YOU'LL DIE!
AND WE CAN NEVER REPLACE YOU.

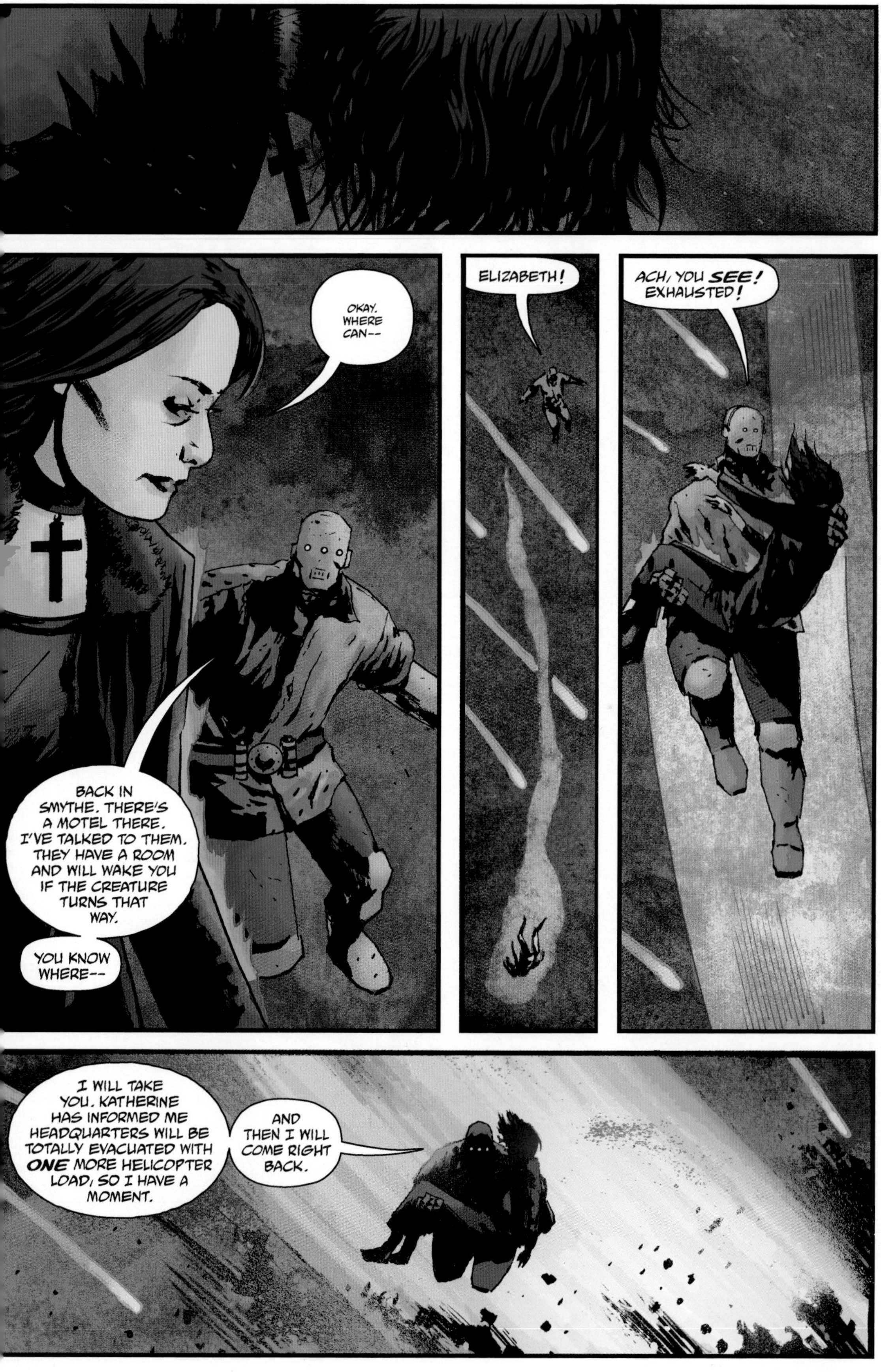
OKAY. WHERE CAN--
BACK IN SMYTHE. THERE'S A MOTEL THERE. I'VE TALKED TO THEM. THEY HAVE A ROOM AND WILL WAKE YOU IF THE CREATURE TURNS THAT WAY.
YOU KNOW WHERE--
ELIZABETH!
ACH, YOU SEE! EXHAUSTED!
I WILL TAKE YOU. KATHERINE HAS INFORMED ME HEADQUARTERS WILL BE TOTALLY EVACUATED WITH ONE MORE HELICOPTER LOAD, SO I HAVE A MOMENT.
AND THEN I WILL COME RIGHT BACK.

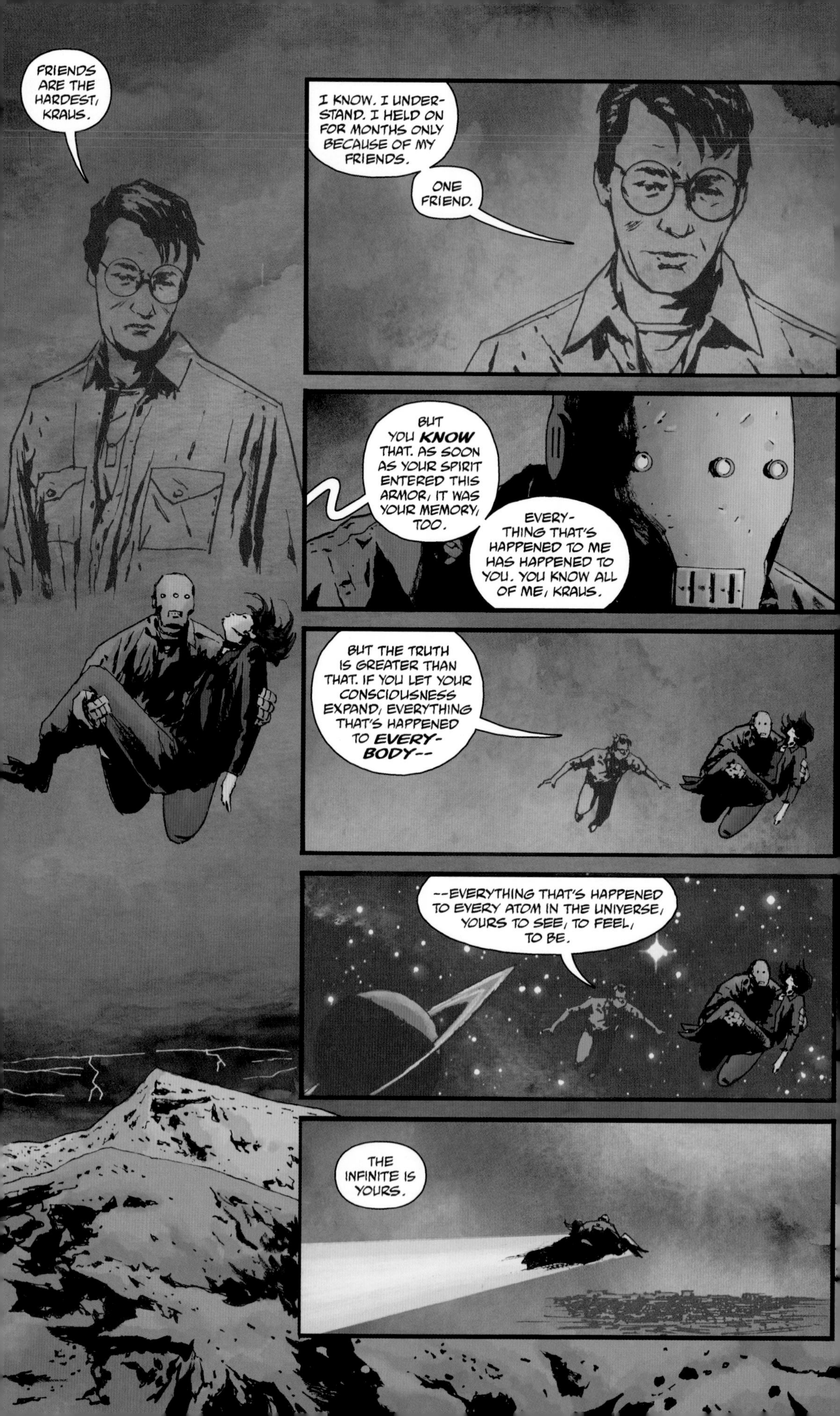
FRIENDS ARE THE HARDEST, KRAUS.
I KNOW. I UNDERSTAND. I HELD ON FOR MONTHS ONLY BECAUSE OF MY FRIENDS.
ONE FRIEND.
BUT YOU **KNOW** THAT. AS SOON AS YOUR SPIRIT ENTERED THIS ARMOR, IT WAS YOUR MEMORY, TOO.
EVERYTHING THAT'S HAPPENED TO ME HAS HAPPENED TO YOU. YOU KNOW ALL OF ME, KRAUS.
BUT THE TRUTH IS GREATER THAN THAT. IF YOU LET YOUR CONSCIOUSNESS EXPAND, EVERYTHING THAT'S HAPPENED TO **EVERYBODY**--
--EVERYTHING THAT'S HAPPENED TO EVERY ATOM IN THE UNIVERSE, YOURS TO SEE, TO FEEL, TO BE.
THE INFINITE IS YOURS.

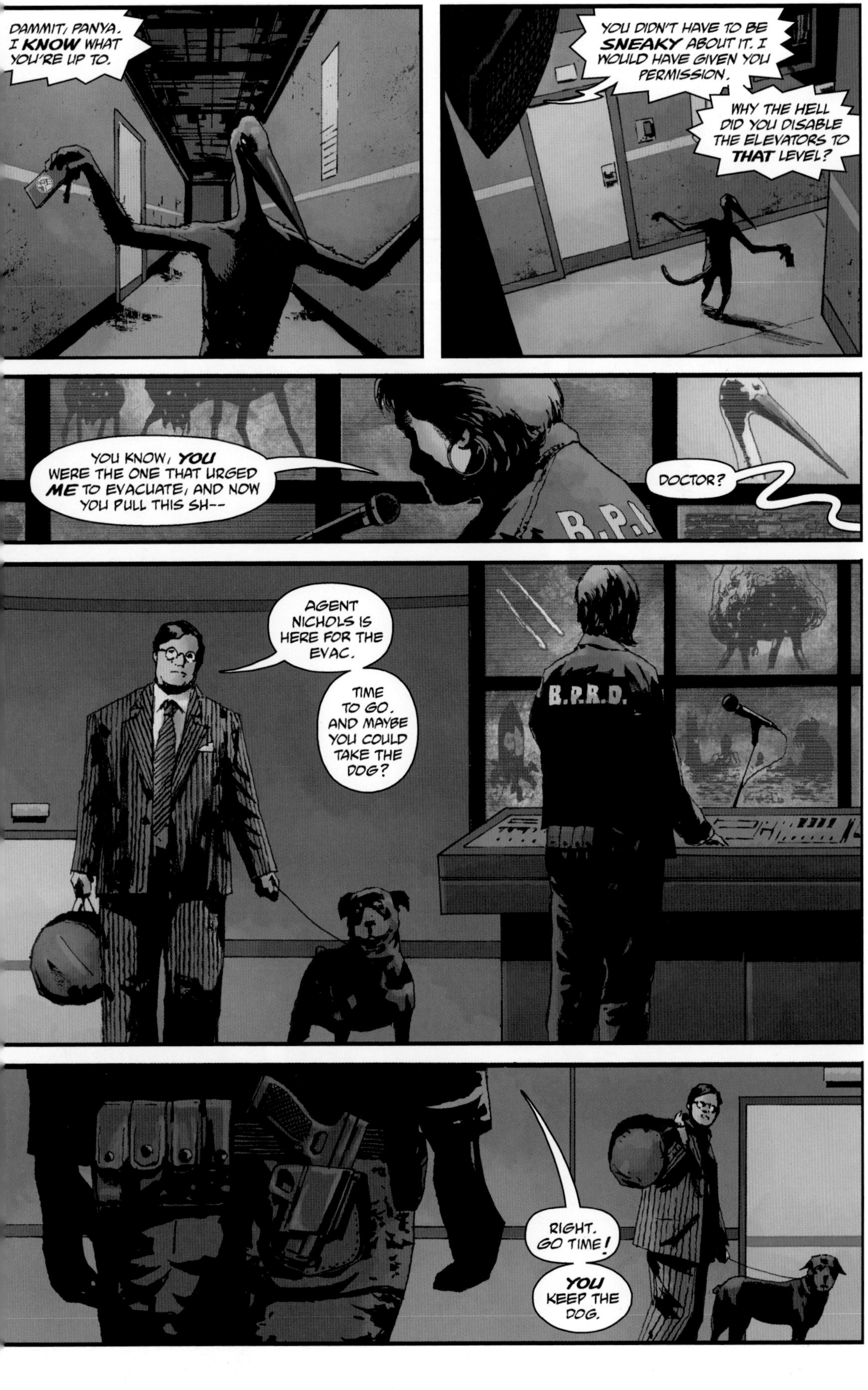
DAMMIT, PANYA. I KNOW WHAT YOU'RE UP TO.
YOU DIDN'T HAVE TO BE SNEAKY ABOUT IT. I WOULD HAVE GIVEN YOU PERMISSION.
WHY THE HELL DID YOU DISABLE THE ELEVATORS TO THAT LEVEL?
YOU KNOW, YOU WERE THE ONE THAT URGED ME TO EVACUATE, AND NOW YOU PULL THIS SH--
DOCTOR?
AGENT NICHOLS IS HERE FOR THE EVAC.
TIME TO GO. AND MAYBE YOU COULD TAKE THE DOG?
B.P.R.D.
RIGHT. GO TIME!
YOU KEEP THE DOG.

HEY, I THOUGHT THIS WOULD BE THE LAST LOAD. WHERE'S THE WHEEL-CHAIR LADY?

I'M WORKING ON THAT.

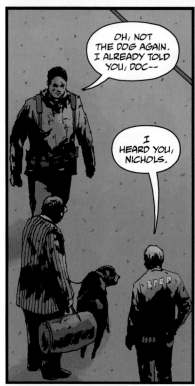

OH, NOT THE DOG AGAIN. I ALREADY TOLD YOU, DOC--

I HEARD YOU, NICHOLS.

YOU DON'T LIKE DOGS, BUT I WANT TO KNOW HOW *MUCH* YOU DON'T LIKE THEM?

RRRRRRRR

DOCTOR...?

Ah, C'MON, DOC. YOU WON'T SHOOT THAT DOG.

NO?

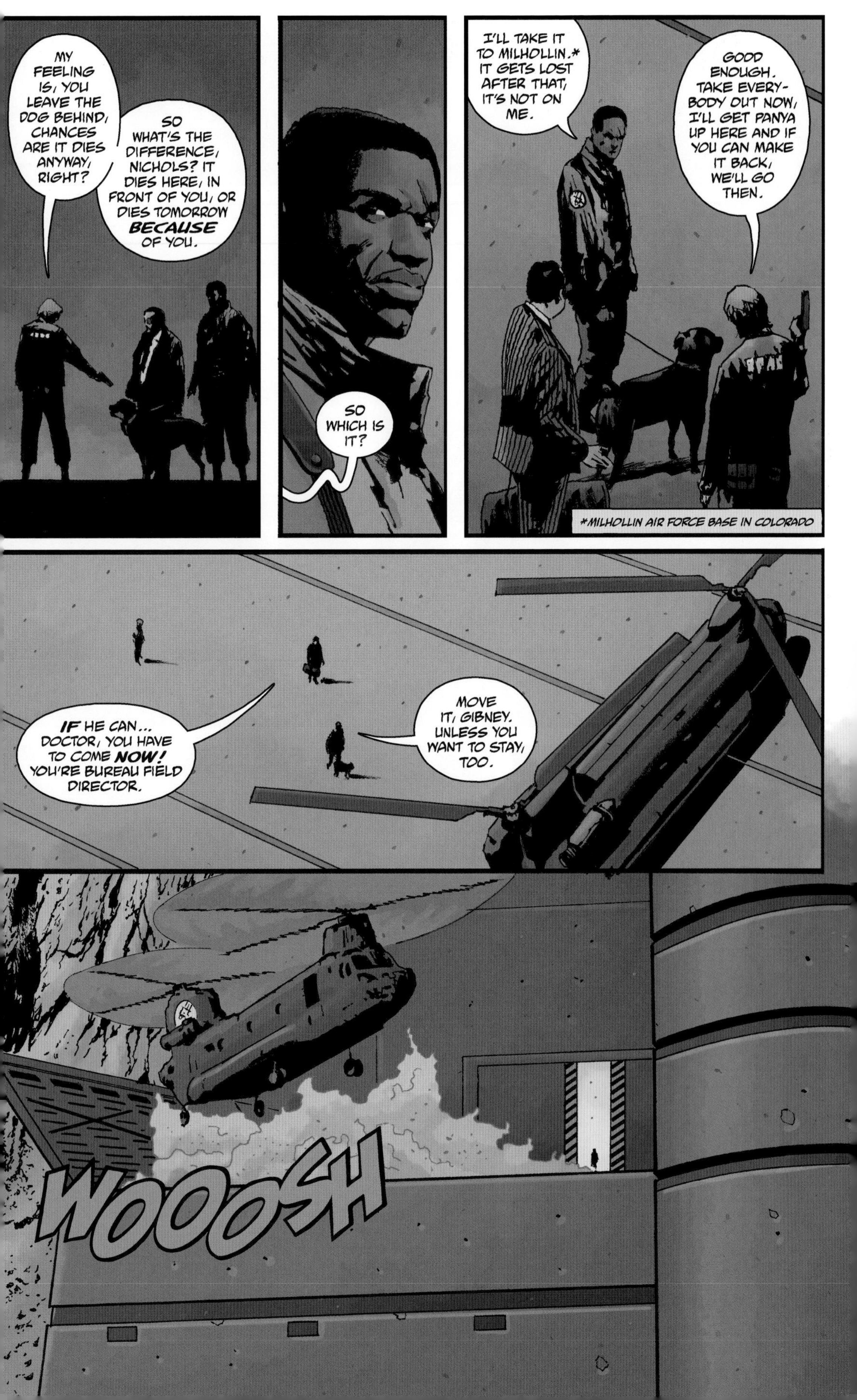
MY FEELING IS, YOU LEAVE THE DOG BEHIND, CHANCES ARE IT DIES ANYWAY, RIGHT?
SO WHAT'S THE DIFFERENCE, NICHOLS? IT DIES HERE, IN FRONT OF YOU, OR DIES TOMORROW BECAUSE OF YOU.
SO WHICH IS IT?
I'LL TAKE IT TO MILHOLLIN.* IT GETS LOST AFTER THAT, IT'S NOT ON ME.
GOOD ENOUGH. TAKE EVERY-BODY OUT NOW, I'LL GET PANYA UP HERE AND IF YOU CAN MAKE IT BACK, WE'LL GO THEN.
*MILHOLLIN AIR FORCE BASE IN COLORADO
IF HE CAN... DOCTOR, YOU HAVE TO COME NOW! YOU'RE BUREAU FIELD DIRECTOR.
MOVE IT, GIBNEY. UNLESS YOU WANT TO STAY, TOO.
WOOOSH

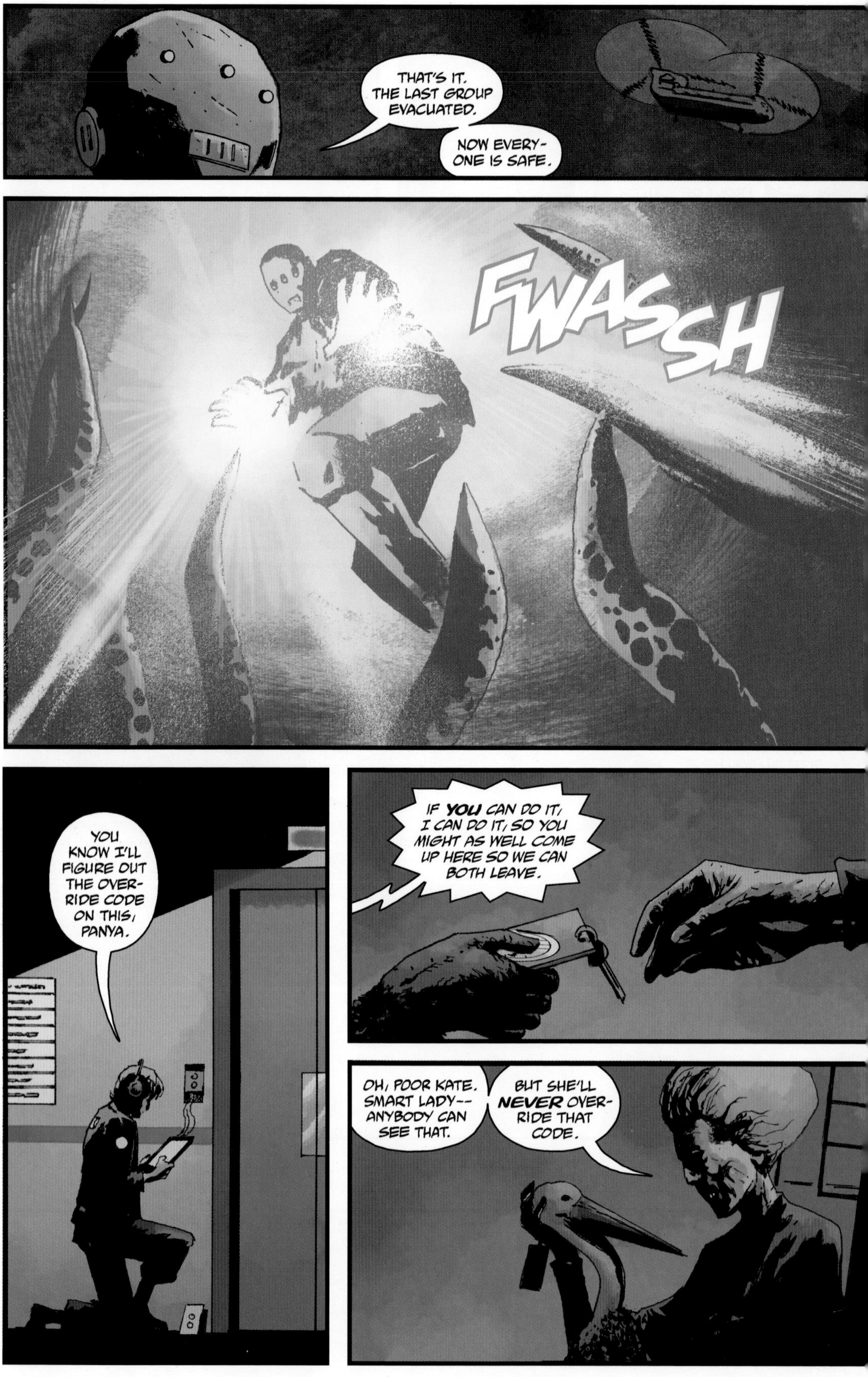
THAT'S IT. THE LAST GROUP EVACUATED.
NOW EVERY-ONE IS SAFE.
FWASSH
YOU KNOW I'LL FIGURE OUT THE OVER-RIDE CODE ON THIS, PANYA.
IF YOU CAN DO IT, I CAN DO IT, SO YOU MIGHT AS WELL COME UP HERE SO WE CAN BOTH LEAVE.
OH, POOR KATE. SMART LADY-- ANYBODY CAN SEE THAT.
BUT SHE'LL NEVER OVER-RIDE THAT CODE.

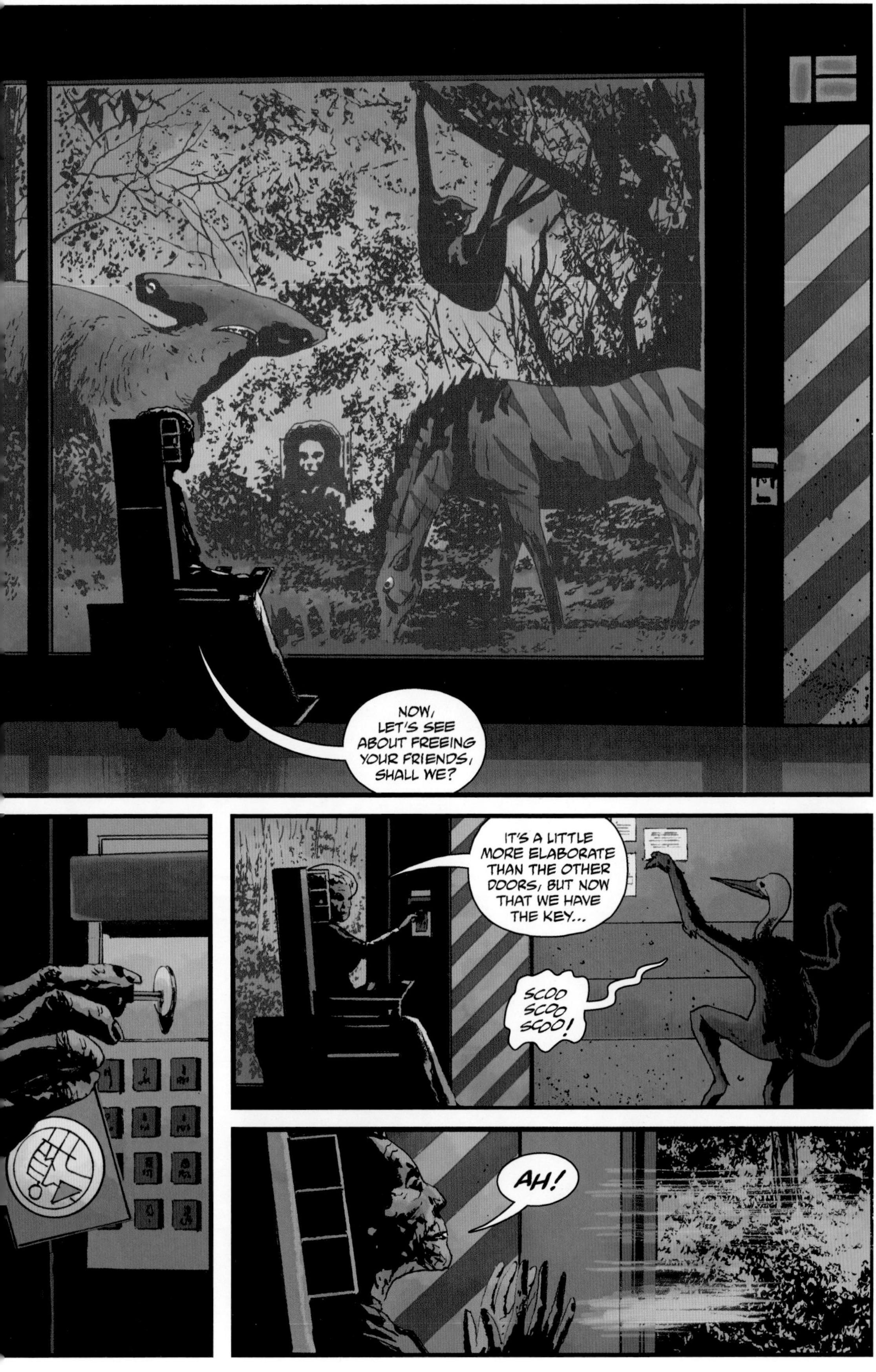
NOW, LET'S SEE ABOUT FREEING YOUR FRIENDS, SHALL WE?
IT'S A LITTLE MORE ELABORATE THAN THE OTHER DOORS, BUT NOW THAT WE HAVE THE KEY...
SCOO SCOO SCOO!
AH!

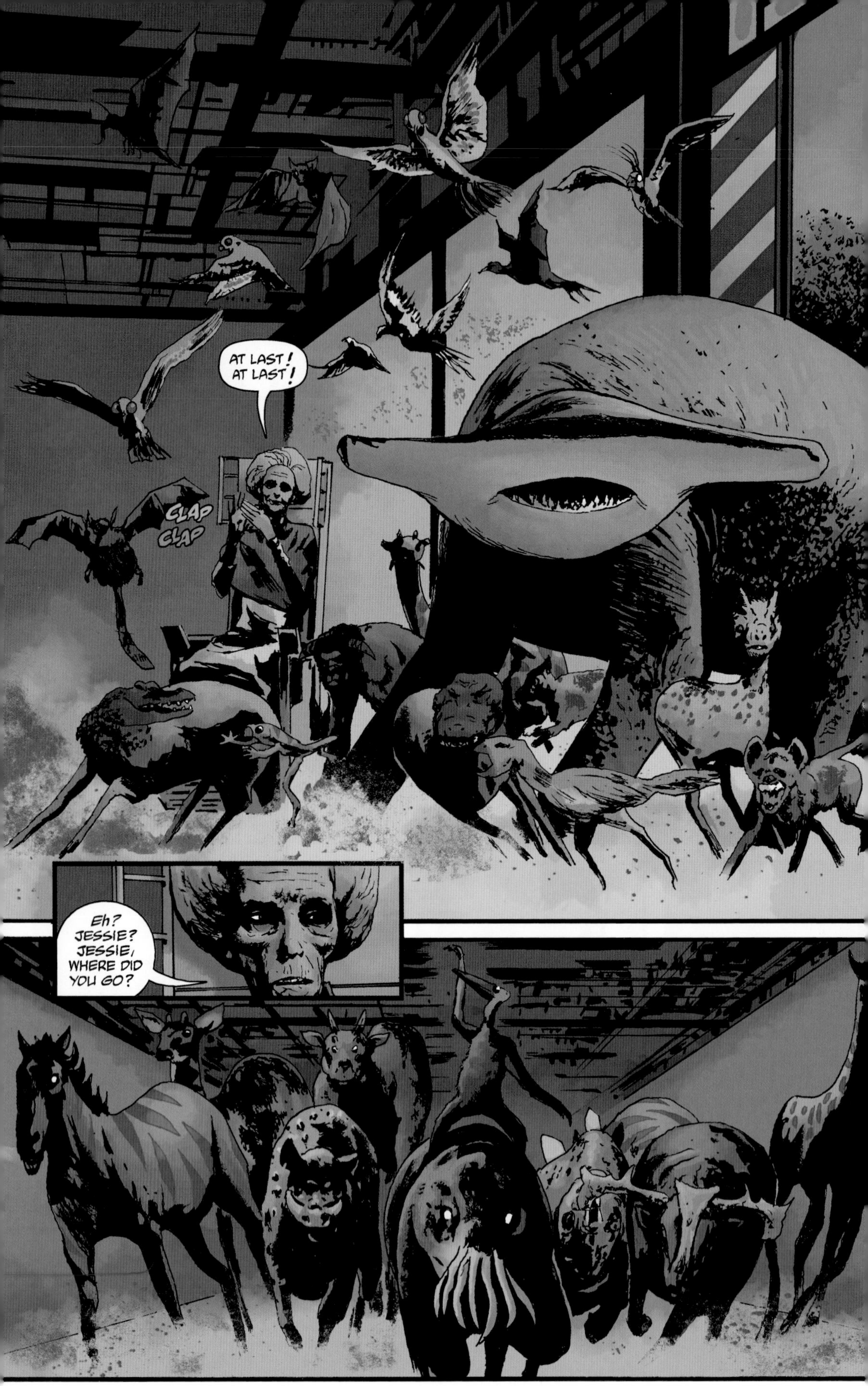
AT LAST! AT LAST!
CLAP CLAP
Eh? JESSIE? JESSIE, WHERE DID YOU GO?

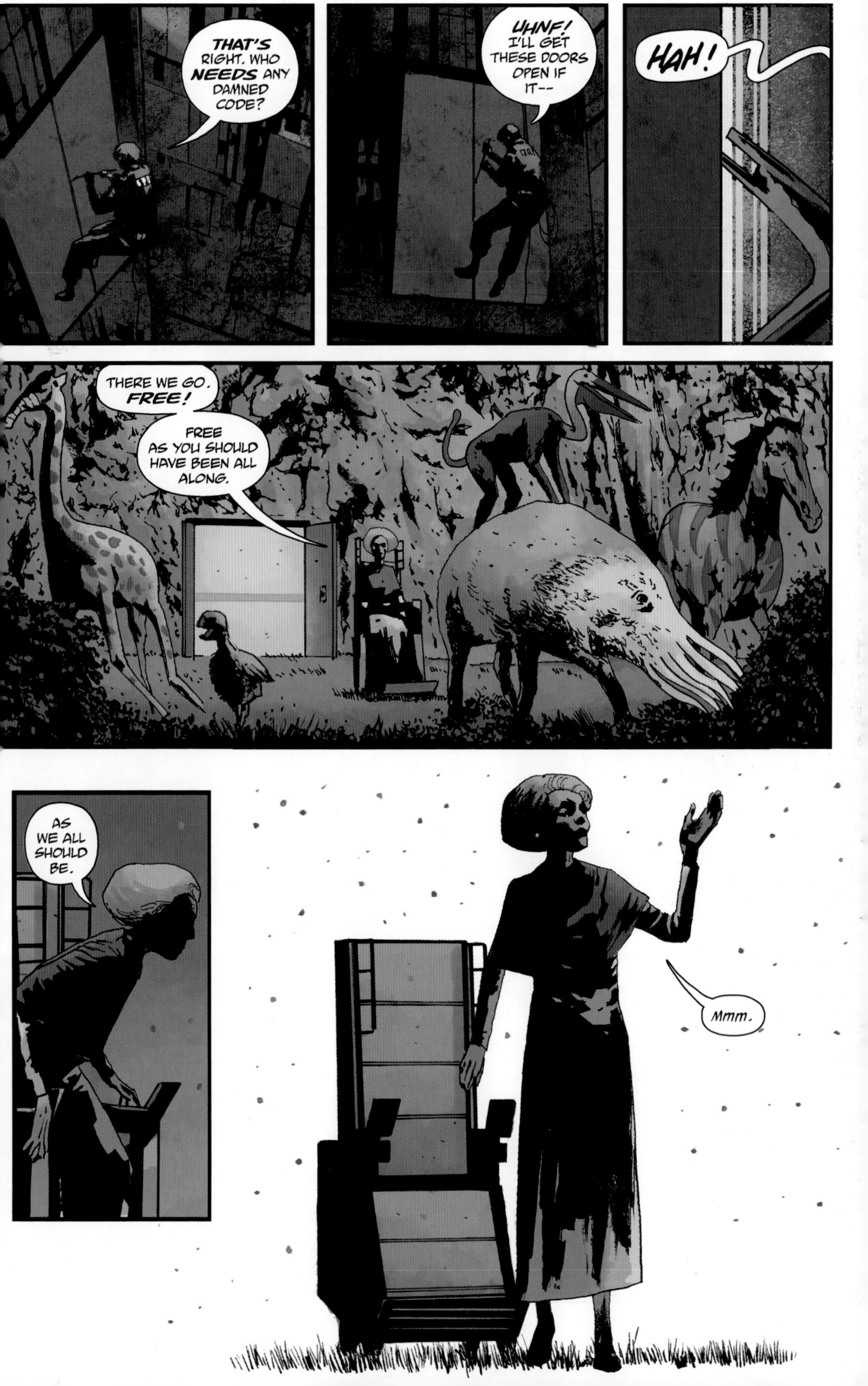
THAT'S RIGHT. WHO NEEDS ANY DAMNED CODE?
UHNF! I'LL GET THESE DOORS OPEN IF IT--
HAH!
THERE WE GO. FREE!
FREE AS YOU SHOULD HAVE BEEN ALL ALONG.
AS WE ALL SHOULD BE.
Mmm.

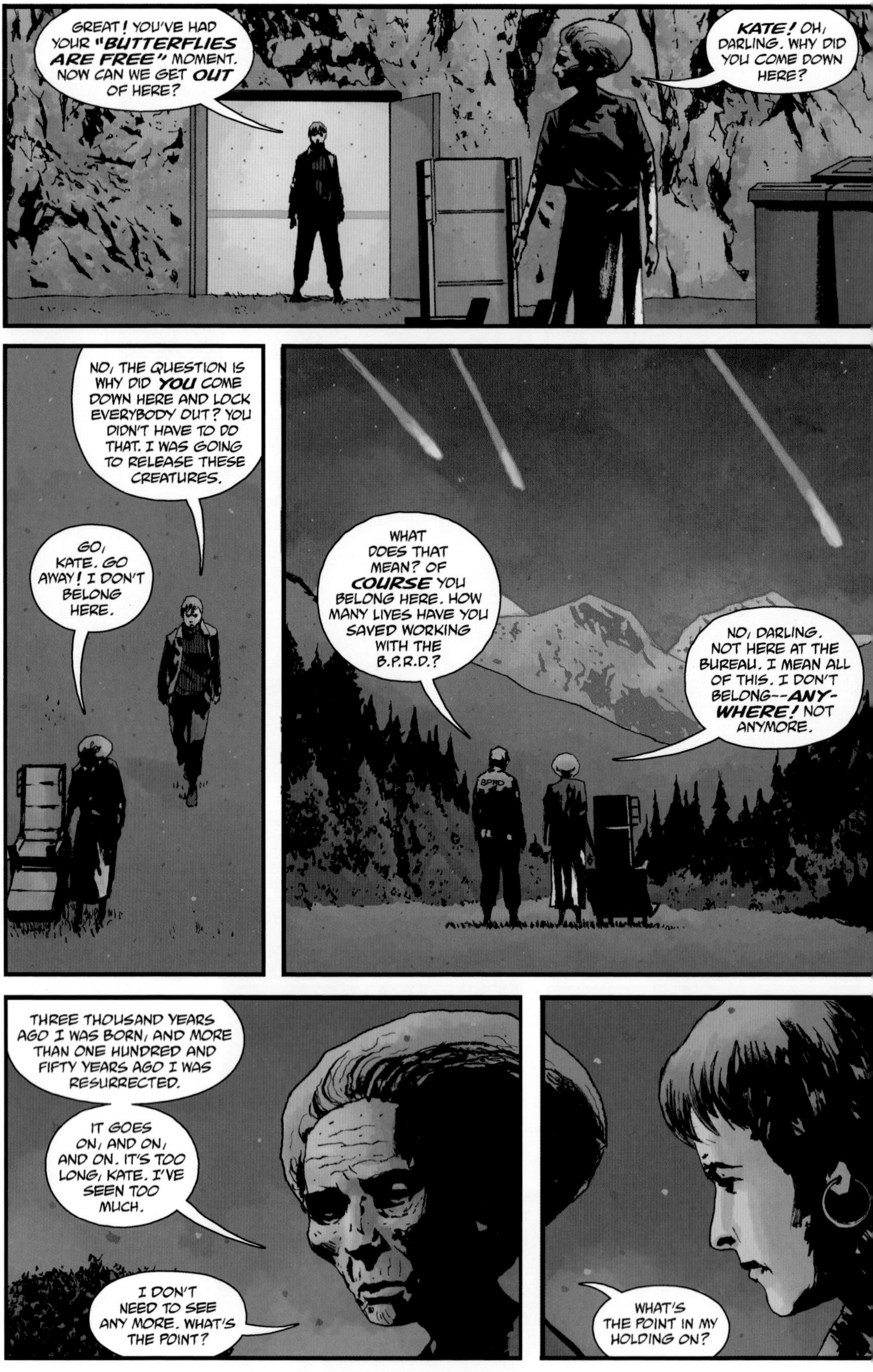
GREAT! YOU'VE HAD YOUR "BUTTERFLIES ARE FREE" MOMENT. NOW CAN WE GET OUT OF HERE?
KATE! OH, DARLING. WHY DID YOU COME DOWN HERE?
NO, THE QUESTION IS WHY DID YOU COME DOWN HERE AND LOCK EVERYBODY OUT? YOU DIDN'T HAVE TO DO THAT. I WAS GOING TO RELEASE THESE CREATURES.
GO, KATE. GO AWAY! I DON'T BELONG HERE.
WHAT DOES THAT MEAN? OF COURSE YOU BELONG HERE. HOW MANY LIVES HAVE YOU SAVED WORKING WITH THE B.P.R.D.?
NO, DARLING. NOT HERE AT THE BUREAU. I MEAN ALL OF THIS. I DON'T BELONG--ANY-WHERE! NOT ANYMORE.
THREE THOUSAND YEARS AGO I WAS BORN, AND MORE THAN ONE HUNDRED AND FIFTY YEARS AGO I WAS RESURRECTED.
IT GOES ON, AND ON, AND ON. IT'S TOO LONG, KATE. I'VE SEEN TOO MUCH.
I DON'T NEED TO SEE ANY MORE. WHAT'S THE POINT?
WHAT'S THE POINT IN MY HOLDING ON?

PANYA, WHY DIDN'T YOU EVER TELL ME ALL THIS?

I WOULD HAVE LISTENED. I COULD HAVE HELPED.

WHAT COULD YOU DO? I DON'T NEED A PILL, KATE. I NEED TO GO!

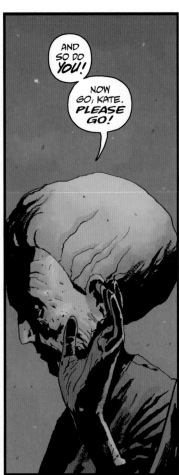

AND SO DO YOU!

NOW GO, KATE. PLEASE GO!

OH, BUT YOU CAME BACK FOR ME.

DEAR, DEAR GIRL. YOU ARE A TREASURE.

PANYA. PLEASE...?

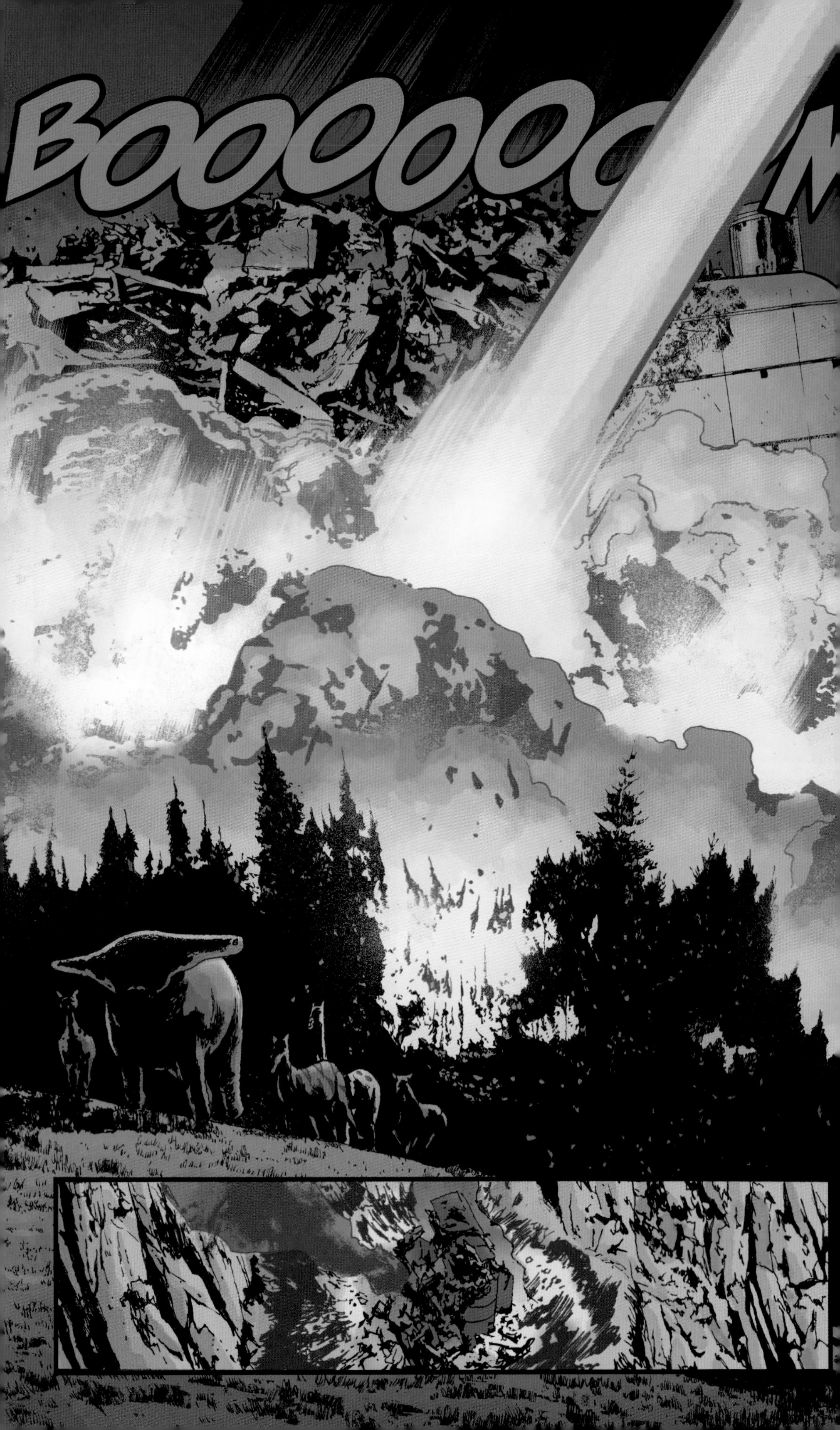
BOOOOOOOM

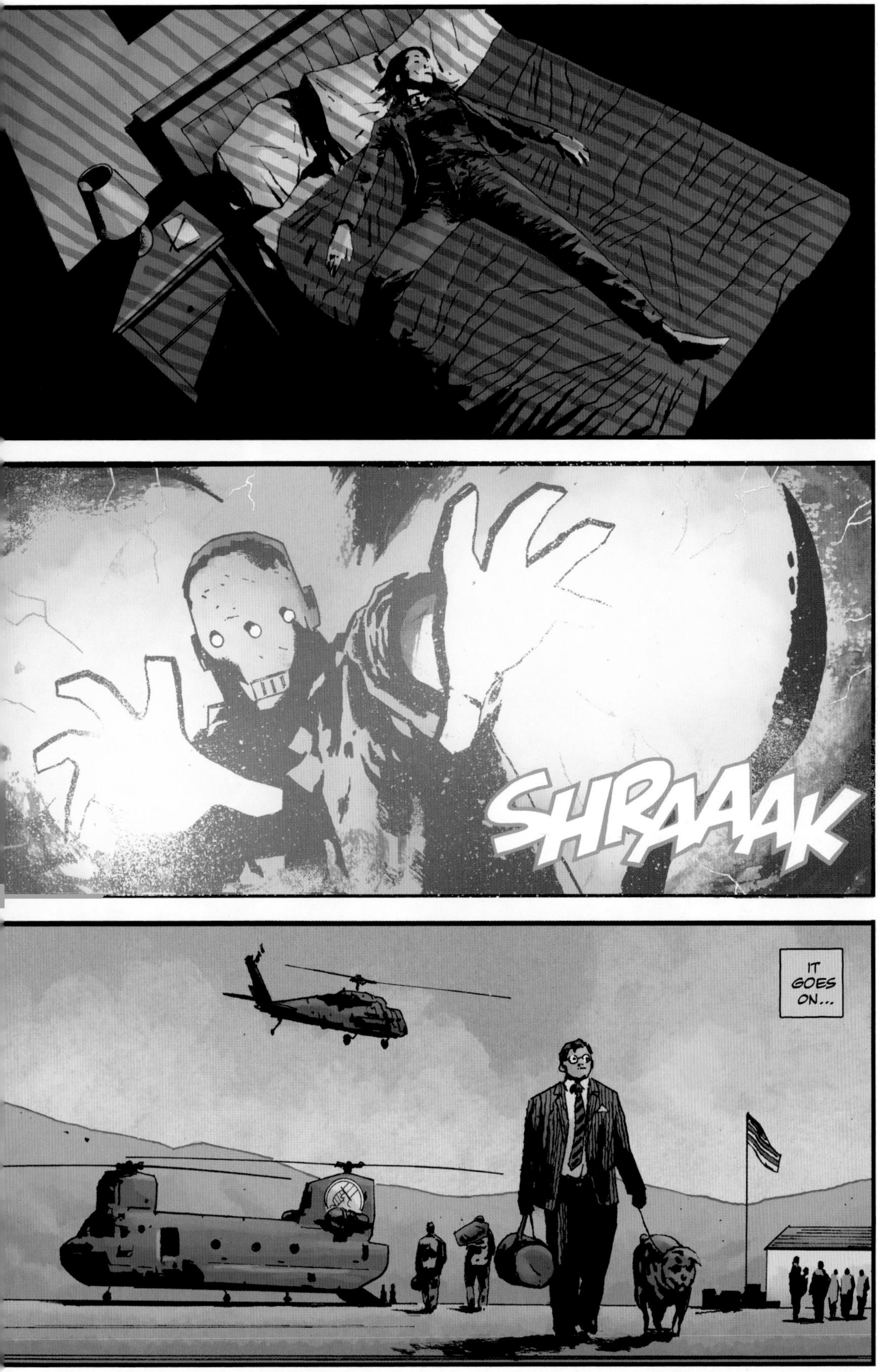
SHRAAAK
IT GOES ON...

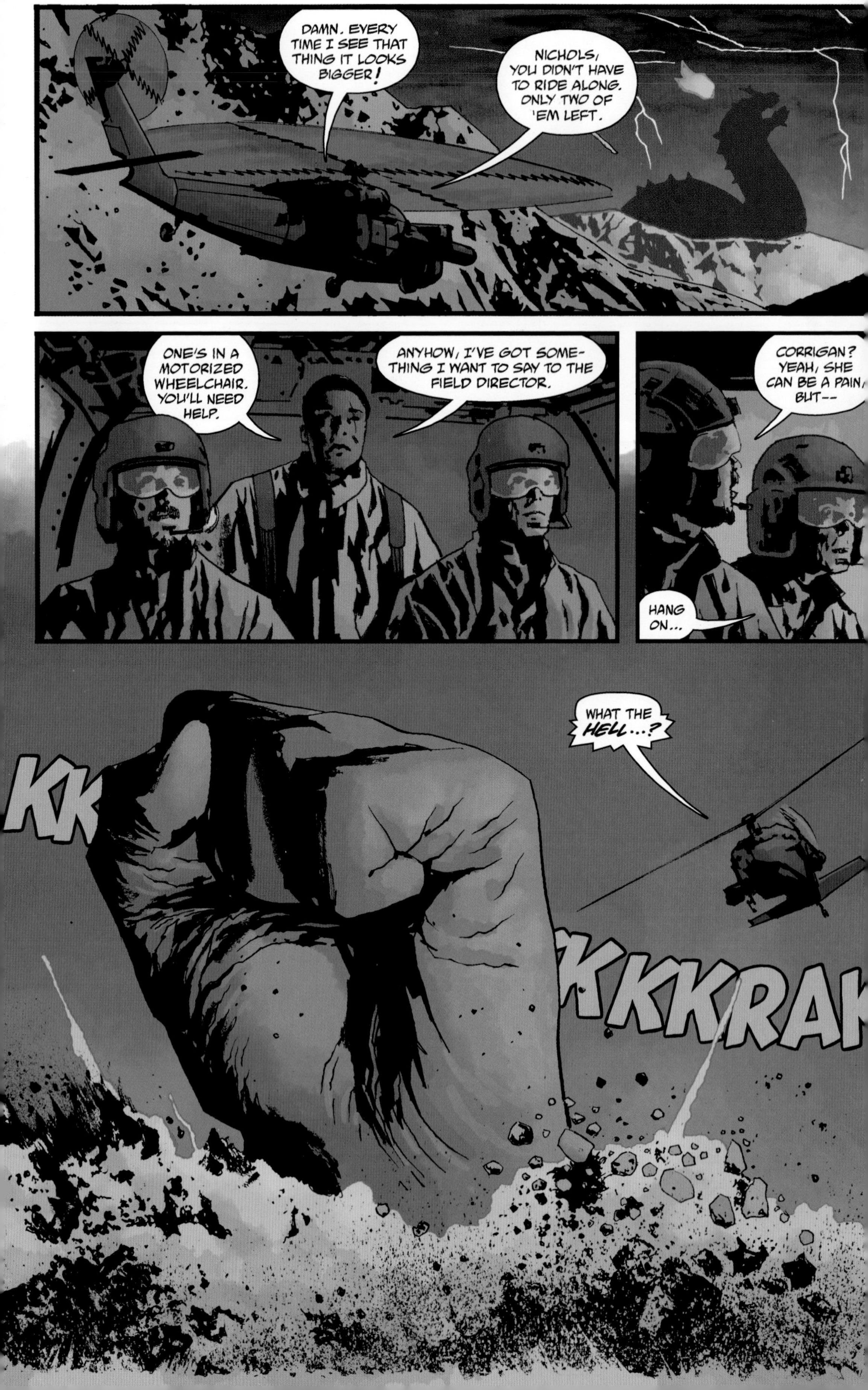

DAMN. EVERY TIME I SEE THAT THING IT LOOKS BIGGER!
NICHOLS, YOU DIDN'T HAVE TO RIDE ALONG. ONLY TWO OF 'EM LEFT.
ONE'S IN A MOTORIZED WHEELCHAIR. YOU'LL NEED HELP.
ANYHOW, I'VE GOT SOMETHING I WANT TO SAY TO THE FIELD DIRECTOR.
CORRIGAN? YEAH, SHE CAN BE A PAIN, BUT--
HANG ON...
WHAT THE HELL...?
KK
KKKRAK

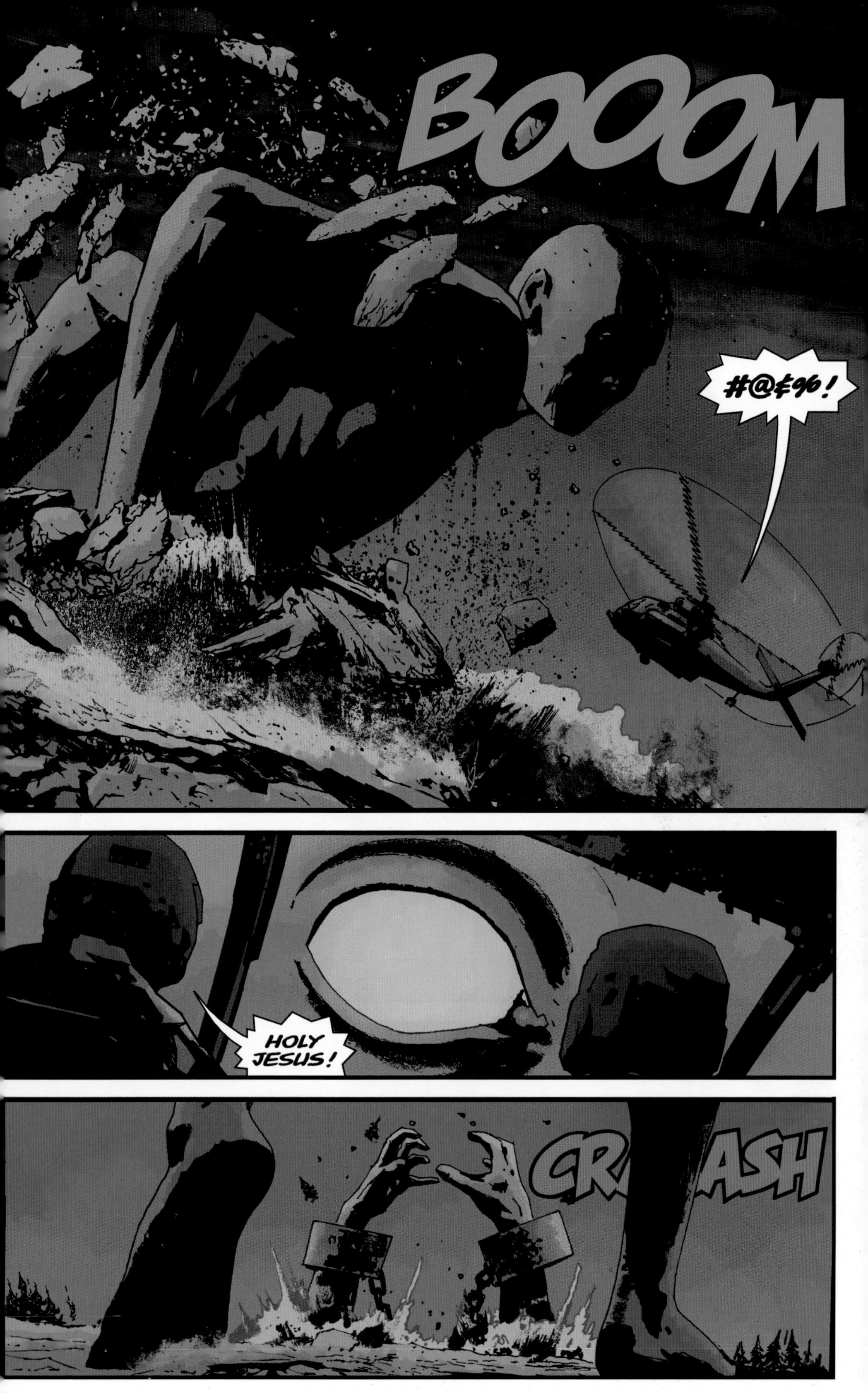
BOOOM
#@£%!
HOLY JESUS!
CRASH

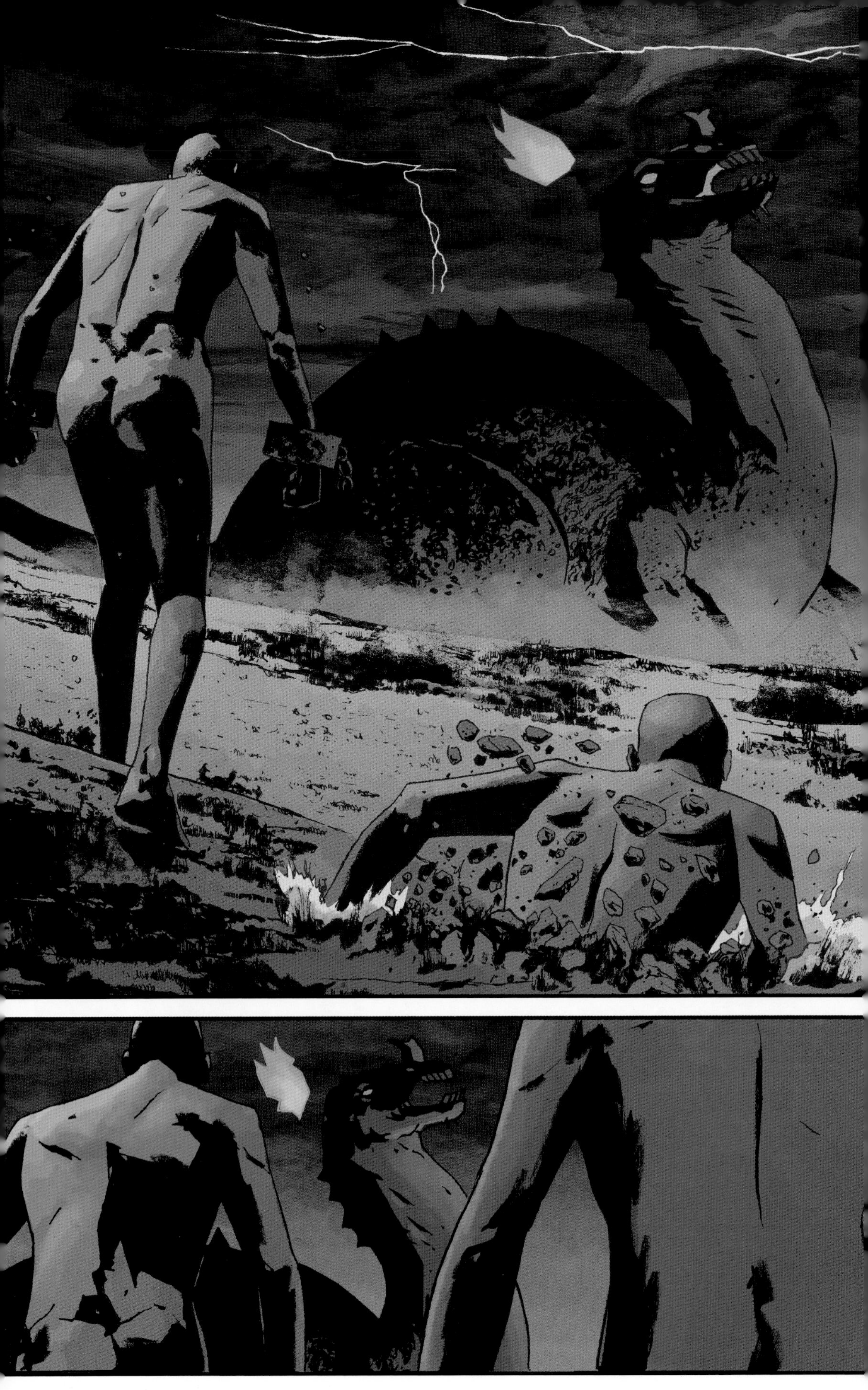

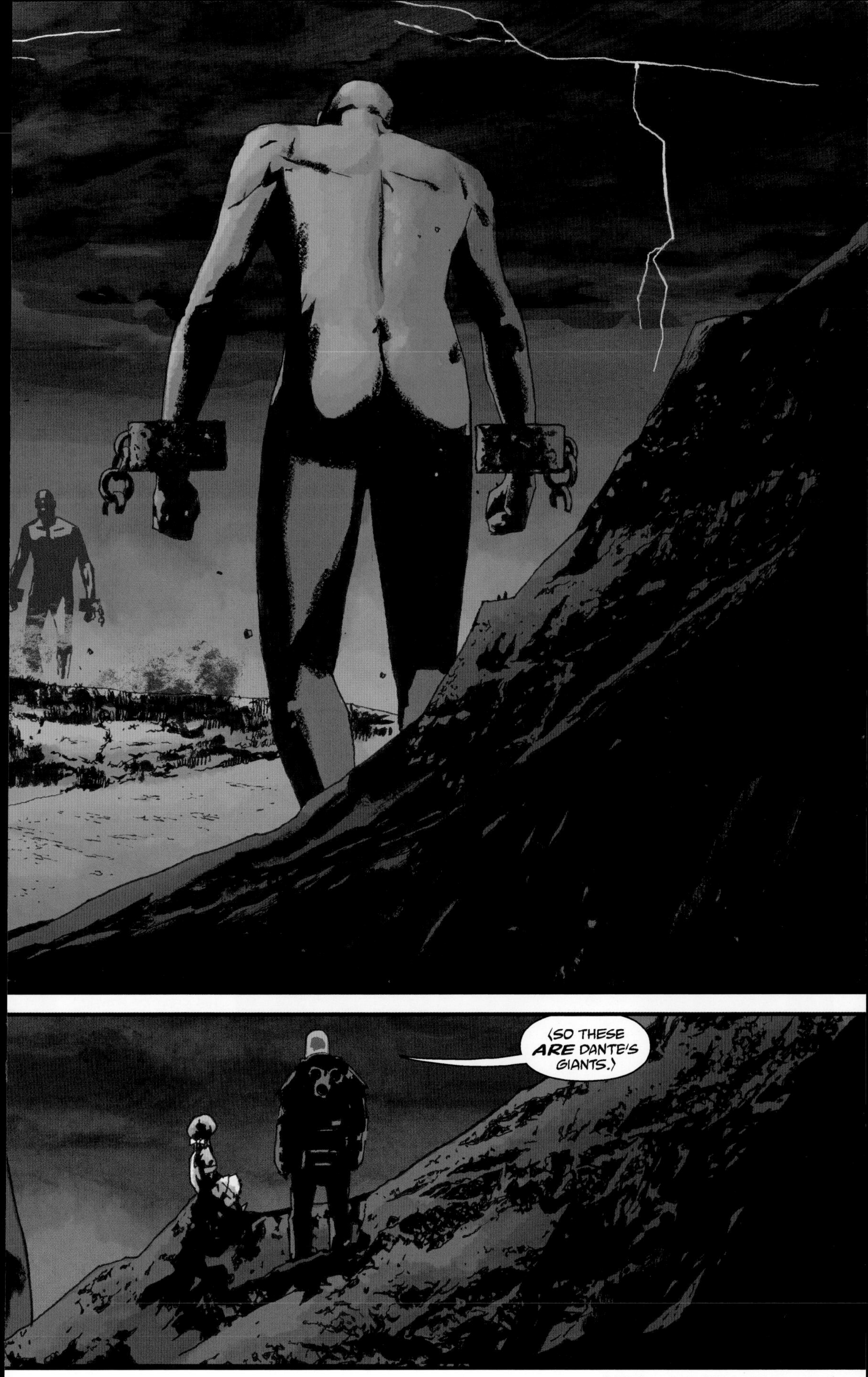
‹SO THESE **ARE** DANTE'S GIANTS.›

‹TRANSLATED FROM THE RUSSIAN›

〈CALL THEM WHAT YOU WANT, NICHAYKO. THEY ARE THE FIRST ANGELS, CAST INTO THE PIT FOR STEALING THE FIRE FROM THE SKY-- AND FOR **WORSE** SINS.〉

"〈THERE IN THE PIT FIRST, BUT WHEN SATAN AND ALL OF US FALLEN ARRIVED, THERE WAS WAR. A WAR FOR THE CONTROL OF DESPAIR.〉

"〈THEY WERE DEFEATED. CRUSHED DOWN, KILLED. ONE WAS ENSLAVED TO BUILD SATAN'S CAPITAL, HIS SEAT OF POWER.〉

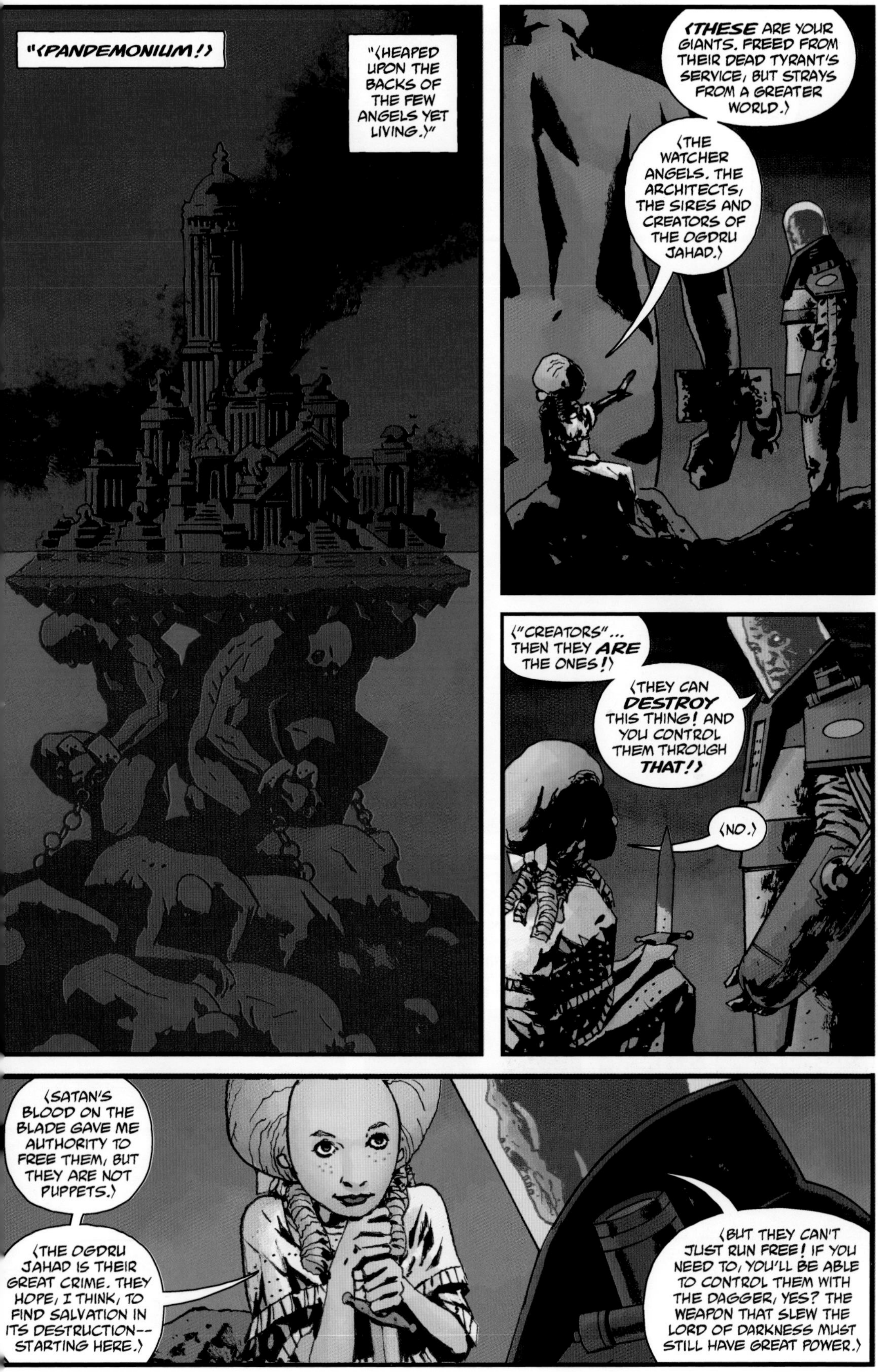
"‹PANDEMONIUM!›
"‹HEAPED UPON THE BACKS OF THE FEW ANGELS YET LIVING.›"
‹THESE ARE YOUR GIANTS. FREED FROM THEIR DEAD TYRANT'S SERVICE, BUT STRAYS FROM A GREATER WORLD.›
‹THE WATCHER ANGELS. THE ARCHITECTS, THE SIRES AND CREATORS OF THE OGDRU JAHAD.›
‹"CREATORS"... THEN THEY ARE THE ONES!›
‹THEY CAN DESTROY THIS THING! AND YOU CONTROL THEM THROUGH THAT!›
‹NO.›
‹SATAN'S BLOOD ON THE BLADE GAVE ME AUTHORITY TO FREE THEM, BUT THEY ARE NOT PUPPETS.›
‹THE OGDRU JAHAD IS THEIR GREAT CRIME. THEY HOPE, I THINK, TO FIND SALVATION IN ITS DESTRUCTION-- STARTING HERE.›
‹BUT THEY CAN'T JUST RUN FREE! IF YOU NEED TO, YOU'LL BE ABLE TO CONTROL THEM WITH THE DAGGER, YES? THE WEAPON THAT SLEW THE LORD OF DARKNESS MUST STILL HAVE GREAT POWER.›

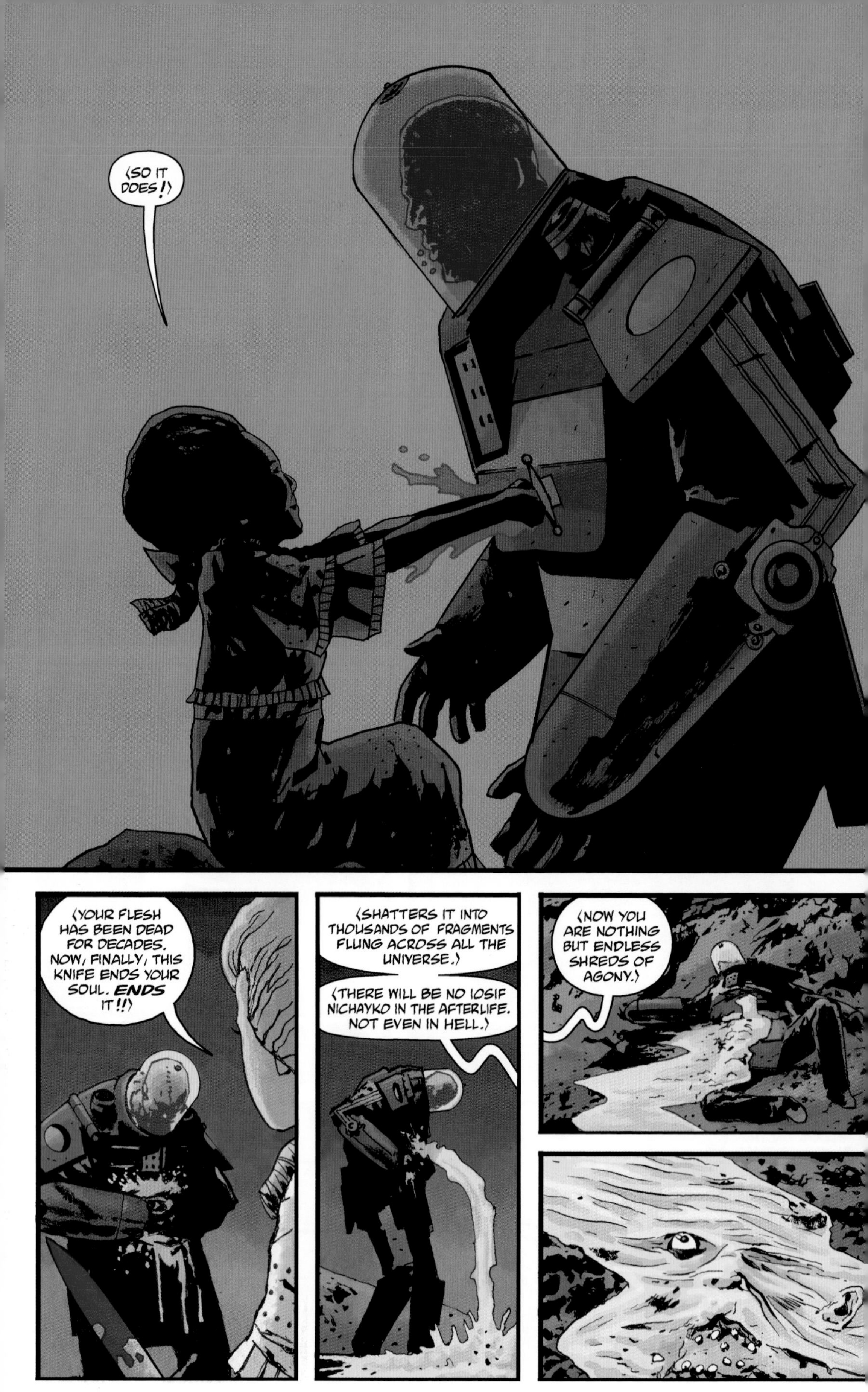
⟨SO IT DOES!⟩
⟨YOUR FLESH HAS BEEN DEAD FOR DECADES. NOW, FINALLY, THIS KNIFE ENDS YOUR SOUL. ENDS IT!!⟩
⟨SHATTERS IT INTO THOUSANDS OF FRAGMENTS FLUNG ACROSS ALL THE UNIVERSE.⟩
⟨THERE WILL BE NO IOSIF NICHAYKO IN THE AFTERLIFE. NOT EVEN IN HELL.⟩
⟨NOW YOU ARE NOTHING BUT ENDLESS SHREDS OF AGONY.⟩

CHAPTER FOUR

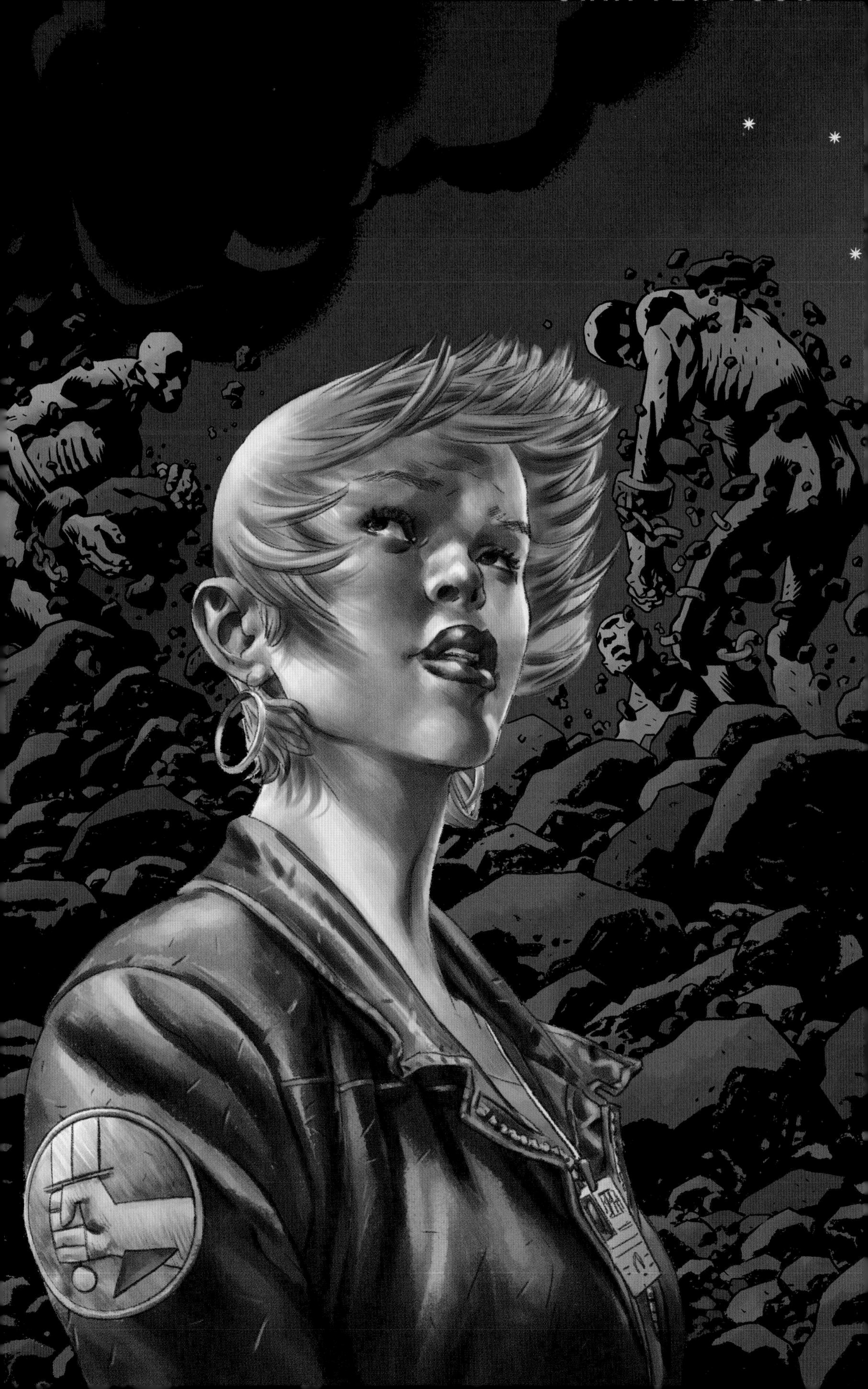

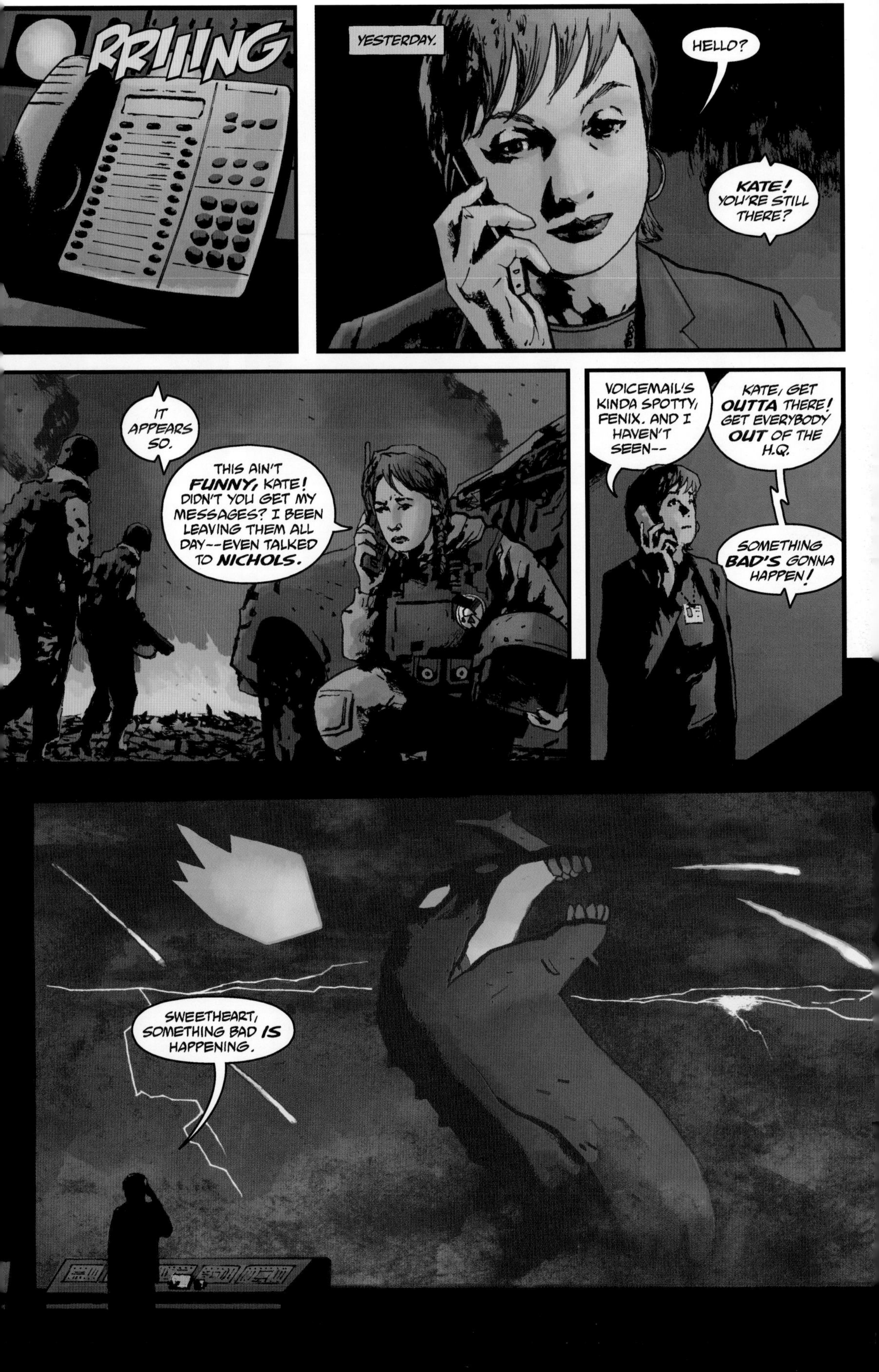
RRIIING
YESTERDAY.
HELLO?
KATE! YOU'RE STILL THERE?
IT APPEARS SO.
THIS AIN'T FUNNY, KATE! DIDN'T YOU GET MY MESSAGES? I BEEN LEAVING THEM ALL DAY--EVEN TALKED TO NICHOLS.
VOICEMAIL'S KINDA SPOTTY, FENIX. AND I HAVEN'T SEEN--
KATE, GET OUTTA THERE! GET EVERYBODY OUT OF THE H.Q.
SOMETHING BAD'S GONNA HAPPEN!
SWEETHEART, SOMETHING BAD IS HAPPENING.

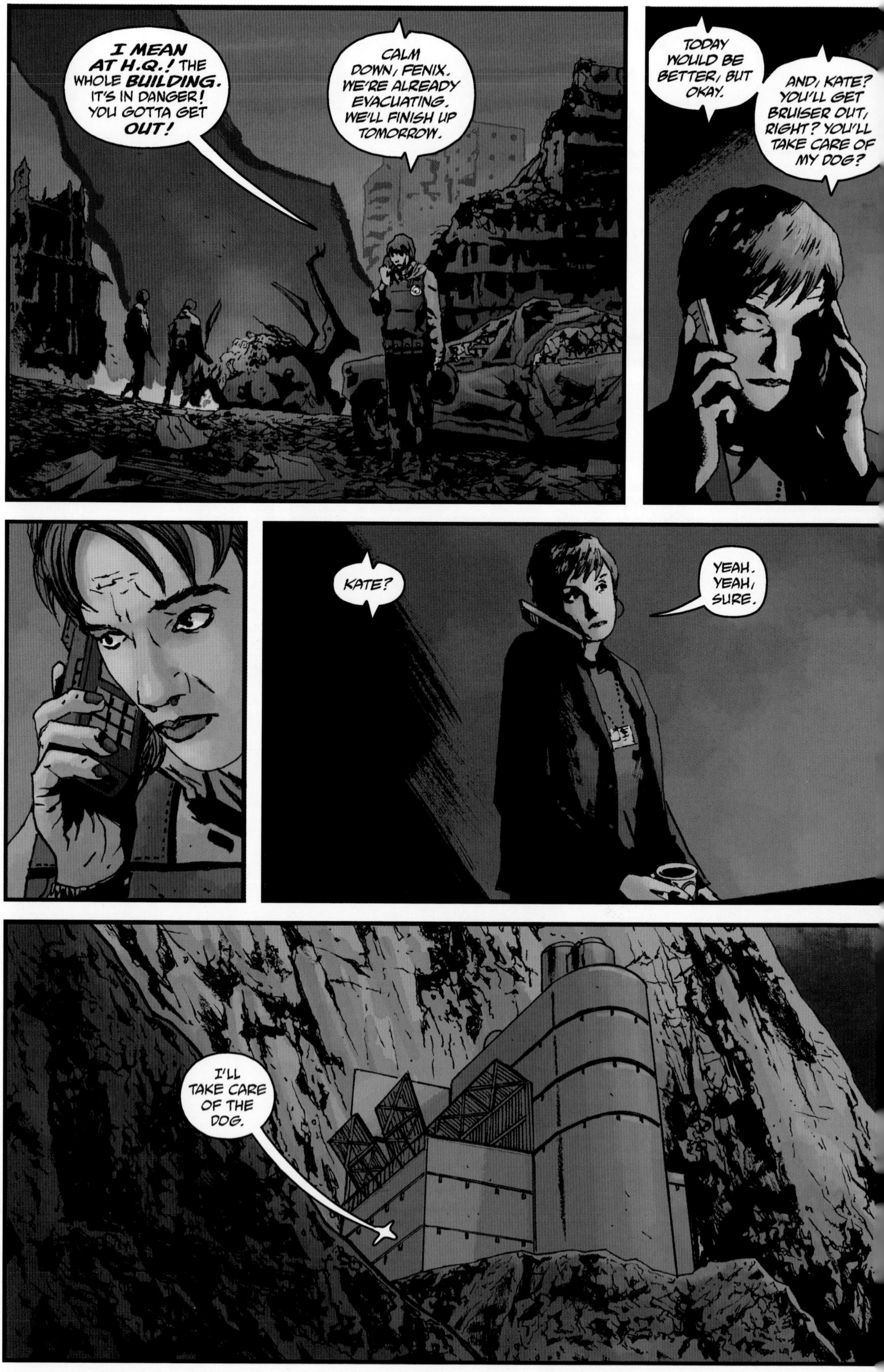
I MEAN AT H.Q.! THE WHOLE BUILDING. IT'S IN DANGER! YOU GOTTA GET OUT!
CALM DOWN, FENIX. WE'RE ALREADY EVACUATING. WE'LL FINISH UP TOMORROW.
TODAY WOULD BE BETTER, BUT OKAY.
AND, KATE? YOU'LL GET BRUISER OUT, RIGHT? YOU'LL TAKE CARE OF MY DOG?
KATE?
YEAH. YEAH, SURE.
I'LL TAKE CARE OF THE DOG.

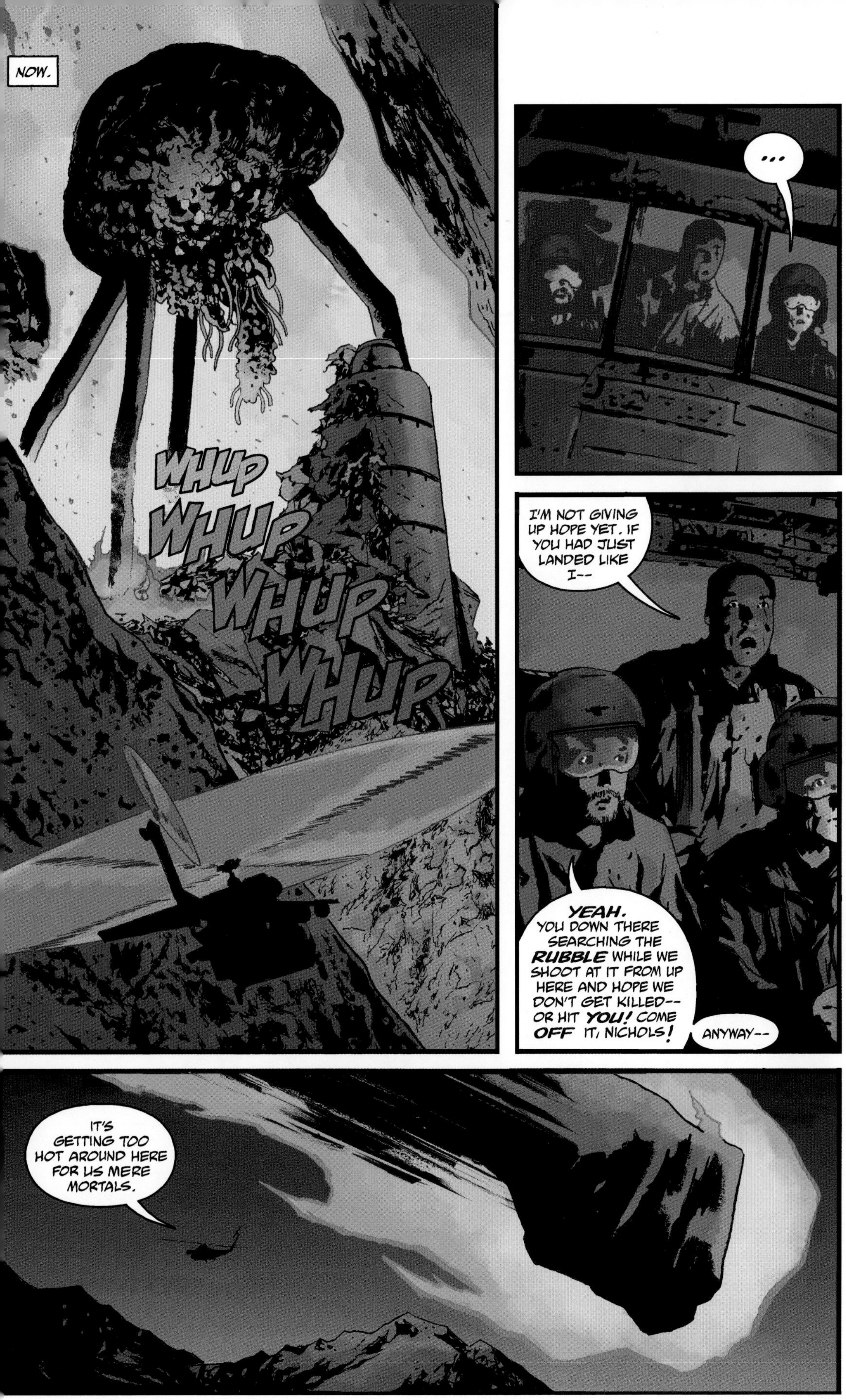
NOW.
WHUP WHUP WHUP WHUP
...
I'M NOT GIVING UP HOPE YET. IF YOU HAD JUST LANDED LIKE I--
YEAH. YOU DOWN THERE SEARCHING THE RUBBLE WHILE WE SHOOT AT IT FROM UP HERE AND HOPE WE DON'T GET KILLED-- OR HIT YOU! COME OFF IT, NICHOLS!
ANYWAY--
IT'S GETTING TOO HOT AROUND HERE FOR US MERE MORTALS.

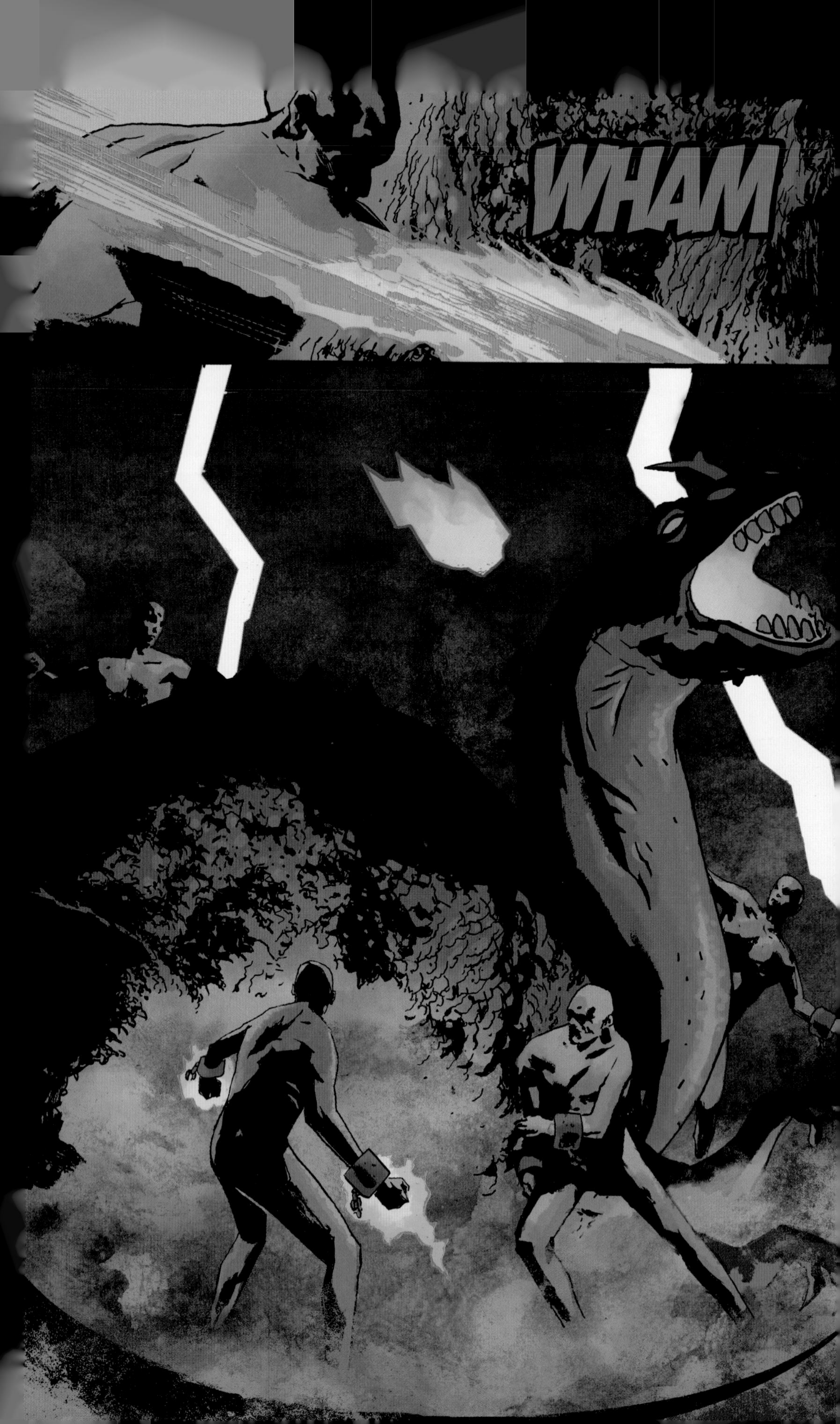
WHAM

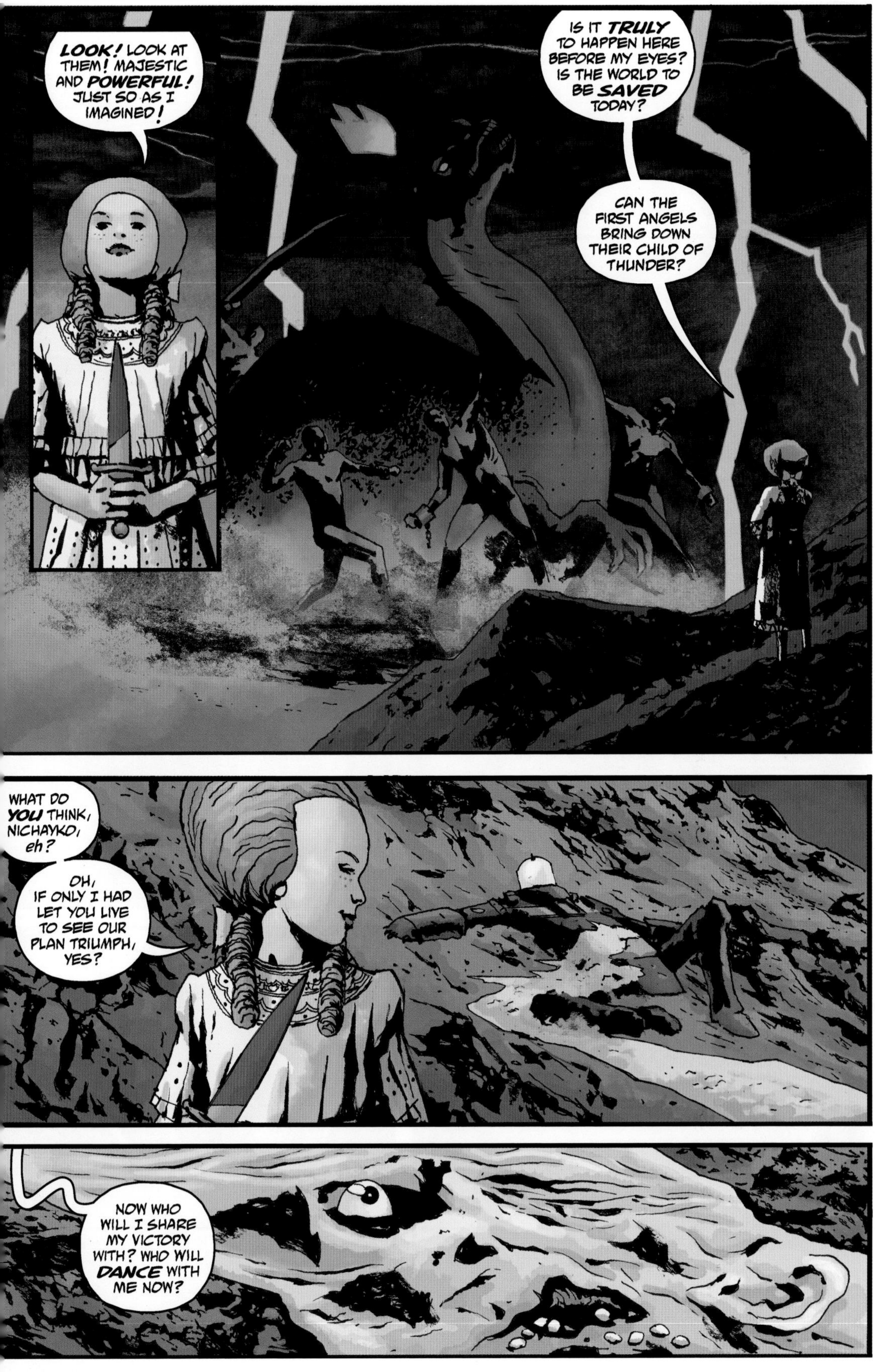
LOOK! LOOK AT THEM! MAJESTIC AND POWERFUL! JUST SO AS I IMAGINED!
IS IT TRULY TO HAPPEN HERE BEFORE MY EYES? IS THE WORLD TO BE SAVED TODAY?
CAN THE FIRST ANGELS BRING DOWN THEIR CHILD OF THUNDER?
WHAT DO YOU THINK, NICHAYKO, eh?
OH, IF ONLY I HAD LET YOU LIVE TO SEE OUR PLAN TRIUMPH, YES?
NOW WHO WILL I SHARE MY VICTORY WITH? WHO WILL DANCE WITH ME NOW?

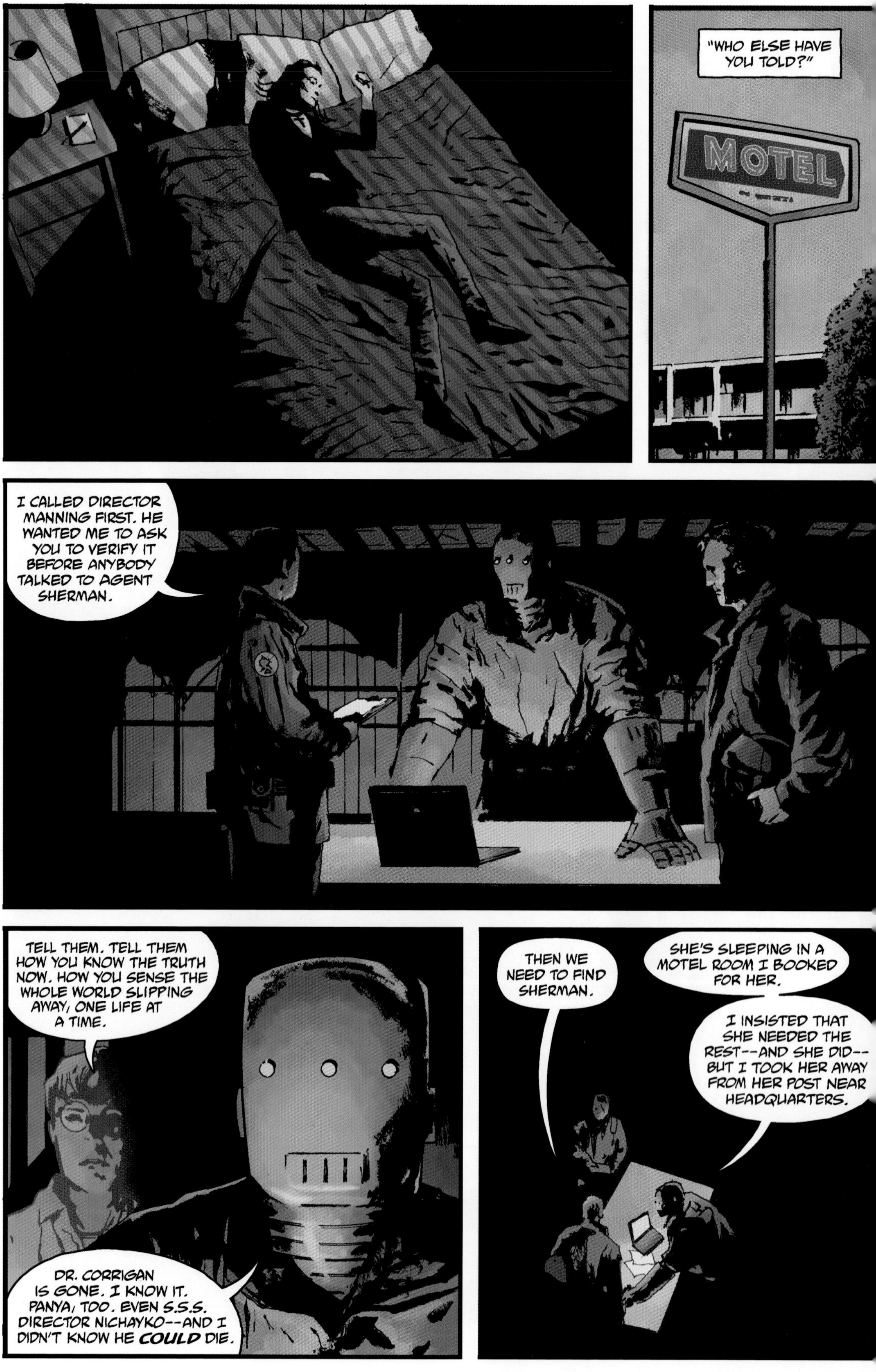
"WHO ELSE HAVE YOU TOLD?"
MOTEL
I CALLED DIRECTOR MANNING FIRST. HE WANTED ME TO ASK YOU TO VERIFY IT BEFORE ANYBODY TALKED TO AGENT SHERMAN.
TELL THEM. TELL THEM HOW YOU KNOW THE TRUTH NOW. HOW YOU SENSE THE WHOLE WORLD SLIPPING AWAY, ONE LIFE AT A TIME.
DR. CORRIGAN IS GONE. I KNOW IT. PANYA, TOO. EVEN S.S.S. DIRECTOR NICHAYKO--AND I DIDN'T KNOW HE COULD DIE.
THEN WE NEED TO FIND SHERMAN.
SHE'S SLEEPING IN A MOTEL ROOM I BOOKED FOR HER.
I INSISTED THAT SHE NEEDED THE REST--AND SHE DID--BUT I TOOK HER AWAY FROM HER POST NEAR HEADQUARTERS.

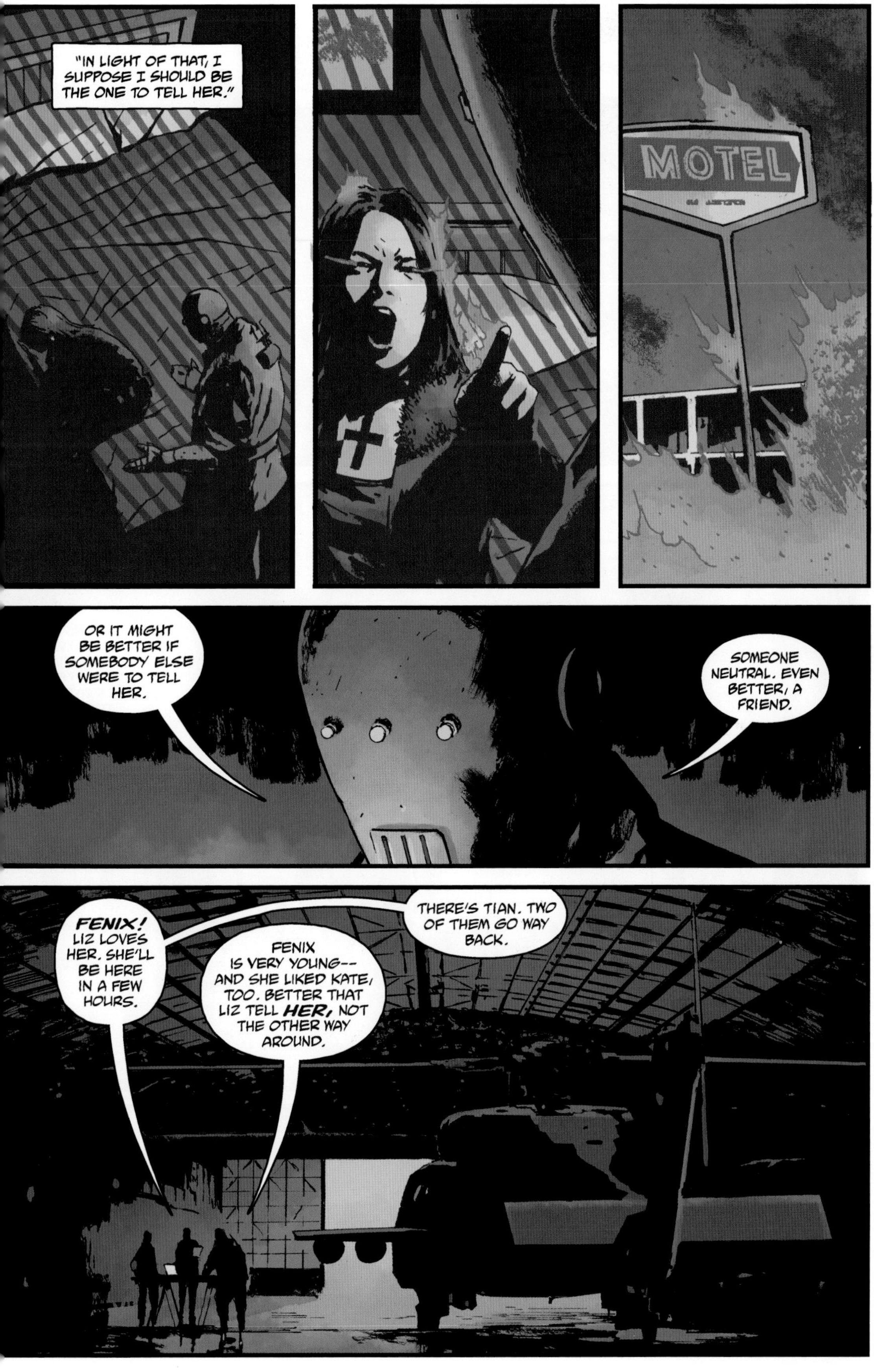
"IN LIGHT OF THAT, I SUPPOSE I SHOULD BE THE ONE TO TELL HER."
MOTEL
OR IT MIGHT BE BETTER IF SOMEBODY ELSE WERE TO TELL HER.
SOMEONE NEUTRAL. EVEN BETTER, A FRIEND.
FENIX! LIZ LOVES HER. SHE'LL BE HERE IN A FEW HOURS.
THERE'S TIAN. TWO OF THEM GO WAY BACK.
FENIX IS VERY YOUNG-- AND SHE LIKED KATE, TOO. BETTER THAT LIZ TELL HER, NOT THE OTHER WAY AROUND.

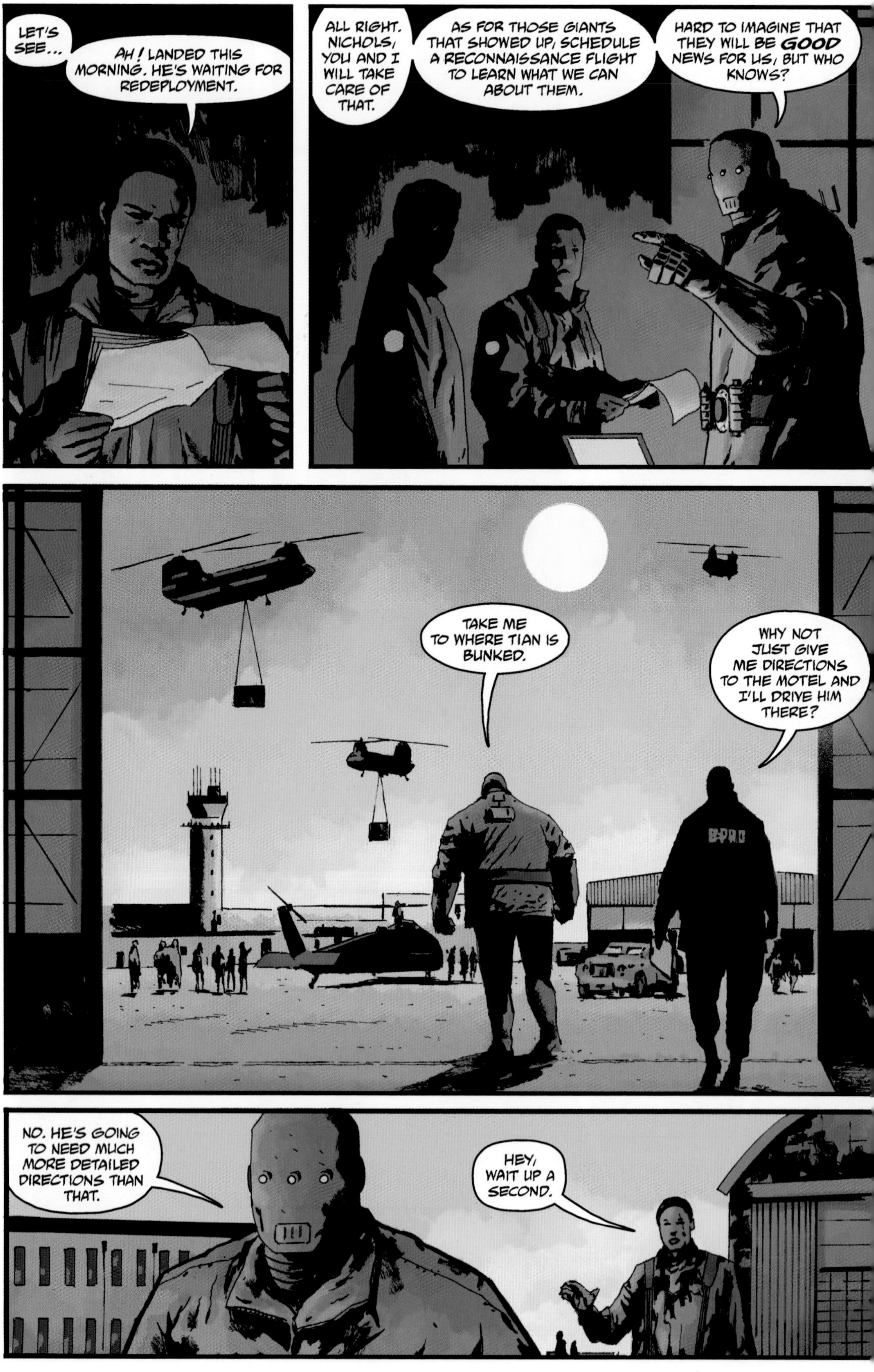
LET'S SEE...
AH! LANDED THIS MORNING. HE'S WAITING FOR REDEPLOYMENT.
ALL RIGHT. NICHOLS, YOU AND I WILL TAKE CARE OF THAT.
AS FOR THOSE GIANTS THAT SHOWED UP, SCHEDULE A RECONNAISSANCE FLIGHT TO LEARN WHAT WE CAN ABOUT THEM.
HARD TO IMAGINE THAT THEY WILL BE GOOD NEWS FOR US, BUT WHO KNOWS?
TAKE ME TO WHERE TIAN IS BUNKED.
WHY NOT JUST GIVE ME DIRECTIONS TO THE MOTEL AND I'LL DRIVE HIM THERE?
NO. HE'S GOING TO NEED MUCH MORE DETAILED DIRECTIONS THAN THAT.
HEY, WAIT UP A SECOND.

WHAT IS IT?

EARLIER, WHEN WE SAW THE HEADQUARTERS, I WANTED TO LAND. TO SEE IF I...BUT IT WOULDN'T HAVE MATTERED, RIGHT? I MEAN, YOU SAID KATE'S DEAD.

SHE IS.

BUT **IS** SHE?

I'M SAYIN', THAT THING YOU DO WHERE YOU USE SOME OF YOUR...YOUR-**SELF** TO RAISE THE SPIRIT OF A... RECENTLY DEAD PERSON--

IF I COULD ACTUALLY BRING ANY OF THE PEOPLE WE'VE LOST BACK TO LIFE, DON'T YOU THINK I WOULD HAVE DONE THAT BY NOW, AGENT NICHOLS?

IN ANY CASE, THIS ARMOR HAS NO VALVES. IT IS COMPLETELY SEALED, WITH NO WAY FOR MY ECTOPLASM TO ESCAPE--UNLESS THE ARMOR IS DAMAGED.

AND IF THAT SHOULD HAPPEN, WITH ALL MY CONTAINMENT SUITS DESTROYED AT HEAD-QUARTERS...

WELL, I'M NOT SURE EXACTLY WHAT WOULD BECOME OF ME.

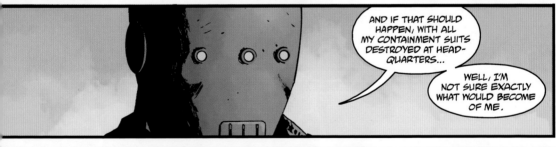

JOIN THE CLUB.

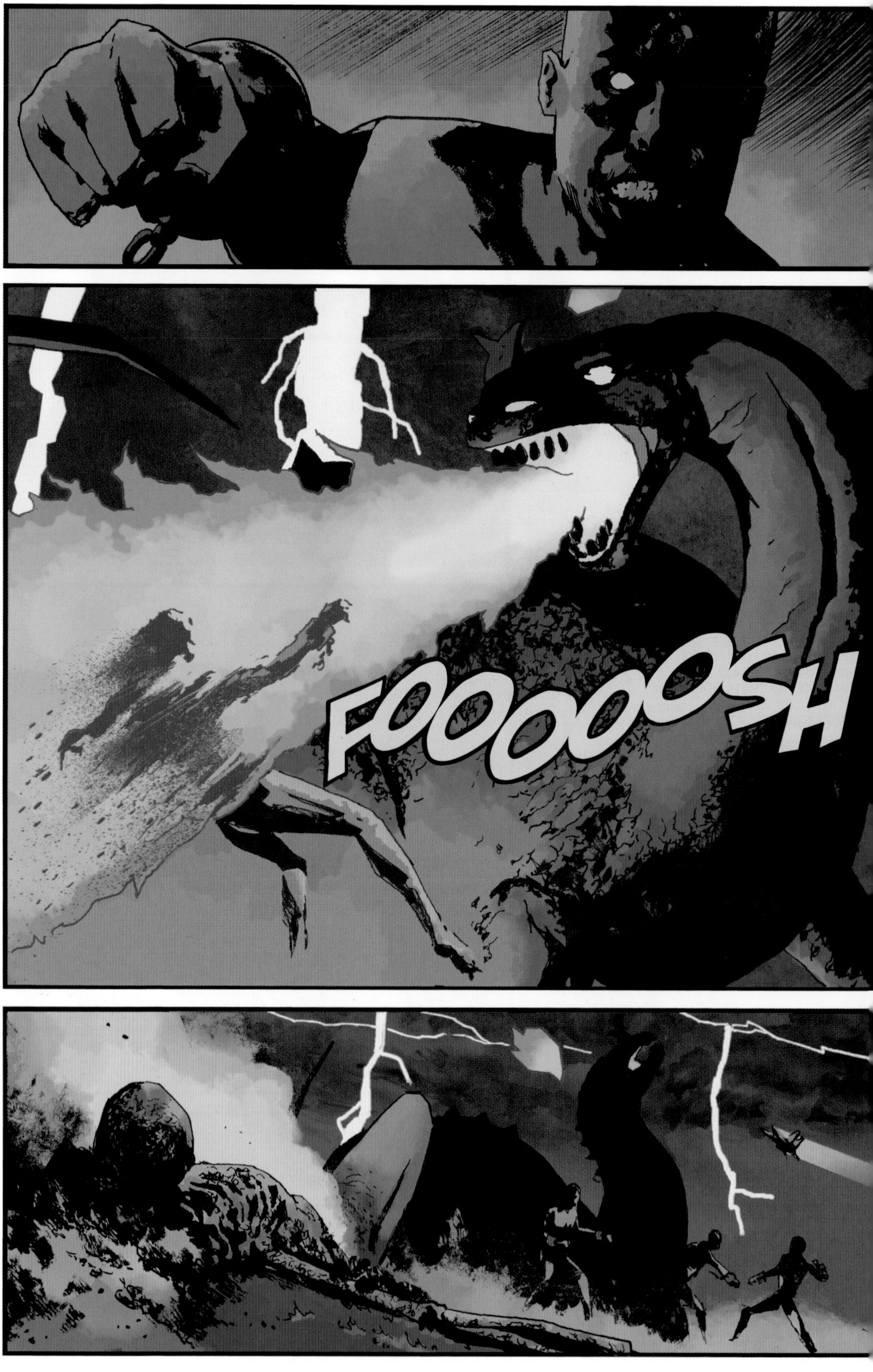
FOOOOOSH

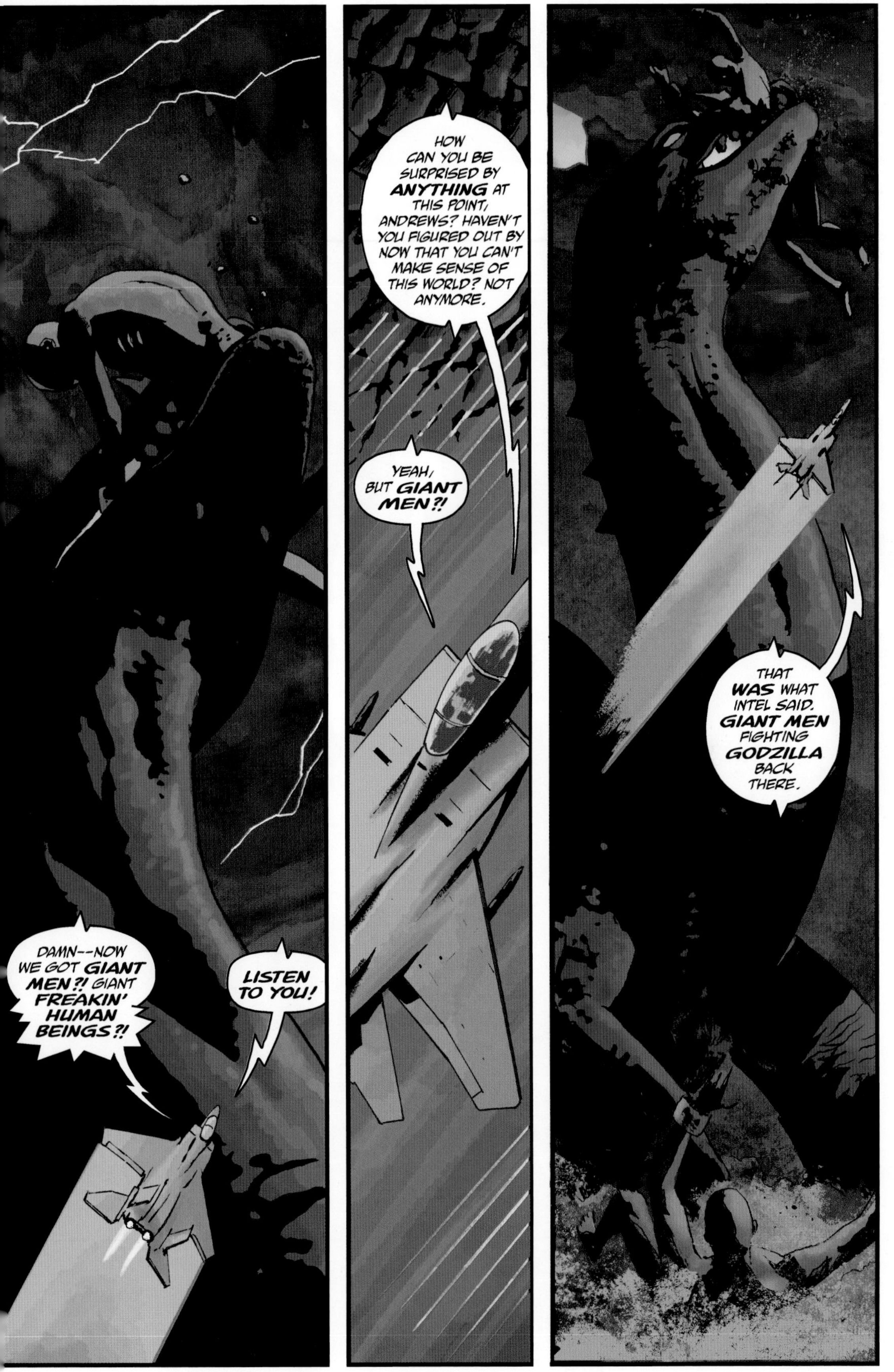
DAMN--NOW WE GOT GIANT MEN?! GIANT FREAKIN' HUMAN BEINGS?!
LISTEN TO YOU!
HOW CAN YOU BE SURPRISED BY ANYTHING AT THIS POINT, ANDREWS? HAVEN'T YOU FIGURED OUT BY NOW THAT YOU CAN'T MAKE SENSE OF THIS WORLD? NOT ANYMORE.
YEAH, BUT GIANT MEN?!
THAT WAS WHAT INTEL SAID. GIANT MEN FIGHTING GODZILLA BACK THERE.

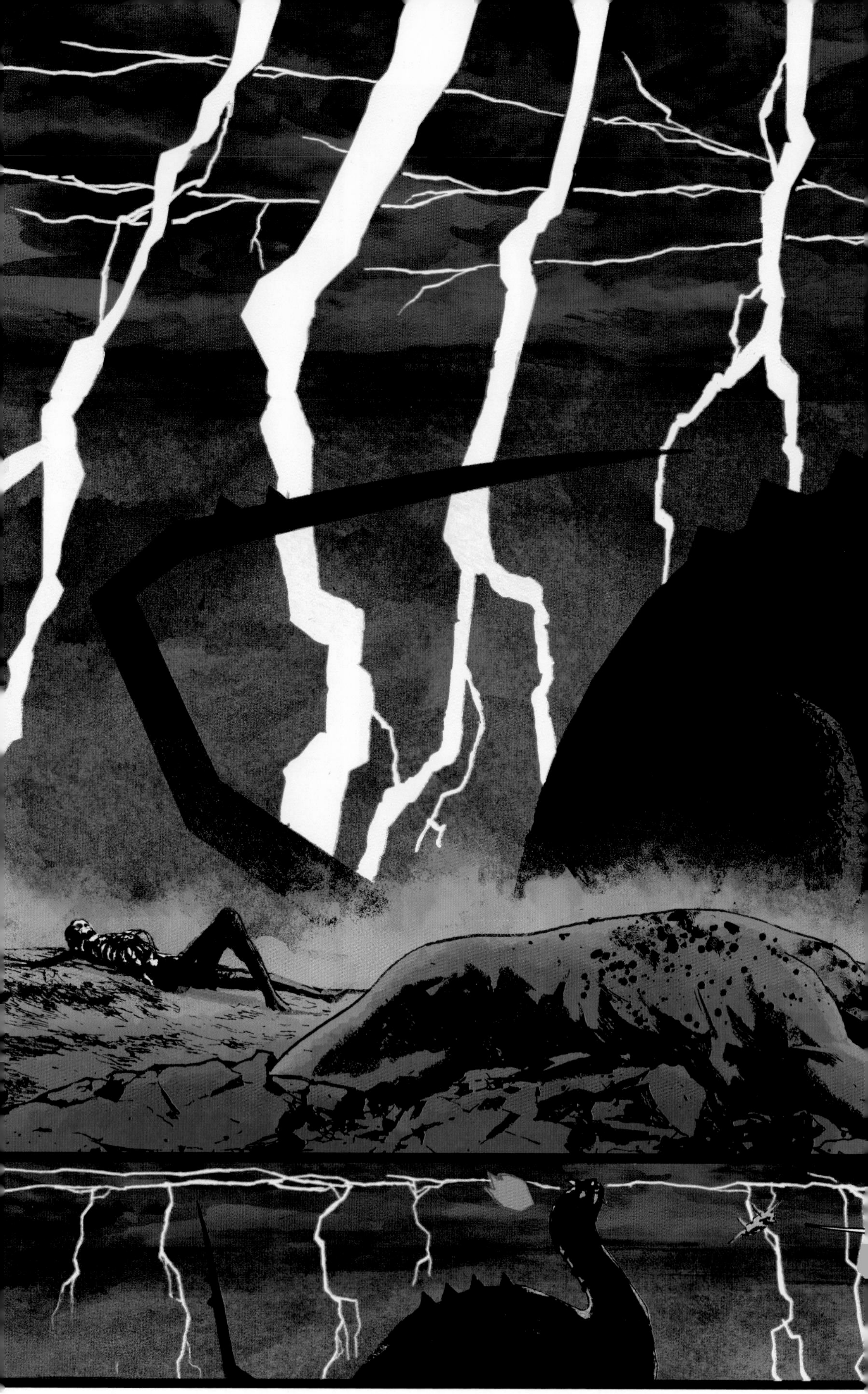

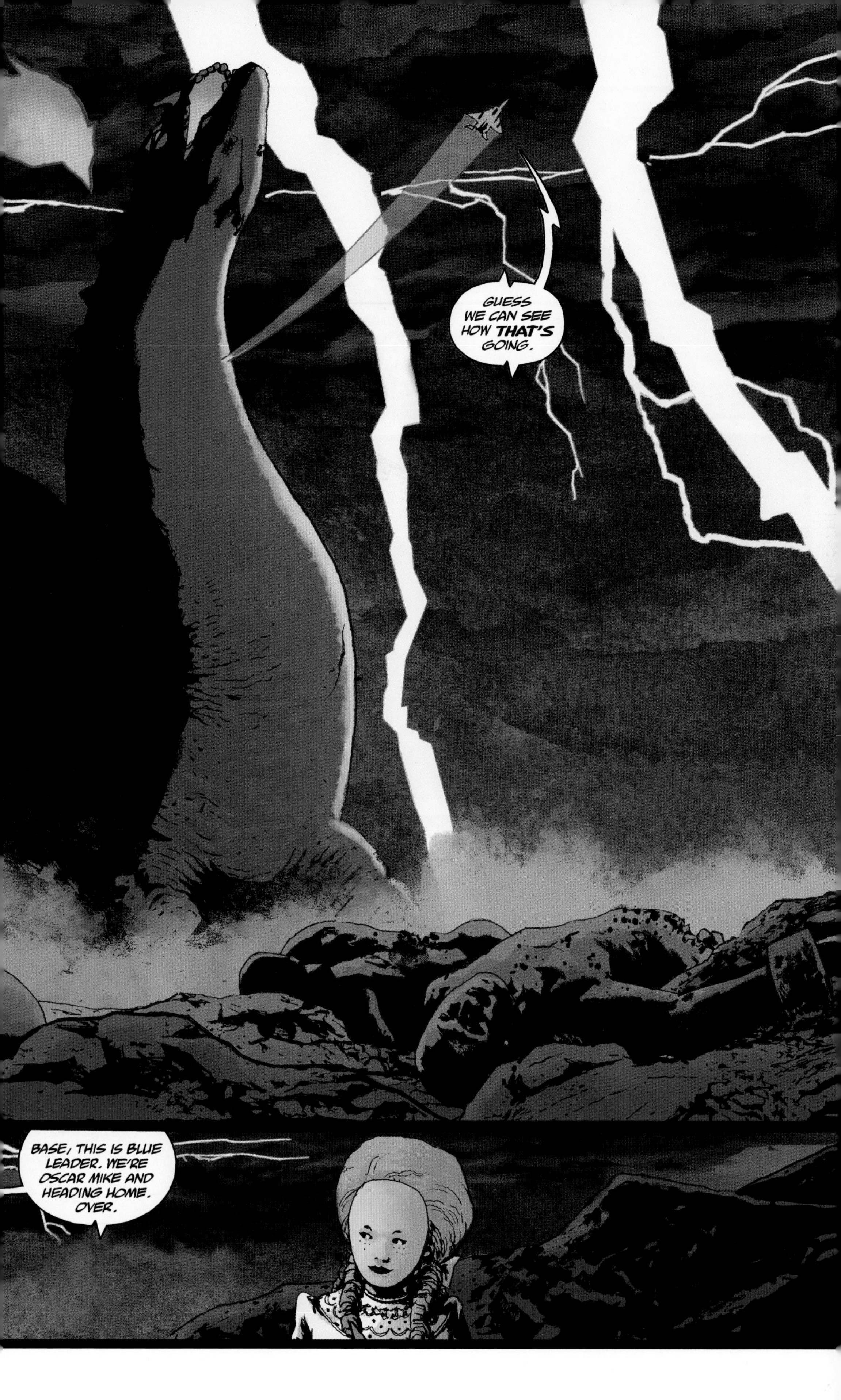
GUESS WE CAN SEE HOW **THAT'S** GOING.
BASE, THIS IS BLUE LEADER. WE'RE OSCAR MIKE AND HEADING HOME. OVER.

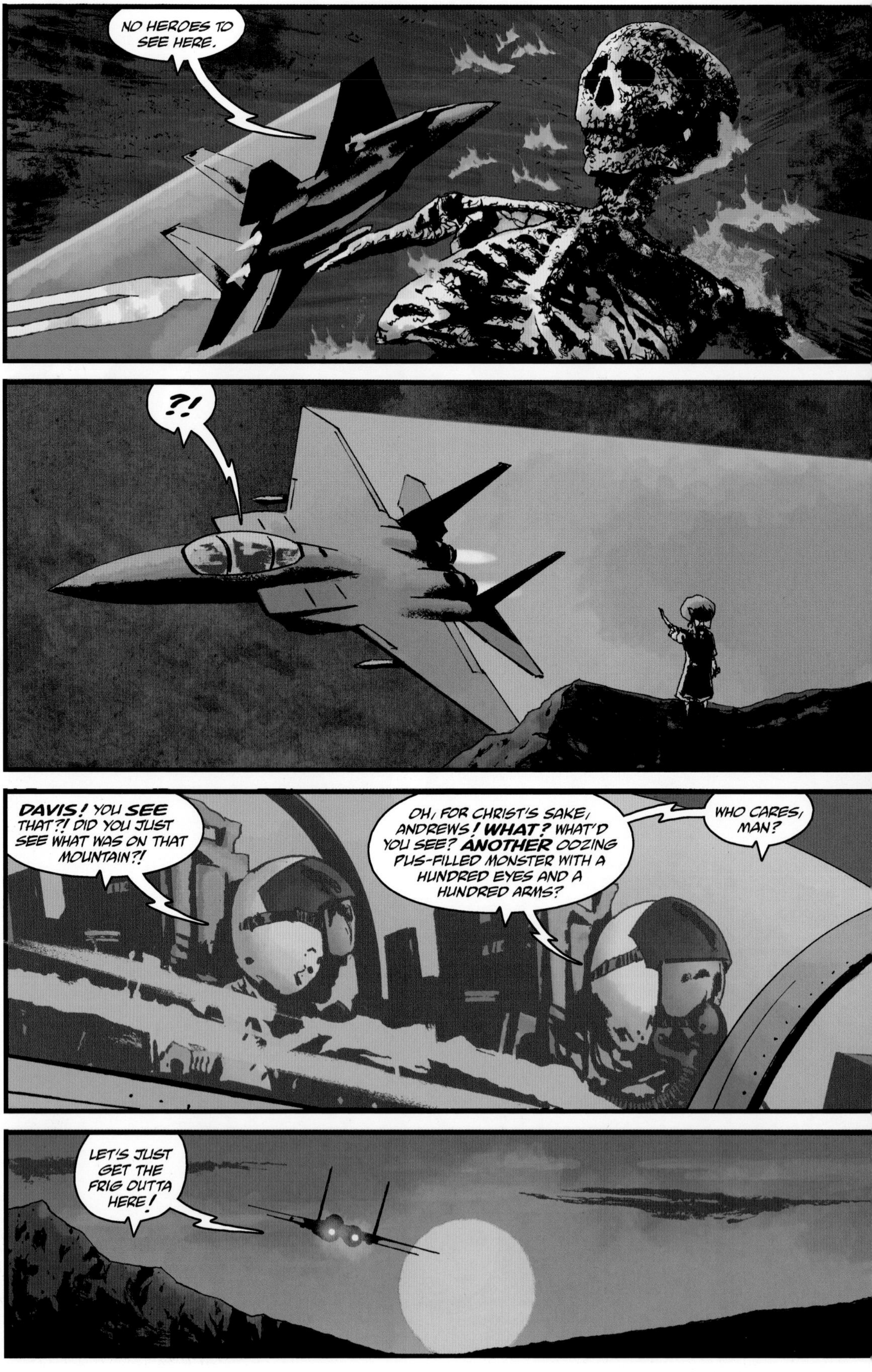
NO HEROES TO SEE HERE.
?!
DAVIS! YOU SEE THAT?! DID YOU JUST SEE WHAT WAS ON THAT MOUNTAIN?!
OH, FOR CHRIST'S SAKE, ANDREWS! WHAT? WHAT'D YOU SEE? ANOTHER OOZING PUS-FILLED MONSTER WITH A HUNDRED EYES AND A HUNDRED ARMS?
WHO CARES, MAN?
LET'S JUST GET THE FRIG OUTTA HERE!

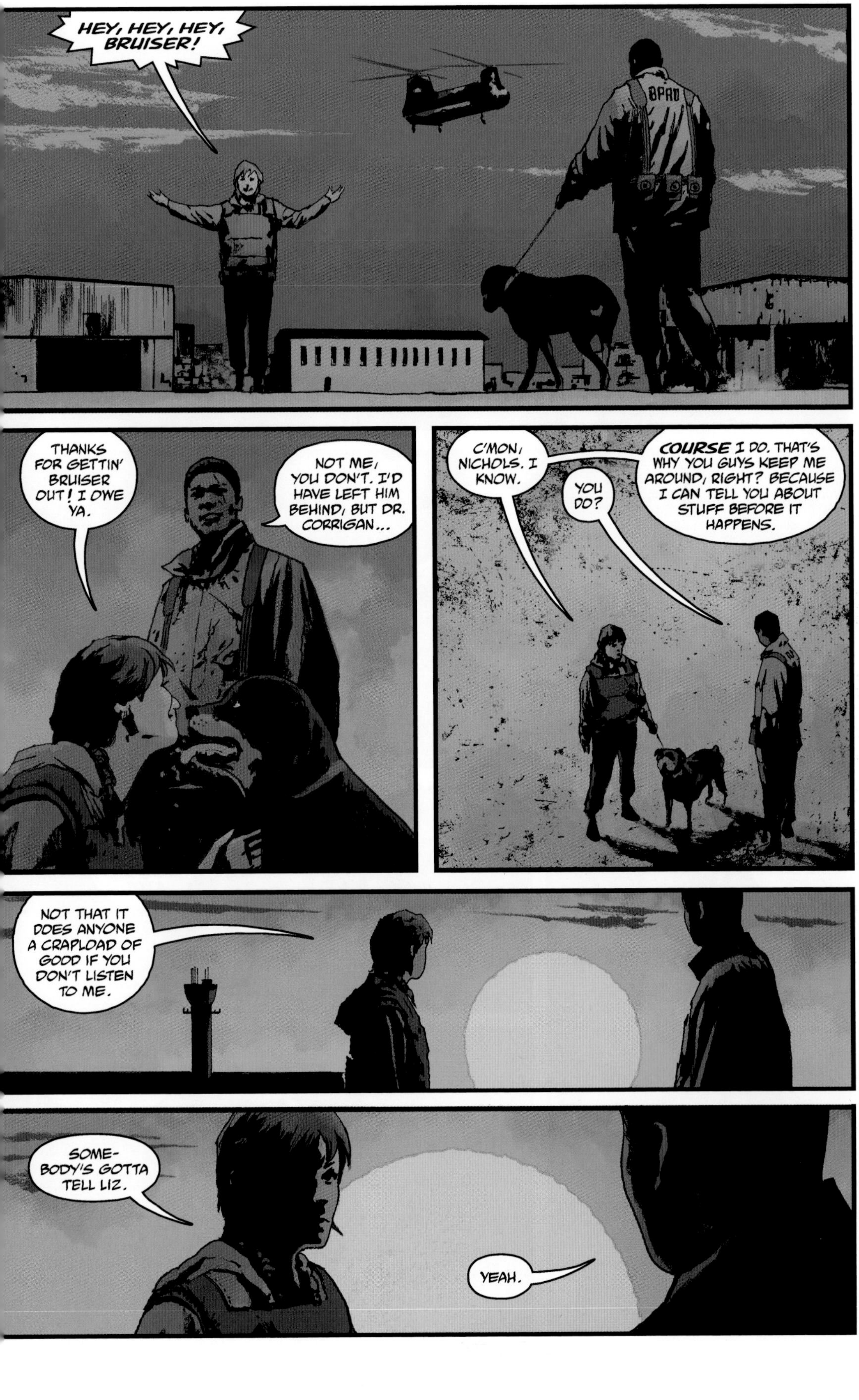
HEY, HEY, HEY, BRUISER!
BPRD
THANKS FOR GETTIN' BRUISER OUT! I OWE YA.
NOT ME, YOU DON'T. I'D HAVE LEFT HIM BEHIND, BUT DR. CORRIGAN...
C'MON, NICHOLS. I KNOW.
YOU DO?
COURSE I DO. THAT'S WHY YOU GUYS KEEP ME AROUND, RIGHT? BECAUSE I CAN TELL YOU ABOUT STUFF BEFORE IT HAPPENS.
NOT THAT IT DOES ANYONE A CRAPLOAD OF GOOD IF YOU DON'T LISTEN TO ME.
SOME-BODY'S GOTTA TELL LIZ.
YEAH.

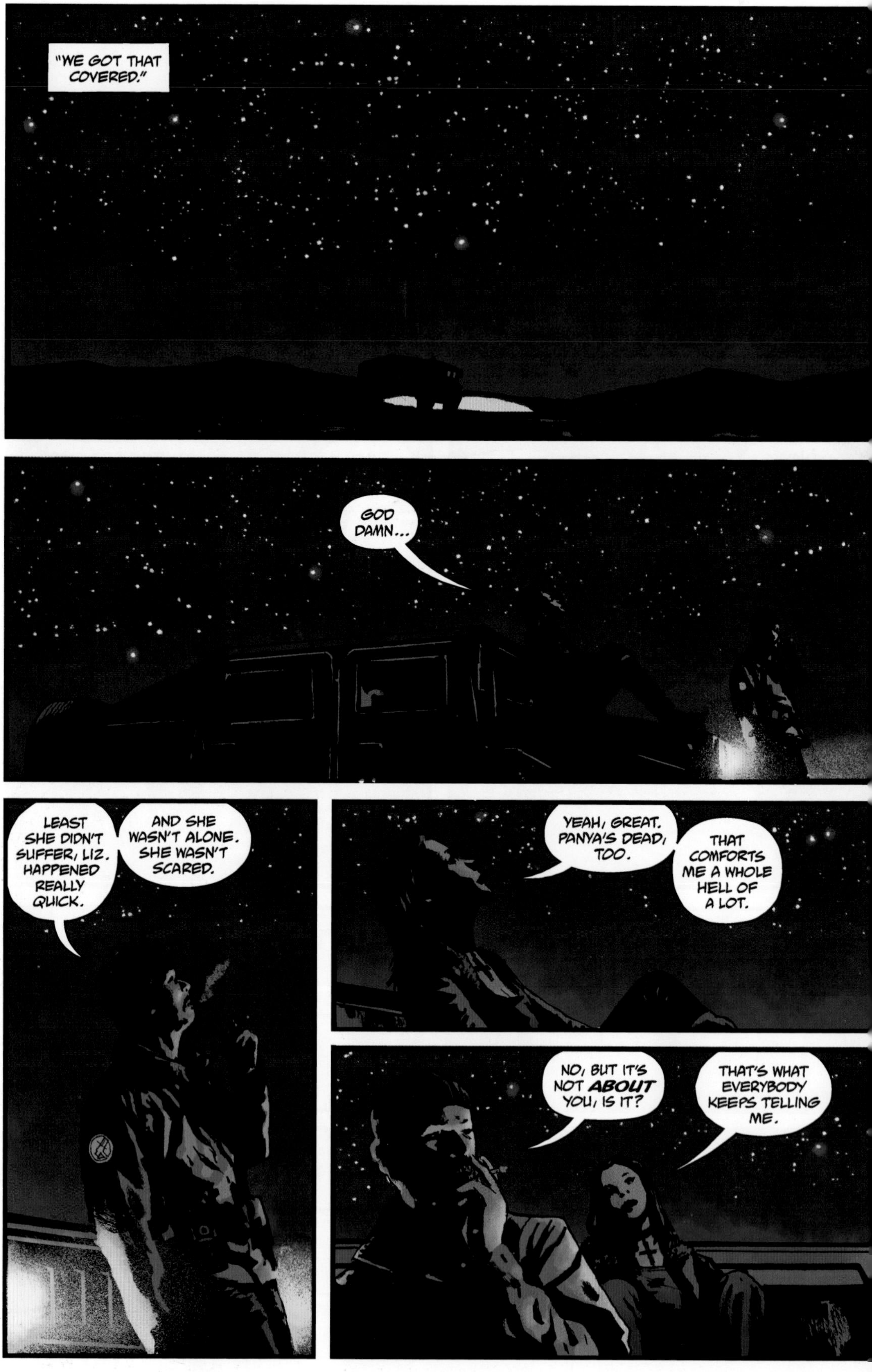
"WE GOT THAT COVERED."
GOD DAMN...
LEAST SHE DIDN'T SUFFER, LIZ. HAPPENED REALLY QUICK.
AND SHE WASN'T ALONE. SHE WASN'T SCARED.
YEAH, GREAT. PANYA'S DEAD, TOO.
THAT COMFORTS ME A WHOLE HELL OF A LOT.
NO, BUT IT'S NOT *ABOUT* YOU, IS IT?
THAT'S WHAT EVERYBODY KEEPS TELLING ME.

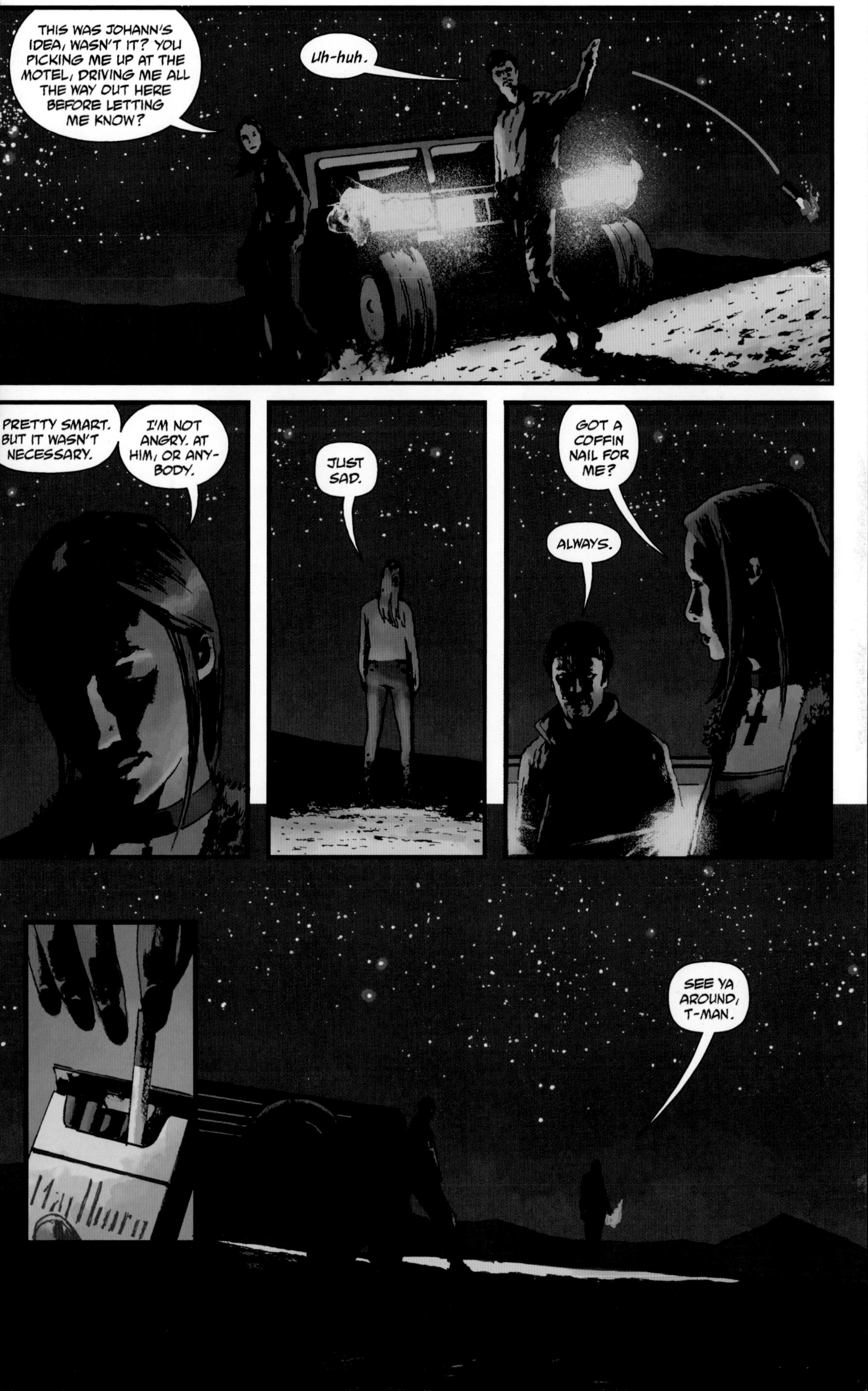
THIS WAS JOHANN'S IDEA, WASN'T IT? YOU PICKING ME UP AT THE MOTEL, DRIVING ME ALL THE WAY OUT HERE BEFORE LETTING ME KNOW?
Uh-huh.
PRETTY SMART. BUT IT WASN'T NECESSARY.
I'M NOT ANGRY. AT HIM, OR ANY-BODY.
JUST SAD.
GOT A COFFIN NAIL FOR ME?
ALWAYS.
SEE YA AROUND, T-MAN.

BOOM

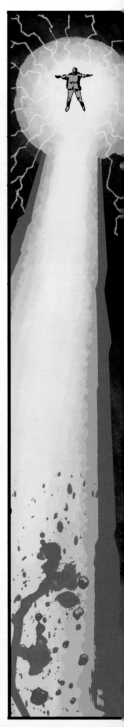

I REMEMBER THAT FEELING.

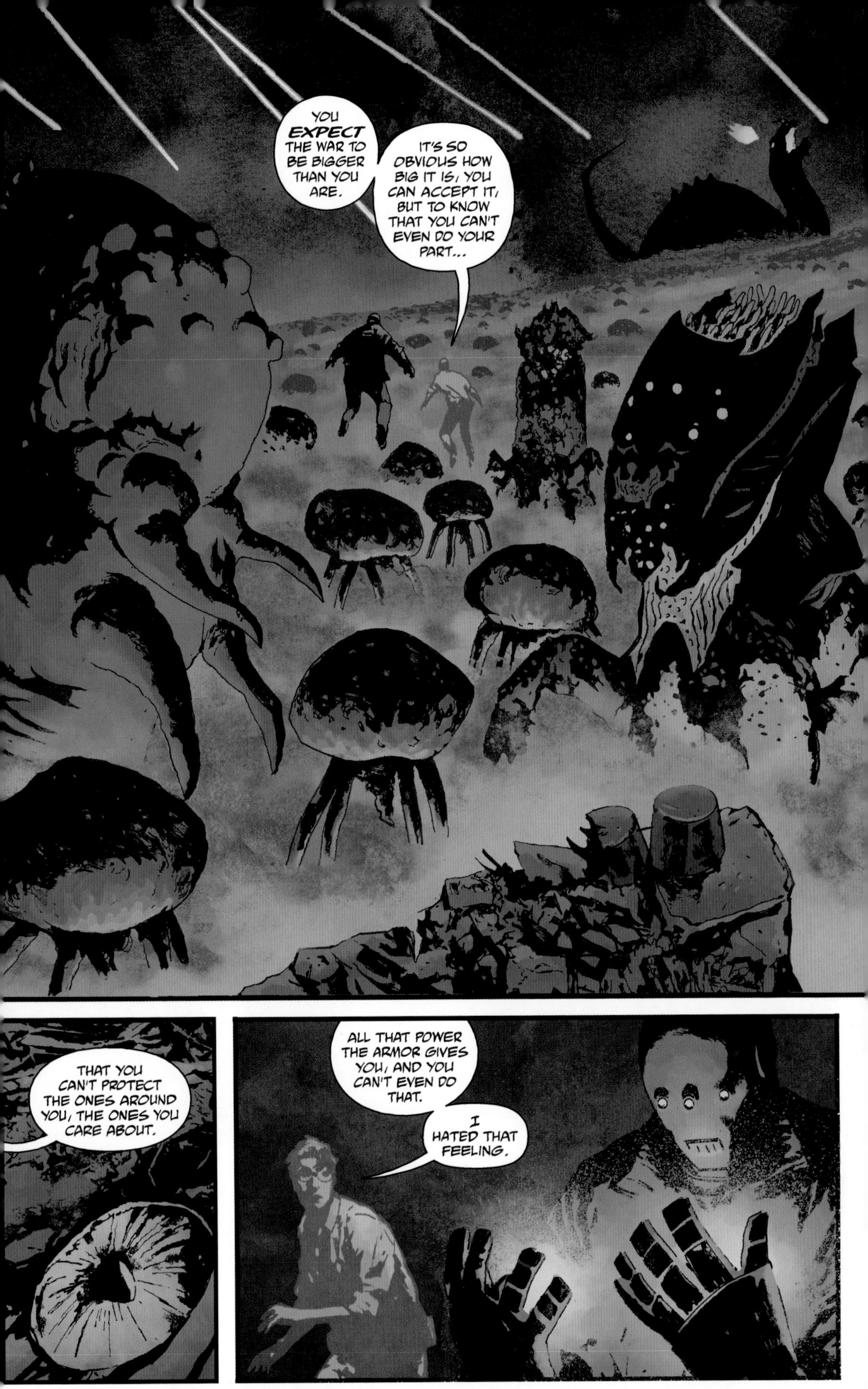
YOU EXPECT THE WAR TO BE BIGGER THAN YOU ARE.
IT'S SO OBVIOUS HOW BIG IT IS, YOU CAN ACCEPT IT, BUT TO KNOW THAT YOU CAN'T EVEN DO YOUR PART...
THAT YOU CAN'T PROTECT THE ONES AROUND YOU, THE ONES YOU CARE ABOUT.
ALL THAT POWER THE ARMOR GIVES YOU, AND YOU CAN'T EVEN DO THAT.
I HATED THAT FEELING.

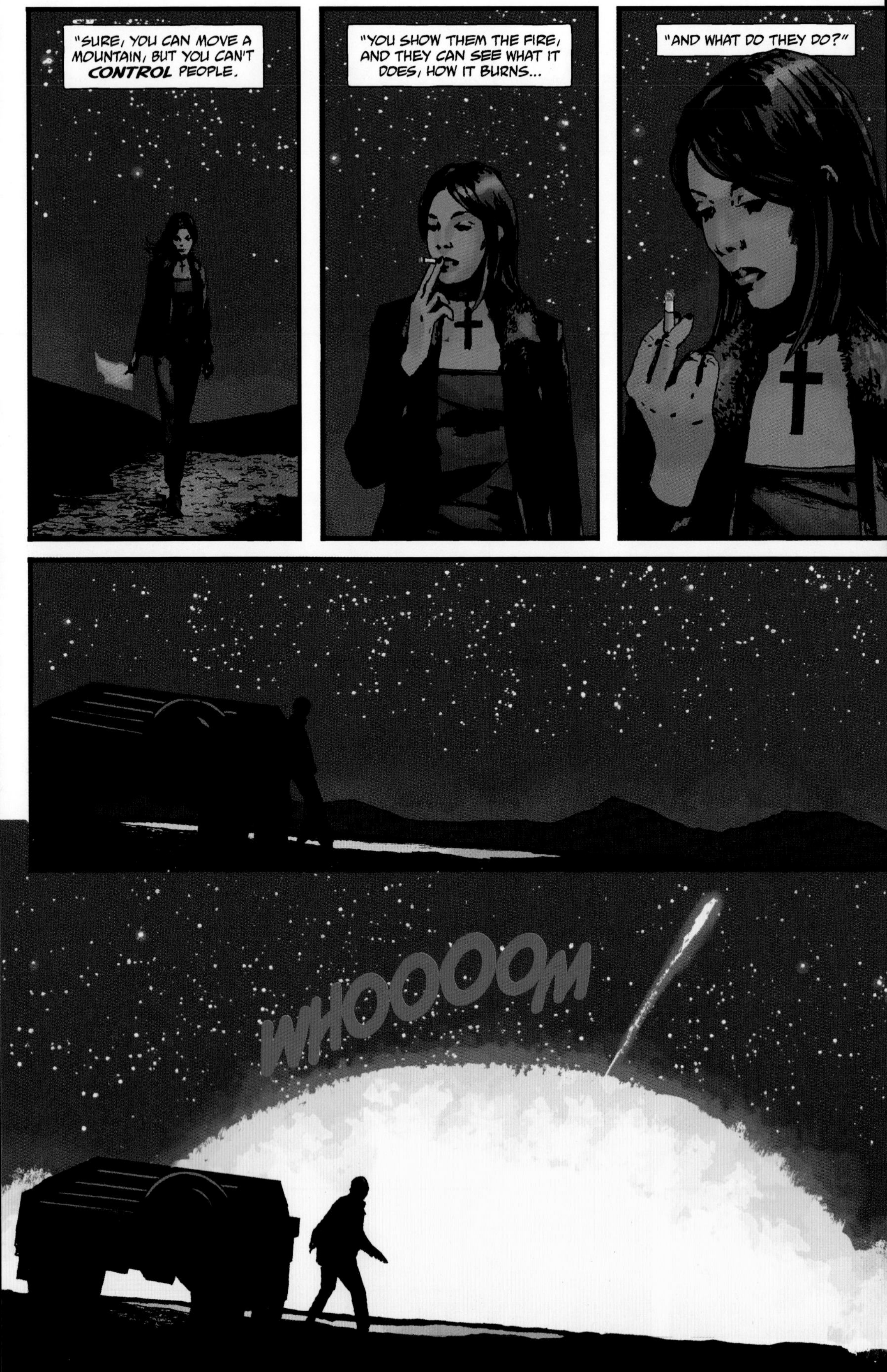
"SURE, YOU CAN MOVE A MOUNTAIN, BUT YOU CAN'T CONTROL PEOPLE.
"YOU SHOW THEM THE FIRE, AND THEY CAN SEE WHAT IT DOES, HOW IT BURNS...
"AND WHAT DO THEY DO?"
WHOOOOM

THEY GO AND STICK THEIR HANDS IN ANYWAY.

ARE WE TALKING ABOUT ME, OR YOU?

YOU'RE STICKING *YOUR* HANDS IN, AREN'T YOU?

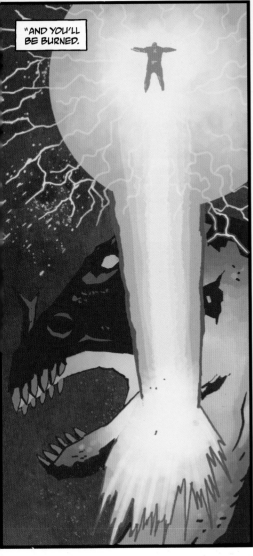

"AND YOU'LL BE BURNED.

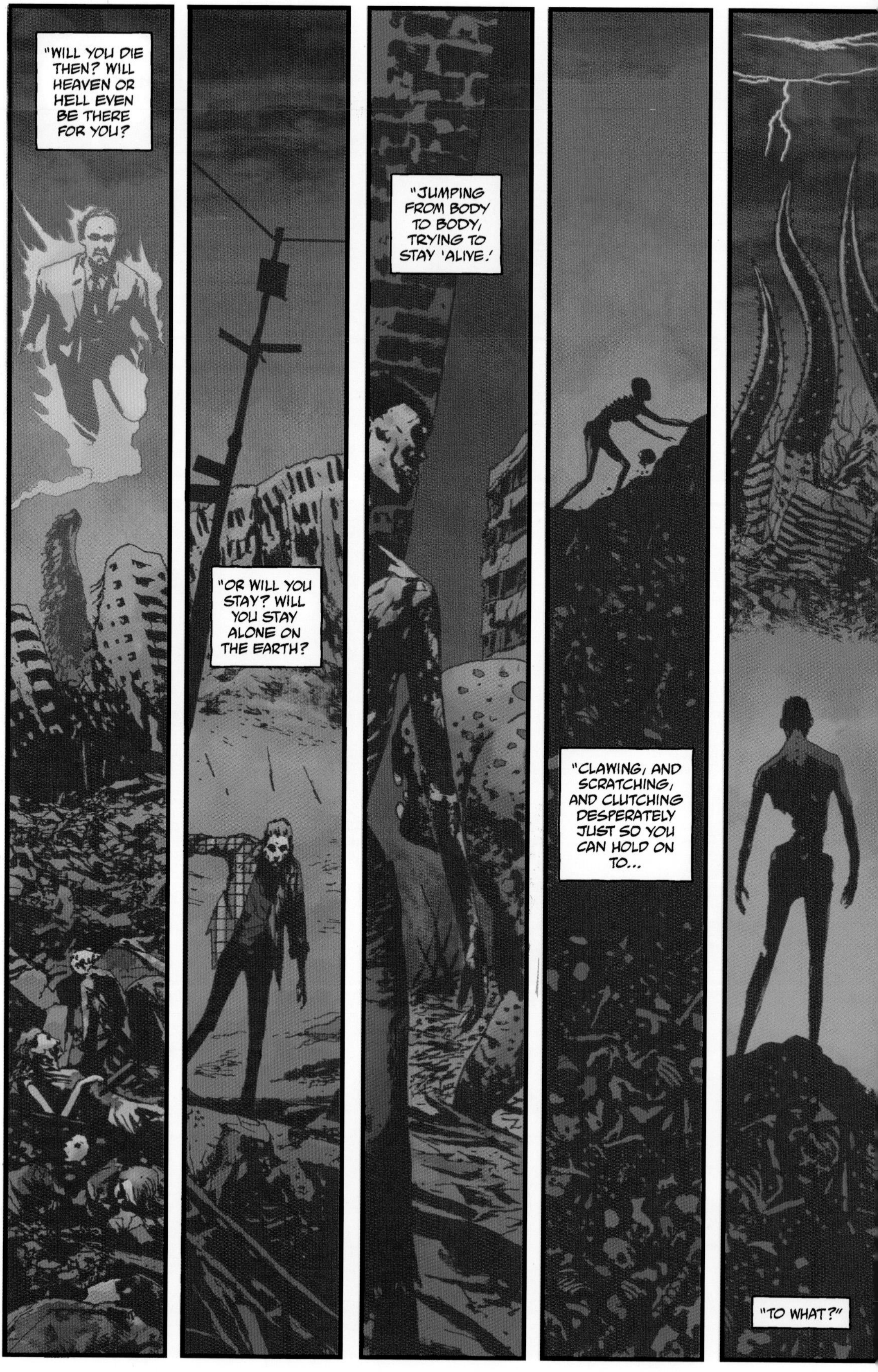
"WILL YOU DIE THEN? WILL HEAVEN OR HELL EVEN BE THERE FOR YOU?
"OR WILL YOU STAY? WILL YOU STAY ALONE ON THE EARTH?
"JUMPING FROM BODY TO BODY, TRYING TO STAY 'ALIVE.'
"CLAWING, AND SCRATCHING, AND CLUTCHING DESPERATELY JUST SO YOU CAN HOLD ON TO...
"TO WHAT?"

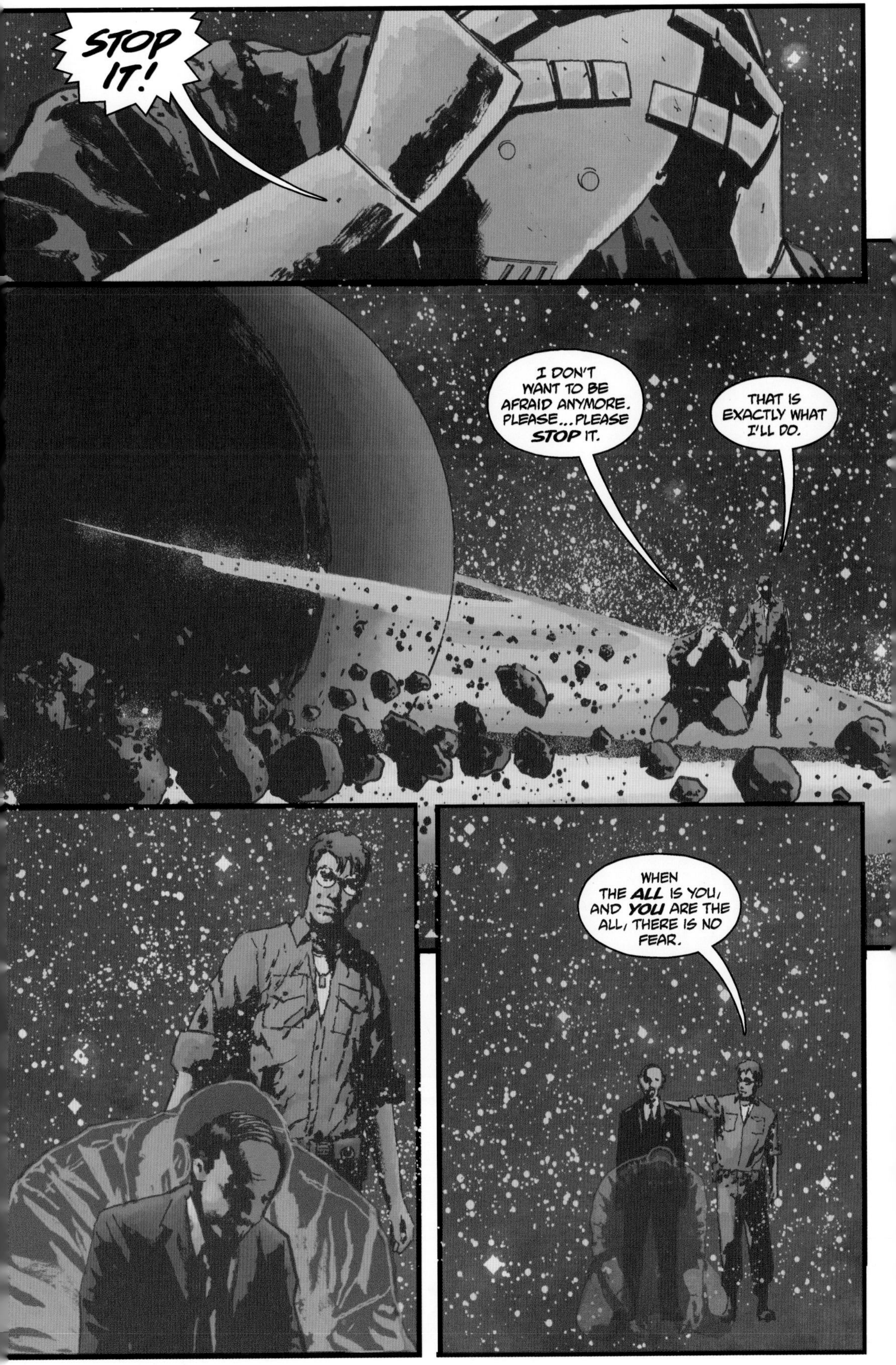
STOP IT!
I DON'T WANT TO BE AFRAID ANYMORE. PLEASE...PLEASE STOP IT.
THAT IS EXACTLY WHAT I'LL DO.
WHEN THE ALL IS YOU, AND YOU ARE THE ALL, THERE IS NO FEAR.

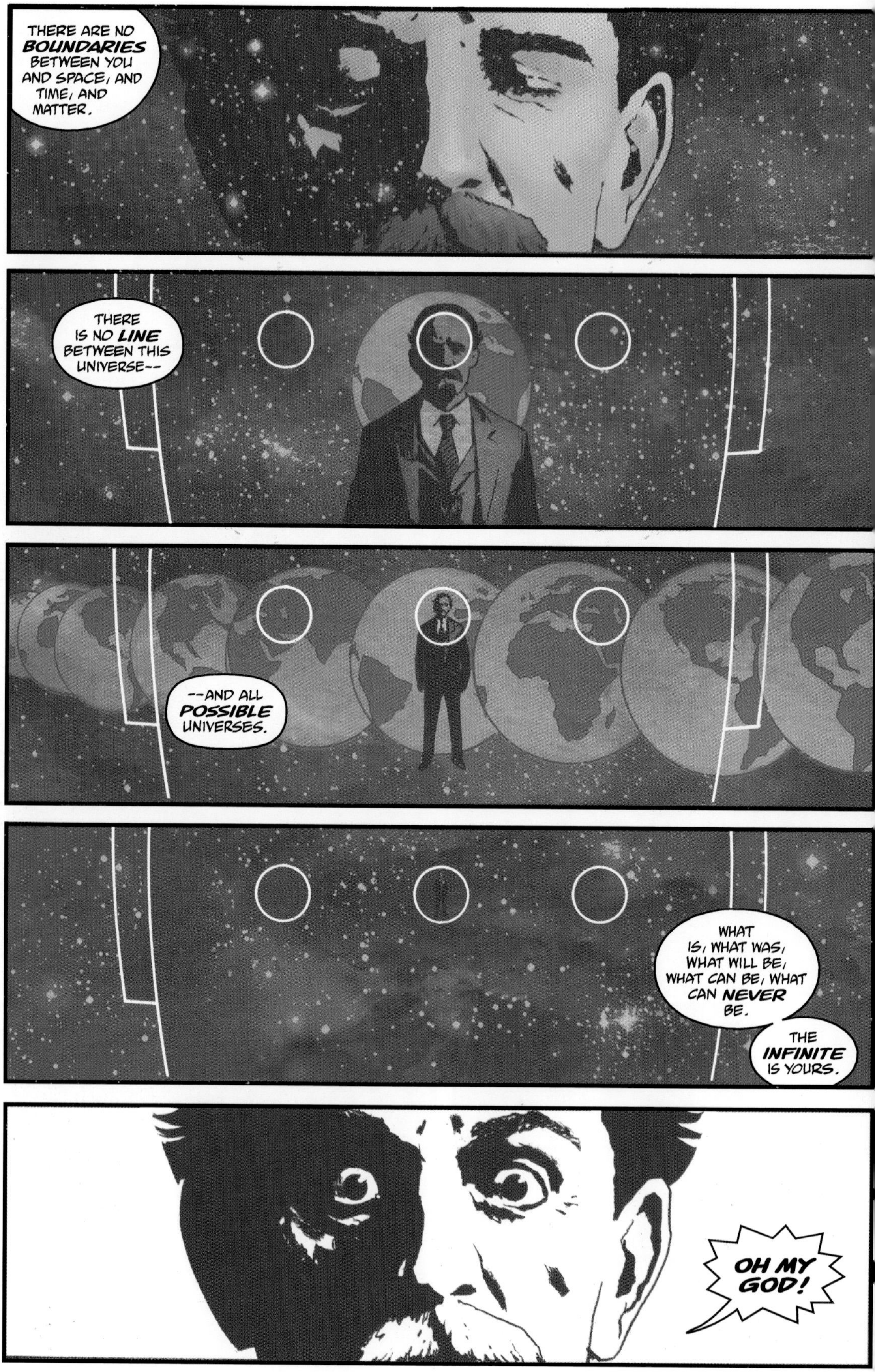
THERE ARE NO BOUNDARIES BETWEEN YOU AND SPACE, AND TIME, AND MATTER.
THERE IS NO LINE BETWEEN THIS UNIVERSE--
--AND ALL POSSIBLE UNIVERSES.
WHAT IS, WHAT WAS, WHAT WILL BE, WHAT CAN BE, WHAT CAN NEVER BE.
THE INFINITE IS YOURS.
OH MY GOD!

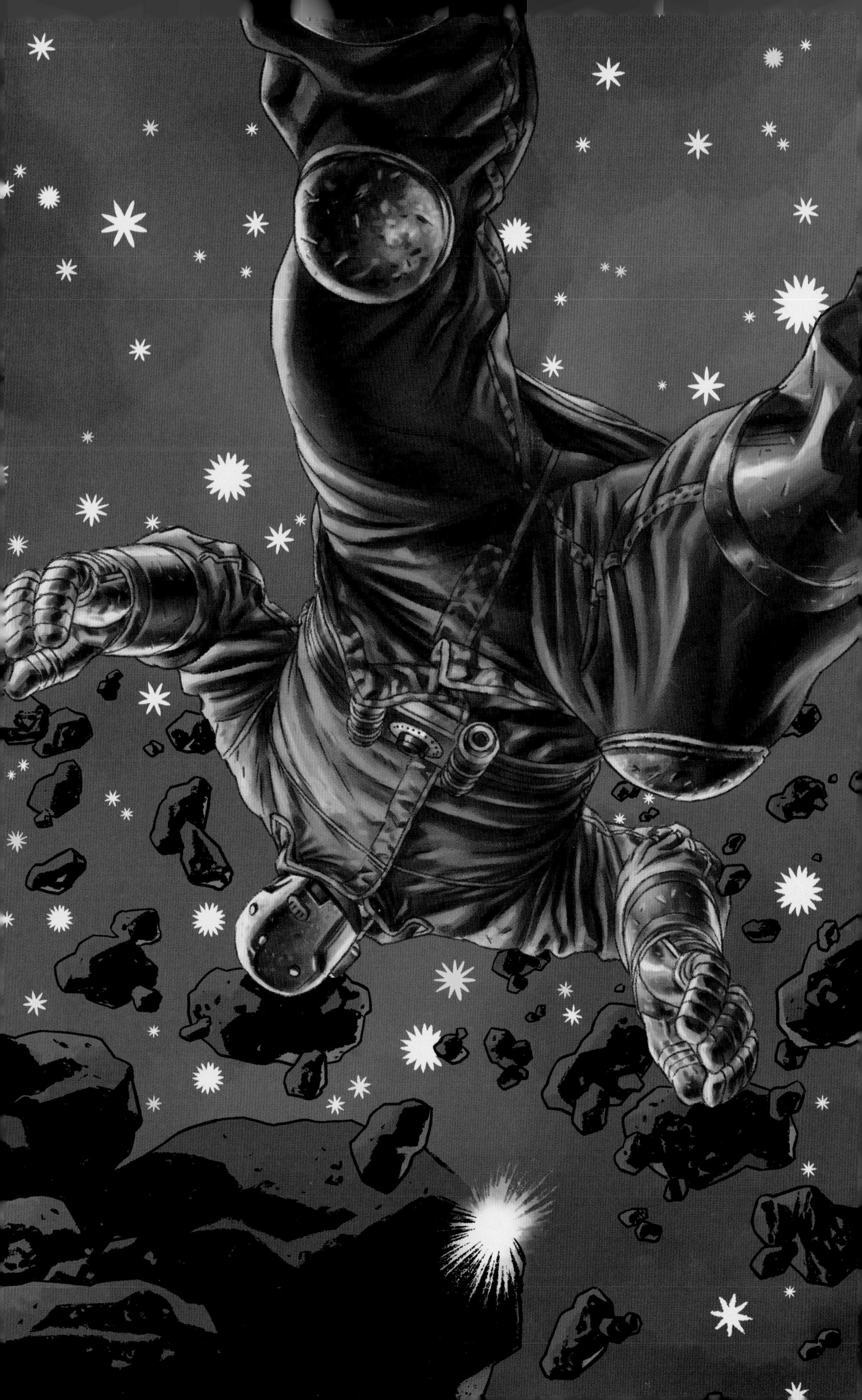

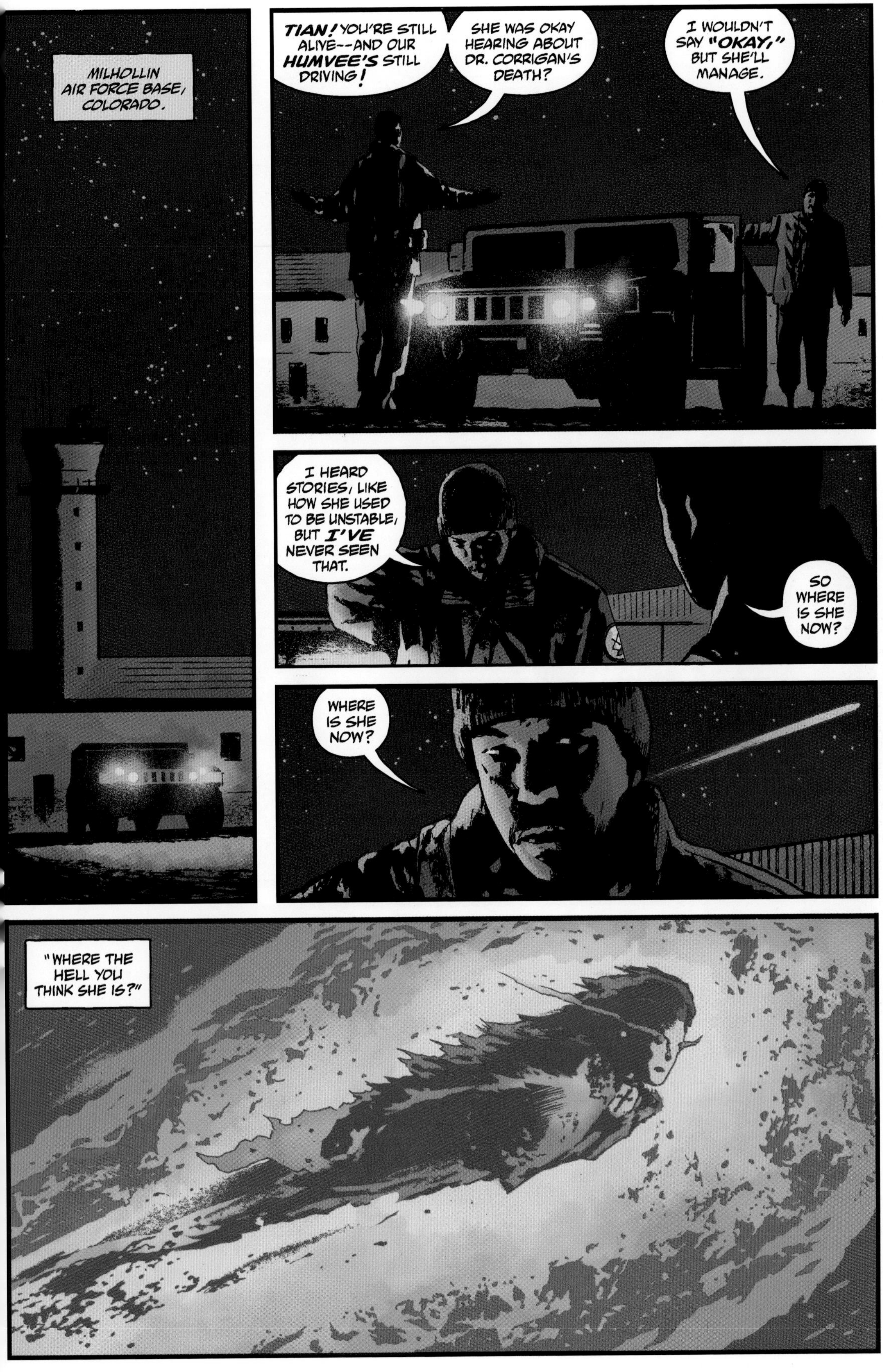
MILHOLLIN AIR FORCE BASE, COLORADO.
TIAN! YOU'RE STILL ALIVE--AND OUR HUMVEE'S STILL DRIVING!
SHE WAS OKAY HEARING ABOUT DR. CORRIGAN'S DEATH?
I WOULDN'T SAY "OKAY," BUT SHE'LL MANAGE.
I HEARD STORIES, LIKE HOW SHE USED TO BE UNSTABLE, BUT I'VE NEVER SEEN THAT.
SO WHERE IS SHE NOW?
WHERE IS SHE NOW?
"WHERE THE HELL YOU THINK SHE IS?"

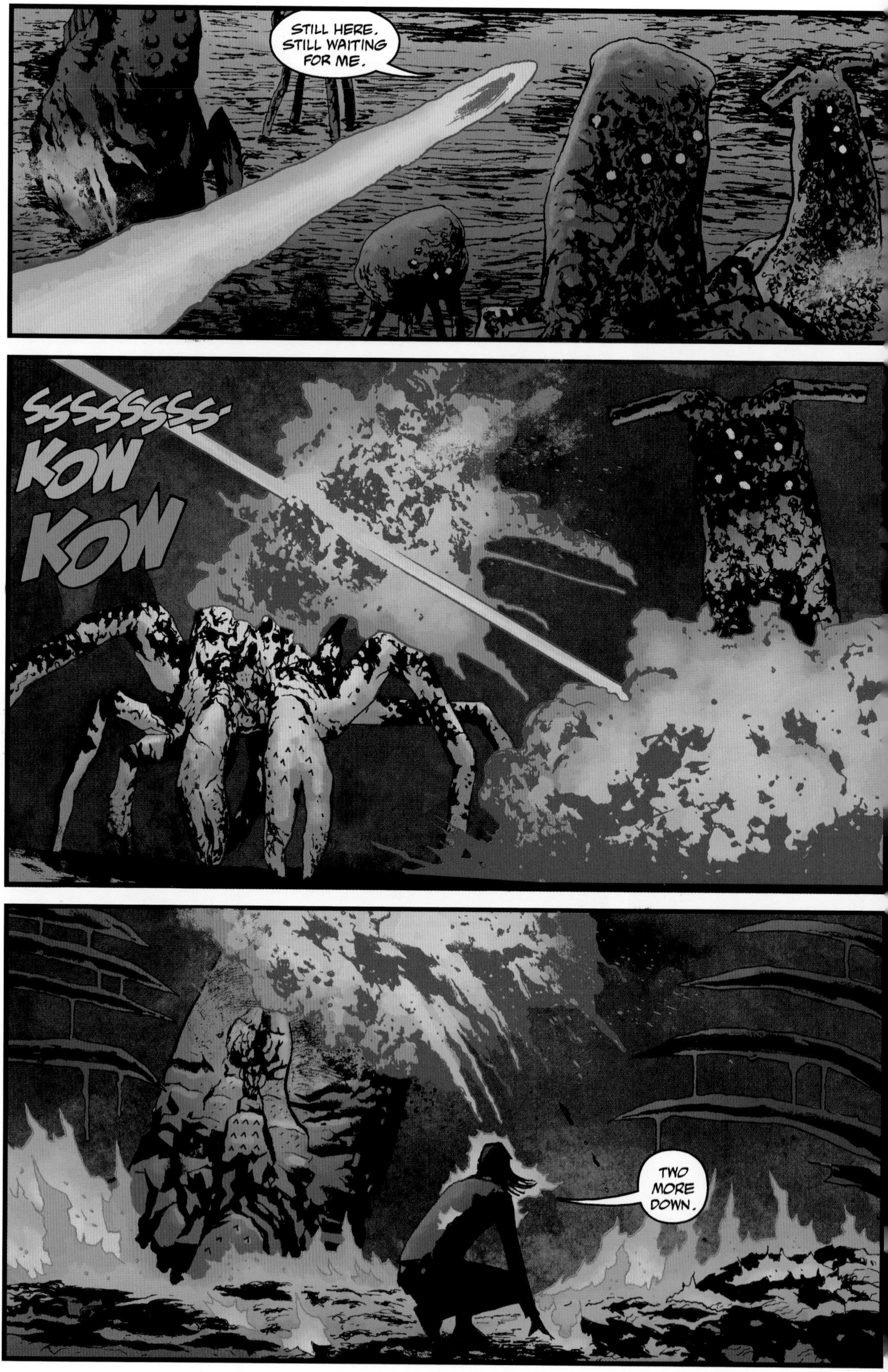
STILL HERE. STILL WAITING FOR ME.
SSSSSSSS-
KOW
KOW
TWO MORE DOWN.

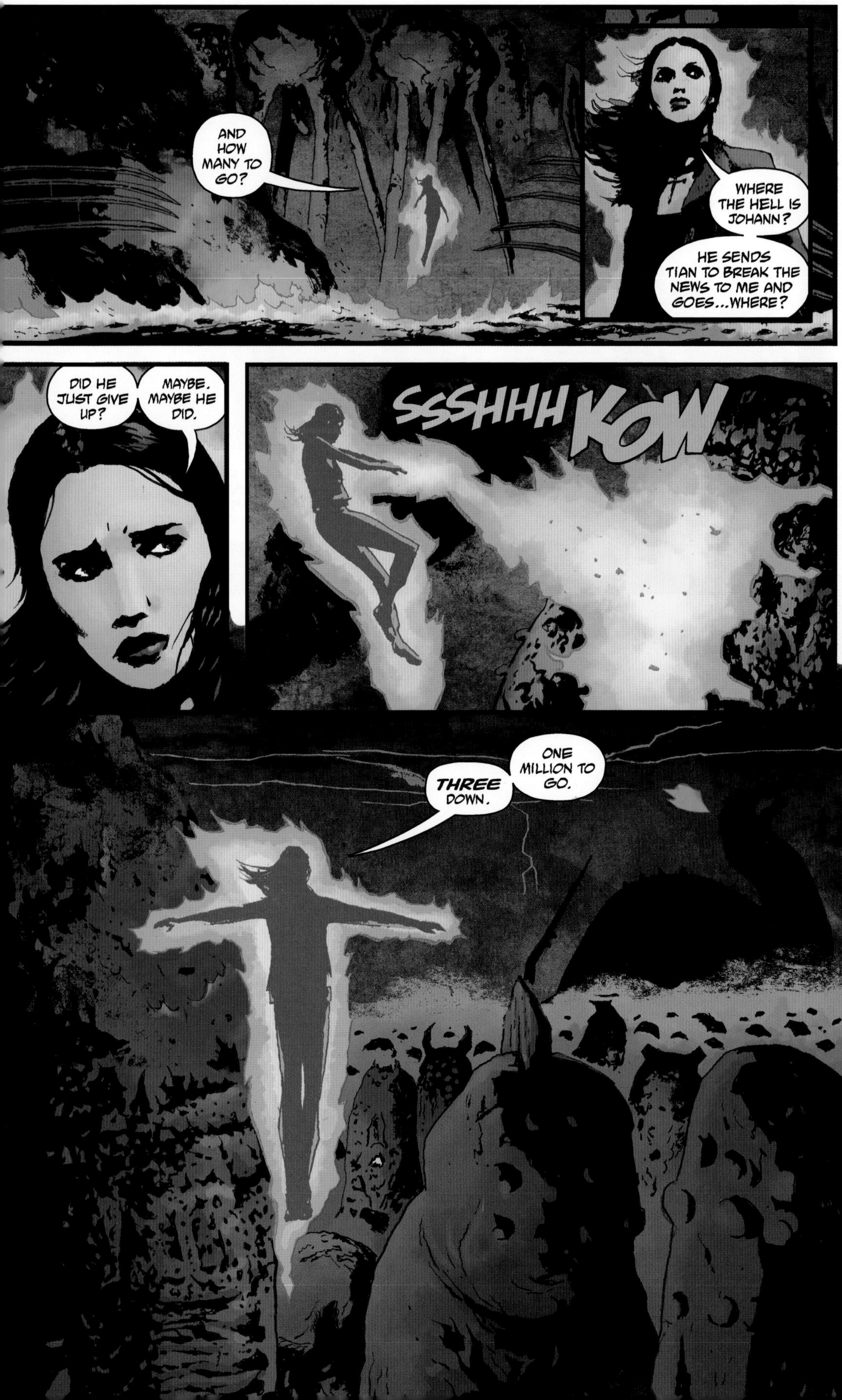
AND HOW MANY TO GO?
WHERE THE HELL IS JOHANN?
HE SENDS TIAN TO BREAK THE NEWS TO ME AND GOES...WHERE?
DID HE JUST GIVE UP?
MAYBE. MAYBE HE DID.
SSSHHH KOW
THREE DOWN.
ONE MILLION TO GO.

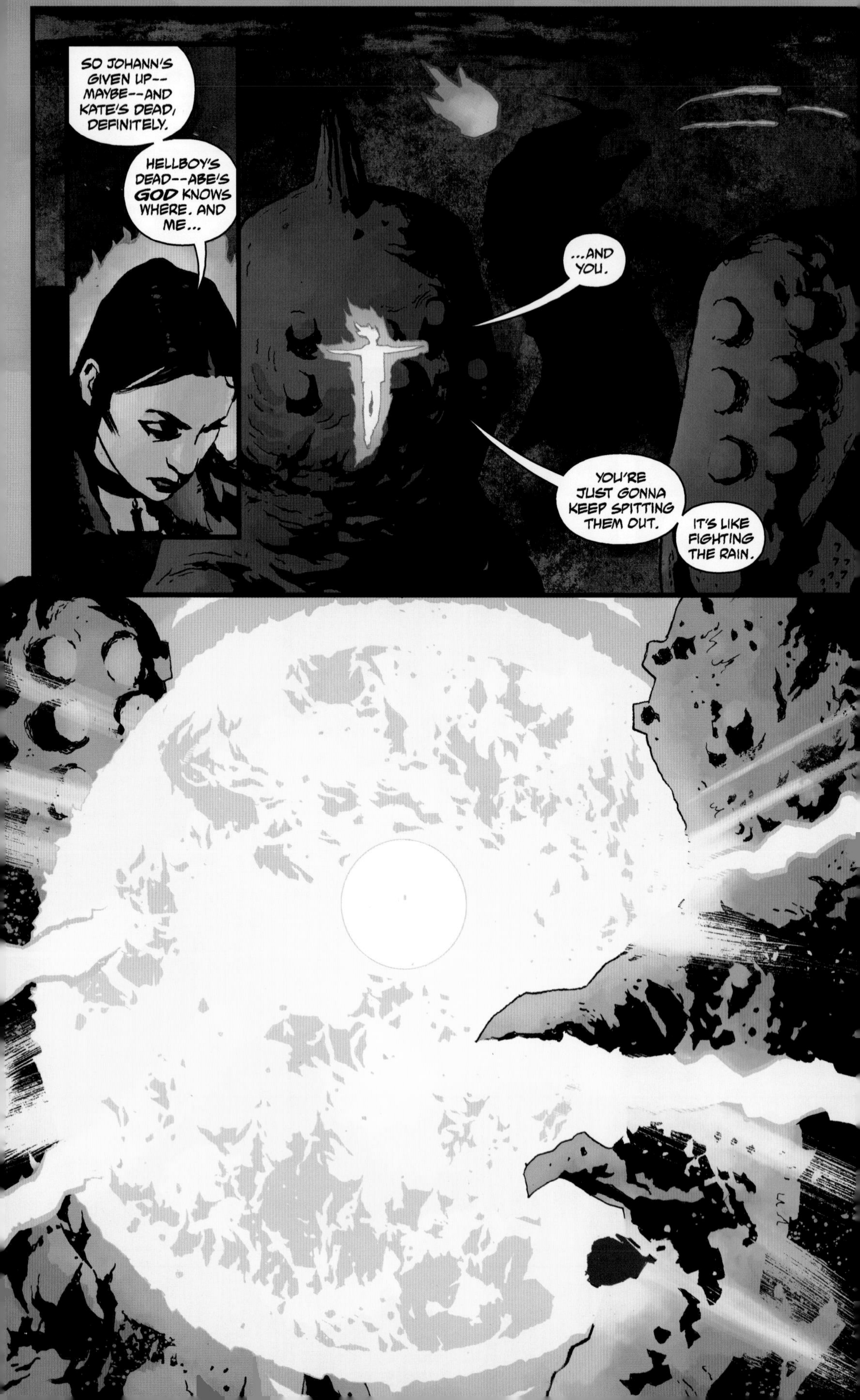
SO JOHANN'S GIVEN UP-- MAYBE--AND KATE'S DEAD, DEFINITELY.
HELLBOY'S DEAD--ABE'S GOD KNOWS WHERE. AND ME...
...AND YOU.
YOU'RE JUST GONNA KEEP SPITTING THEM OUT.
IT'S LIKE FIGHTING THE RAIN.

FINE BY ME!! YOU GOT A MILLION MORE BABIES? I'LL KILL 'EM ALL!

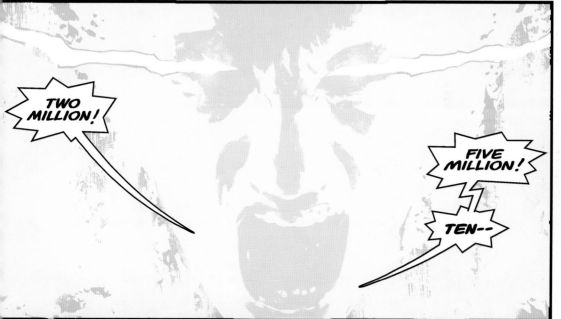

TWO MILLION!

FIVE MILLION!

TEN--

...

JO--

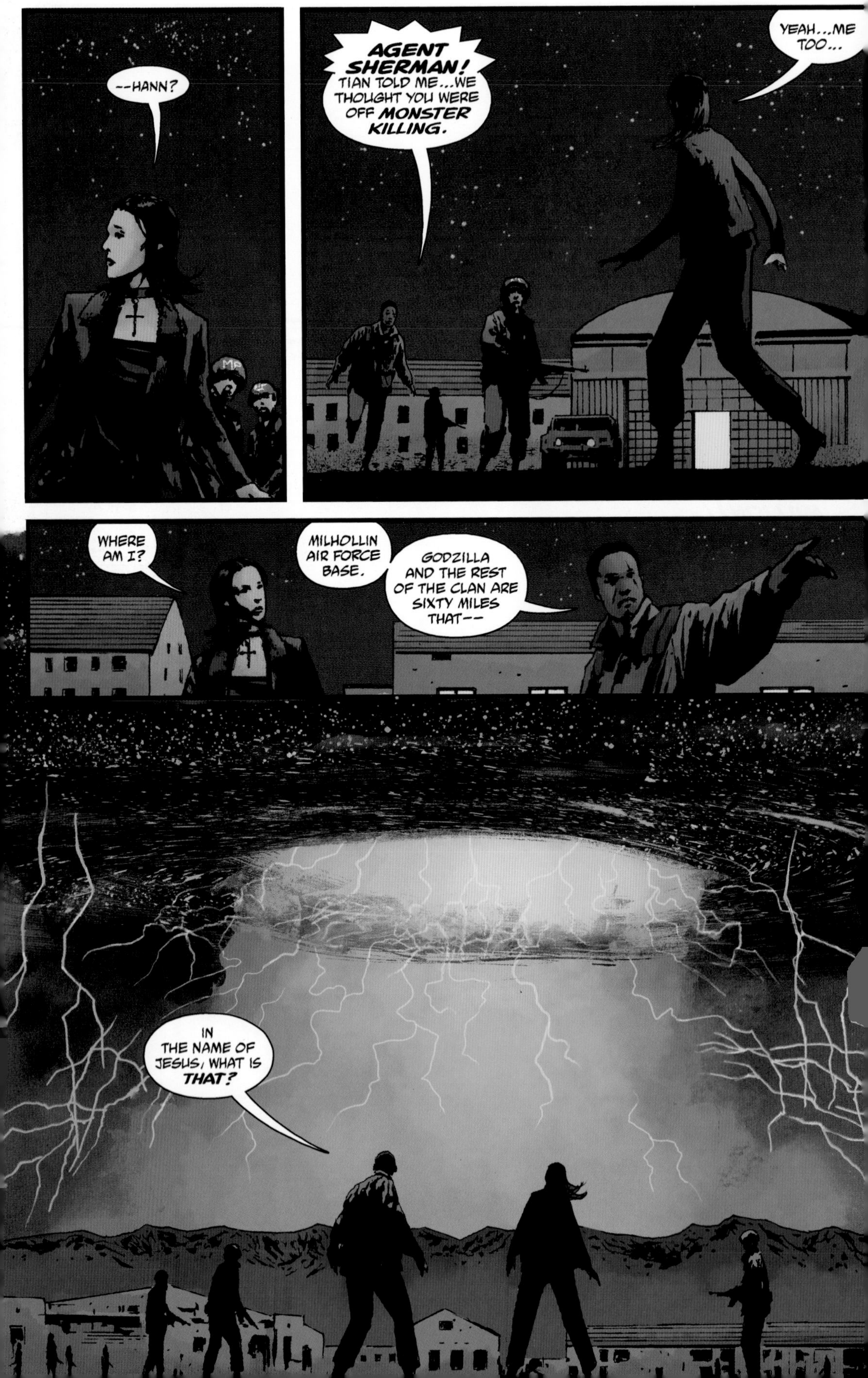
--HANN?
AGENT SHERMAN! TIAN TOLD ME...WE THOUGHT YOU WERE OFF MONSTER KILLING.
YEAH...ME TOO...
WHERE AM I?
MILHOLLIN AIR FORCE BASE.
GODZILLA AND THE REST OF THE CLAN ARE SIXTY MILES THAT--
IN THE NAME OF JESUS, WHAT IS THAT?

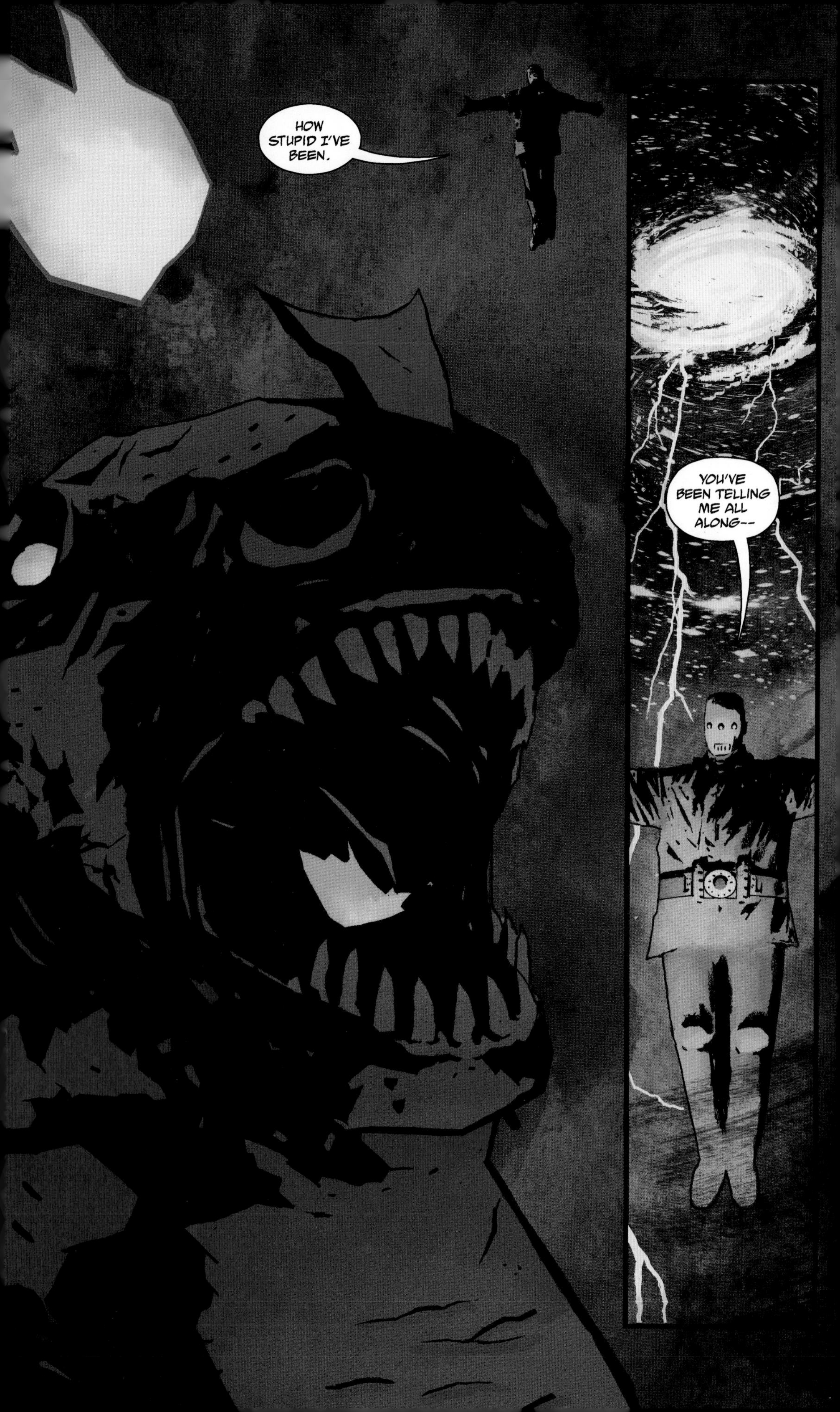
HOW STUPID I'VE BEEN.
YOU'VE BEEN TELLING ME ALL ALONG--

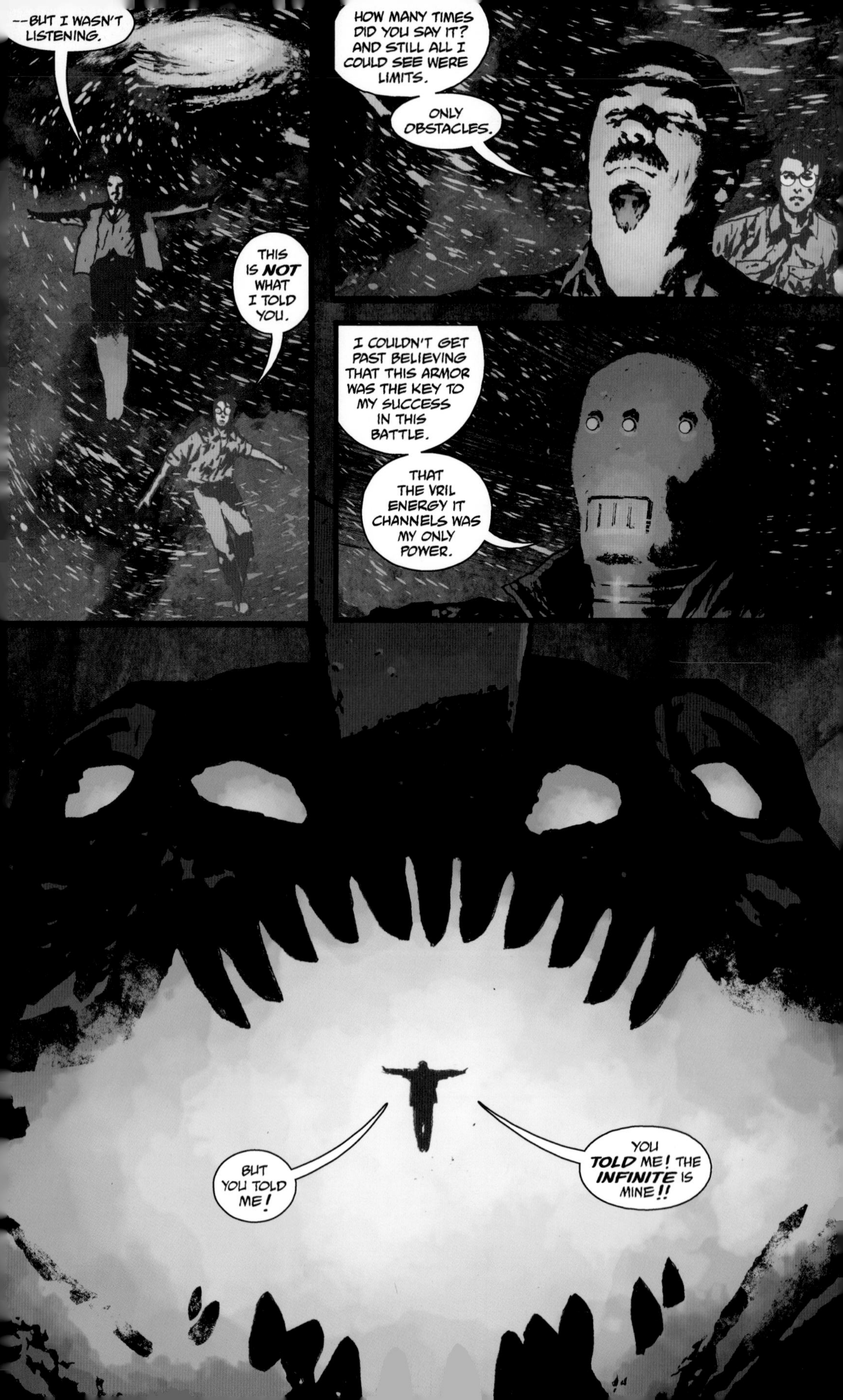
--BUT I WASN'T LISTENING.
THIS IS NOT WHAT I TOLD YOU.
HOW MANY TIMES DID YOU SAY IT? AND STILL ALL I COULD SEE WERE LIMITS.
ONLY OBSTACLES.
I COULDN'T GET PAST BELIEVING THAT THIS ARMOR WAS THE KEY TO MY SUCCESS IN THIS BATTLE.
THAT THE VRIL ENERGY IT CHANNELS WAS MY ONLY POWER.
BUT YOU TOLD ME!
YOU TOLD ME! THE INFINITE IS MINE!!

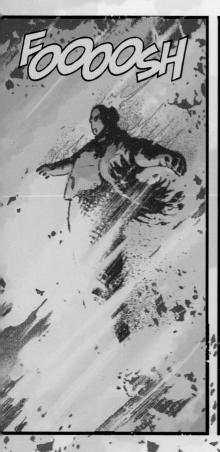

FOOOOSH

YES. IF YOU LET GO AND BECOME ONE WITH THE INFINITE, IT'S YOURS.

NO.

I WILL NOT BECOME ONE *WITH* IT.

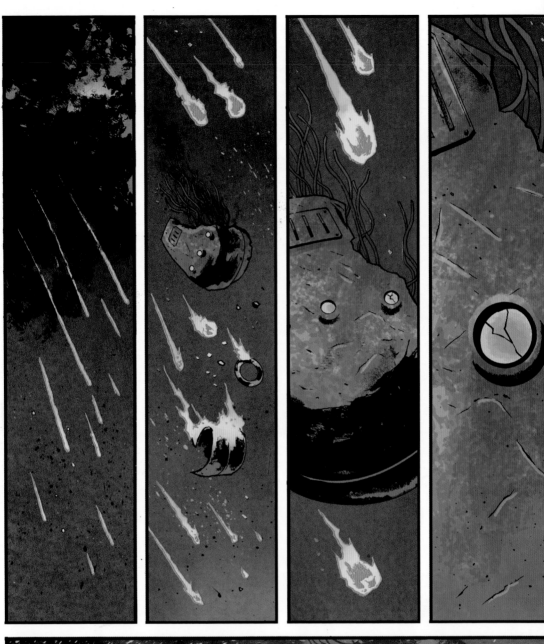

IT'S ALREADY MINE.

I HAVE THE POWER OF THE INFINITE.

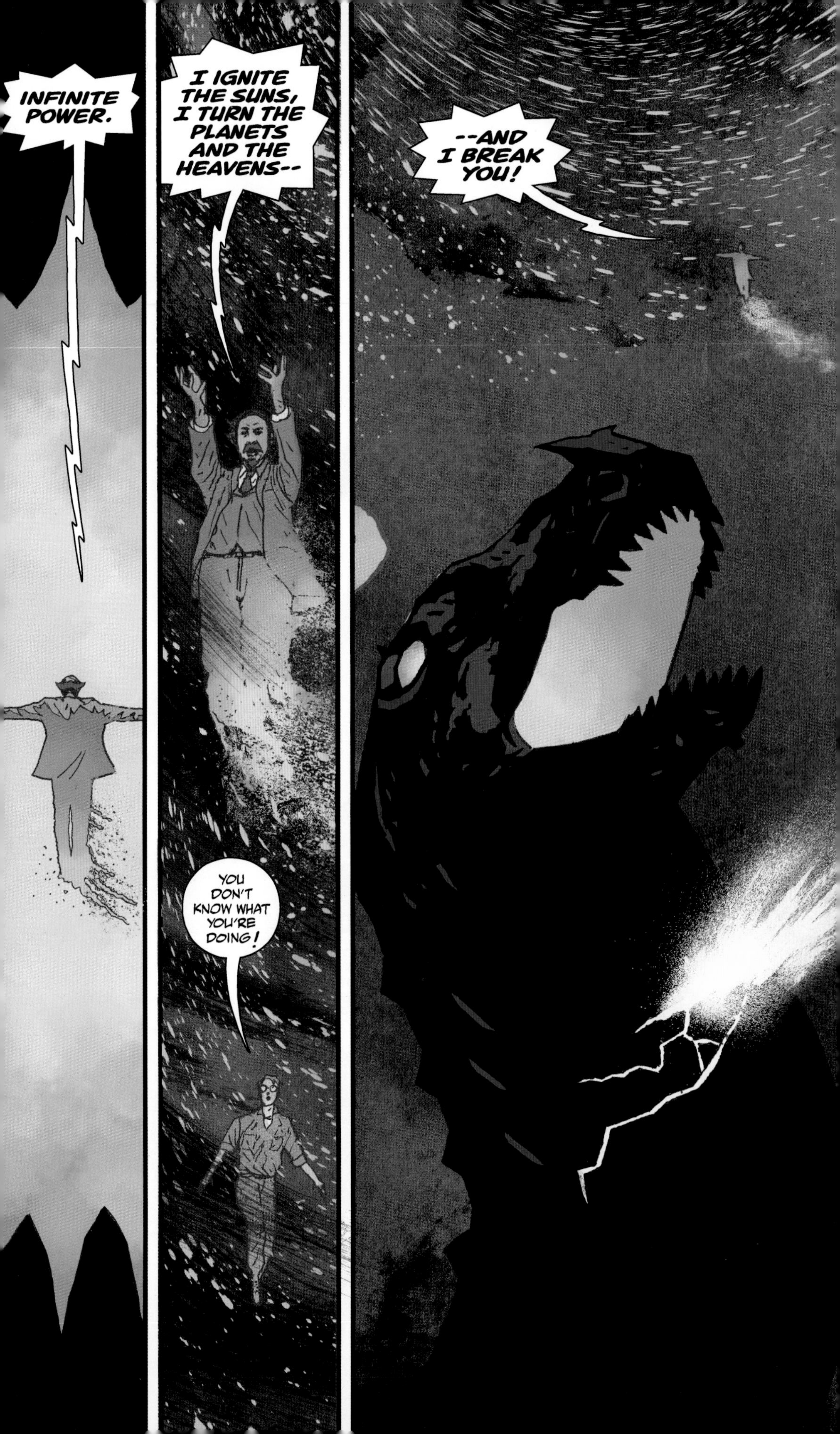
INFINITE POWER.
I IGNITE THE SUNS, I TURN THE PLANETS AND THE HEAVENS--
YOU DON'T KNOW WHAT YOU'RE DOING!
--AND I BREAK YOU!

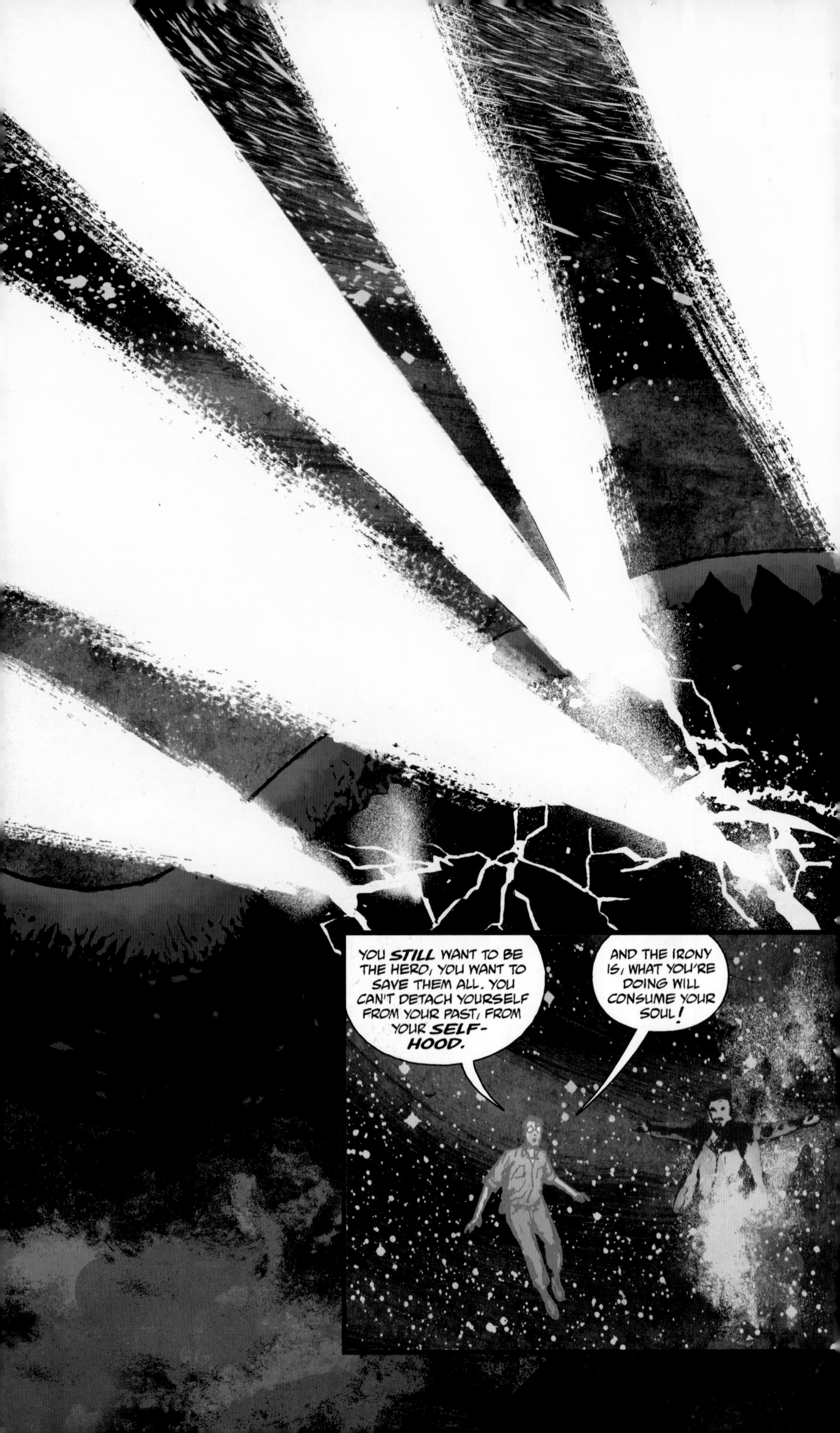
YOU STILL WANT TO BE THE HERO, YOU WANT TO SAVE THEM ALL. YOU CAN'T DETACH YOURSELF FROM YOUR PAST, FROM YOUR SELF-HOOD.
AND THE IRONY IS, WHAT YOU'RE DOING WILL CONSUME YOUR SOUL!

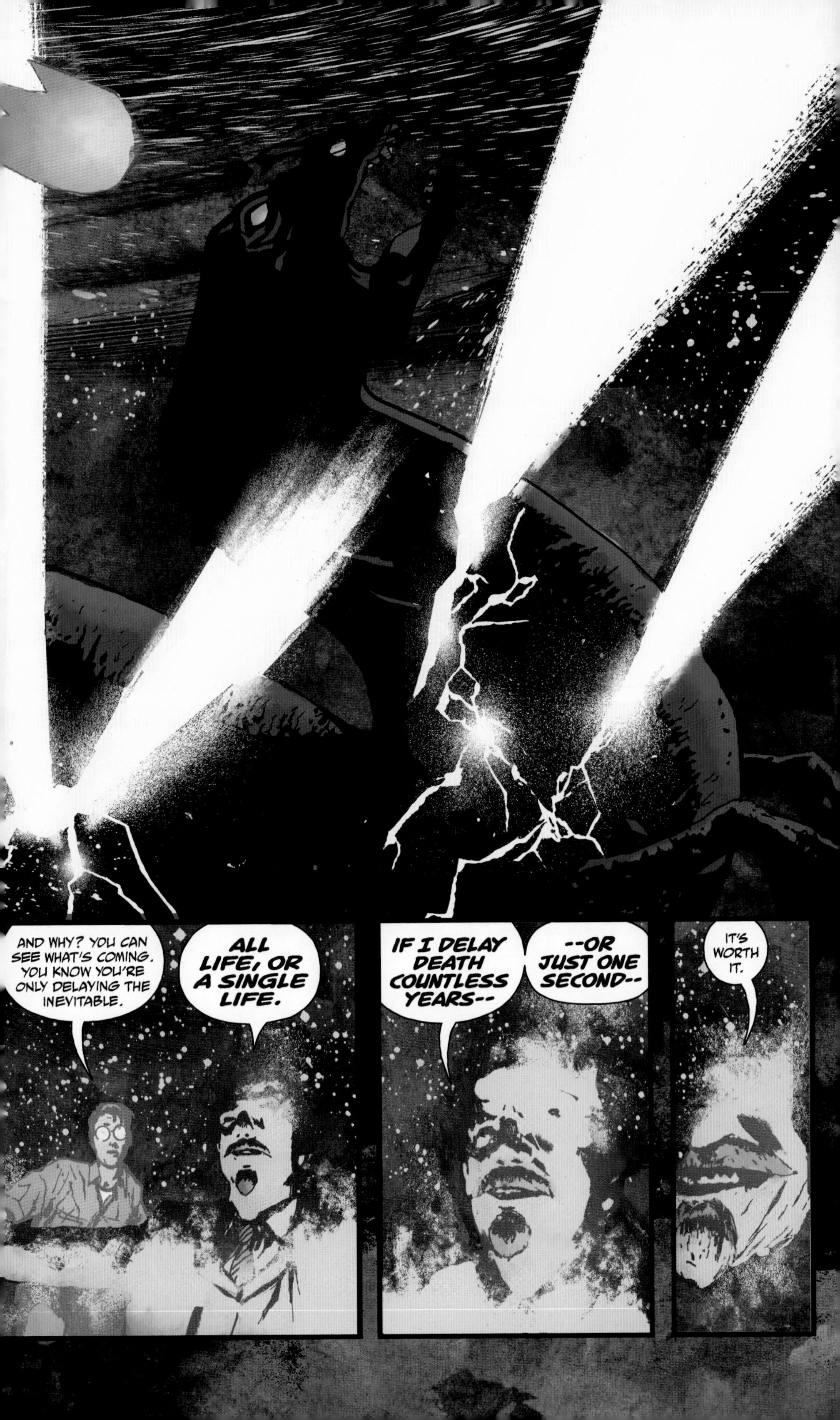
AND WHY? YOU CAN SEE WHAT'S COMING. YOU KNOW YOU'RE ONLY DELAYING THE INEVITABLE.
ALL LIFE, OR A SINGLE LIFE.
IF I DELAY DEATH COUNTLESS YEARS--
--OR JUST ONE SECOND--
IT'S WORTH IT.

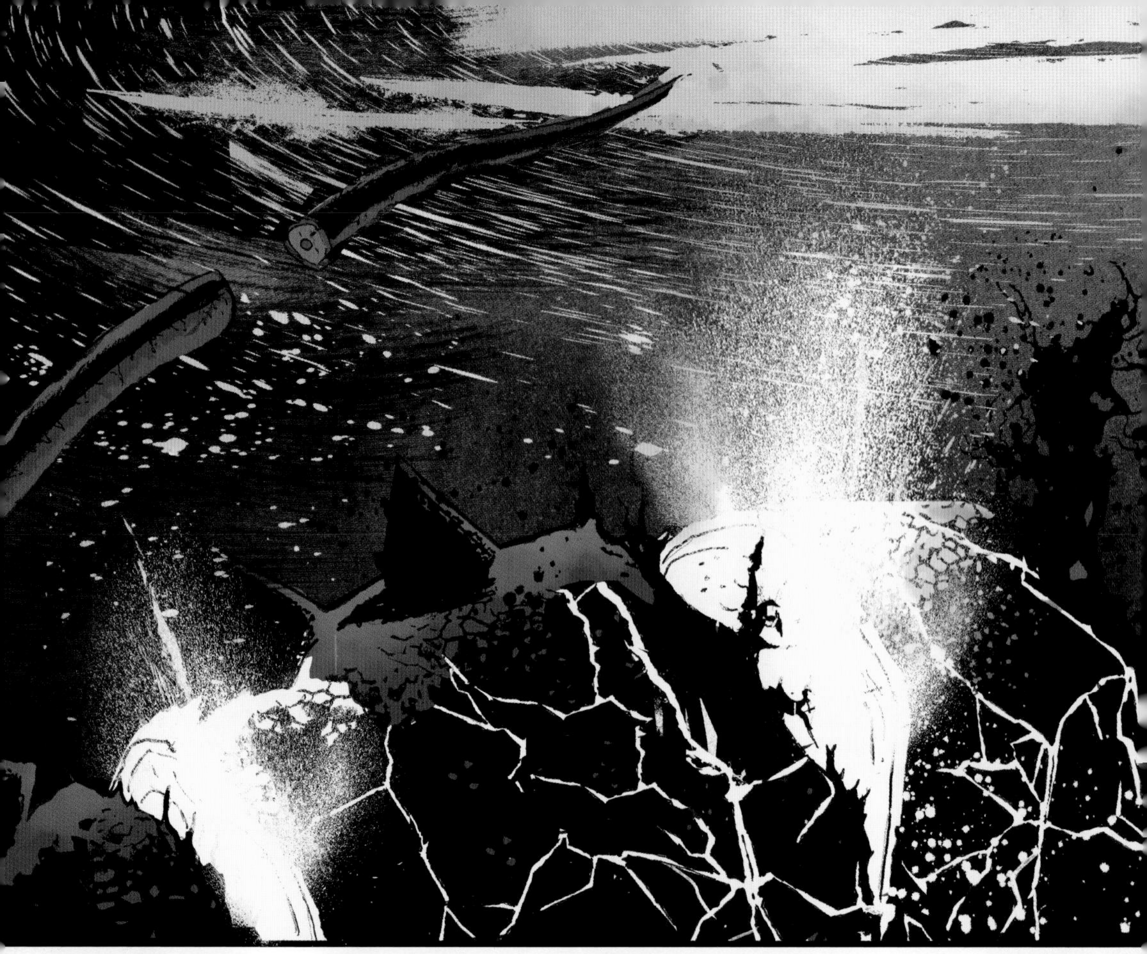

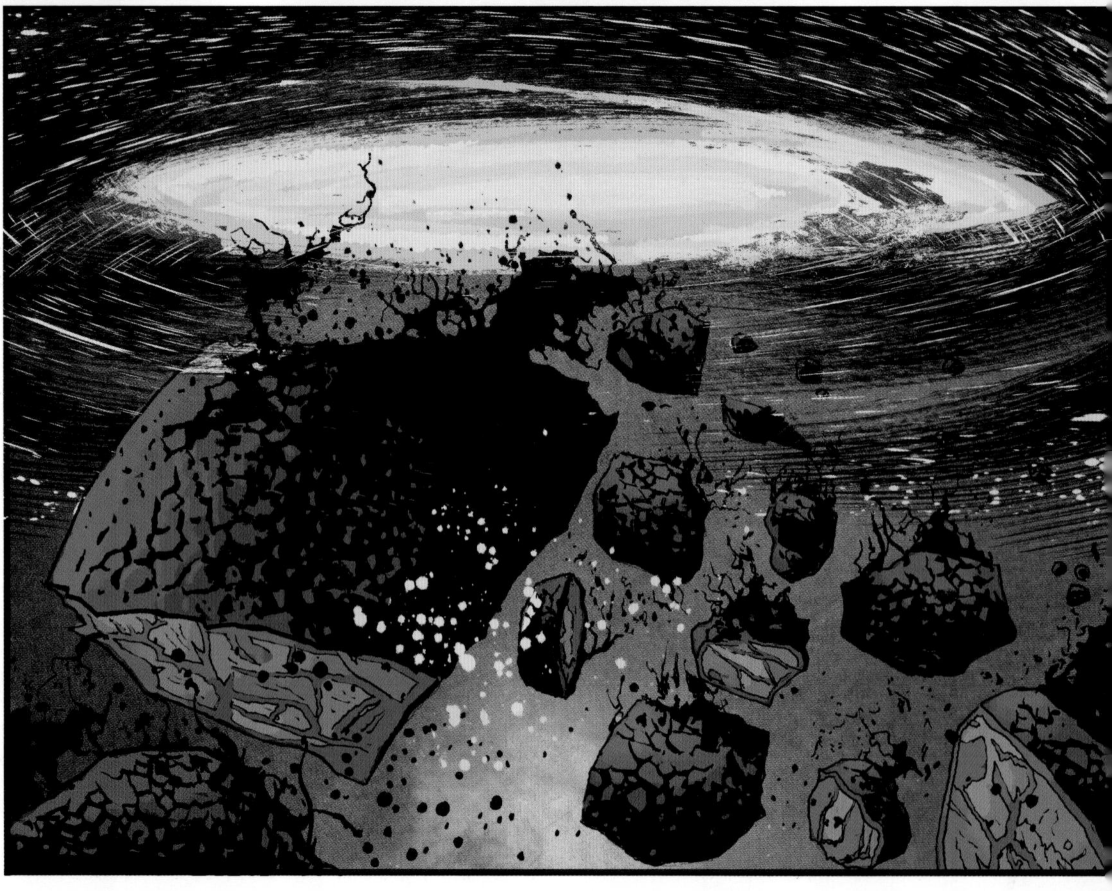

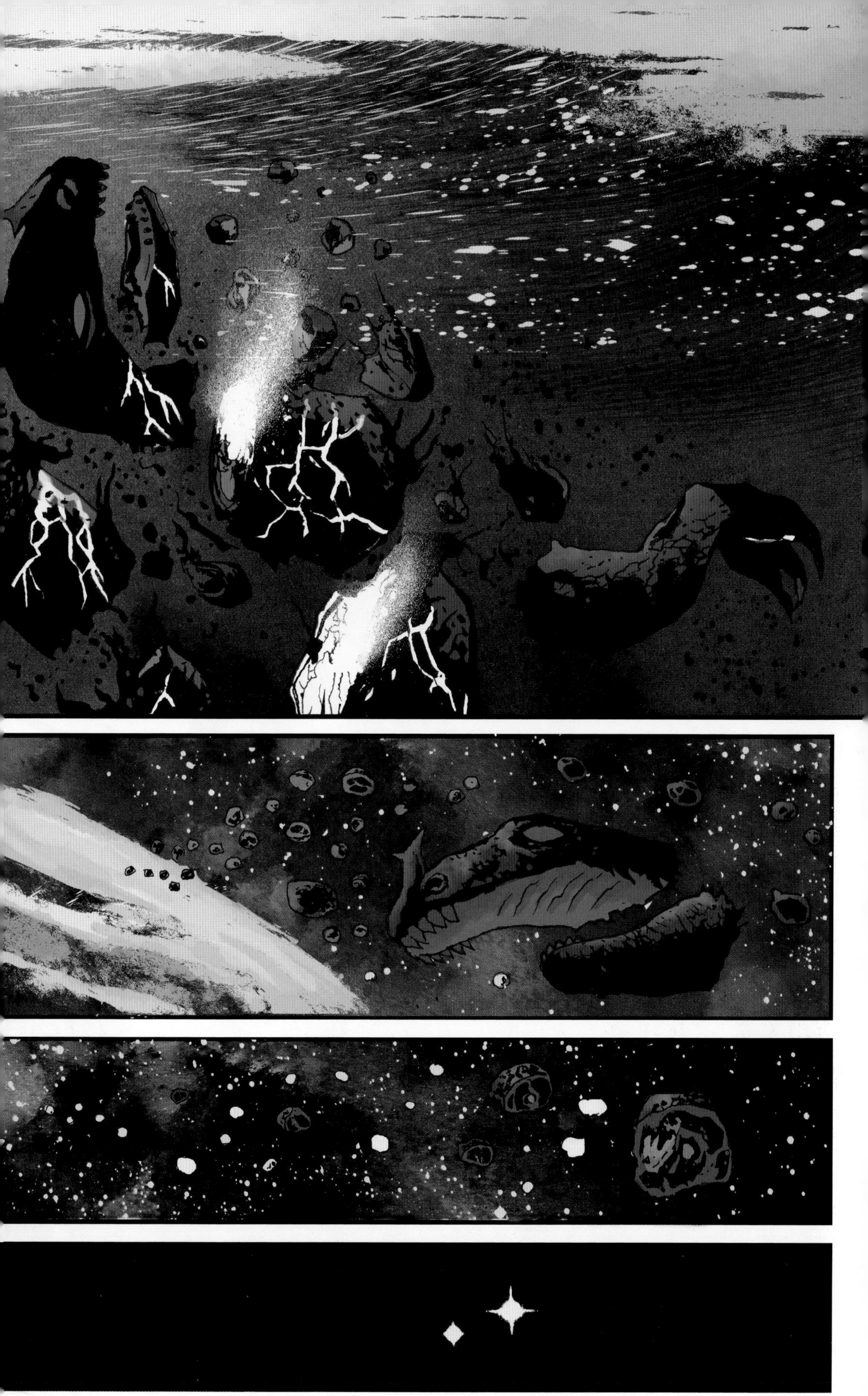

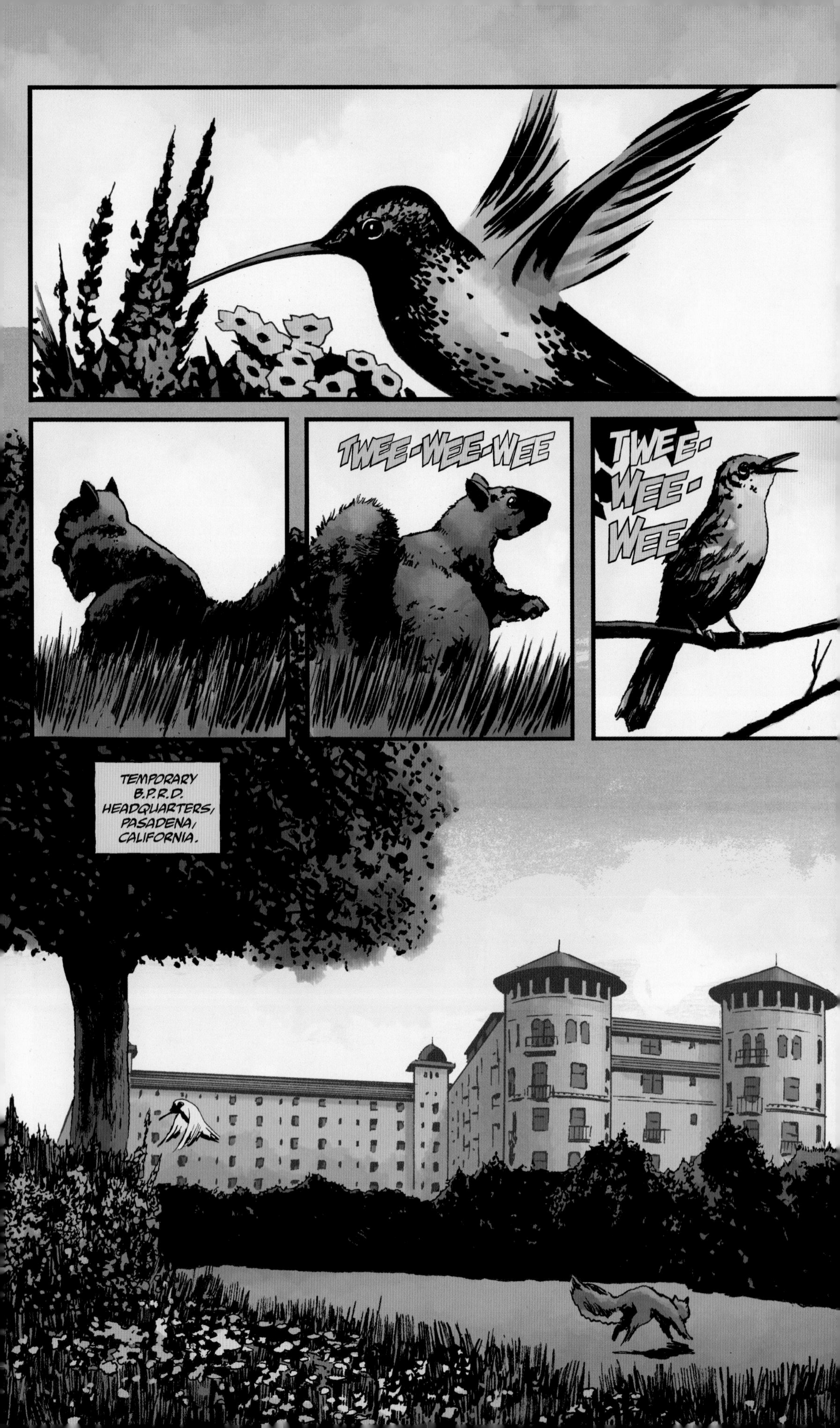
TWEE-WEE-WEE
TWEE-WEE-WEE
TEMPORARY B.P.R.D. HEADQUARTERS, PASADENA, CALIFORNIA.

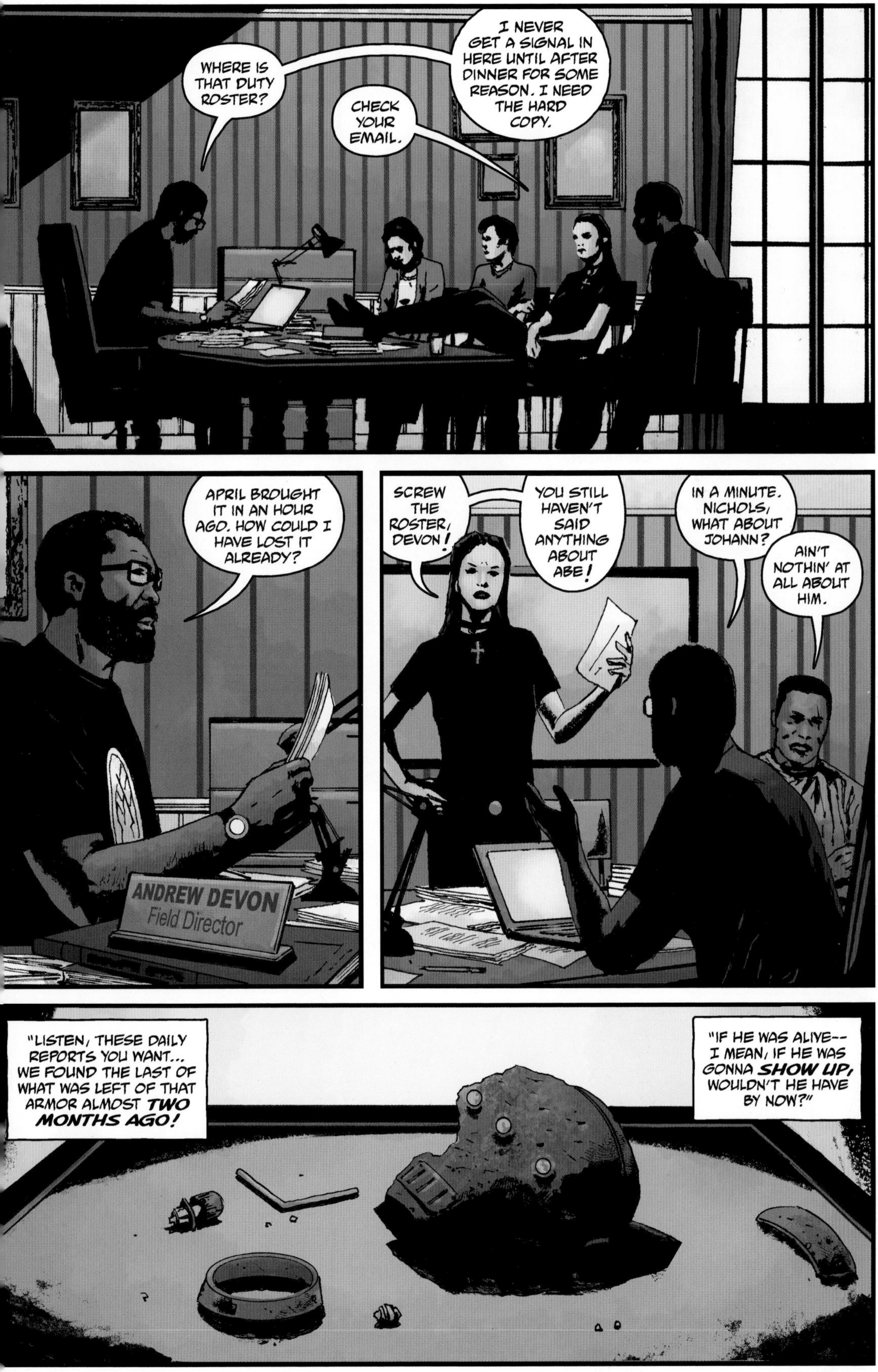
WHERE IS THAT DUTY ROSTER?
CHECK YOUR EMAIL.
I NEVER GET A SIGNAL IN HERE UNTIL AFTER DINNER FOR SOME REASON. I NEED THE HARD COPY.
APRIL BROUGHT IT IN AN HOUR AGO. HOW COULD I HAVE LOST IT ALREADY?
ANDREW DEVON
Field Director
SCREW THE ROSTER, DEVON!
YOU STILL HAVEN'T SAID ANYTHING ABOUT ABE!
IN A MINUTE. NICHOLS, WHAT ABOUT JOHANN?
AIN'T NOTHIN' AT ALL ABOUT HIM.
"LISTEN, THESE DAILY REPORTS YOU WANT... WE FOUND THE LAST OF WHAT WAS LEFT OF THAT ARMOR ALMOST **TWO MONTHS AGO!**
"IF HE WAS ALIVE-- I MEAN, IF HE WAS GONNA **SHOW UP,** WOULDN'T HE HAVE BY NOW?"

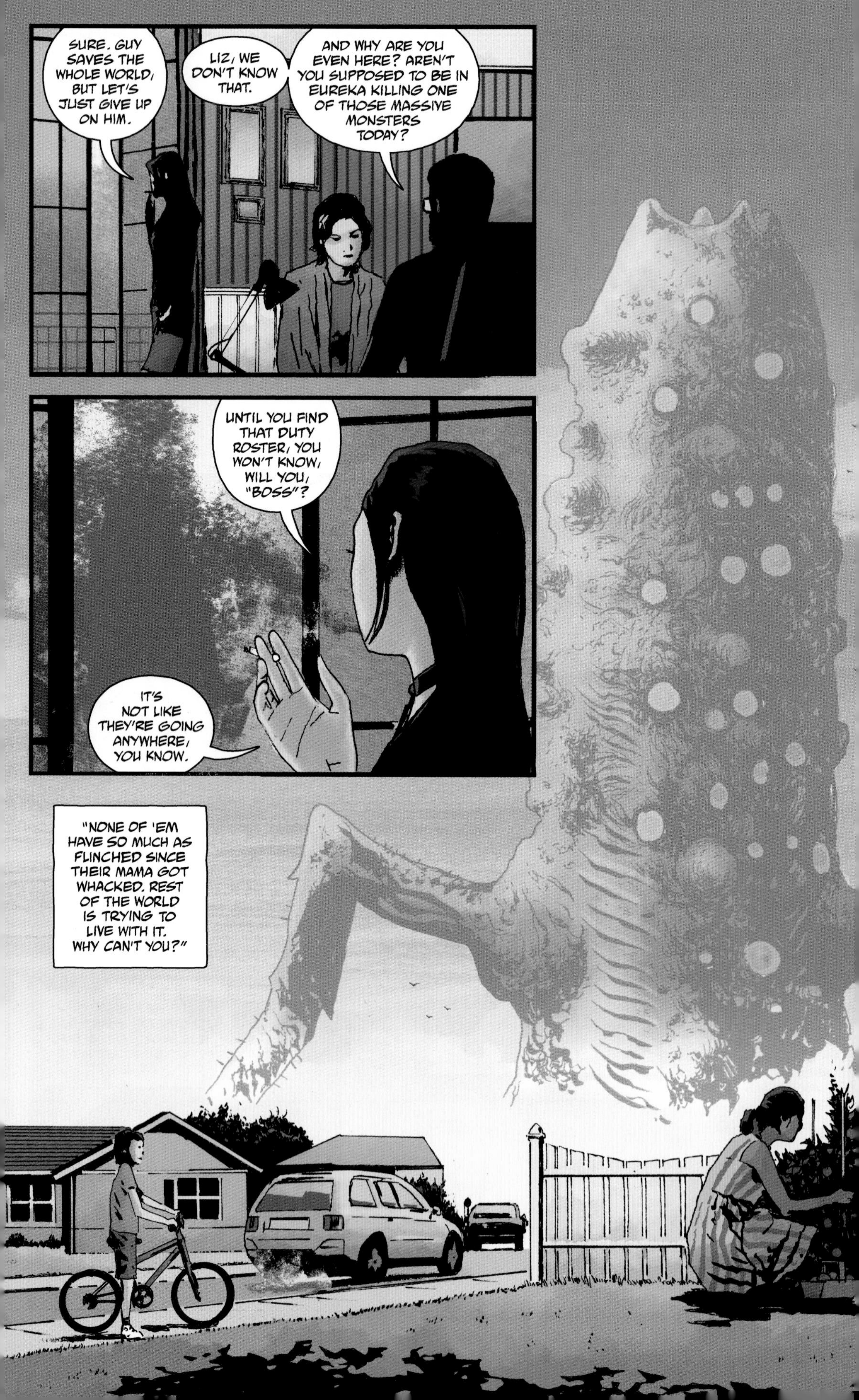

SURE. GUY SAVES THE WHOLE WORLD, BUT LET'S JUST GIVE UP ON HIM.
LIZ, WE DON'T KNOW THAT.
AND WHY ARE YOU EVEN HERE? AREN'T YOU SUPPOSED TO BE IN EUREKA KILLING ONE OF THOSE MASSIVE MONSTERS TODAY?
UNTIL YOU FIND THAT DUTY ROSTER, YOU WON'T KNOW, WILL YOU, "BOSS"?
IT'S NOT LIKE THEY'RE GOING ANYWHERE, YOU KNOW.
"NONE OF 'EM HAVE SO MUCH AS FLINCHED SINCE THEIR MAMA GOT WHACKED. REST OF THE WORLD IS TRYING TO LIVE WITH IT. WHY CAN'T YOU?"

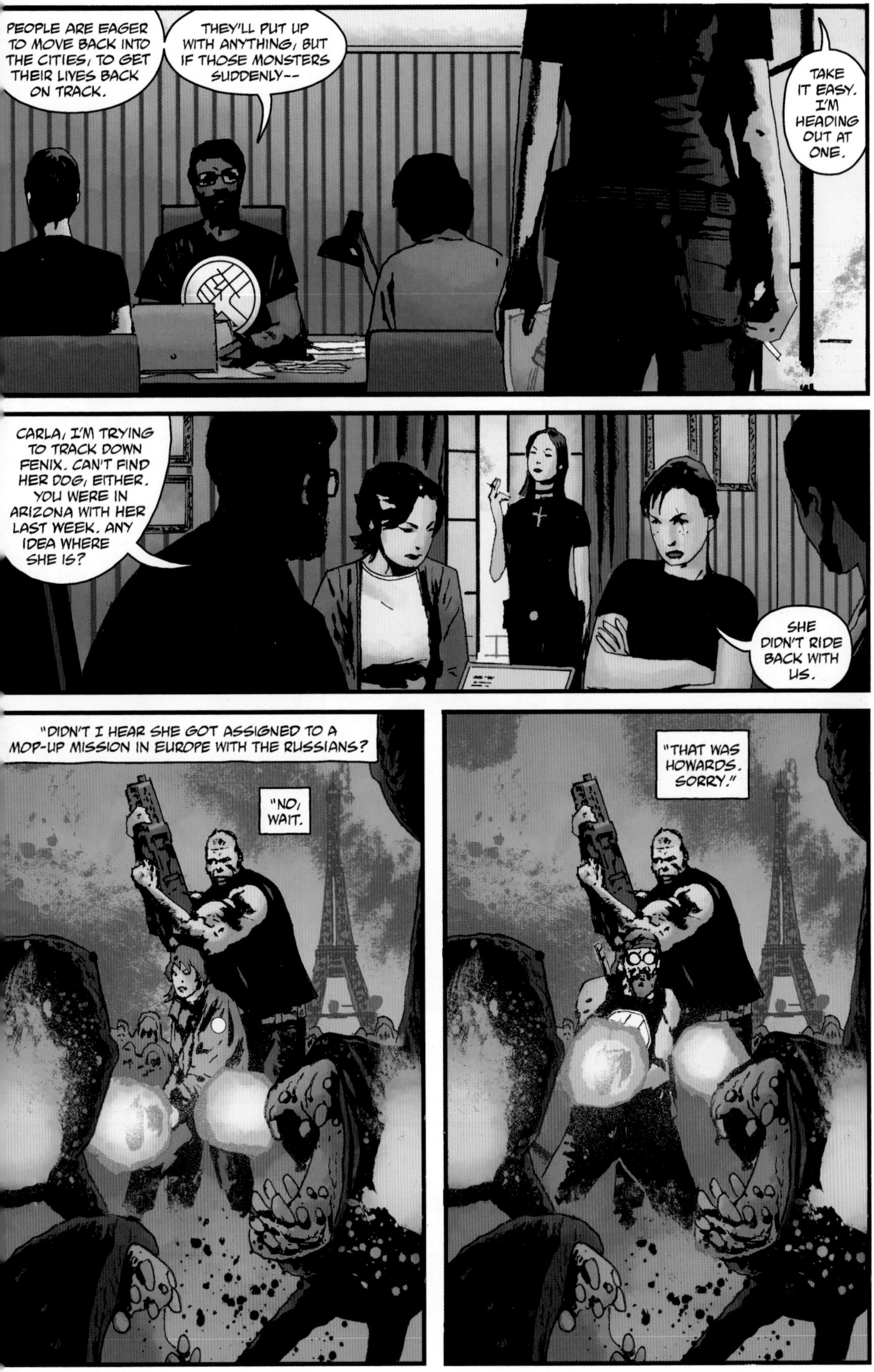
PEOPLE ARE EAGER TO MOVE BACK INTO THE CITIES, TO GET THEIR LIVES BACK ON TRACK.
THEY'LL PUT UP WITH ANYTHING, BUT IF THOSE MONSTERS SUDDENLY--
TAKE IT EASY. I'M HEADING OUT AT ONE.
CARLA, I'M TRYING TO TRACK DOWN FENIX. CAN'T FIND HER DOG, EITHER. YOU WERE IN ARIZONA WITH HER LAST WEEK. ANY IDEA WHERE SHE IS?
SHE DIDN'T RIDE BACK WITH US.
"DIDN'T I HEAR SHE GOT ASSIGNED TO A MOP-UP MISSION IN EUROPE WITH THE RUSSIANS?
"NO, WAIT.
"THAT WAS HOWARDS. SORRY."

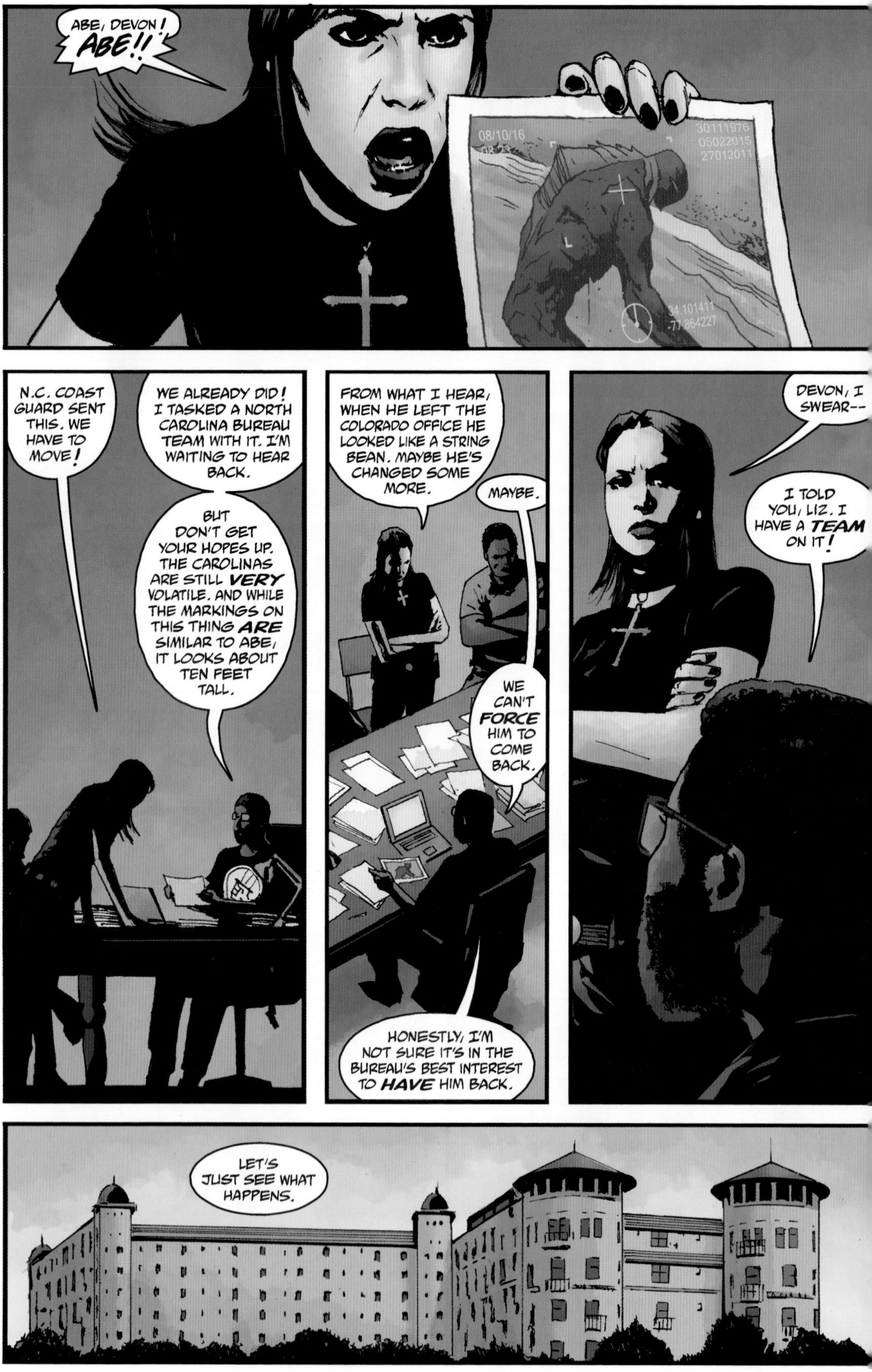
ABE, DEVON! ABE!!
08/10/16
30111976
05022015
27012011
34.101411
-77.864227
N.C. COAST GUARD SENT THIS. WE HAVE TO MOVE!
WE ALREADY DID! I TASKED A NORTH CAROLINA BUREAU TEAM WITH IT. I'M WAITING TO HEAR BACK.
BUT DON'T GET YOUR HOPES UP. THE CAROLINAS ARE STILL VERY VOLATILE. AND WHILE THE MARKINGS ON THIS THING ARE SIMILAR TO ABE, IT LOOKS ABOUT TEN FEET TALL.
FROM WHAT I HEAR, WHEN HE LEFT THE COLORADO OFFICE HE LOOKED LIKE A STRING BEAN. MAYBE HE'S CHANGED SOME MORE.
MAYBE.
WE CAN'T FORCE HIM TO COME BACK.
HONESTLY, I'M NOT SURE IT'S IN THE BUREAU'S BEST INTEREST TO HAVE HIM BACK.
DEVON, I SWEAR--
I TOLD YOU, LIZ. I HAVE A TEAM ON IT!
LET'S JUST SEE WHAT HAPPENS.

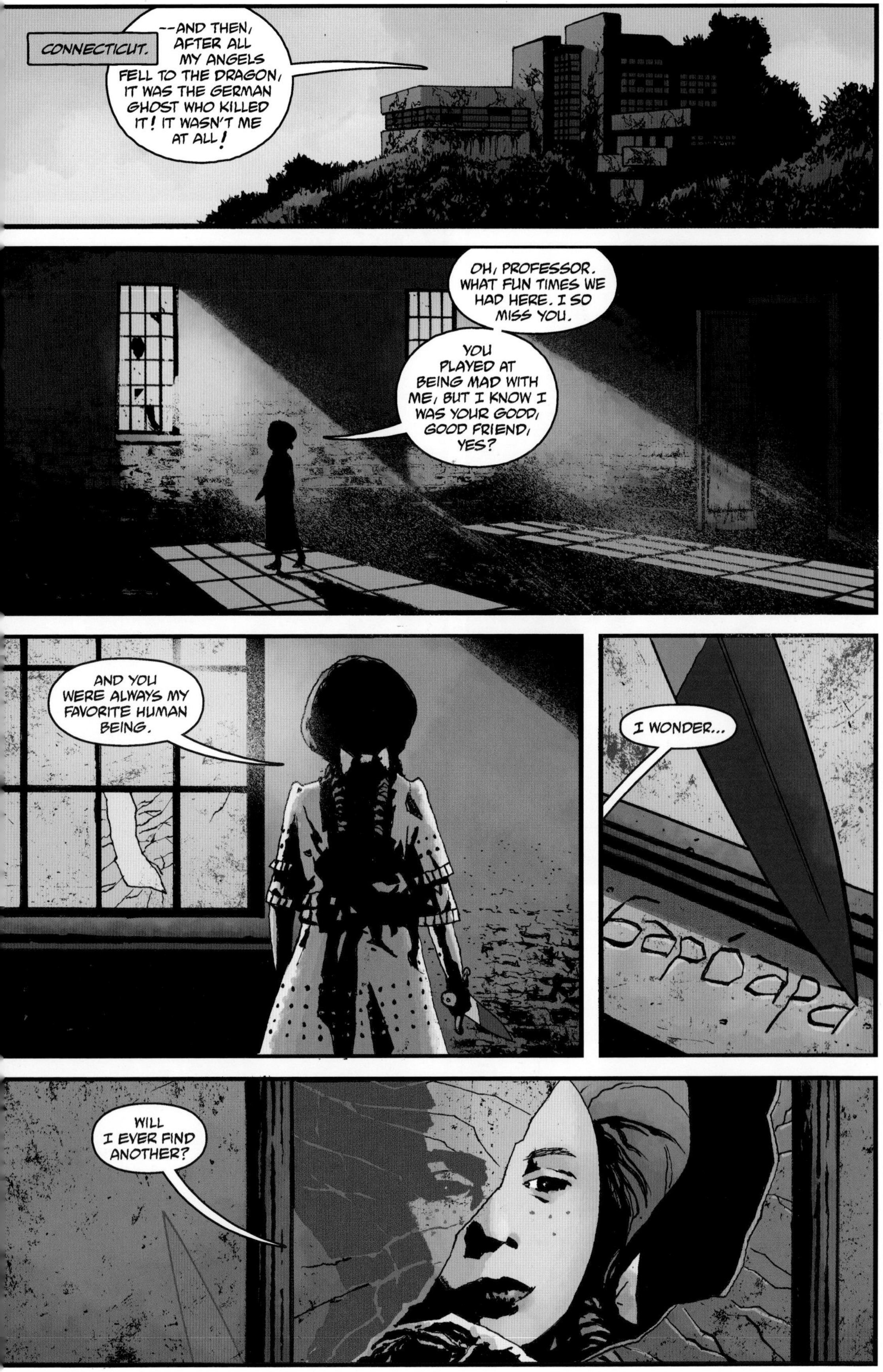
CONNECTICUT.
--AND THEN, AFTER ALL MY ANGELS FELL TO THE DRAGON, IT WAS THE GERMAN GHOST WHO KILLED IT! IT WASN'T ME AT ALL!
OH, PROFESSOR. WHAT FUN TIMES WE HAD HERE. I SO MISS YOU.
YOU PLAYED AT BEING MAD WITH ME, BUT I KNOW I WAS YOUR GOOD, GOOD FRIEND, YES?
AND YOU WERE ALWAYS MY FAVORITE HUMAN BEING.
I WONDER...
WILL I EVER FIND ANOTHER?

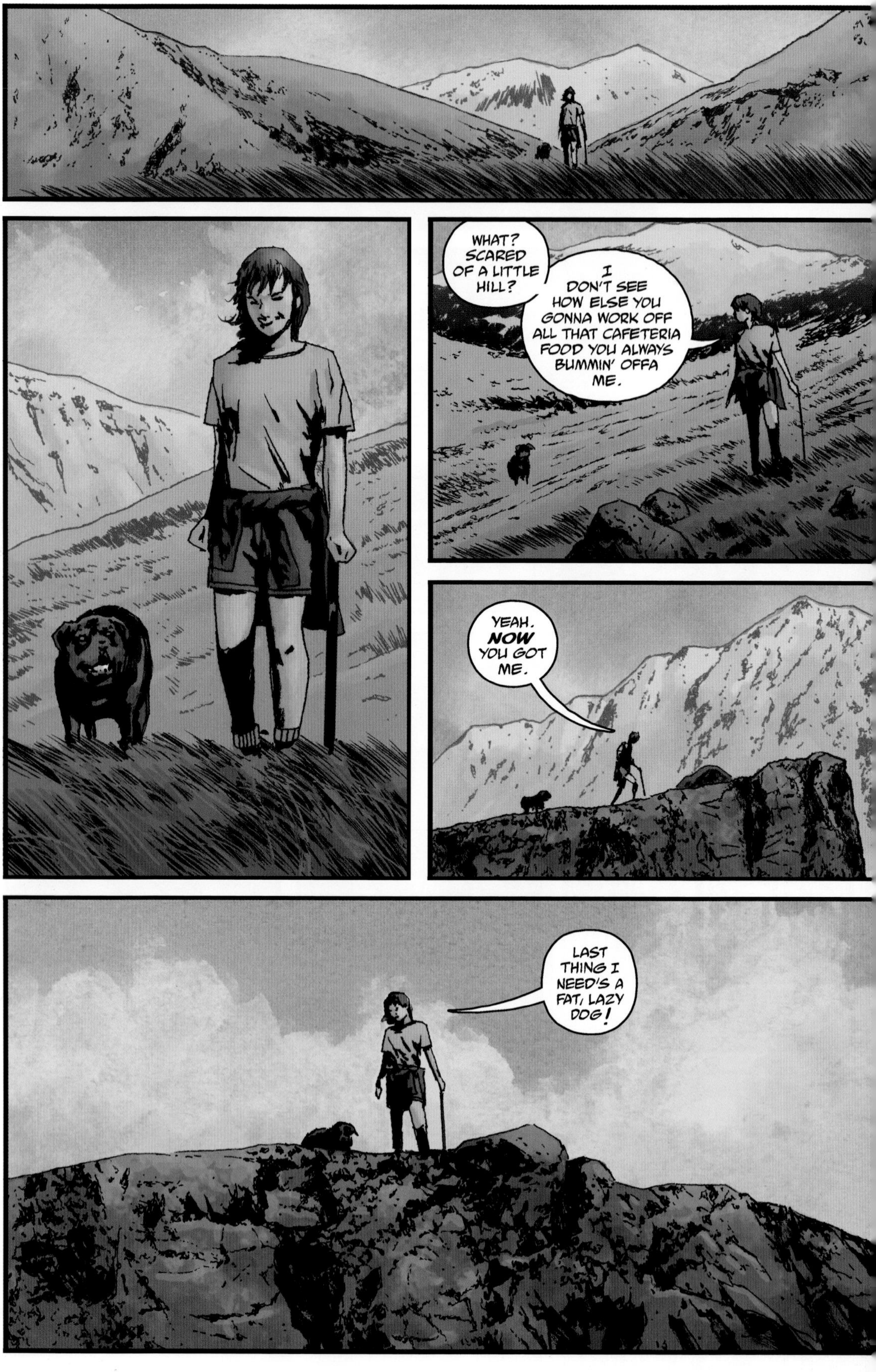
WHAT? SCARED OF A LITTLE HILL?
I DON'T SEE HOW ELSE YOU GONNA WORK OFF ALL THAT CAFETERIA FOOD YOU ALWAYS BUMMIN' OFFA ME.
YEAH. NOW YOU GOT ME.
LAST THING I NEED'S A FAT, LAZY DOG!

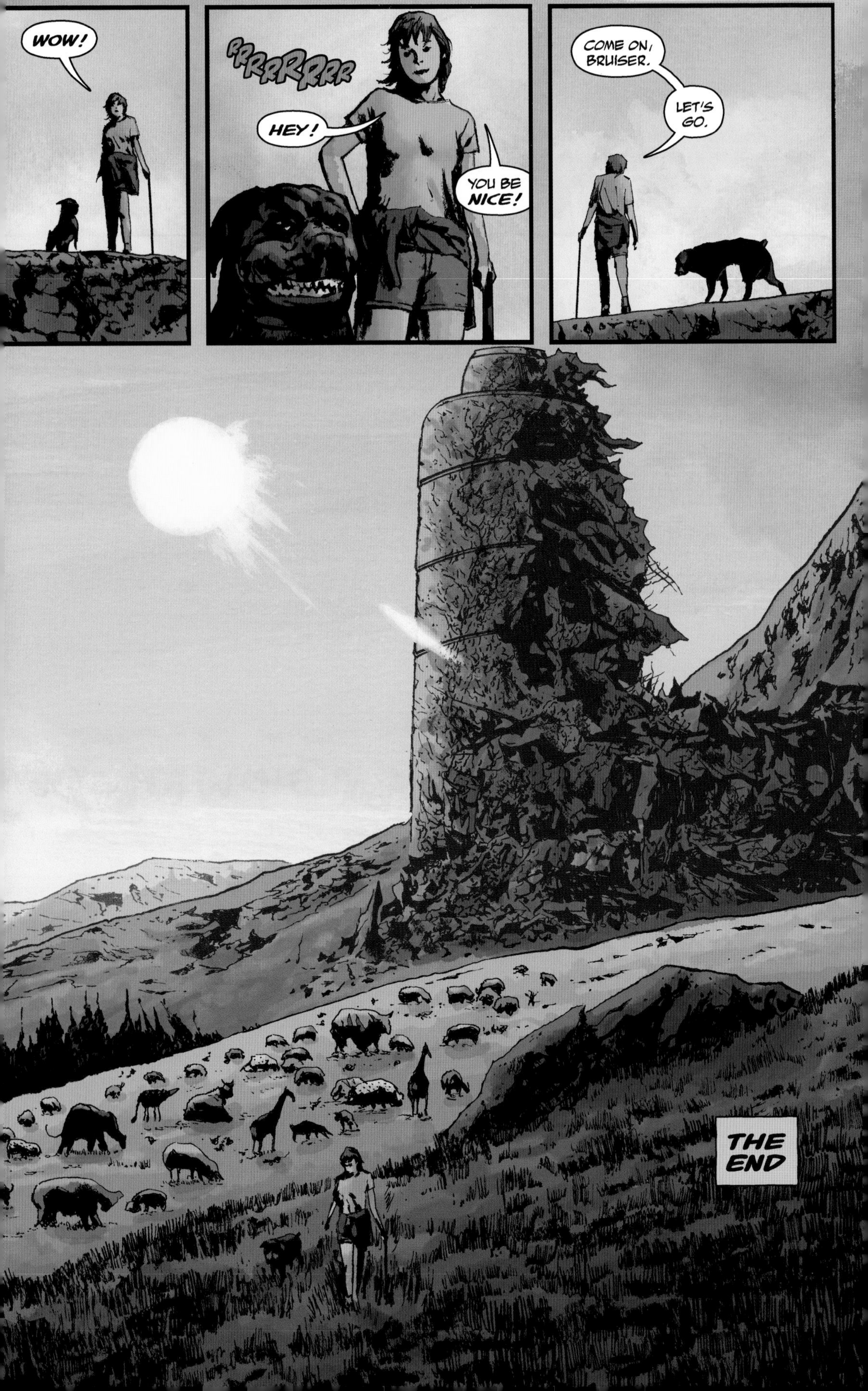
WOW!
RRRRRRRRR
HEY!
YOU BE NICE!
COME ON, BRUISER.
LET'S GO.
THE END

B.P.R.D.™

SKETCHBOOK

Notes by Duncan Fegredo and Laurence Campbell

Duncan Fegredo: Ideally when you do a run of covers for a story arc you want them to be linked either by design or theme, and this series was no exception. Scott suggested that a different character could be featured on each of the covers, and after I read the synopsis and available scripts, it was clear to me that Kate should feature on the fourth cover—a memorial, as it turns out, as I saw her as the heart of both the story and the covers themselves.

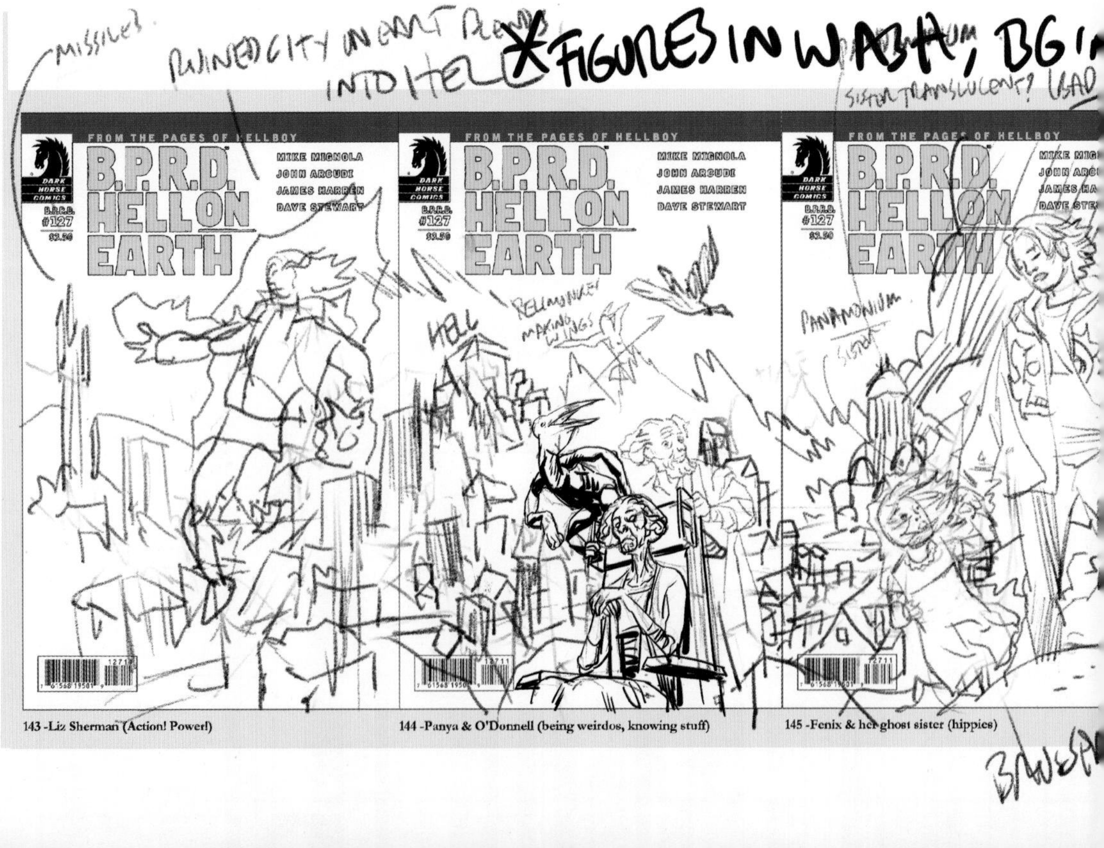

FROM THE PAGES OF HELLBOY
B.P.R.D. HELL ON EARTH
MIKE MIGNOLA
JOHN ARCUDI
JAMES HARREN
DAVE STEWART
HELL
PANDAMONIUM
SISTER
143 -Liz Sherman (Action! Power!)
144 -Panya & O'Donnell (being weirdos, knowing stuff)
145 -Fenix & her ghost sister (hippies)

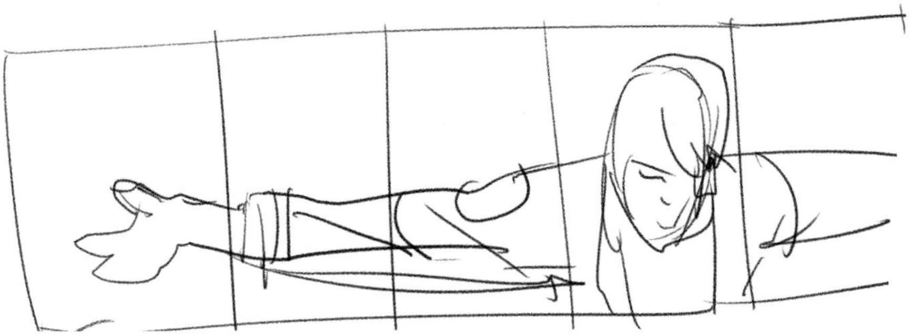

Among the first sketches I drew was one that showed Kate spreading her arms across the covers. It was an interesting image: she was either embracing the cast across the covers or it was an act of sacrifice that really fit with her character. The problem was that this image would only make sense months after the release of the first of the books; until then it would be fragmented and unreadable. The individual covers needed to be strong in and of themselves. If they worked as five linked images, then that was a bonus.

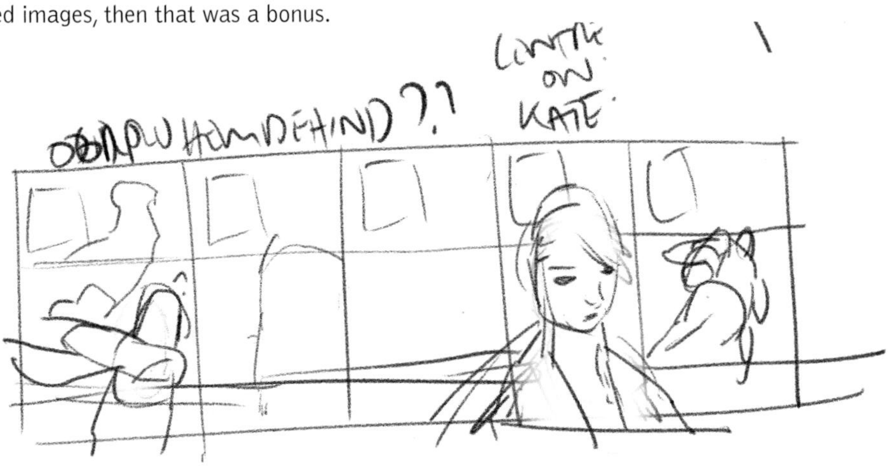

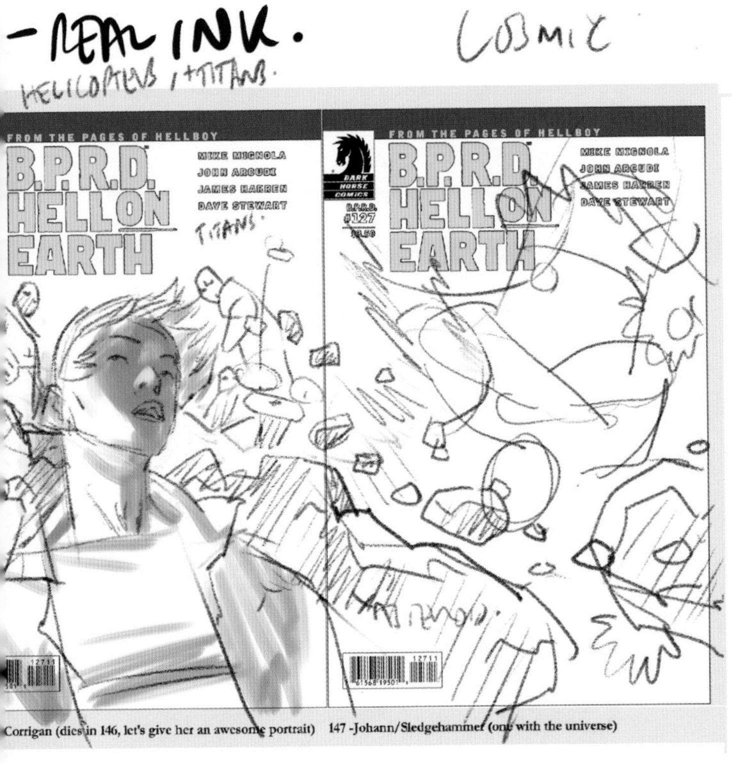
-REAL INK.
COSMIC
HELICOPTERS / TITANS.
FROM THE PAGES OF HELLBOY
B.P.R.D. HELL ON EARTH
MIKE MIGNOLA
JOHN ARCUDI
JAMES HARREN
DAVE STEWART
TITANS
FROM THE PAGES OF HELLBOY
DARK HORSE COMICS
B.P.R.D. HELL ON EARTH
MIKE MIGNOLA
JOHN ARCUDI
JAMES HARREN
DAVE STEWART
Corrigan (dies in 146, let's give her an awesome portrait)
147 -Johann/Sledgehammer (one with the universe)

BPRD 143–147: FIGURES IN WASH, CONTINUOUS B/G LANDSCAPE IN LINE.

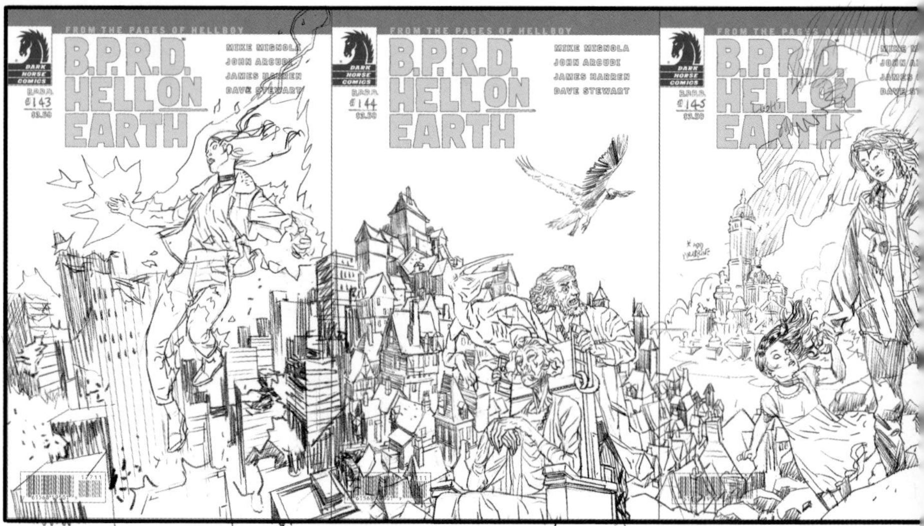
FROM THE PAGES OF HELLBOY
B.P.R.D. HELL ON EARTH
MIKE MIGNOLA
JOHN ARCUDI
JAMES HARREN
DAVE STEWART
#143
#144
#145

EARTH RUINED CITY → HELL → PANDEMONIUM! →
+CORMORANT.

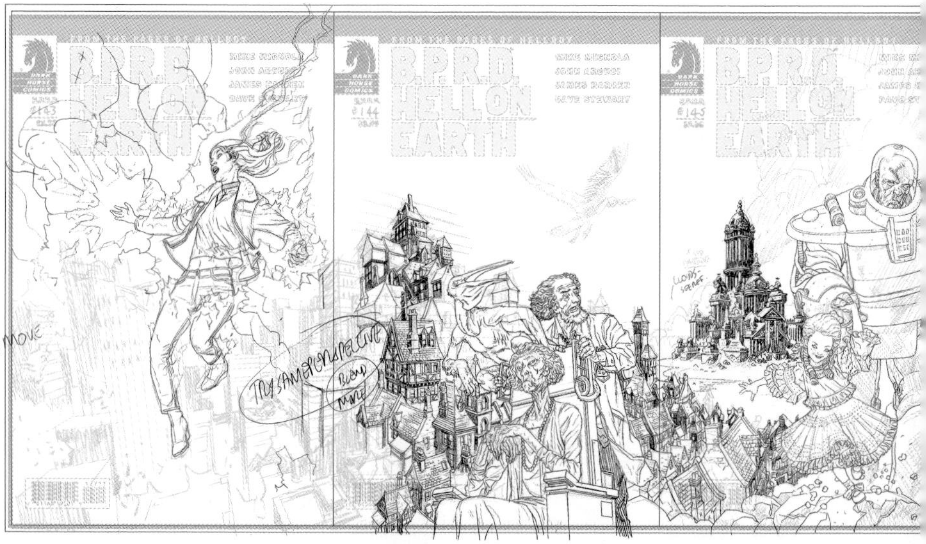
FROM THE PAGES OF HELLBOY
B.P.R.D. HELL ON EARTH
#143
#144
#145
TRY SAME PERSPECTIVE
BLEND MORE

SMOKE

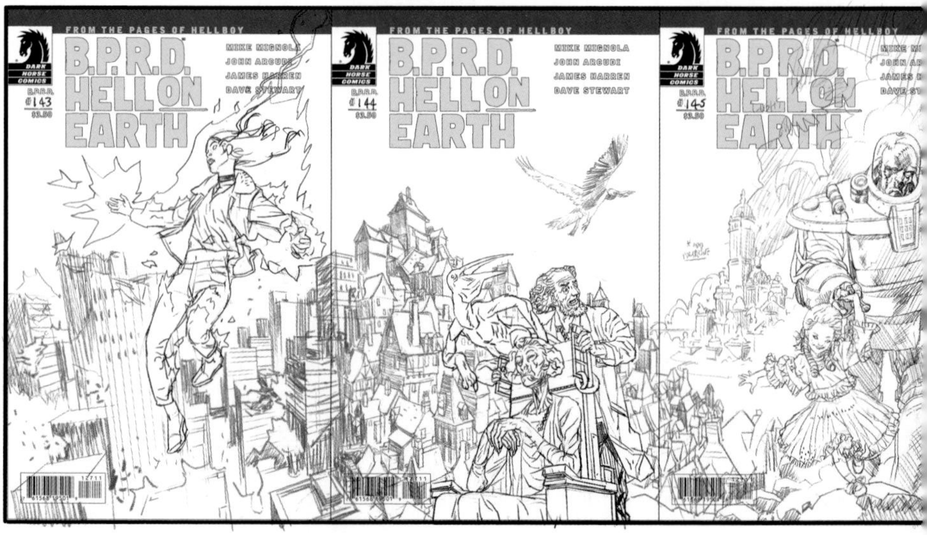
FROM THE PAGES OF HELLBOY
B.P.R.D. HELL ON EARTH
MIKE MIGNOLA
JOHN ARCUDI
JAMES HARREN
DAVE STEWART
#143
#144
#145

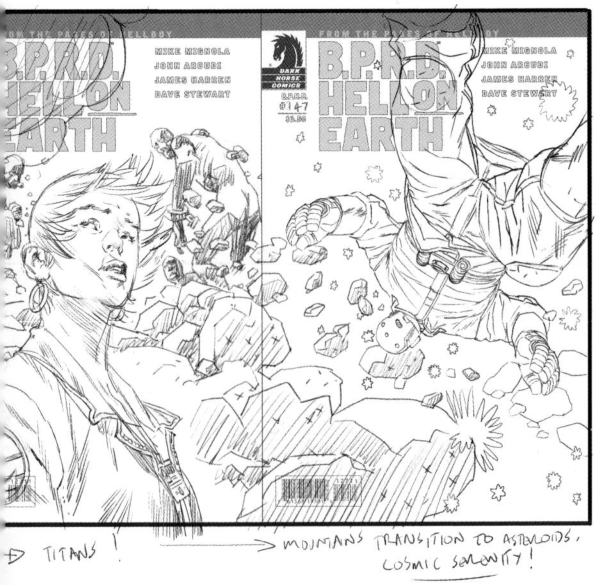
FROM THE PAGES OF HELLBOY
B.P.R.D. HELL ON EARTH
MIKE MIGNOLA
JOHN ARCUDI
JAMES HARREN
DAVE STEWART
#147
$3.50
TITANS!
MOUNTAINS TRANSITION TO ASTEROIDS, COSMIC SERENITY!

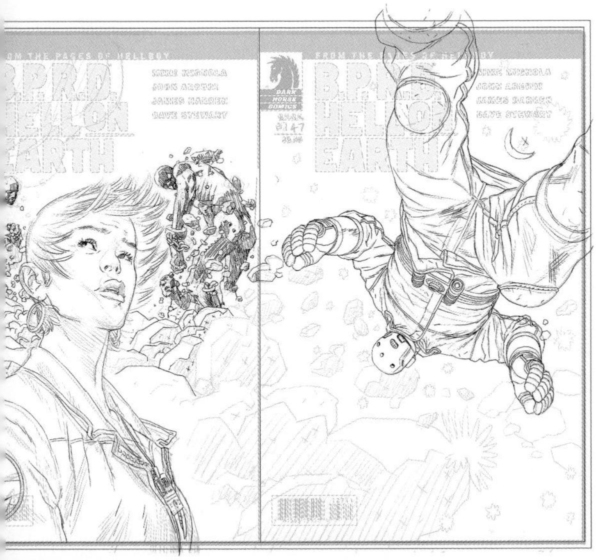

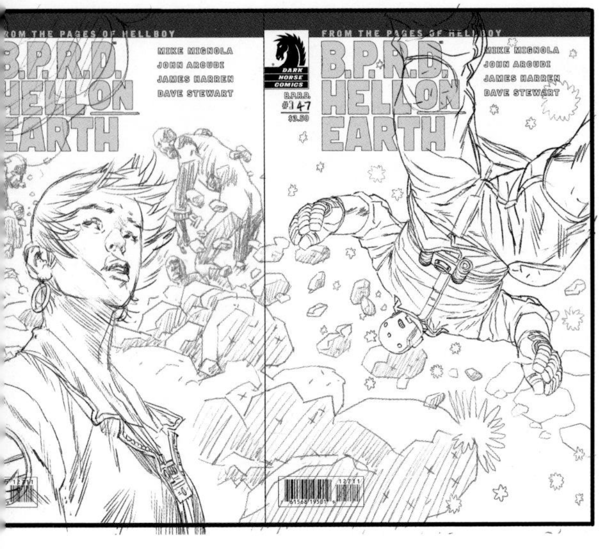
FROM THE PAGES OF HELLBOY
B.P.R.D. HELL ON EARTH
MIKE MIGNOLA
JOHN ARCUDI
JAMES HARREN
DAVE STEWART
#147
$3.50

Working around Kate, I assigned characters to each cover. The choice was determined by the events of each issue. As I indicated backgrounds for each, I realized that would be the way to link the covers. The clincher was the way the modern cityscape joined the tumbledown coastal towns of Hell. I could see a natural progression and so I pushed that link across the subsequent covers. The backgrounds indicated a journey through the five books. It felt right.

The only change that was asked of me was to substitute Iosif and Varvara for Fenix and Eris on the third cover. It was a better fit, and it fit with a cover idea that Laurence came up with. Eris was easily replaced by Varvara, although she was now leading the rather more bulky Iosif. That took a little more effort to recompose.

The characters decided, I worked up final pencils. You can see from the note that I was attempting to match the perspectives of the city and Hell to better lead the eye through the covers. In retrospect I regret not making Hell more chaotic.

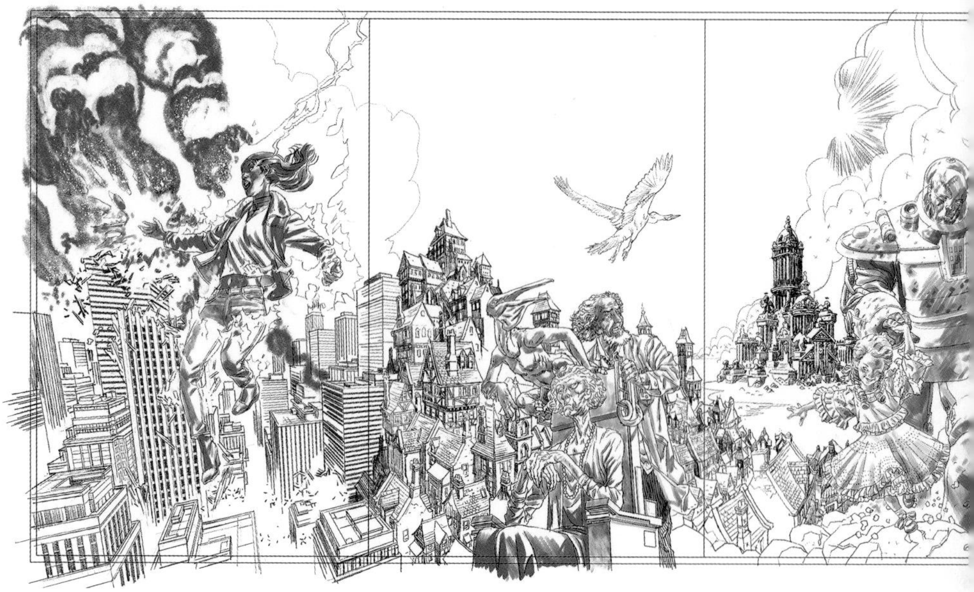

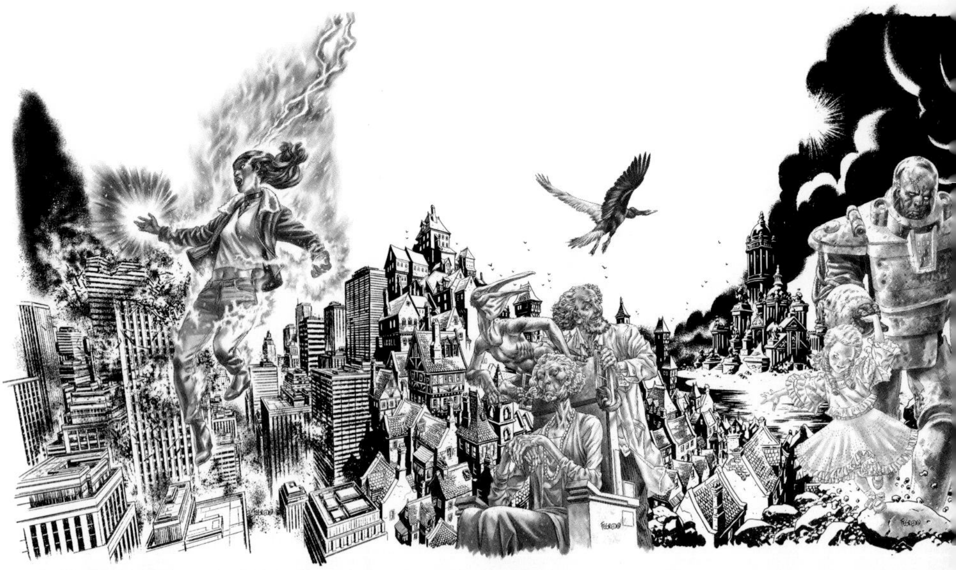

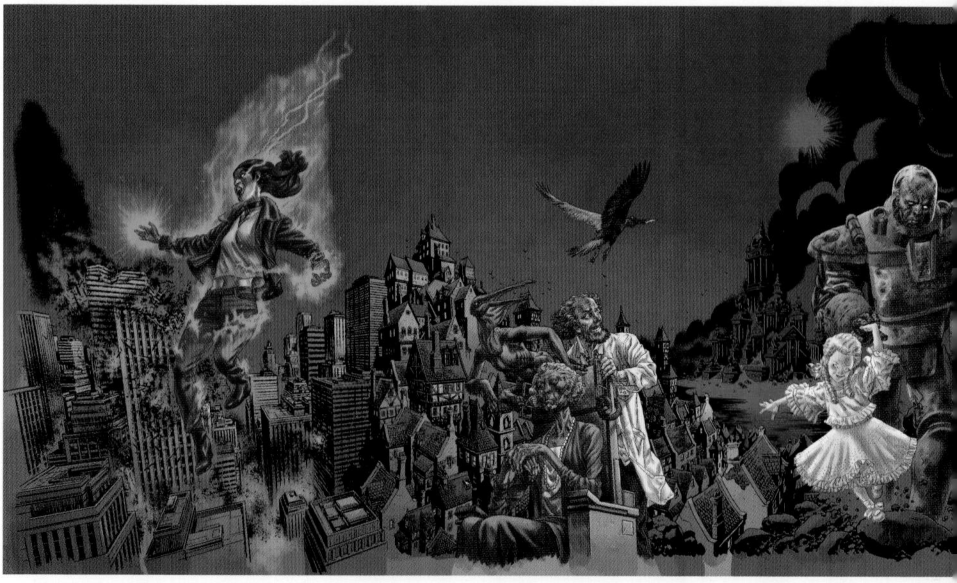

After finishing the pencils I roughly painted gray tones under the figures. I wanted the characters to stand out on the covers and decided to do something similar to my work on *Hellboy: The Midnight Circus*. In that story there is a point at which young Hellboy crosses over from the real world into another realm, not unlike Dorothy crossing over to Oz. I drew this as a mix of Hellboy in pen and ink and the other realm in watercolor. I was aiming to reverse that for these covers. Up until this point I drew everything digitally, but I was intending to print out the art as a blue line and ink the backgrounds traditionally, painting the figures in watercolor. After half an hour painting Liz on the first cover, I came to my senses and reverted to completing the entire run of covers digitally. What started out as rough gray tones became part of the final art.

I only had one color note to Dave Stewart, and that was that the central light source for all five covers should be the hellish sun on the third cover.

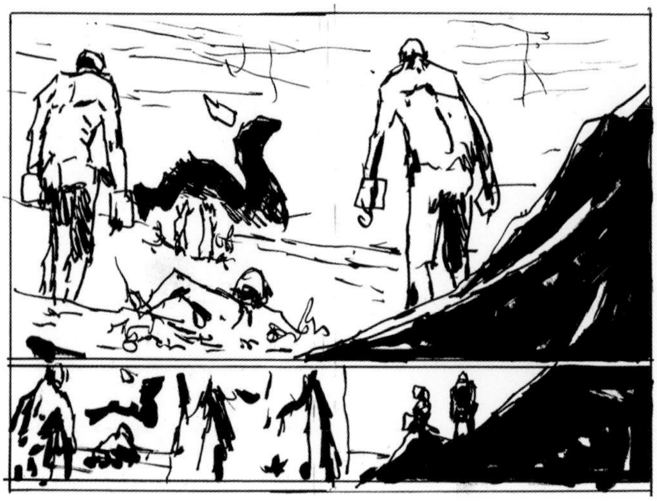

Laurence Campbell: This was a huge arc with lots of incredible moments, one of which was the Titans from underneath Pandemonium arriving on earth to battle the Ogdru Jahad. The final image for this spread is pretty faithful to the thumbnail (*left; below, pencils*). With so many giant creatures, I still had to capture the size and scale of the situation. Having Varvara and Iosif in the second panel helps convey that. We tried a version of the second panel with one of the giants closer (*top right*), but found the chain blocked the panel too much, cutting it in two.

Of course Dave's colors took the page to a different level for me.

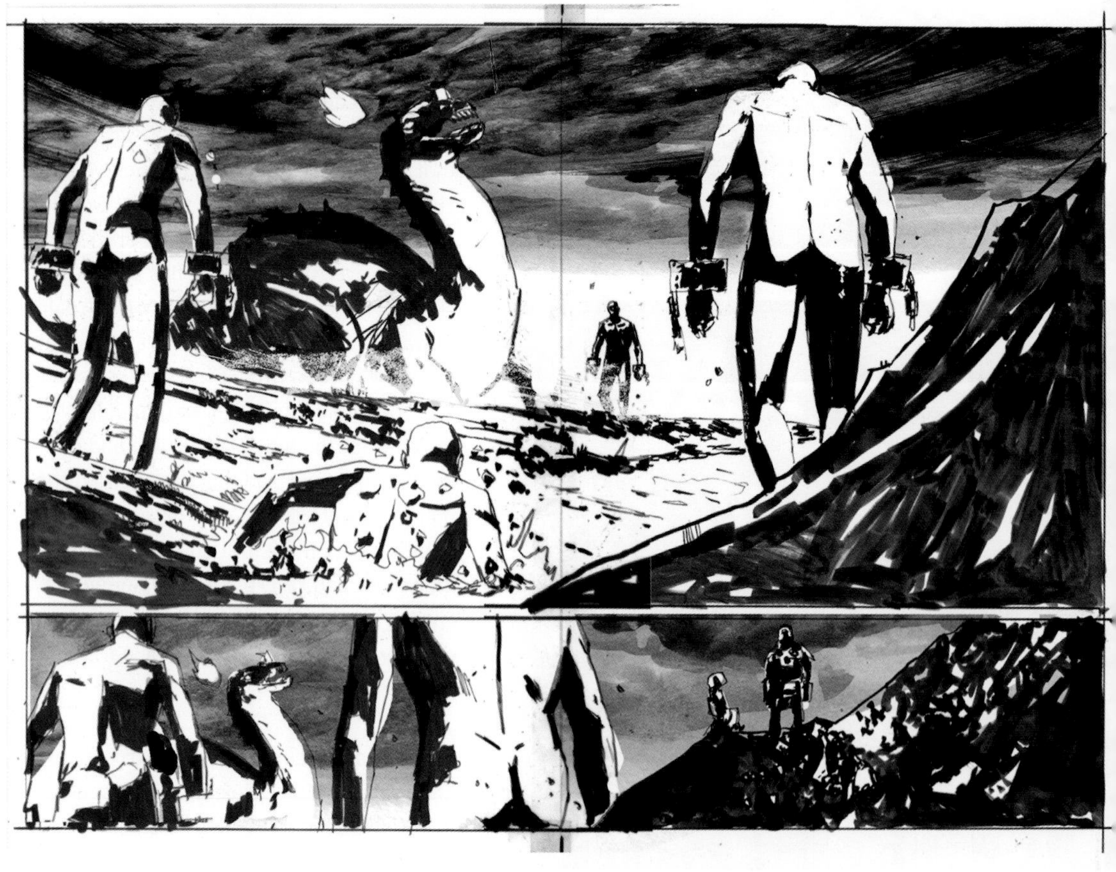

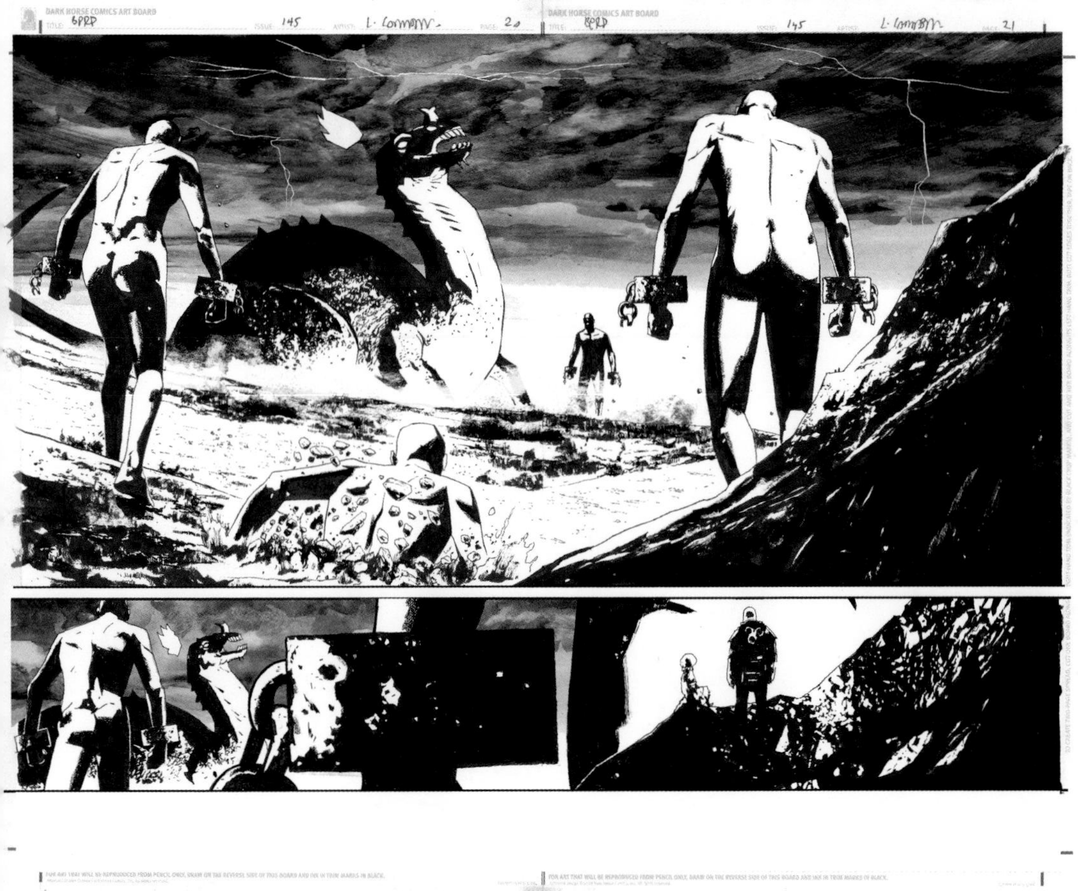

DARK HORSE COMICS ART BOARD
TITLE: BPRD ISSUE: 145 ARTIST: L. Cormack PAGE: 20
DARK HORSE COMICS ART BOARD
TITLE: BPRD ISSUE: 145 ARTIST: L. Cormack PAGE: 21

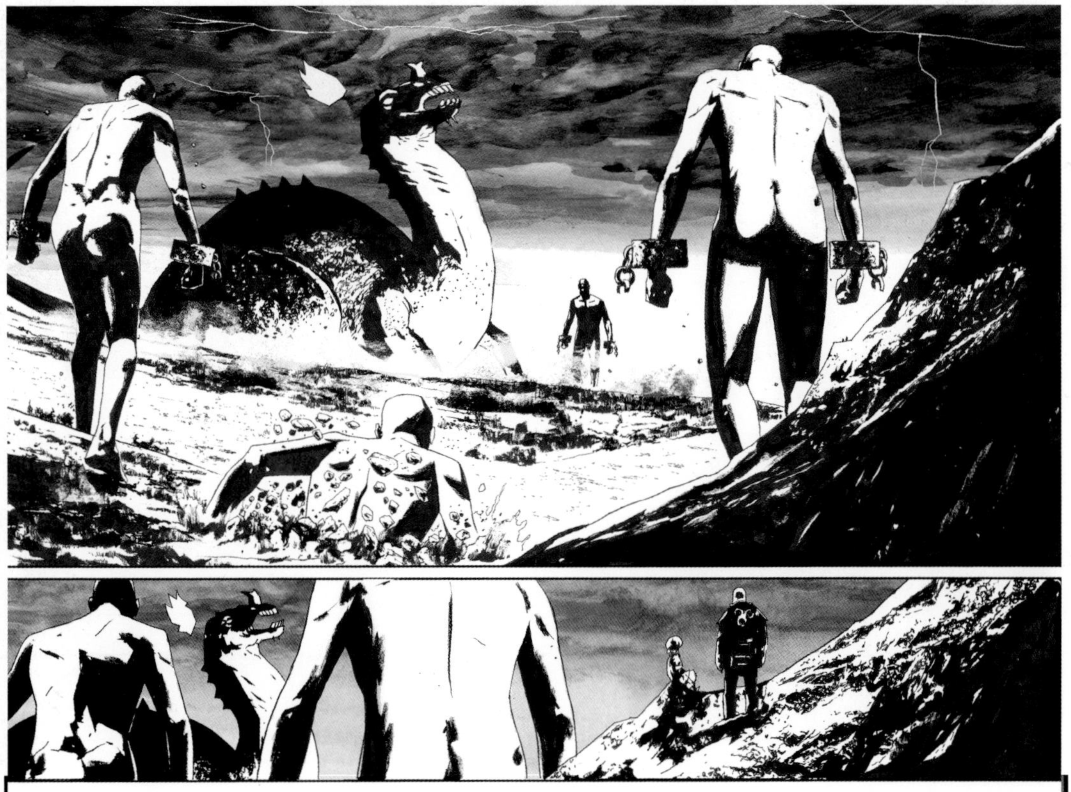

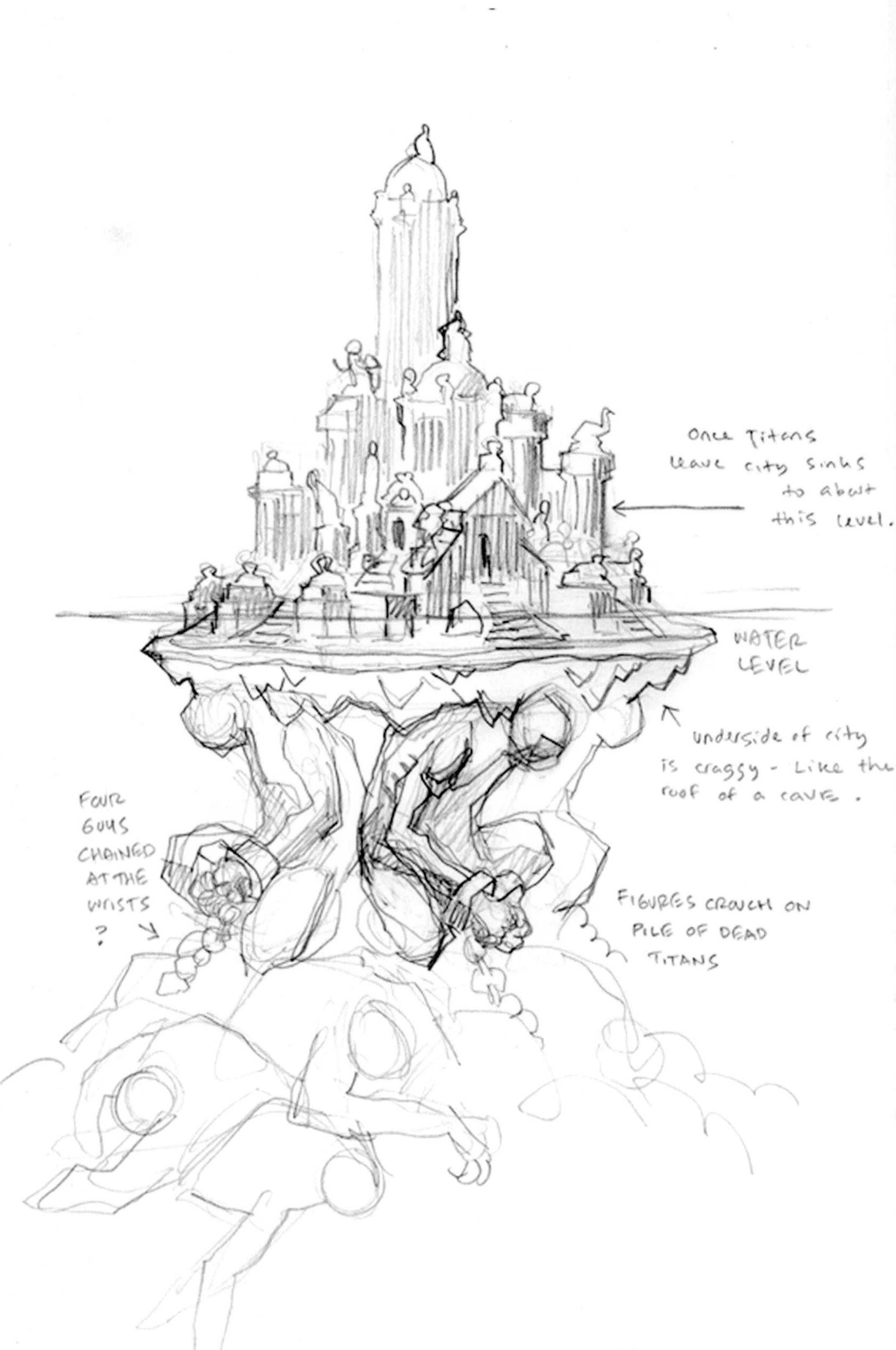

Once Titans leave city sinks to about this level.
WATER LEVEL
underside of city is craggy - Like the roof of a cave.
FOUR GUYS CHAINED AT THE WRISTS ?
FIGURES CROUCH ON PILE OF DEAD TITANS

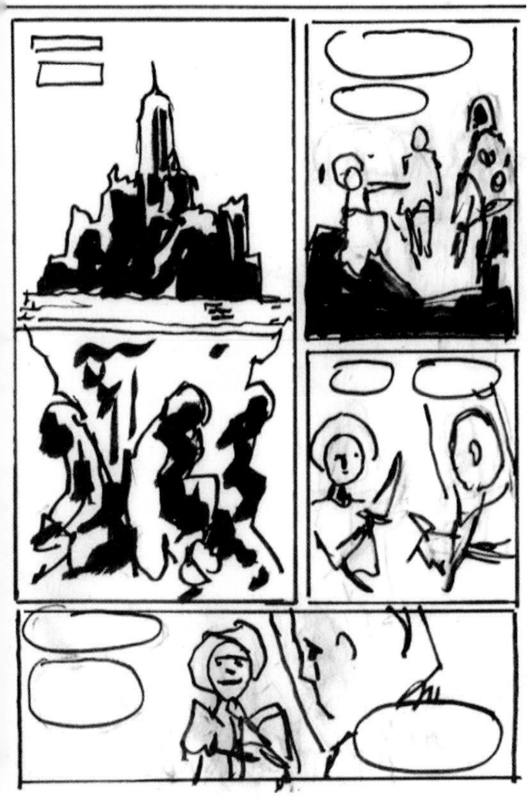

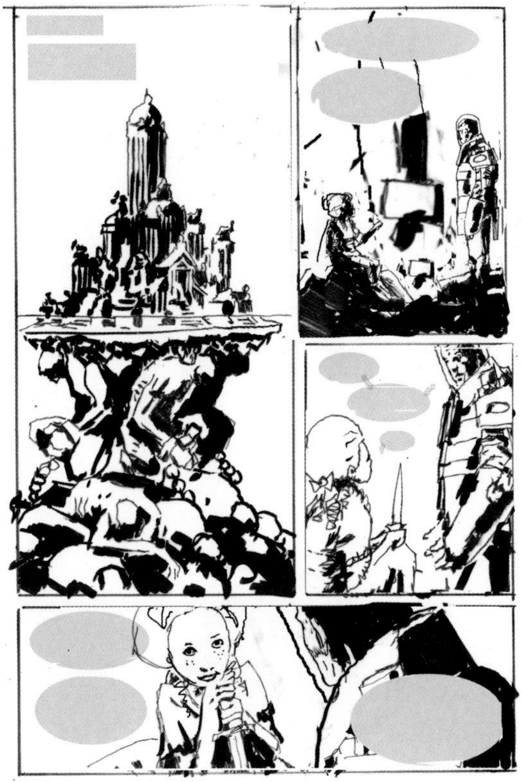

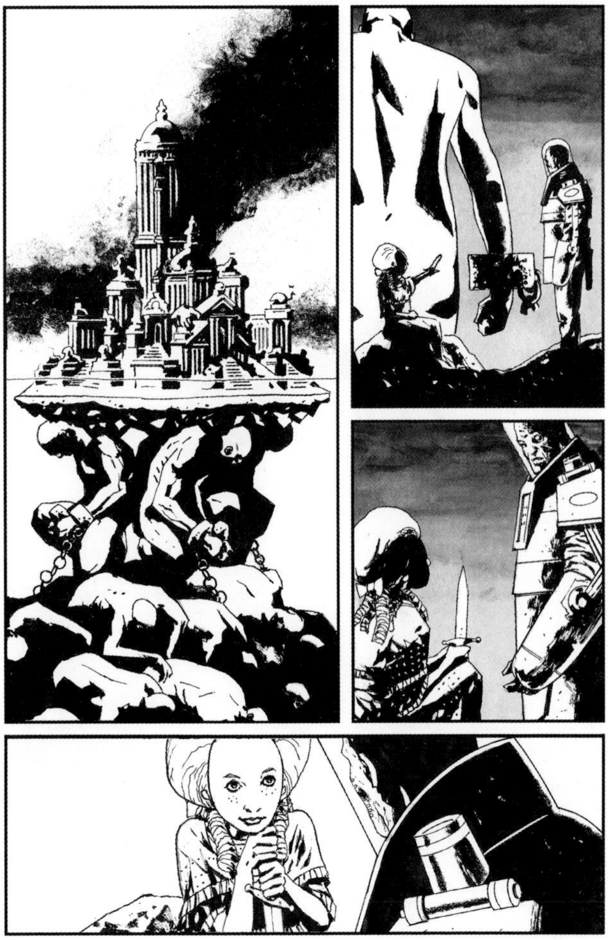

Facing: Always good getting drawn notes from Mike, and this one knocked me out when I first looked at it. The idea of the Titans holding up Pandemonium blew my mind. Getting to draw this image was a huge buzz for me, along with drawing the other scenes in Hell.

Clockwise from top left: thumbnail, pencils, and inks.

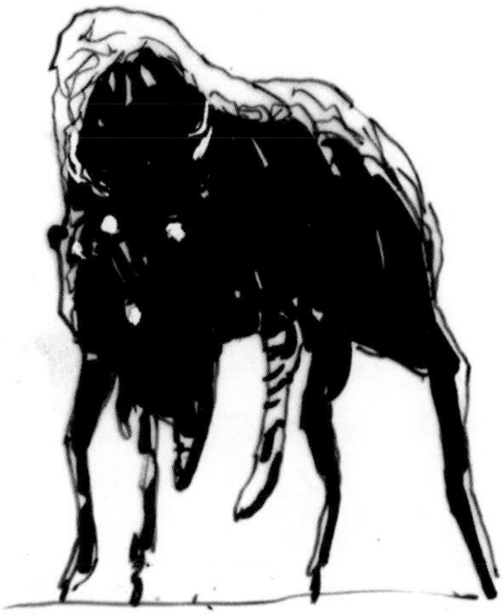

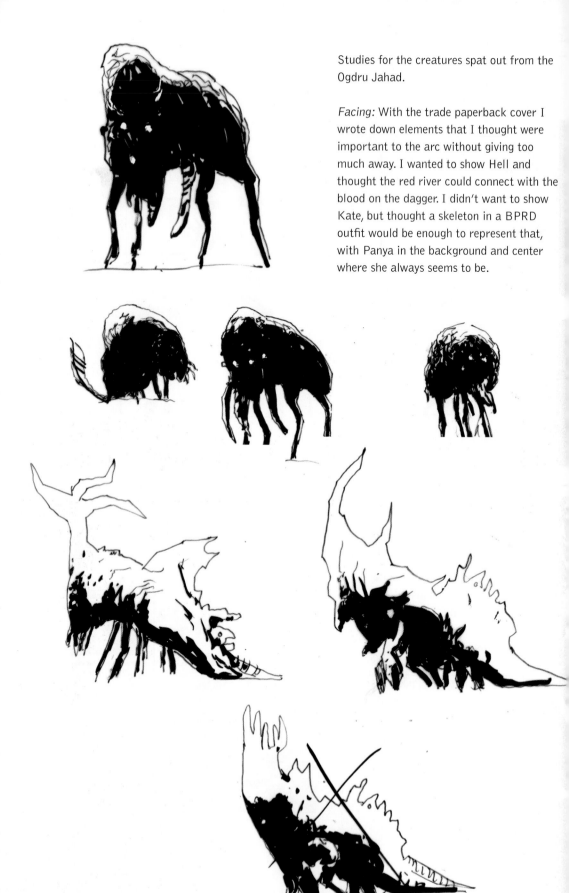

Studies for the creatures spat out from the Ogdru Jahad.

Facing: With the trade paperback cover I wrote down elements that I thought were important to the arc without giving too much away. I wanted to show Hell and thought the red river could connect with the blood on the dagger. I didn't want to show Kate, but thought a skeleton in a BPRD outfit would be enough to represent that, with Panya in the background and center where she always seems to be.

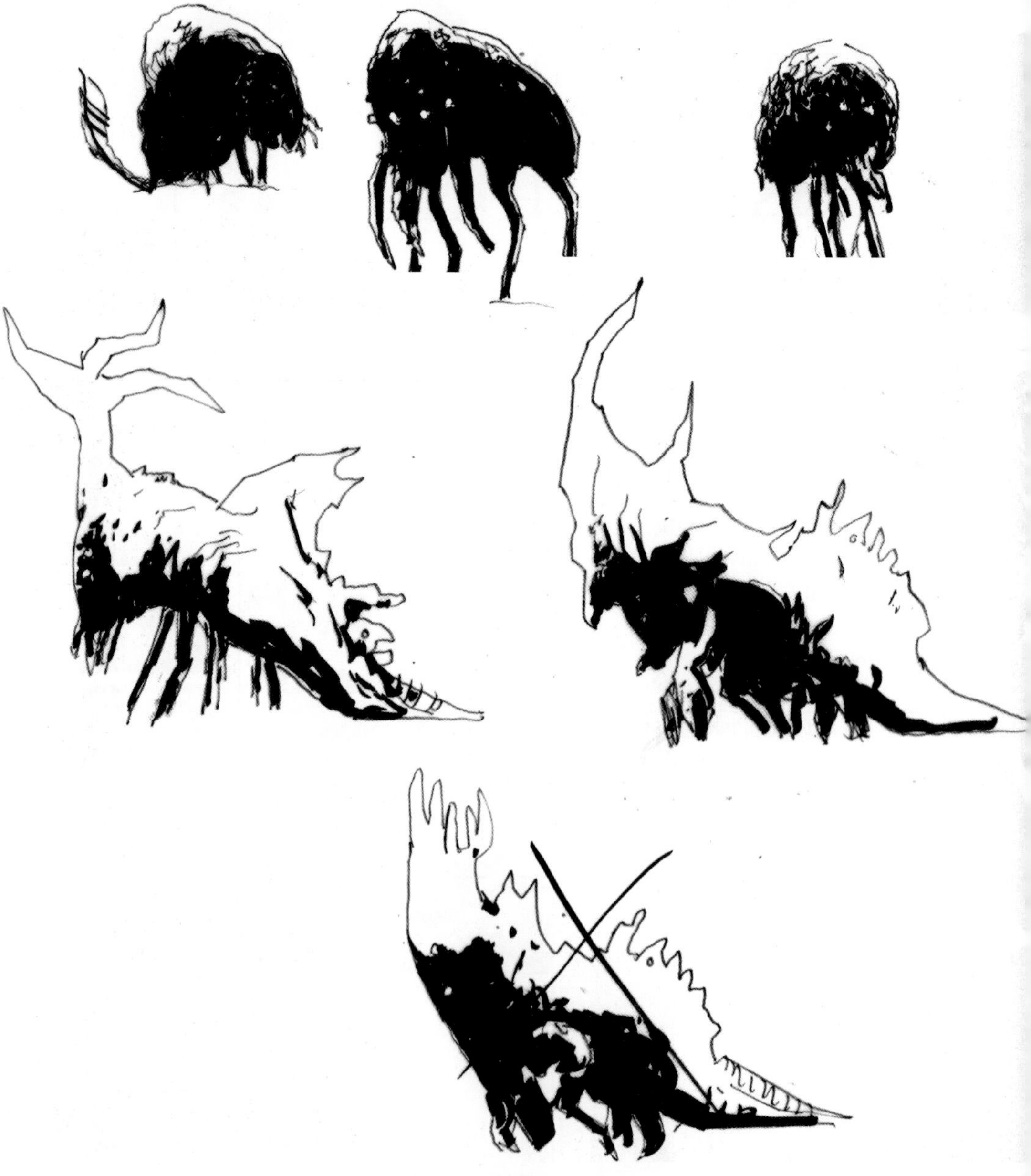

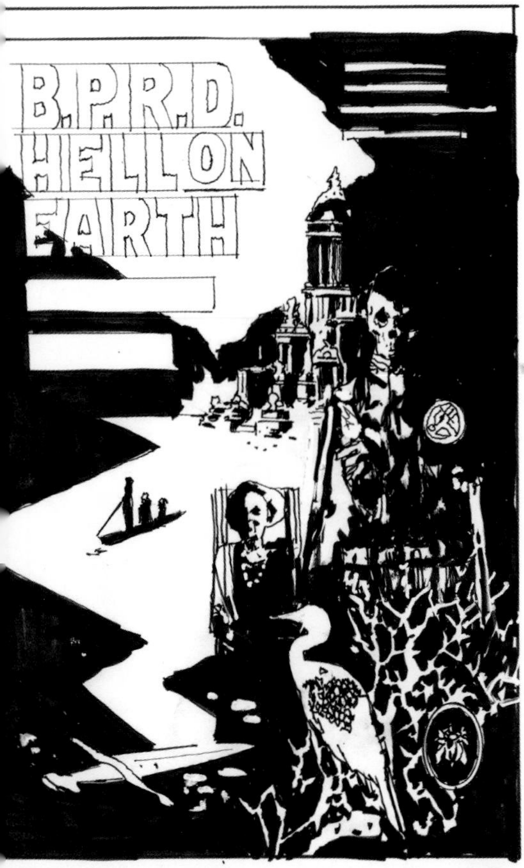
B.P.R.D.
HELL ON
EARTH

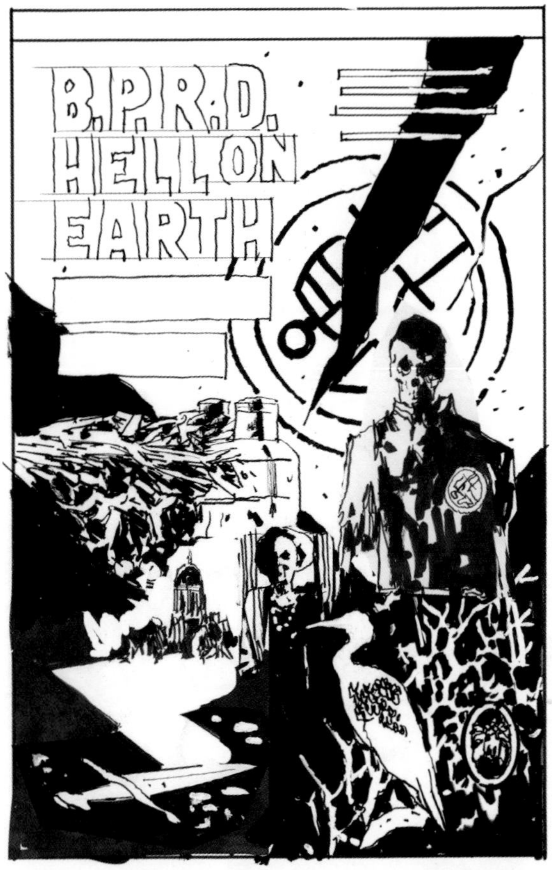
B.P.R.D.
HELL ON
EARTH

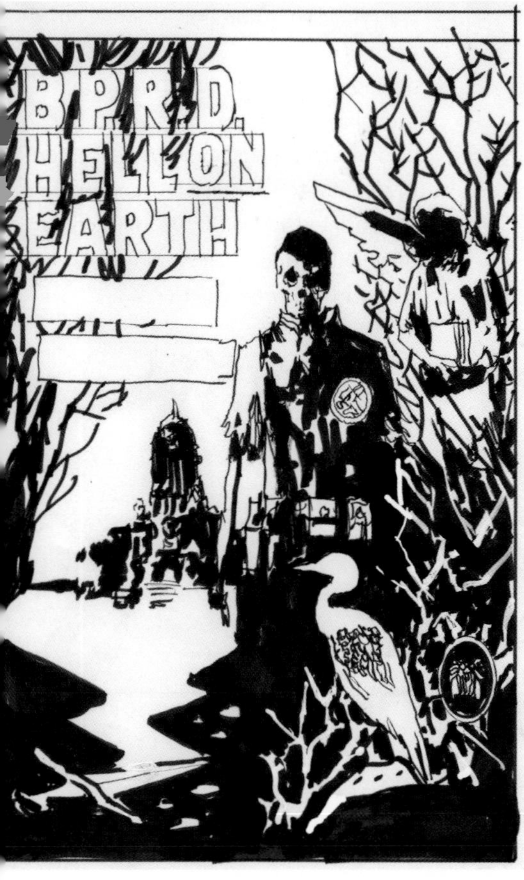
B.P.R.D.
HELL ON
EARTH

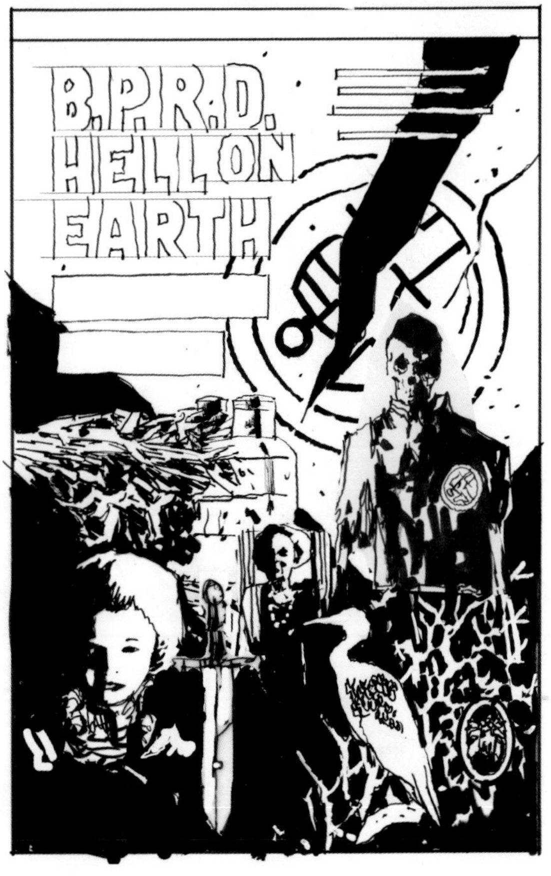
B.P.R.D.
HELL ON
EARTH

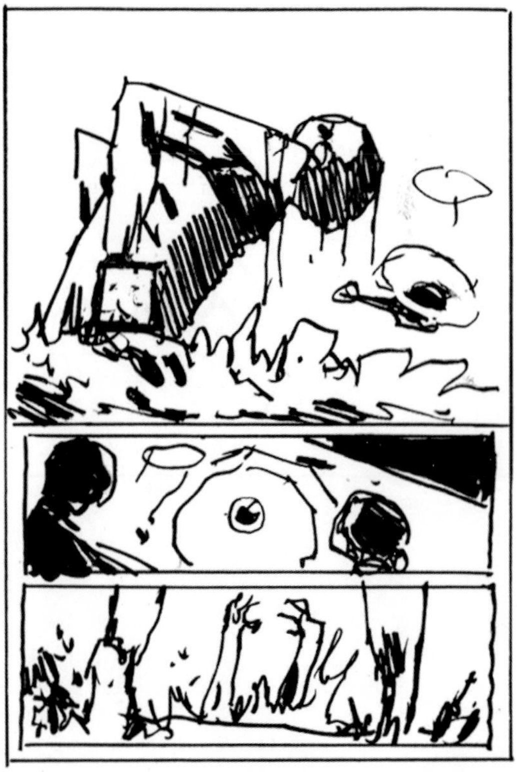

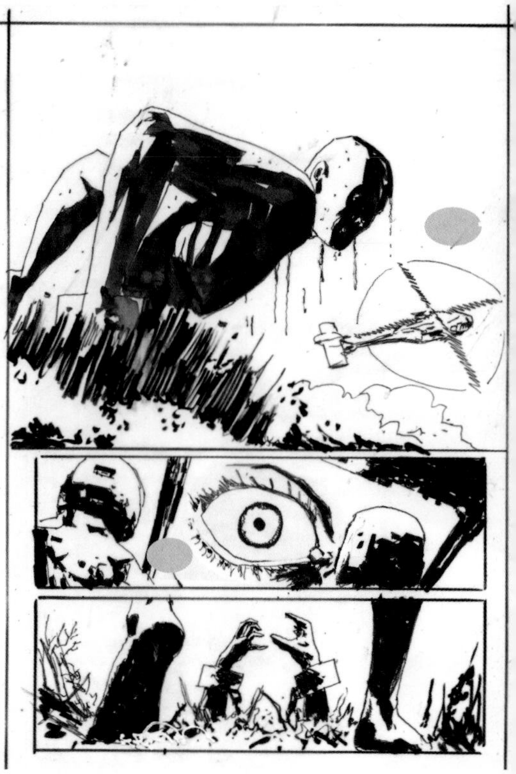

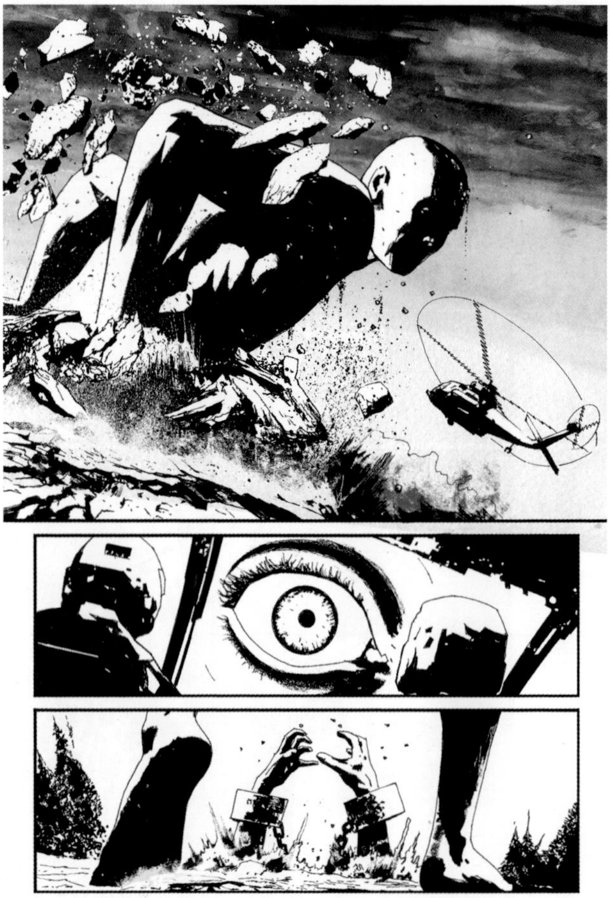

The Titans bursting out of the earth was fun to draw. I was thinking Ray Harryhausen at the time of drawing them. I remember Scott suggested adding more debris, which I did, and it brought a real sense of power to it. I also moved the angle of the helicopter to give it a touch more tension. In the final printed version Dave knocked out the pupil to make it less human-like, which I think works better.

Also by MIKE MIGNOLA

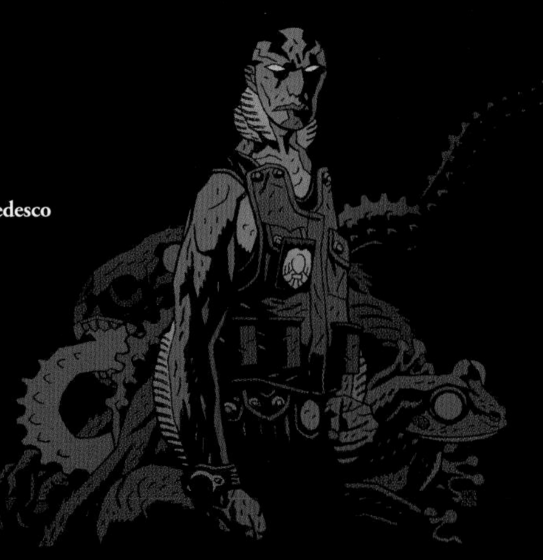

P.R.D.
AGUE OF FROGS
lume 1
th Chris Golden, Guy Davis, and others
B: ISBN 978-1-59582-675-6 | $19.99

lume 2
th John Arcudi, Davis, and others
B: ISBN 978-1-59582-676-3 | $24.99

lume 3
th Arcudi and Davis
B: ISBN 978-1-61655-622-8 | $24.99

lume 4
th Arcudi and Davis
B: ISBN 978-1-61655-641-9 | $24.99

46–1948
th Joshua Dysart, Paul Azaceta, Fábio Moon,
briel Bá, Max Fiumara, and Arcudi
3N 978-1-61655-646-4 | $34.99

ING HUMAN
th Scott Allie, Arcudi, Davis, and others
BN 978-1-59582-756-2 | $17.99

MPIRE
th Moon and Bá
BN 978-1-61655-196-4 | $19.99

P.R.D. HELL ON EARTH
EW WORLD
th Arcudi and Davis
BN 978-1-59582-707-4 | $19.99

ODS AND MONSTERS
th Arcudi, Davis, and Tyler Crook
BN 978-1-59582-822-4 | $19.99

JSSIA
th Arcudi, Crook, and Duncan Fegredo
BN 978-1-59582-946-7 | $19.99

IE DEVIL'S ENGINE
ND THE LONG DEATH
th Arcudi, Crook, and James Harren
BN 978-1-59582-981-8 | $19.99

IE PICKENS COUNTY
ORROR AND OTHERS
th Allie, Jason Latour, Harren,
d Max Fiumara
BN 978-1-61655-140-7 | $19.99

IE RETURN OF THE MASTER
th Arcudi and Crook
BN 978-1-61655-193-3 | $19.99

COLD DAY IN HELL
th Arcudi, Peter Snejbjerg, and
urence Campbell
BN 978-1-61655-199-5 | $19.99

HE REIGN
F THE BLACK FLAME
ith Arcudi and Harren
BN 978-1-61655-471-2 | $19.99

HE DEVIL'S WINGS
ith Arcudi, Campbell,
e Querio, and Crook
BN 978-1-61655-617-4 | $19.99

AKE OF FIRE
ith Arcudi and Crook
BN 978-1-61655-402-6 | $19.99

LESH AND STONE
ith Arcudi and Harren
BN 978-1-61655-762-1 | $19.99

METAMORPHOSIS
with Arcudi, Snejbjerg, and Julián Totino Tedesco
ISBN 978-1-61655-794-2 | $19.99

END OF DAYS
with Arcudi and Campbell
ISBN 978-1-61655-910-6 | $19.99

THE EXORCIST
with Cameron Stewart, Chris Roberson,
and Mike Norton
ISBN 978-1-50670-011-3 | $19.99

COMETH THE HOUR
with Arcudi and Campbell
ISBN 978-1-50670-131-8 | $19.99

ABE SAPIEN
THE DROWNING
with Jason Shawn Alexander
ISBN 978-1-59582-185-0 | $17.99

THE DEVIL DOES NOT JEST AND
OTHER STORIES
with Arcudi, Harren, and others
ISBN 978-1-59582-925-2 | $17.99

DARK AND TERRIBLE
AND THE NEW RACE OF MAN
with Allie, Arcudi, Sebastián
Fiumara, and Max Fiumara
ISBN 978-1-61655-284-8 | $19.99

THE SHAPE OF THINGS TO COME
with Allie, S. Fiumara, and M. Fiumara
ISBN 978-1-61655-443-9 | $19.99

SACRED PLACES
with Allie, S. Fiumara, and M. Fiumara
ISBN 978-1-61655-515-3 | $19.99

A DARKNESS SO GREAT
with Allie, S. Fiumara, and M. Fiumara
ISBN 978-1-61655-656-3 | $19.99

THE SECRET FIRE
with Allie, S. Fiumara, and M. Fiumara
ISBN 978-1-61655-891-8 | $19.99

THE DESOLATE SHORE
with Allie, S. Fiumara, and M. Fiumara
ISBN 978-1-50670-031-1 | $19.99

LOBSTER JOHNSON
THE IRON PROMETHEUS
with Jason Armstrong
ISBN 978-1-59307-975-8 | $17.99

THE BURNING HAND
with Arcudi and Tonci Zonjic
ISBN 978-1-61655-031-8 | $17.99

SATAN SMELLS A RAT
with Arcudi, Fiumara, Querio,
Wilfredo Torres, and Kevin Nowlan
ISBN 978-1-61655-203-9 | $18.99

GET THE LOBSTER
with Arcudi and Zonjic
ISBN 978-1-61655-505-4 | $19.99

WITCHFINDER
IN THE SERVICE OF ANGELS
with Ben Stenbeck
ISBN 978-1-59582-483-7 | $17.99

LOST AND GONE FOREVER
with Arcudi and John Severin
ISBN 978-1-59582-794-4 | $17.99

THE MYSTERIES OF UNLAND
with Kim Newman, Maura McHugh, and Crook
ISBN 978-1-61655-630-3 | $19.99

CITY OF THE DEAD
with Roberson and Stenbeck
ISBN 978-1-50670-166-0 | $19.99

FRANKENSTEIN UNDERGROUND
with Stenbeck
ISBN 978-1-61655-782-9 | $19.99

JOE GOLEM: OCCULT DETECTIVE—
THE RAT CATCHER & THE SUNKEN DEAD
with Golden and Patric Reynolds
ISBN 978-1-61655-964-9 | $24.99

BALTIMORE
THE PLAGUE SHIPS
with Golden and Stenbeck
ISBN 978-1-59582-677-0 | $24.99

THE CURSE BELLS
with Golden and Stenbeck
ISBN 978-1-59582-674-9 | $24.99

A PASSING STRANGER
AND OTHER STORIES
with Golden and Stenbeck
ISBN 978-1-61655-182-7 | $24.99

CHAPEL OF BONES
with Golden and Stenbeck
ISBN 978-1-61655-328-9 | $24.99

EMPTY GRAVES
with Golden and Bergting
ISBN 978-1-50670-042-7 | $24.99

THE APOSTLE AND THE WITCH OF HARJU
with Golden, Stenbeck, and Peter Bergting
ISBN 978-1-61655-618-1 | $24.99

THE CULT OF THE RED KING
with Golden and Bergting
ISBN 978-1-61655-821-5 | $24.99

NOVELS
LOBSTER JOHNSON: THE SATAN FACTORY
with Thomas E. Sniegoski
ISBN 978-1-59582-203-1 | $12.95

JOE GOLEM AND THE DROWNING CITY
with Golden
ISBN 978-1-59582-971-9 | $99.99

BALTIMORE; OR, THE STEADFAST TIN
SOLDIER & THE VAMPIRE
with Golden
ISBN 978-1-61655-803-1 | $12.99

HELLBOY
by MIKE MIGNOLA